Crimsy

Michael Martin

To the rebels, who make science
the wonder that it is.

Join the Heart Beat Books Email List

Receive our newsletters
https://heartbeatbookstore.com/

Published in the United States by Heart Beat Publications, LLC.

Library of Congress Cataloging-in-Publication data available on request.

Printed in the United States of America.

DC

One

This much was clear: We had to determine whether the most phenomenal discovery in the history of science was nothing more than a fluke. Was *Crimsococcus halocryophilus* really and truly from Mars? Or was it just a remnant from past Mars missions?

We and our partners were convinced our mission had discovered Life on Mars. Others insisted *Crimsococcus*—Crimsy, for short—was little more than the offspring of an Earthling bug, one of thirty-or-so thousand bacteria that hitch rides from Earth to the Red Planet, despite our best efforts to sterilize probes, rovers, robotic arms, and landing vehicles.

Harold Hale, the Harvard astrobiologist, led the latter, soul-crushing camp. If Crimsy were merely a "forward contaminant"—a germ forwarded from Earth to Mars—"How do you explain its discovery nowhere near any previous landing sites? And below ground?" Those were the kinds of press questions Dr. Hale routinely dismissed.

"Extraordinary claims require extraordinary evidence," he said. "All we have at this point are extraordinary claims."

"That isn't true, and he knows it," our principal investigator Marcia Levitt said. "What the hell changed?"

"He didn't expect us to find anything," said Mike Brando, our lead microbiologist. "Nobody did."

I SAT IN THE audience on Capitol Hill before our mission began, watching the House Committee on Science, Space, and Technology grill Dr. Levitt, looking for any reason to take NASA—and taxpayers—out of the loop.

I remember the morning Dr. Hale testified. We held our collective breath: What would *he* say? He was skeptical in the media, doubtful on grant application reviews.

"Do you solemnly swear to tell the truth, the whole truth, and nothing but the truth, so help you God?"

"I do," Dr. Hale said, his right hand raised before the phalanx of inquisitors, camera crews, interns, aides, and water glasses on the table of truth before him.

"It is my professional and scientific opinion . . . "

Uh oh. Here it comes.

" . . . after much consideration and intimate involvement in the planning and funding process . . . "

Dragging out the agony. Get it over with! Plunge in the knife!

" . . . that if we fail to support a mission of this magnitude, our people, the American People, will be the worse off for it," he read from a prepared statement.

"What Dr. Levitt and her hand-picked team of scientists and researchers promise is the payoff of Mars mission spending that dates to 1964 and Mariner Three.

"Our last Mars rover, *Foresight*, found the strongest evidence yet of extremophile life below the planet surface and along the slopes lineae.

"Coupled with new techniques to distinguish between life native to Mars and possible contaminants from previous missions that somehow survived; and a new method to identify microbes on the planet, MarsMicro presents our best opportunity yet to find life on the Red Planet.

"Carl Sagan—whose lifelong dream was to find life on Mars —said the evidence for it was not yet extraordinary enough. Now, I believe that it is."

I was almost in tears. I craned my head and looked around. In the crowded room, I could only see the back of Dr. Levitt's head, but Dr. Brando caught my gaze and smiled. I smiled back, big and wide, and rolled my eyes. Dr. Hale had knocked it out of the park. For us.

IT WAS FUN WATCHING the post-docs doing the congratulatory shoulder grip thing on Dr. Levitt and mugging for selfies as we sat down for lunch at a cafe blocks from the Capitol.

"However this turns out, I want to thank you guys for all your love and support," Levitt said.

"To our fearless PI," Dr. Shonstein said, toasting our

principal investigator with her Pepsi.

"Here, here," Dr. Marcum agreed, raising his lox-and-cream-cheese-lathered bagel.

"For she's a jolly good fellow, for she's a jolly good fellow, for she's a jolly good fellow," we sang. "That nobody, not even Hale, can deny."

We got our funding and our ride-along ticket, only the second round trip in Martian history. Drs. Levitt, Shonstein, Marcum, Brando, and me, the PhD-to-be, weren't wasting taxpayer money after all.

JPL

Two

"The best scientific papers and mathematical equations are brief, so in that spirit I'd like to publish a one or two pager in a place like *Nature* or *Science* ala Watson, Crick, and the double helix," Dr. Levitt explained at our weekly staff meeting. "But *we* will assure full credit for our *entire* team," she continued. "No Rosalind Franklins."

"I should *hope* we'd be a bit more egalitarian than the old norms," Dr. Marcum said.

"What about the nitty-gritty?" Dr. Brando asked. "The details, our travails, my secret recipe for saltwater taffy?"

"I have an idea, but I wanna put it to a vote," Dr. Levitt said. "I'd like us to consider making Jennifer's diss the primary compendium of the nitty-gritty."

As in, my dissertation, the novel to Dr. Levitt's Cliff's Notes.

"Interesting idea," Dr. Marcum said.

"We can and should publish individual papers about our own contributions," Levitt said. "I'm just concerned that we establish provenance quickly, via the one route that's already well under way: her dissertation."

"I have a question about that," I said. "How do I cite everyone? Without publications to footnote?"

"You have some of mine already," said Dr. Marcum. "My predictive algorithms, analysis of Hale's work on microbial movement. Already published."

"Why not oral testimony, papers in process?" Dr. Shonstein said. "We've got some not-ready-for-prime-time stuff on the Arxiv," a vast online repository of science.

"Notes on napkins?" Dr. Brando said.

"Worked for Steve Jobs," Dr. Shonstein said.

"Well, sort of," Marcum said. "How many years have been spent litigating that stuff? All those pseudonymous patents and people claiming it was their handwriting tucked away in the 'one more thing' safe they found—what? In an old house?"

"Under it," I piped up. "The Jackling House. After Steve tore it down. Little safe they found years later."

"That's a trivial pursuit question right there," Shonstein said.

"Sounds like we're good on using papers in process," Levitt said. "U-Dub has deep pockets, but it's up to us to protect our provenance."

"How much does the University own of our work?" Dr. Brando asked.

"One hundred and ten percent," Dr. Shonstein said. "The ten percent is the pound of flesh they took after they tenured us."

"Speak for yourself," Brando said.

"That's right," Marcum said. "You're still up to bat."

"We need to vote," Levitt said. "All in favor of making Jennifer's dissertation our MarsMicro compendium, say 'aye.'"

The 'ayes' carried.

"Thank you," I said. "I'm honored."

Brando squeezed my forearm and smiled.

"Don't thank us yet," Shonstein said.

THE FIRST QUEST I mapped was the search for a way to detect bacteria on a planet that, at its closest to Earth, was thirty four million miles distant; at its farthest, two hundred and fifty million miles (401 million km) away. Even on Earth, "ship sample to lab" was a critical part of the testing process. That's fifteen minutes in Kenosha, Wisconsin, my hometown; two hours in LA traffic; six to eight months from Mars to Earth. And no telling if the samples would survive the trip.

Biolite technology promised ten times faster results without the need to grow a colony in nutrient-rich agar, baby food for bacteria. It lit up the bacteria on site. Food production companies used the technology in their plants; our team bacteriologist, Rebecca Shonstein, wondered if we couldn't use it on Mars.

Dr. Levitt liked the idea. So did the scientists who peer-reviewed Shonstein's paper for the journal Microbe: *A new method to detect bacterial microorganisms in non-Earth environments in situ.* But Dr. Brando wasn't convinced a key part of the test called a "phage" would survive the journey. Short for bacteriophage, a phage is a virus that infects a bacteria. Biolite figured out how to get phages to light up inside a germ.

"If the phages don't make it, we've got no test," Brando proclaimed.

"You're starting to sound like Hale," Shonstein said at one of our staff meetings. "Melissa finally getting to you?"

"What do you mean *finally*?" Brando said.

"We need a viral extremophile. One we can use as a well-lighted phage," a problem Dr. Shonstein proceeded to tackle with scientific gusto.

She found some thirty-year-old work by a group of Dartmouth bioengineers—Gupta, Lee, and Yin—that made a bold claim: "We demonstrate that a bacteriophage can, over a number of generations, be adapted to tolerate a hostile and unnatural environment." Their technique made the phage three hundred fifty times more capable of surviving harsh conditions.

Though she stayed out of the lab and away from contact with her muscular phages when she was pregnant with Malachi, Dr. Shonstein put in some wicked office hours grinding out protocols, spreadsheets, and grant applications.

"Okay—time for the big test," she said, eyeing the pillow contraption we constructed for back support on a swivel chair larger than the one she has now. She sat down and settled her back. "Ahh. Glorious. And now we set sail for Cape Disappointment." She turned to her monitor and pulled up a seemingly endless scroll of phage survivability data. "Dammit. Jennifer—we've got to get these temps down."

"When we raise the salt concentration, the phages croak."

"I know," she said. "*Oy vey iz mir.*"

We were facing another catch-22: Every time we lowered our test temperatures to replicate Mars, the phages died *unless* we also lowered our salt concentrations, which made the test less like Mars, and made the water freeze faster.

Martian salt is mostly magnesium and calcium perchlorate. The water on Mars gets trapped in the perchlorate crystals, where it stays liquid all the way down to minus ninety four degrees Fahrenheit, or minus seventy degrees Celsius, aka really fricking cold.

"So we're using calcium perchlorate, right?" Dr. Shonstein said. Before I could answer, "must be right. He just kicked me," she said. She smiled and looked at me. "What else have we tried? Refresh my tired memory."

"Magnesium perchlorate," I replied.

"Let's try potassium, sodium, and lithium perchlorate."

"Lithium?"

"It's got some interesting properties," she said. "Brandy suggested it at our first protocol meeting. I just wanna see if we can get our phages on board."

Malachi arrived, a pink, healthy eight pounds and change, two weeks before our salt-and-temp-tested bacteriophage emerged.

"Sodium worked," Dr. Brando texted our new mom, who would not be back in the office, classroom, or lab for several weeks, but who was as eager for us to be successful at phage rearing as she was trying her hardest and most exhausted to be at child rearing.

Shonstein dialed into a conference call sounding weary but happy. "Okay," she said. "Our phage is cool with Martian-level low temps and sodium perchlorate concentrations. But this ain't Martian salt."

"What about a two-step process?" Dr. Brando asked. "We acclimate the phages to sodium perchlorate, then gradually introduce calcium perchlorate."

"I like that idea," said Dr. Levitt, our team geologist. "Calcium and sodium perchlorate dissolve about the same in water. We kind of got lucky that the phage likes sodium."

"What if it's a different kind of water on Mars?" Dr. Shonstein asked. "Something our mapping and testing somehow missed."

"What kind of water?" Levitt asked.

"Heavy water, say."

A different kind of water on Mars? I mean, why not? Normal water is H_2O. Heavy water is D_2O. Heavy water freezes and boils at higher temperatures. It will kill fish and tadpoles. But bacteria can live quite nicely in heavy water. So why not?

"I think the odds are significantly against heavy water or anything other than good old H_2O," said Bill Marcum, the mathematician known as The First Man in Dreads to Win a Fields Medal, with the added gravitas of his British elocution. "I can show everyone mathematically why we shouldn't worry about anything more exotic than calcium perchlorate," Dr. Marcum added.

"I'm down with that," Dr. Shonstein said over the speaker phone. "Dr. Brando?"

"Fine by me."

"Dr. Levitt?"

"It was a wild idea, but good to explore all possibilities."

"So we have a motion on the floor," Shonstein said, probably from her bed. "We take our sodium perchlorate-acclimated phages and gradually introduce calcium perchlorate. We don't worry about hypotheticals like heavy water. And we see what happens. Sound like a plan?"

Agreeable nods and noises circled the table.

"We are close, people," Shonstein concluded. "We are so close."

After a night of colic, breast-feeding refusal, Mom and Dad frantically trying to restore wee-hour calm and catch some rare Z's, Dr. Brando made the call.

"Hullo?" Dr. Shonstein said in her best exhausted new mom voice.

"It worked," he said. "Phage halocryophilus reporting for duty, ma'am."

"Oh, Brandy," she said. "That's the second best news I've had all year."

TO OUTFIT BIOLITE FOR space travel, we specified exotic materials like carbon nanotubes; extra strong, contaminant-free glass; and metal with glass-like properties aptly called "metallic glass." I overheard an argument about that payload from Shonstein's office in the Physics-Astronomy Building or PAB, which rhymes with HAB, the habitation module that kept Mark Watney safe in *The Martian*.

"Arjan," she told me beneath headphones, as in Arjan Kadabe "Integrated Planning & Execution Team Chief" at the Jet Propulsion Lab in Pasadena.

"I'm wondering if we shouldn't just include your stuff as part of environmental monitoring," Dr. Kadabe said.

"Our 'stuff'?" Dr. Shonstein said to me later.

"They're still in SAM mode," I said. "We're in BAM mode."

Past rovers equipped with SAM, aka Sample Analysis at Mars, looked for the building blocks of life—hydrogen, carbon, oxygen, nitrogen, amino acids, water vapor—or evidence of past life, like fossils or ancient seas. But our mission was BAM —Biological Analysis on Mars.

"It has to be clear that MarsMicro is *organism* focused." I walked past her office and overheard her on her headset again. I peered in to see her in the chair at her desk, swiveled around to Malachi stacking puzzle blocks.

"I know. I realize that," Dr. Shonstein said. "But our tests require an even stricter level of sterility. Everything's designed to fit. I can resend those specs if you want."

She looked at me and rolled her eyes. Malachi's eyes followed the blocks in his mother's hand.

"Okay. Thanks." She set the headset on her desk and leaned back and stretched, both arms free in the air. "Why are we still having these discussions?" she asked me.

"How are you, buddy?" I said to Malachi. He was too absorbed to notice me.

"Martin was supposed to pick him up from daycare, but got called into a late meeting."

"If you ever need me to watch him."

"Thank you." She sounded surprised. "I may take you up on that."

"Still haggling?"

"Interminably," Dr. Shonstein said. "You do not know how much I'd love to scream."

"You think it's deliberate?" I asked. "SpaceTek wants to fold our research into theirs?"

"For what possible reason, my dear?"

"Ha!" I exclaimed. I started connecting bricks with Malachi, building an elaborate nothing-in-particular. We heard first raindrops patter on the window. Dr. Shonstein turned to watch, those big, round, individual splashes that herald a downpour.

"How's your diss going?"

Like with said PhD dissertation, I placed another block in its proper spot. "Awaiting data."

"Won't that be the day," she said. "What if we find something?"

"We're gonna find something. Remember?"

"Marcum's predictive algorithm? I'm not the mathematical genius he is, so I've taken that part on faith."

"I know we're gonna find something," I said. "Is that faith? Or science?"

Shonstein smiled. "God, I love your optimism. And what if this thing we find starts a pandemic. Or if it's like the thing in that movie years ago."

"It's too small."

"That thing was small. At least, it started small. What was the name of that movie?"

"It wasn't *Alien*."

"No, no. Alien didn't start out as a germ."

"Calvin?"

"I think that was the name of the critter. It crushed a guy's hand. I need my hands. I still change an occasional pullup, and diapers are on the horizon."

"Are you pregnant?"

"Oh god no. At least, god no for now. But Martin and I aren't finished. Malachi needs a Malachette—or a Ben. Maybe even a Betty, too."

"You want three?"

"Maybe. Maybe four."

"I don't want kids," I said. "Look at Dr. Brando."

Shonstein reached down with both hands and raised Malachi to her lap. He cuddled against her shoulder and she met his cheek with hers. "He's my peach," she said. "Aren't you, sweet boy?"

"Since you put it like that."

"I hope the Brandos work it out," Shonstein said. "I can't imagine."

"I don't want to," I said. "I'm married to my work."

"That's what I said. Then I met Mr. Mine. And this one came along. Didn't you?" She kissed her son and he took her nose in his hand and grinned.

I WITNESSED THE MARS fakes vs. uniques dilemma on our first visit to the Jet Propulsion Lab, watching engineers in biohazard suits load BAM onto the MarsMicro rover. It's an interplanetary catch-22—we can't explore Mars or any other planet without "forward contaminating" it with Earth's own extremophiles—bacteria that can survive the harsh trip's heat and cold extremes. The best we can do is reduce the probability that Earth microbes will contaminate a Mars mission.

"The Coleman-Sagan equation," Dr. Bill Marcum, our team mathematician, began this morning's meeting with a list of factors on the conference room whiteboard.

How many Earthling microorganisms are on the rover before it launches?

How many bacteria would heat sterilization of the mission apparatus kill before it launched?

How many microbes would survive launch?

How many microbes would survive entering the Martian

atmosphere?

How many contaminant microbes would then reproduce and thrive?

"Per our much-vaunted *planetary protection standards*, the International Committee on Space Research has decided a one in ten thousand chance of forward contamination is *acceptable*." Marcum said the last word with a shudder.

"We need one in a million," Shonstein said. "Only way to keep Hale at bay."

"How?" Dr. Levitt asked. "Hard to see any way to keep the risk that low."

"Brandy?" Shonstein asked Dr. Brando.

"Lasers and ultraviolet light—a ramped-up version of what they do in hospitals," Dr. Brando said. "I'll give Bill the preliminary data. He can run the numbers. It may not be one in a million, but it'll be a lot higher than the standard."

Marcum plugged that data into the Coleman-Sagan equation and voila! We wound up with a contamination probability of one in 774,000. MarsMicro would be a lot cleaner than its one-in-ten thousand predecessors.

DR. COOPER. WELCOME, WELCOME," Dr. Levitt said, to the post-doc walking down the aisle in Sparks Hall, our building's auditorium. "How are things at the Hale Lab?"

"We miss you," astroclimatologist Alonzo Cooper told her, as I took the chair beside him.

"Hal misses me?"

"Of course. And Jennifer, too. How are you?" We shook

hands.

"Everyone know Dr. Cooper?" Levitt asked.

"Coop." Shonstein reached over and shook his hand. "What wonderful providence prompted Dr. Hale to share you like this?"

"Industrial—or is it academic—espionage," Cooper said, smiling. "Why you guys are ranked first and we're pulling up the rear at a distant second."

"And I've got a Space Needle to sell you," Dr. Levitt said.

"You're upstaging him on RateMyProfessor," Marcum said.

I agreed with the red peppers and praise like, "Coop makes the Nine Circles of Hale almost heavenly." I was his teaching assistant and a speaker at Howard to Harvard week. Dr. Cooper came to Harvard from the NOAA Center, a Howard University-led climate research venture.

Dr. Levitt looked around the table. "Where's Brandy?"

"Court, I think," Dr. Shonstein said. "Visitation hearing."

"Are you kidding?"

"I wish I were. Melissa's got him in court, on the phone, or answering email 24/7."

"Okay, well. Onto Valles Marineris, the Grand Canyon of Mars," Dr. Levitt said. "Do we land there and if so, how?"

"Don't hold me responsible if the rover smashes up on the canyon walls," Dr. Marcum said.

"You're sending us there," Levitt quipped. "Of course I'm holding you responsible."

Marcum's mathematical model strongly suggested we put MarsMicro down on Coprates Chasma, a once-volcanically active region in Valles Marineris, named for the old Mariner missions. Superimposed over these United States, the 4,000 km —2,500 mile—long canyon almost swallows them whole.

"Visuals of the Valles suggest rivers and lakes and other signs of ancient hydration, coupled with high canyon walls that provided shade and cooler temperatures," Cooper added.

"Water water everywhere, and maybe a drop to analyze. Woot! " Shonstein said.

"So I'll throw in, being the team geologist," Levitt said. "Earlier expeditions spotted suggestive geologies around Coprates Chasma, including opals, which can contain up to twenty percent water. *Odysseus* identified highly-probable stromatolites in the same area."

"Remind me again what a stromatolite is," Dr. Cooper said.

"Fossilized bacteria," Levitt said. "The earliest known fossils on Earth."

"So how do we land in the middle of a jagged-edged canyon peppered with dormant volcanoes?" Cooper asked.

Dr. Levitt turned to the projector, stage right in Sparks Hall. "Sire," she commanded the voice-activated device. "Valles Marineris, Coprates Chasma, Levitt's Landing, please."

"Levitt's Landing?" Dr. Shonstein said.

"Commander Ryong suggested the name," Marcum said. "For esprit de corps, and an old-fashioned good luck wish from Deep Space Gateway."

An exquisite 3D rendering of the Martian canyon punctuated by pitted, cone-shaped objects thought to be old volcanoes appeared before us. It stretched the width of Sparks Hall's stage, compliments of the most amazing three-dimensional projection system in the world.

"It worked," Dr. Brando said.

"Sire the sinister behaves," Marcum said. "I still prefer my keyboard."

Levitt walked around the projection and with a laser pointer, identified Levitt's Landing, a flat, sturdy-looking spot close to the recurrent slope lineae that hinted of ancient water and life.

"This is approximately at the center of Chapman-Harrison Lake," Levitt said. "It's shallow, about as big as Earth's Caspian Sea. If we land here, we have the best chance of avoiding a mesa or a rock pile that could strand or crush our rover. Arjan Kadabe tells me the new navigation and propulsion systems are hypothetically, at least, capable of delivering the rover inside the canyon."

"Hypothetically?" Dr. Cooper asked. "And what about getting the samples out? If we think landing will require delicacy, launching back out . . . especially with wind, dust."

"The usual treachery," Dr. Marcum noted.

"We'll have to re-position the return vehicle somewhere around here." Levitt pointed to an area where the canyon walls were farther apart, presenting less of a flight hazard. A closer shot of this dirt patch looked more like the Martian surface I'd grown up wondrously viewing: dry, barren, rocky. No recurring slope lineae. No suggestive mineral deposits. No hints that anything might live or have lived there.

"And SpaceTek can do this?"

"We ran the simulation," Shonstein said. "Seemed doable to me."

"Speaking of the usual treachery: What about convection currents and the kind of unexpected turbulence you expect in a canyon?" Dr. Cooper asked.

"Sara Goode applied the Martian turbulence studies of Chen and Lovejoy to the Grand Canyon," Marcum said.

"Chen and Lovejoy. Let me think. Turbulence on Earth is statistically similar, if not identical, to turbulence on Mars," Cooper said.

"Indeed," Marcum said. "If Sara's right, and she always is, the Chen-Lovejoy findings hold in canyons as well as on surfaces. We can therefore use Grand Canyon turbulence to predict Valles Marineris turbulence, and map our route accordingly."

"Sara Goode," Dr. Brando said. "She just dash this off?"

"I wouldn't call it a dash-off, exactly," Marcum said. "But she did the bulk of the calculations in about two weeks."

Dr. Levitt was looking up, toward one of the lecture hall doors. I turned and saw Parada, who even from this distance was exquisite. Dr. Levitt flinched and fidgeted.

"Looks like we're holding up a class," Dr. Cooper said.

"That's Parada," Dr. Shonstein whispered to Cooper. "Marcia's fiancée."

"With two 'e's'," Dr. Marcum leaned in and reminded.

"That's all I have," Dr. Levitt said. She stuck her pointer in her pocket and I watched her ascend the aisle, say something to Parada, then the two women vanish behind the soft click of the closing door.

"Everything all right?" Dr. Marcum asked.

"I wouldn't know," Shonstein replied. But the tone of her voice suggested otherwise.

AFTER MONTHS OF ARGUING, debating, squabbling, cajoling, negotiating, and screaming after the phone or headset went down, our team made "The Pilgrimage," as Dr. Cooper called it, to Mission Control in Pasadena, a joint effort between SpaceTek, NASA, and JPL. A newly-remodeled geek's paradise, Mission Control offered one-touch adjustments to space travel parameters like planetary entry velocity and landing gear deployment unheard of with earlier missions.

Gate sentries scanned our microchips (the main reason I finally relented and had the Orwellian bug implanted) and a receptionist led us to a Mission Control "Simulation Station," which looked like the latest in 3D interactive movie theaters.

"If you'd all take your seats," said an engineer whose name tag read "A. Reed." "I'd like to introduce your simulation co-host, Pei Lin. I'm Argosy Reed, and this is the JPL MarsMicro simulator, the most immersive practice experience on this planet. Welcome."

"Welcome", "mornin'", and "hi" percolated around the

room, with a lone Brit-accented "howdy" from Dr. Marcum.

"We will be simulating entry into the Martian atmosphere and subsequent landing, with camera-eye views of precisely what Mission Control will see when we launch. We wanted you all to walk through this with us, help us work out any bugs, and assure we land the rover where you want it without incident."

Dr. Levitt turned to us and smiled. Dr. Marcum raised his hand in that polite halfway-way bidders use at an auction.

"Yes sir."

"I'm fascinated with this new navigation system we've been hearing about," Marcum said. "Quantum-entangled computers? That's never been more than theory."

"We have some surprises on this trip, including limited ability to use quantum entanglement with our landing computers," Dr. Lin said. "We've prepared a video presentation that will make a good segue into the simulation."

The lights went down and I felt my chair tilt back.

"Watch the ceiling, folks," Dr. Reed said.

A resonant space-faring voice narrated as a beam of light traveled through space from Earth to Mars. "With the Red Planet 34 million miles, or 55 million kilometers, from Earth at its closest, two-way communication with a rover or planetary laboratory used to take eight to twenty minutes, as signals traveled from Earth to Mars and back again, at no faster than light speed," the voice, which sounded suspiciously like Carl Sagan, explained. "This time delay hindered any instantaneous controls, like delicately steering into a canyon for a picture-perfect landing."

We saw a hypothetical vessel land in a hypothetical place deep within Valles Marineris. The slopes lineae were exaggerated: they looked like true rivulets of icy fresh spring water.

"If only," Dr. Shonstein whispered.

"MarsMicro," the voice continued, "offers the first test of our new quantum entanglement navigation system, also known as Quant-Quest, where the unusual properties of sub-atomic particles like photons allow an Earth-based computer to send instructions to Mars and receive feedback instantly. With Quant-Quest, we can guide the rover to a safe Mars landing with the same precision as parking a car outside."

We saw a split screen of a Mission Control engineer using a joystick to guide the craft down, down, down, three, five, maybe seven kilometers (at its deepest), into the dark heart of the Valles. No one knew exactly what the sides of the canyon walls looked like up close, but the imagined version was sufficiently mind-blowing. Valles Marineris is three times as deep as our Grand Canyon, and seven times as wide.

"Einstein called this quantum entanglement phenomenon 'spooky action at a distance,'" the narrator continued, "which roughly translated means that two entities cannot communicate with one another faster than the speed of light unless something spooky is going on. Light takes roughly three minutes to reach Mars from Earth when the two planets are at their closest, hardly the split second timing we need for precision craft control.

"Einstein wasn't wrong. Two separate entities cannot talk to one another at faster than light speed. But the key word is *separate.* Using a device known as an Einstein-Podolsky-Rosen (EPR) Bridge—named for a famous paradox about spooky action—we are able to fuse two computers, one on Earth and one on the MarsMicro rover, at the quantum level. This single functional unit uses a property of sub-atomic particles known as 'spin' to calculate and communicate instantly."

The film used animations to illustrate: colorful tops spinning clockwise and counterclockwise, aka up and down. "Spin Up and Spin Down are the quantum entanglement versions of the famous zeroes and ones at the heart of traditional computer systems. With the EPR Bridge, a Spin Up command on Earth instantly becomes a Spin Down action on Mars. Press a button here, get an action there. No waiting for light or radio signals to travel deep space."

The lights came up.

"Amazing," Dr. Marcum said. "So you have full control from Mission Control."

"Yes, but only of the landing apparatus at this point," Lin said. "Rover control is still in beta testing."

"That has to be a huge advantage," Dr. Cooper said. "You still have any minutes of terror?"

"No," Reed said.

"What are minutes of terror?" I asked.

"Before, because of the signal delay, we had no idea if we had landed in one piece for about seven minutes," Lin said. "Was the landing successful? Or did we crash? We could only cross our fingers, agonize in terror, and wait the requisite minutes for the signal from Mars to travel home."

"Is everyone comfortable and ready?" Reed asked.

We nodded and mumbled agreeably. "I'd say so," Dr. Levitt said.

The lights went out again and what happened next I can only describe as a Disney ride on steroids. I felt like I was being hurdled forward, as the MarsMicro spacecraft pierced the Martian atmosphere at roughly fifteen thousand miles per hour. Seat warmers even simulated the heated entry we were witnessing on screen, getting a few laughs.

The action on the walls and ceiling had us completely immersed, as the spaceship released the newest generation of sky crane, a flying version of Spiderman villain Doc Ock, that would plunk the rover on the planet surface with precision mechanical arms.

Cameras on the ship followed the crane, which deployed a parachute on one end, then a suite of rocket engines to keep it aloft. We watched first from cameras on the spaceship; then from cameras on the crane, as a panoramic view of the Martian surface unfolded.

And holy—! Valles Marineris came into view.

I broke out in goosebumps and saw Drs. Levitt and Shonstein join hands out the corner of my eye. I've hiked and camped the Grand Canyon, viewed it from a helicopter and its awe-inspiring rim, where it looks like a surreal painting that at any moment might vanish into your imagination.

But you can't see across Valles Marineris, which like the Great Lakes presents the illusion of an infinite horizon. Up here, from the landing vehicle's perspective, it was an awesome, endless cavern that looked like a planet unto itself.

I don't know how JPL pulled off this simulated vision. No vehicles have ever navigated the Valles extensively, and past missions have turned back mostly grainy close shots. MarsMicro was in for one helluva ride.

Our seats returned upright.

"Please direct your attention to the control sticks and Cloud screens rising from the floor," Argosy Reed said. "Dr. Levitt, would you do the honors? Take the stick and navigate into the canyon."

"It's a very intuitive system," Pei Lin said. "You have a large margin for error, so don't be shy."

Dr. Levitt raised a "thumbs up" over her head and grasped the controller, flying crane and rover toward the Valles, more glorious with every airborne second.

"Dr. Brando," Reed said. "If you will bring up the coordinate guide on your cloud screen and enter the Coprates quadrangle, latitude south: thirteen point four degrees; and longitude west: sixty one point four degrees, we will be on our way to the Coprates Chasma."

The flying crane gracefully turned, soaring above the canyon floor. The characteristic dimpled cones came into view, and I got a distant glance of recurring slope lineae.

"Guide the craft toward a green X that will appear as you near the landing site," Reed said.

Dr. Levitt moved the vehicle in said direction, until it was hovering high over what was apparently the Coprates Chasma.

"So far, so good," Reed said. "You're using our latest version of Range Trigger, by the way, developed for *Perseverance*."

"Any volunteers to begin our descent into the Valles floor?" Pei Lin asked.

"I'll be the guinea pig," Dr. Shonstein said. "But if I crash—"

"We're hoping Terrain Relative Navigation and MEDLI4 make that a remote possibility," Reed said. "Are you all familiar with TRN and MEDLI4?"

"Only at their most rudimentary," Dr. Marcum responded.

"MEDLI for sure," Cooper added.

"With Terrain Relative Navigation," Lin said, "our orbiters have created a detailed map of the landing site, which you guys are calling 'Levitt's Landing'?"

"We are," Dr. Marcum said.

"The sky crane and rover constantly video and photograph the landing site, comparing the visuals with the Orbiter maps stored in their navigation computers," Reed explained. "The continual updates allow the ensemble to avoid small obstacles. MEDLI4 adds the most up-to-date atmospheric information and analysis."

"Okay now," Lin said to Shonstein. "Take the controller and steady as she goes. You'll use the buttons on its right hand side to cut back the rockets and decrease altitude; left hand side for extra thrust."

The sky crane began its descent.

"We're particularly pleased with our simulated Valles interior," Lin said. "We think you're in for some astonishing visuals."

Imagine a line of Mount Everests as long as the United States, on two sides. That's what we were dropping into. Lights and more cameras switched on as the sky crane descended, the planet's horizon gradually giving way to the Valles. Total—and I mean *total*—chills, as the crane broke the canyon's crest and sunlight and shadows played on layer upon layer of Martian minerals, billions of years of sedimentation, hints of water, and the most exciting signs I'd ever seen that something other than rocks and dust once inhabited this eerie expanse.

"Incredible," Cooper exclaimed.

There was no sense that we were on Mars anymore; nothing anywhere suggested anything but Valles. We stayed near one side of the canyon, as the other side gradually gave way to the hundred mile distance that divided the canyon walls.

In the Grand Canyon, you can see the other side. You can see to the top from the bottom. You know you're on Earth. But not here. We had left Mars for yet another new world, where only one side of the Valles reminded us where we were. Down, down, down. The crane's lights grew brighter, sunlight dimmer, with the descent.

"Let's move her toward the interior. Better light there," Reed directed. "Keep descending. I'll tell you when to enter our landing site coordinates."

The crane moved away from the valley wall, soaring over

hundreds of dead volcano mounds that looked like mud piles.

"Lots of obstacles in here, so slow and steady, slow and steady," Reed said.

"Watch out!" I blurted. The crane ran headlong into one of the mounds. Lights and warning buzzers shattered our collective trance.

"Whaddid I did?" Shonstein said.

"Damage report," Reed said.

A synthetic voice came back with "no damage."

"A lot of these mounds we think are just dried mud left virtually undisturbed this far into the Valles," Reed explained. "Still, we have to maneuver around them."

The crane flew deeper into the abyss and the most incredible bloom of recurring slope lineae appeared. The way the rivulets bent the sunlight made them appear like flowing rainbows, weaving down the sides of hills and canyon walls and mud volcanoes, fanning out into what may have been diluvium, the soil-engraved remains of a Noah-sized flood as it gradually receded.

MMM. MMM. MMM: A beeping noise that sounded like the letter M between pursed lips.

"That's our landing coordinates signal," Lin said. "Dr. Brando: On your Cloud screen, would you please enter the following coordinates: thirteen point four degrees."

"Thirteen point four degrees," Brando repeated, touching the control panel, hovering like a ready specter next to his seat.

"Twenty one minutes."

Brando followed.

"Four point three seconds South."

"Done," Brando said.

"Now: Sixty one point four degrees, forty seven minutes, seven point eight seconds West."

He completed the entry and this appeared on our monitors: 13.4° 21′ 4.3″ S and 61.4° 47′ 7.8″ W. The crane veered to our right, away from the mud domes and rocks and craters.

"Entering powered descent," the synthetic voice said. "Autopilot to Levitt's Landing."

A miraculous thing happened: the MarsMicro Rover, three times the size but only the twice the weight of her immediate predecessors, the *Foresight* and *Odysseus* rovers, emerged from the sky crane like an elaborate blossom. Then the simulation did something I don't think I can ever forgive: it heightened our already towering emotions with the tremulous first notes of Johann Strauss' *Blue Danube Waltz*.

"Begin sky crane rover separation," the synthetic voice told us. "Five minutes to first contact."

One by one, like petals on a rose, arms, tracks, wheels, lasers, cameras, battery-charging solar panels opened in time to the waltz, below the crane's cameras, where we could see our equipment approaching the Valles floor.

"Nice touch," Cooper's voice boomed, as the waltz played and the sky crane sailed.

"Our chief flight engineer," Reed said. "He loves setting things to music."

"Three minutes to contact and counting," the simulation

voice instructed.

I rubbed my hands through my hair and stared. Triumphant strands of Strauss, sunlight and crane lights frolicking on the rover and the looming canyon floor. And this was just a simulation. What would the real thing be like?

"One minute to contact and counting."

On cue, the crane's arms released its precious payload.

"Hovercraft ignition," and the crane was free and itself hovered, preparing for its own landing and eventual reuse.

The rover's hover engines forced out air-filled cushions, like car air bags, which replaced the balloons that used to protect rovers of old as they bounced to a graceless but effective landing.

"Ten, nine, eight, seven, six, five, four, three, two, one. Surface contact established. Hover engines cease."

And MarsMicro was on the ground, just like that. The air bags deflated and retracted, for re-use of course.

"You can cheer now," Reed said.

And we did, with woots and yeahs and hell yeahs.

"Gotta know how to do the JPL cheer."

Dr. Levitt, Dr. Shonstein, and I looked at each other.

"That was amazing," Shonstein whispered. And in that instant, any acrimony between Rebecca Shonstein and the Jet Propulsion Lab vanished.

"DUST STORM PROTECTION: BRINGING certainty to cleaning events" was the subject of Wednesday's hour-long demonstration during our Simulation Week at JPL in Pasadena.

"You know how those Styrofoam peanuts cling to damn near everything," began our guide, Argosy Reed, brushing a handful of the white packaging bits off his sweater sleeve. "Now imagine a storm of these peanuts. That's what a Martian dust storm is like. Martian dust can have enough static cling that it sticks like Velcro."

An animation of a dust devil in hot pursuit of a solar-and-nuke-powered rover driving across the planet surface appeared on the screen over our lecture hall stage.

"Guess who wins this race?" Reed continued. The dust devil passed over the rover, leaving it covered with fine, dull, reddish grit. "Dust won't affect power sources like plutonium-238 and batteries," Reed said. "But we still need the solar panels, for backup, battery recharge, heli-drone power. And dust can gum up other things. Our only hope to keep the rover running smoothly after a dust storm is a cleaning event."

A friendly wind blew off most of the dust.

"A cleaning event is basically a dust-free breeze," Dr. Cooper announced.

"We used to rely on cleaning events to get the dust off and restore power," Reed said. "With primary nuclear power and solar backup, that's not as big a problem. But onboard control is a huge problem."

"Breezes are unpredictable," Cooper continued. "And cleaning events aren't much help keeping the other equipment clean."

"Which is why we developed a better method," Reed interjected.

While the rover's robotic arms sampled soil and photographed ice in another animation, a dust storm loomed amid light flashes in the dark. We heard a soft hum. The storm got closer and closer, finally passing over and around, staying about four feet on all sides from the rover, which looked like it was in a transparent bubble.

"Some kind of force field?" Dr. Marcum said.

"An 'electrodynamic screen,'" Reed said. "We use dynamic electricity—the kind that flows through wires—to repel the static electricity that makes Martian dust so clingy."

"When can I get one for my clothes dryer?" Marcum said.

"Some of our investors hope quite soon," Reed said.

"I've seen a system like this in clean rooms," Dr. Shonstein said. "But nothing portable."

"Sounds like you took the advice of our collaboration," Dr. Levitt said. "I was part of a group that studied and characterized the dust *Odysseus* brought back."

"We did," Reed said. "Think of the electrodynamic screen as a pop-up storm cellar. Good for the rover to hunker down in until the storm passes and the coast clears."

"But you have to know when the tornado's coming to know when to get into the storm cellar," Midwestern me said.

"Same idea applies here."

"So we actually have to predict small dust storms for this system to work?" Cooper said. "It can't just be on all the time?"

"The electrodynamic screen isn't without its drawbacks. It interferes with the EPR Bridge and other controls. We can't send or receive instantaneous signals—commands, audio, video, whatever. We're back to the old ten to fifteen minute wait times, each way. So we stop rover operations and wait," Reed explained.

"And hope the storm doesn't last too long." Cooper swept us with his eyes. He looked at Reed.

"How much lead time does the onboard computer need to turn that thing on?" Shonstein said.

"Let's see," Dr. Cooper said. "Thin atmosphere, weak gravity, sand like snow: A six mile-an-hour breeze could kick up a helluva dust cloud in seconds."

"That's not much lead time," Brando said.

I CAN'T BELIEVE THEY'D drop something like this on us so close to launch," Cooper said that night at dinner around a big table at Mijares, my fave Mexican restaurant when I lived here.

"We can predict everything else," Dr. Levitt said. "Why not dust devils?"

"Dust devils are about as unpredictable as weather gets," Cooper said. "Plus, you've got a totally different type of air, different gravity, different lightning, and hella different dust."

"It *is* strange stuff," Levitt said. "We wore hair covers and gas masks whenever we handled it in the lab. When we stirred it, even slightly, it rose and hovered like smoke and took forever to settle. And it wouldn't wash off, no matter what we tried. We had to use those dryer sheets to get it off glassware. And forget it if it got on your lab coat or pants. No detergent on Earth will take it out."

"Truly the devil's dust," Marcum said.

"Any way to adapt what we used to predict canyon turbulence?" Brando asked. "What was it called—Love-something?"

"Chen-Lovejoy. With more time, maybe. But I barely have time to get done what's already on my desk," Cooper said. "Hale's breathing down my neck for the grant report he promised the House Science Committee. If it's not in, they could pull our funding."

"Dust devils are a kind of turbulence," Marcum said. "My good friend Sara Goode might appreciate the challenge."

A LOT OF BACK and forth later, Drs. Marcum, Cooper, and Goode from her academic perch in Australia, had designed a kind of Terrain Relative Navigation system for everything dust. Clouds, storms, devils, haze, even micro-particulate swirls invisible to the naked eye became another kind of terrain. Probes and monitors delivered temperature, pressure, wind velocity, solar activity, even humidity readings (Mars does get surprisingly humid, especially at night) to the rover's onboard computer, which translated the data into a "dust storm probability." A high storm likelihood switched on the electrodynamic force field. The rover then sat idle until the probability dropped to an acceptable level (like zero).

The system worked in simulations, and once after the rover had landed on Mars, when a dust devil about thirty meters away triggered the shield. A low-slung haze developed that gradually settled during about a Martian day of dead time, as the rover hunkered down in its invisible storm cellar, emerging cheerfully clean thereafter.

Three

I was taking my final set—ever—of brain-frying finals when MarsMicro launched, so I didn't get to share the excitement of live takeoff at Cape Canaveral. But I was there, at Mission Control with my brothers David, Brian, and Mom, when MarsMicro landed.

And when the rover got stuck the next day.

On touchdown eve, we were seated on lawn chairs in the cool, desert air outside JPL with an audience of mission staff and media, watching closed-circuit big screens of the action inside Mission Control.

But unlike previous audiences, we weren't watching pre-recorded space travel simulations or time-delayed video. With the new Quant-Quest gear, we saw the landing craft and rover touch down in real time, guided and steered by blue-shirted engineers and navigators from six nations.

We were glued to rolling data—Distance, Altitude, Velocity, Time to Entry, Time to Touchdown—monitoring the rover as it entered Mars' orbit and descended to the surface. The camera panned a few brown suits inside Mission Control—investors and Senator Alan Scherr, a decades-long NASA supporter—and Dr. Levitt, who smiled and waved.

On the back wall, *NASA/SpaceTek Jet Propulsion Laboratory, California Institute of Technology* overlooked the proceedings in bold 3D lettering next to a montage of flags from the nations involved in our venture. Patriotism, the scientific method, international teamwork, Cal Tech alma loyalty (me). What emotional button weren't they pushing?

As the rover neared the planet surface, each small milestone merited applause. "Comm support established." Applause. "Quantum linkup complete." Applause. "EM drives engaged." There it was, the announcement of this incredible new propulsion technology, and I missed it. Must have been because of the applause. The blue shirts looked like an orchestra from out here, manipulating joysticks and touchscreens and Cloud screens like musicians stroking harps, tickling keys, coaxing violins.

My anxiety peaked when the chief flight engineer started pacing the floor. He peered over shoulders, made hand signals: thumbs up, thumbs down, a wave, three fingers, one finger, a stare, a frown, a tentative smile.

"We have a heartbeat," I heard. Tones from the landing craft let Mission Control know signals were coming through. More applause. Lots of smiles. All eyes on the flight data.

Distance 2,100 miles/3379.6 km and dropping.
Altitude 1,034 miles/1664 km and dropping.
Time to entry -00:05:47.3 and falling.
Velocity 15,079 miles/24,267.298 km per hour and holding.

Everybody watching, watching. "Who put these filberts in

the peanuts?" I heard someone quip. Everyone was eating peanuts, inside and out here. It's a NASA touchdown tradition.

"No more freakin' seven minutes of terror," someone else said.

"Heartbeat tones continuing. Navigation systems engaged."

"Three minutes to entry."

Altitude 402 miles.

Mom squeezed my hand and lay her head on my shoulder. Parada waved with two fingers and a grin. The rest of our team was spread around in lawn chairs, faces in the crowd.

"This is too cool," Brian said. David leaned over and gave me the biggest smile.

Entry. Descent. Landing. Those three words pulsated on our screens, while flight engineers called out MarsMicro's progress.

"EM thrusters now online," we heard. "Still getting heartbeat tones. Everything looking good."

The camera panned Mission Control again. Dr. Levitt was focusing intently on a monitor.

"Coming up on entry. Engaging live feed." Minor applause.

"Approaching entry interface. Starting guided entry." Bigger applause. A few woo-hoos.

"We are now receiving data." Cheering.

"Heading toward target. Heat shield holding. Temperatures stable."

"Range Trigger engaged. Terrain Relative Navigation [TRN] online."

"Mach two point four. Altitude twelve kilometers."

"Mach two and falling. Heartbeat tones okay."

"We have atmospheric clearing and live video." Big applause. And there was MarsMicro, on all of our monitors and the 3D imaging ports at each flight navigation station. I shivered in the warm air.

"Parachutes deploying." Mom's hug grew tighter, as we watched the parachute—that symbol of safe landings—expand.

"Heat shield separated. EM reverse thrusters engaged. Comparing TRN data."

"Altitude six kilometers and falling."

"Hover systems online. Watch the rocks, people."

"We are in powered flight." Applause and cheers.

"Range Trigger moving us one degree west" and other stuff I didn't catch.

"We have canyon."

That's when the goosebumps hit and *hard,* as the vast and this time, *real* walls of Valles Marineris opened up. And the first notes of that Straussian homage to Stanley Kubrick—*The Blue Danube*—waltzed off with our emotions.

"Oh my god!" my mother chirped, as the rover and the landing crane glided into the canyon. Brian and David just stared. In fact, no one moved. Not in Mission Control, not out here. Even the chief flight engineer stopped pacing to stare. It was an awesome, awesome sight.

The waltz faded as the voices returned.

"Descending at 0.8 meters per second. Sky crane holding."

"Hover engines engaged. EM Drive stable."

"TRN takin' us in."

Down, down. Lights getting brighter, illuminating the canyon wall. Then suddenly, unexpectedly, "Touchdown Coprates site. We are safe on Mars."

In unison out here and inside, we jumped and cheered and fist-bumped and high-fived and high-tenned. Brian kissed Mom. He kissed me. He kissed David. Mom was hugging me so tightly it almost hurt and she grabbed me around the neck and whispered into my ear, "I'm so so proud of you," she cried.

And I almost cried. I've never felt anything so crushingly joyous.

"I wish your father were here to see this," Mom said.

"Me, too."

I saw Parada standing, all six plus feet of her, looking bewildered. I pushed through the crowd. "Parada." She turned and we hugged.

"*That* was amazing," she said.

AFTER THE LANDING, WE ate at Flintridge, a JPL-fave restaurant open late nearby. I went with the fam, Dr. Brando, and Lexi. Dr. Levitt, Parada, Dr. Shonstein and the rest of our University of Washington Astrobiology Department walked in shortly after we were seated.

Dr. Levitt came over to our table.

"I didn't get to see you guys and I wanted to meet your family," she said.

I stood and went around the table. "My baby brother Brian. My big brother David. And last but always first, my most wonderful mother," I said. "Patrice Zendeck."

Dr. Levitt shook each hand in turn. "Marcia Levitt," she said.

"And I don't know if you've met: Dr. Mike Brando and his daughter, Lexi," I teased.

"We have indeed met," Dr. Levitt said. She shook Lexi's hand. "Future human on Mars?"

Lexi smiled.

"Jennifer is one of our superstars, I want you all to know," Dr. Levitt said. "She has been such a trooper."

"Wow," Mom whispered to the table.

"My sister's very humble," Brian said. "Never brags on self, so we don't always hear all this great stuff."

"She certainly brags on all of you," Dr. Levitt said. "I know where she gets her intelligence and drive."

Mom took my arm. "Chip off the old block," she said.

I couldn't remember the last time she was this affectionate. The idea that flying to Mars was bringing our family together, if even briefly, was as stupendous as the idea that life existed in such barrenness. I loved seeing Mom light up. I loved seeing Brian so animated. I loved seeing David look relaxed for a change.

"I'd invite you over to our table, but this place is packed and we're crammed together," Dr. Levitt said.

"Count on me to represent the team," Dr. Brando said.

"How did we get separated?" Dr. Levitt asked.

"Lexi. She wanted to go with Jennifer." She must have

communicated this flattering desire privately, because it was the first I'd heard.

"We love having Lexi," my mother said, leaning over and hugging her shoulders.

"Come by tomorrow," Dr. Levitt said. "We're firing up the rover and driving in the Valles."

"Really?" Brian said.

"Really. Real time controls. Dr. Cooper likens it to 3D video games, only much cooler."

I SIDLED UP TO David on the way to the car in the parking lot. "You're awfully quiet," I said.

"Just enjoying the moment."

"You mean the mom?"

"Oh yeah. Brian, too. Maybe it's this weather."

The night was cool, clear, easy. The days were warm, but not humid like Kenosha. The Sun had a lilting quality, pleasant, gentle, soft, never harsh nor bright-yet-freezing. I saw Lexi hugging on Mom as she and her dad slipped into their rental car.

"That doesn't hurt, either," David said observantly.

THE YOU-KNOW-WHAT hit the rover's hovercraft fans early the next morning. Dr. Levitt texted me. "Get over here if you want excitement."

I was barely awake. "Wat's up?" I texted back.

"They'll let you in."

"Fam?"

"Asleep, right?"

Good point. It was 3:30 AM. I slipped on clothes and sandals and told our rental car to drive me to JPL. The gate guard scanned my chip.

"Hands on steering wheel at all times, ma'am," she said.

The car parked and a blue-shirted staffer escorted me to Mission Control. Drs. Levitt, Shonstein, Marcum, and Cooper were gathered around a large monitor, gawking over the shoulders of a GN—ground navigation engineer—nudging a joystick.

"What's going on?" I whispered.

Dr. Levitt pressed her finger to her lips and pointed at the screen. The rover looked stuck in what was maybe a rock-and-dirt slide down the side of a Valles Marineris wall.

"Any luck?" the chief flight engineer (CFE) asked.

"Nada. She's tighter than a drum."

"This is not good, people," the CFE announced, over everyone's headphones.

"You've tried hover mode?" Marcum said.

"Yeah."

Marcum went to a 3D projection of the rover and rock outcropping. "You mind?" he asked.

"What's the plan?"

"Want to see what's stuck in the rocks."

Marcum moved the rover image, looking at its tires, hover

ports, and two side-mounted objects that looked like small cones positioned large end out. "What are these?" Marcum asked.

"Have to ask the chief," the navigator replied.

Marcum turned and motioned the CFE over. "Was wondering what these were."

"Top secret prototypes," he said. "If I tell you, I'll have to kill you."

"That wouldn't be good for you in front of all these witnesses," Marcum quipped. "But seriously."

"Seriously. Top secret prototypes."

"What do they do?" Marcum asked.

"We're not supposed to say until they've passed all their tests. Which aren't scheduled for weeks."

Marcum looked at the cones. Cooper walked over and looked, too. "They look like little jets," he said.

"If they were, they might get us untangled," Marcum said. "Just eyeing the angular and rotational momentum they could generate."

"Hear that?" the ground navigator (GN) said, rocking the rover with the joystick, forward, backward, forward, backward, trying to get it unstuck.

The navigator and CFE conferred.

"We haven't tested it."

"Worth a try."

"Not ready. Could break the thing apart."

"What other choice?"

I don't know what they said—or did—next, but the audio feed relayed a noise like a pound on a kettle drum and two of the impeding rocks moved back.

"I'll be damned," the CFE said.

"How did that happen?" Dr. Levitt asked.

"Rock and roll," the CFE said.

As the GN moved the joy stick back and forth again, the rover started breaking free.

"Another burst?" he asked his boss.

"Why not?"

Kettle drum noise again. Some unseen force drove one of the rover's tires onto an adjacent rock.

"Now what? We can't just drive forward."

"If you're using those mysterious jets," Dr. Marcum interrupted, "turn off the one on the left, then turn on the right hover motor and use it to push off that rock."

The CFE nodded to the GN.

I watched one side of the rover rise in a dust cloud as the hover motor forced air underneath. "Okay," the chief flight engineer said. "Pray." He motioned to the navigator, who ramped up the hover motor. "On one," he said. "Five, four, three, two, one."

Kettle drum noise. The rover whipped left, and in a clumsy, glorious move, broke free of the rocks.

"Full hovers. Forward thrusters," the CFE said. "Now!"

The rover flew forward about six feet and emerged from a dust cloud and the navigator set it down with a hard bounce on clear Martian soil. Cheers, applause, all that NASA high-five stuff.

"How's that for Earthly ingenuity?" Dr. Levitt said.

Dr. Marcum followed up on the mysterious prototype, electromagnetic-drive rover engines. SpaceTek and JPL had miniaturized the same technology that gave the rockets a boost on the way to the planet. And with this big save, the miniaturized model passed one test weeks early.

"EM drive will be huge someday, for auto, aircraft, any industry that uses engines," the CFE told Marcum. "That's why we're being careful about how much we disclose."

Four

I stayed in my office later than usual, catching up on my diss after our week in Pasadena, reading, and I guess, nodding off. An odd, high-pitched whimper awakened me and I thought an injured dog had found its way into the building. What *is* that? I tried the door to the stairwell and the janitor's closet (locked) and to the only place in our now-empty building that might create an echo, Sparks Hall.

No dog.

I followed the intermittent cries to Dr. Brando's office, where his door was ajar. I stood torn between bursting in—what if he was injured?—and pushing his door slowly so it wouldn't squeak, allowing me a discreet peek. I opted for a hurried adaptation of the latter.

I saw him crouched against the wall on the floor, head in his arms on his knees, next to the elaborate book case that lined his walls. He had the largest collection of real, palpable books among our team, ever fearful of a repeat of Fahrenheit 2031. I was relying on my Ember Blaze e-reader to get me through a General Relativity class, and I remember when Avalon turned off every Ember and Ember Flame and Ember Blaze in the world. I was without my digital compendium for three agonizing days. I remember the news media called it a *hacking*, the tech media a "cloudburst," a massive failure of the servers that host Avalon's cloud computing infrastructure their

PR flacks assured the world "would never happen again."

But Mike Brando would have none of it.

"This," he told me, proudly displaying his voluminous wall, "is my book shelter."

I wanted to enter, ask him what was wrong. But I stayed near the door, heard him sniffle, and saw him move his head. I don't know if he saw me. I didn't linger. I didn't want to embarrass him. And my selfish side didn't want to hurt me, either.

Embarrassing a high-ranking male colleague, even in the throes of compassion, threatened negative consequences for the subordinate, especially a female subordinate. Had I been one of the guy post-docs, I probably could have just marched in and said, "Hey bro? Get your ass up. Let's grab a beer." But that option was not one of mine.

I'd known Dr. Brando for a year. He seemed like a great dad, and a smart, super-dedicated researcher caught between two planes—science and justice—with sharp edges.

The justice part of Dr. Brando's life he called "Commissioners Court" aka Family Court, a harmless name for what I decided was a peculiar hell, known only to its asylum seekers—divorcing moms and dads and kids—and its border patrol agents: lawyers, judges known as "commissioners," court-appointed "advocates," guardians ad litem, and other Latinate incarnations.

If our microbial discovery returned alive and well, we had

Mike Brando to thank. He formulated the microbiological version of space food for the long trip home, a gelatinous goo that tasted "like the saltiest caviar you never want to eat," he said. "Think habanero anchovies."

He offered me a bite on the tip of plastic spatula in his lab —"it's perfectly edible"—and ever the curious scientist, I extended the tip of my tongue. My mouth almost caught fire. "That is *nasty*," I said.

"Thank you," he said. "Our bug will love it." He looked at the wall clock. "And now I have a soccer game."

"Arsenal or Manchester United?"

"My daughter's team," he said. "Lexi's good; really good, actually. But her mom wants a doctor in the family, not a soccer player. I'm the cheering fan."

VISITORS. I COULD HEAR them in the hallway, strange voices, grave chuckles, faint echoes of power. I peered around the post-doc door toward Dr. Levitt's office.

"Jennifer." I turned to Dr. Shonstein. She nodded her heard toward the entourage emerging from Dr. Levitt's office: three men, including the university president. When they turned toward us, I recognized Alexander Sparks. The other man spoke with an accent and carried himself officially.

"Wonder what this is about," Shonstein said. They were upon us before I could guess, Dr. Levitt tagging up the rear.

"Jennifer," she said. "Rebecca. Let me introduce—"

"Rebecca Shonstein," she interjected, jutting out her hand.

Dr. Levitt cleared her throat and frowned. "Allow me to

introduce Yuri Kaleptikov, with RosCosmos, the Russian Space Agency. And Alexander Sparks."

"Who needs no intro," Dr. Shonstein said with a facetious smile.

"Delighted, madam," Kaleptikov said, taking our hands in turn. "Madam," he said to me.

"Jennifer Zendeck," I said.

"Hi," and "Hello," Sparks said, I thought awkwardly. I was meeting the world's first trillionaire, one of only three (or was it two), and I was thinking about the personal quality of his greeting. No wonder I'm not rich.

"These gentlemen are touring our offices," Dr. Levitt said. "They have been fully briefed on the need for—"

"Discretion," President Beane said.

"I'll be writing report for my government that will, of course, be strictly classified," Kaleptikov said. "As I was saying to the very hospitable Dr. Levitt, you are to be congratulated. I understand this is largely speculative journey that relies on faith and deep pockets."

"One deep pocket, mainly," Sparks said, in a low, smooth tone that reminded me of purring. "I was glad to help. Seattle one. Silicon Valley, zero."

"What each of you do?" Kaleptikov asked.

"Bacteriologist," Shonstein said. "Virologist."

"Indeed. Double threat."

"Triple if you count motherhood," she said.

"And husband."

"Motherhood," Shonstein repeated.

Kaleptikov smiled, turned to me.

"I'm working on my dissertation."

"A student," he said.

"Astrobiology," I said.

"The oxymoronic science," Sparks said. I was beginning to see why Shonstein was suspicious.

"You think so?" Kaleptikov said. "Why you finance?"

"Prove my point," Sparks said. "To find life on Mars, we'll have to put it there."

"I completely dis—" Shonstein said.

"We also have a world-renowned mathematician, a rising star in astro-climatology, and a microbiologist who will win the Nobel some day for his theories on microbial physiology," Dr. Levitt said.

"And a Vetlesen Prize-winning geologist," Dr. Shonstein said, looking at Levitt.

"Just an inveterate rock hound."

"Such impressive team," Kaleptikov said. "What is the Vetlesen Prize?"

"Geology's highest honor," Shonstein said. "Marcia is too humble to brag."

"Well, gentlemen—we should probably be on our way," the president said. "We still haven't seen Sparks Hall. Ladies— good meeting you," he said to me, "and seeing you again." He kind of gave Shonstein a look.

"A word," Levitt said, heading to her office. I didn't think she meant me, but being scientifically curious, I followed.

"Rebecca—was that really necessary?" Dr. Levitt said, as she closed the door to her office.

"Was what necessary?"

"You were very short with him."

"Who? Sparks? I don't trust him."

"That doesn't mean you have to be rude to him."

"I wasn't being rude. I was being snarky. There's a difference."

"We talked about your concerns before taking his money. I thought you were on board," Dr. Levitt said.

"He's the one who's not on board," Shonstein said. "You heard what he said. We're just elaborate guinea pigs—" She looked at me. "He's hoping and praying we don't find anything."

"I don't get it," I said.

"War of the Worlds Dilemma," Shonstein said.

"Well—he's just gonna have to get over it," Levitt said. "Both of you are."

DR. BRANDO WAS IN his office with his daughter Lexi, moving around the bodies in our recently-expanded solar system on a 3D model in the Cloud.

"Hey girlfriend."

"Hey," she said. We did the perfunctory pandemic elbow bump. Some habits die hard.

"Dad got you working?"

Dr. Brando grabbed her shoulders and kissed her cheek. She made a yuck face and he kissed her again. "She's all mine," he said. "All mine!" like some crazed Dr. Frankenstein announcing his creation. "For the weekend."

"Take home quiz," Lexi told me. She was trying to remember where bonafide planets Debos and Nedra had been uncloaked, hiding behind the same strange interstellar shadow beyond dwarf-demoted Pluto. "Gotta put all the planets where they belong."

"Mars is—"

"Fourth planet from the Sun, right after Earth," she said. "Then gotta tell why only Earth has life." She smiled.

"You had some salinity data you wanted me to graph?" I asked her dad.

"I *would*," he said. "*If* I had it." He whispered in my ear. "Been in and out of court all week."

"I heard that," Lexi said.

"So—what's the War of the Worlds Dilemma?" I asked.

He went around his desk. "Been talking to Bex, I take it."

"Um, yeah, it came up. Never heard of it."

"Ever seen the movie? Heard the broadcast?"

"Of course," I said, reversing Mars and Venus on Lexi's Cloud screen. "Orson Welles was from Kenosha."

"Didn't know that. Any way, the Martian invaders were 'slain by the putrefactive and disease bacteria against which their systems were unprepared.' No immunity—to us."

"I remember."

"So what happens if we humans find life there? On Mars?"

"We won't be finding it," I said. "MarsMicro will."

"Same difference. What did we just spend tons of time and money doing?"

"You mean sterilizing it."

"Yep."

"Nedra here," I whispered to Lexi. "I know it's confusing, with Pluto."

"If we find life on Mars, we can't visit Mars," Brando said.

"Cuz we might kill it," Lexi said, adjusting Earth's orbit.

"No humans. Maybe no more missions, period," Brando said. "That's the War of the Worlds Dilemma."

Five

I heard running down the hallway. Dr. Levitt stuck her head into the post-doc office. "You seen Coop?" she asked breathlessly.

"Not lately." Before I could ask what was up, she was off.

Dr. Cooper flew out later that day to JPL. They needed his expertise on site stat, Dr. Levitt told us, to navigate an approaching "weather event." He was on speaker during a special team meeting she called later that week.

"Weird problem," he said.

A 3D image of the rover moving below a recurring slope lineae projected from the planet surface across our conference table. Mars' version of lightning crackled faintly in the background, raising dust charged with static electricity.

"Storm's interfering with quantum communications," Cooper said.

"How far away is that storm?" Shonstein asked.

"Not far enough," Cooper said. The static cling from another lightning crackle shot up a dust geyser.

"Shield's up, right?" Brando said.

The electromagnetic force field designed to repel dust. I thought of it as a small-scale version of the *Starship Enterprise's* famous deflector shield.

"That's the other problem," Cooper said. "If we power up the shield, we lose the EPR Bridge."

"With a requisite delay in signal travel," Marcum said.

"Yep. Talking about twelve minutes for the rover to receive a command, another twelve for us to see the response," Cooper said. "We can try to outrun the storm without the shield, or let it pass and hope the shield holds. Hard to outrun anything when max speed is twenty or so miles an hour."

A lot faster than past rovers, which made a mile an hour, but slower than a speeding dust storm.

"Quite the catch-22," Shonstein said.

"Is the storm promising to get any bigger?" Marcum asked. "As in *disastrous*?"

"Don't know," Cooper said. As I watched images of the storm fade to punctuated uncertainty, I heard Cooper's breathing over voices around the mission control room. He mumbled something.

"I tried to warn everybody," he said. "We needed more time to design the shield, the predictive algorithms, the onboard program. If the shield goes down during a storm—"

"It's not going down," Levitt said.

"I tried," Cooper said. "I begged. I pleaded."

"We understand," Levitt said. "Predicting weather on Earth is hard enough."

"Only if you play by house rules," he said. "I play by Coop's rules. Rule One: No surprises."

I felt for him trying to navigate this surprise beside nervous flight engineers who sounded like short order cooks, yelling commands and rushing around to avoid the aerospace equivalents of burned food—inoperable robots, dirty solar panels, wrecked equipment, and "adverse weather events."

Cooper's forecasts were supposed to insure against bad weather. With Marcum's help and support from the Hale Lab, he mapped planet-wide predictions covering the duration of our voyage. We timed MarsMicro based partly on his prediction that Mars would be free of a menace that recurs every few years: dust storms which can cover the entire planet in a dense haze for months, shutting down solar panels, gumming up precision equipment, burying rover wheels in sand so fine it feels like baby powder but acts like quicksand.

All that planning wasn't enough. Cooper's Martian weather map was more like the Farmer's Almanac than the nightly news: good for general, long-term forecasts but unreliable for daily, location-specific events, like the dust devil we were nervously watching. He simply hadn't enough time to fine tune his forecast models.

"WE'VE MADE THE DECISION to stop the rover and turn on the shields manually," Cooper said on our second conference call from JPL late that afternoon. We received the time-lagged video of the rover stopping several minutes later.

"How far off is the storm?" Brando said.

"Best guess—about an hour," Cooper said "It shifted course, but the dust cloud it created is so large we expect it to engulf everything within a two mile radius."

We watched the 3D projections refresh every few minutes,

mission control chatter in the background. Then the projection phased in and out, getting snowy like an old TV.

"Bad news," Cooper said. "We can't get the shield up."

"Why not?" Levitt said.

"We're thinking storm interference," he said. "If we don't get it up soon, we're screwed."

"Will the computer turn it on, or is it just you can't get manual over-ride to work?"

"We know manual isn't working. No idea about the computer."

The computer would definitely turn on the force field if it detected even small amounts of dust around the rover, a probability of almost one that a dust storm was imminent. Too bad the rover's tires were too slow to spin out in the sand. Too bad it didn't have a big engine fan that might churn up some dust. Too bad—

"What about the outgassers?" Brando asked. "Or is it offgassers? Remember the demo?"

I could see the wheels of recall turning in Dr. Levitt's mind.

"Several things on the rover give off volatile gases," Pei Lin had told us during Sim Week. The famous "new car smell" is from gases like these, she said.

"But Mars' light, thin atmosphere gives these gases more than just smell power." From the plastic circuit boards to Crimsy (when she boarded later), volatile gases could contaminate precision components, fog up camera lenses, or even spark combustion (Crimsy's methane). "The rover's outgassers capture and exhaust them."

"Turn on the outgassers," Levitt yelled to Cooper. The entire mission control team probably heard.

On our 3D rover projection at JPL, we started seeing puffs of dust rise around the rover, several minutes after the outgasser's lower jets hit the ground.

"Any way to pump up the volume?" Levitt asked.

The puffs got larger, more frequent.

"I'm likin' it," Cooper said. "If this works—"

Pop! The dust shot away from the rover, like smoke hitting a sudden gust. The shield was on. We heard the flight crew high-fiving.

WE HEARD AN EXPLOSION, like a bomb, somewhere beyond the rover. Drs. Levitt and Cooper watched the monitors with me. We were back at JPL Pasadena, inside Mission Control a couple weeks after the Great Dust Storm Dust Up.

"What was that?" a JPL GN said, covering the microphone on his headset. In my open ear, I heard disconcerted rumblings from the people around me. In my headset ear, engineers and navigators.

"Thunder?"

"Something hit the planet?"

"Damage report."

They rotated the 3D rover projection, over, around, under. "No exterior damage."

"All systems online and functional."

"Didn't sound like thunder to me," Dr. Cooper said. "Not even Martian thunder."

The rover was parked next to a canyon wall, so high that from the ground, you couldn't see the top. It had driven around the Valles Marineris, taking core samples, examining ice, analyzing weather readings, looking for signs of microbial life not far from where *Odysseus* found the first stromatolites.

Dr. Levitt pointed to dust rising behind the rover. "Let's move before the shields go up," she said.

The ground navigator pushed the joystick and drove the rover clear.

"Why's that kicking up?" Dr. Cooper asked. "It's totally still down there."

"I haven't seen a quieter day since we landed," our chief ground engineer said. "And we're in one of the most sheltered parts of the planet."

"Can we get a balloon cam shot?" Levitt asked. That video from above the canyon showed nothing unusual.

"Maybe too high," Cooper said.

Like *Odysseus* before it, MarsMicro launched several camera-equipped balloons for mapping and navigation. Seriously upgraded versions, the balloons reconnoitered and monitored our "areas of interest." But they had to fly high enough to avoid unpredictable turbulence near the canyon crest, one of few places on Mars that experienced high enough winds, Cooper explained, to throw the balloons off course or even destroy them.

"We're picking up some unusual radar," I heard in my earphone.

"Turn up the volume on the rover mikes," Cooper said.

"Sounds like thunder again," I said.

"I don't think so," Cooper said. "Listen carefully." It was getting louder. "Thunder doesn't move like that."

Levitt's face turned white. I mean, white. I'd never seen that before—on anyone.

"Get us out of there," she said. "Now! Move!"

The navigator looked at her.

"Avalanche," she said.

He shoved the joystick forward and the rover picked up speed. "Where's it coming from? Where is it?"

"We have a possible avalanche, people," the CGE announced. "Listen up: We need directions."

"How 'bout the drone?" Dr. Cooper said.

"Turbulence," the CGE said. "It'll be smashed before we can get it high enough."

"We just need to get our bearings," Cooper said.

I was glued to the big wall monitor watching MarsMicro trying to outrun rumbling becoming a roar. I heard buzzing and whirring and watched the observation drone take flight from a launch platform on the rover that looked like a helicopter pad. It was, in fact, more helicopter than drone, its four blades spinning twelve times faster than they would on Earth because of Mars' thin atmosphere. As it ascended in a jittery trajectory, separate smaller screens on the wall monitor appeared with images from its cameras, showing the rover moving away.

"Enlarge drone cam views," which now took over a third of the big screen monitor. Helidrone rising, rover speeding, the drama captured so vividly I got chills.

Then—dust. Lots of dust, nearing the drone cam as navigators controlling the wily flying pie plate maneuvered to evade it. The images were jittery again, making me a little nauseous.

"Turbulence," I heard in my headset.

"Head south," Cooper intervened. "As far into the center of the canyon as you can."

Tossing, turning, almost flipping, the helidrone moved farther away from the canyon wall. As it pulled clear of the dust, our amorphous nemesis took shape.

"Holy—" another GN exclaimed next to me.

"Jennifer: We are witnessing the largest avalanche any human has ever laid eyes on," Levitt said, in a hush meant only for me. It looked like the entire canyon wall was collapsing, and at incredible speed. "This is sand on ice, people," she announced into her mic. "No friction to slow it like snow on snow."

"Look!" I heard.

We saw the rover on the drone cam now, a tiny David fleeing the sliding Goliath.

"Turn! Turn! Turn! Turn! Turn!" I heard. The rover made a

quick turn around a corner.

"Slide's moving at a couple hundred," the CGE said.

"If not faster," Levitt said. "What's our speed?"

"Holding at twenty five."

As the helidrone lost sight of the rover, the rover's own cams caught it hitting bumps that became ruts that became gullies, signs of increasing water flow. The GN throttled it back, but the chief ground engineer put his hand over the navigator's hand and pushed the joystick forward. The rover slapped the ruts, then jumped over what looked like a sandbar, landing hard and spinning. The cameras cut out and my earphones went crazy.

"What'd we hit?"

"What was that?"

"All communications offline."

"Systems down."

The drone cam's screen was screwed up, too. Static and snow replaced clear images.

"Where's the drone? Bring it in."

"Lost contact."

"So am I interpreting right?" Levitt said. "We're effed?"

"We're not letting Hale off that easily," Cooper said.

We watched the three screens: rover cams dark, drone cams snow, balloon cams finally picking up the massive slide, as dust from deep inside the canyon started taking to the sky like an atomic mushroom cloud. Then—hope. Wavy lines replaced the snow.

"We're getting signals from the drone," I heard.

Something clearer came into view.

"What is that?"

"We have control?"

The drone navigator fiddled with its joystick. The screen view moved, then flipped.

"Maybe . . . Let's . . . see."

The screen righted and cleared, dust from the avalanche more distant now.

"Three sixty sweep," the CGE said. The helidrone cam circled until we saw a large patch of scalloped ground, pockmarked layers of dirt that formed a crust. I saw something whitish, bluish, translucent kinda, beneath the crust.

"Is that ice?" Levitt said.

"If it is, SHARAD hasn't recorded it," Cooper said. "We got ice beneath the north and south poles, Utopia Planitia, and a few other places. But nothing here."

"Signal from the rover," the GN said, to muted cheers.

"Lock the drone onto it."

Gradually dropping, the helidrone flew across the scalloped ground.

"Let's get a shot from the balloon."

"Be a few."

"Rover!" I heard. The rover cams showed it sailing across the funny-looking patch of ground, going round and round in a gradually slowing orbit, crunching and churning the crust.

"Definitely ice," Cooper said. "We gotta be on a frozen lake. Can you control this thing?"

"Nope," the GN said.

As the helidrone caught up, the rover came into view, turning and sliding like a loopy skater.

"Balloon's in range. Upper left screen, please."

And there it was, a frozen sheet distantly surrounded by Valles walls. If not for the dirt layer over top of it, we might have been staring at the mega-Martian equivalent of the winter skating pond at grandma's house.

"Can we get a read on the embankment?" the CGE asked.

"Radar screen four."

"Bank in ten point seven kilometers, more or less," the GN said.

"Engage wheel. Left front, forward."

"Speed?"

"Use your best judgment."

The rover turned as this wheel rotated.

"Right rear, backward."

This wheel turned and the rover started to straighten.

"Left rear, backward."

"Slow. Keep it slow. But no brakes! Do not brake."

"Slowing front tire."

The rover was straight now, but still careening toward the bank.

"We've got about a thirty knot tailwind, chief," the GN said. "We may have to deploy the airbags."

"Gradually accelerate rear wheels," the CGE said.

We saw the wheels turn, then spin like a car stuck in mud, as the rover moved across the ice-dirt. From the balloon's perspective, the cloud from the avalanche loomed near the lake like an ominous fog. We didn't know it yet, but we were watching the most inauspicious of debuts unfolding.

"Full speed reverse, all wheels."

The rover's wheels spun and spun, but since this wasn't your grandma's frozen pond, I had no idea what was fixing to happen. I wasn't sure whether the ice was made of water, carbon dioxide (aka dry ice) or something more alien. Whatever it was, it was slick and hard.

"Deploy air bags," the chief ground engineer said.

Out they popped, covering the rover and its cameras. The ground navigation engineers watched the radar of the approaching embankment. The drone cam showed it coming up fast.

"Prepare for impact," prompted a launch-style countdown. "Ten, nine, eight, seven, six, five, four, three, two—"

The helidrone banked upward as the rover slammed into an embankment about a football field away from another towering wall of the Valles Marineris. The airbags deflated. Mission control cheers burst from the room when a systems check showed only minor damage. The red returned to Dr. Levitt's cheeks. Dr. Cooper's hands stopped shaking. The CGE stopped pacing. The GN smiled and wiped his brow. The helidrone descended, locking itself onto its launch pad. Though Mission Control made remote repairs and ran the rover through a battery of post-collision tests, we didn't have far to go.

The rover had abruptly stopped a few meters from Crimsy's front door.

Six

I got to know Parada better when she visited JPL during what I nostalgically call "anchor week," when our combined teams—the Levitt Lab, NASA, and JPL—made the momentous decision to drop anchor, as it were, where the MarsMicro rover had skidded to a dramatic halt against the bank of a frozen lake.

The landslide and the dust storms it created forced the decision upon us: steep cliffs surrounded the rover, leaving one open path, where the dust cloud would take weeks to settle. We were stuck for the duration, so why not make the best of it?

The only thing left to do was get permission from the Planetary Protection Officer (PPO) to drill through the dirt and ice and sample any liquid water that might be lurking beneath it.

Parada joined Drs. Brando and Shonstein on their flight down to meet with the PPO, who was supposed to assure we didn't cross-contaminate any potential sources of Martian life with hitchhiking bacteria (or viruses) from Earth. The flight was delayed and there was a rental car screw-up—Brando and Shonstein were left without a car—so Parada drove them to the meeting. She would have dropped them off, but Dr. Levitt insisted she come in, to the JPL conference room where the rest of us were gathered.

We had an additional complicating factor, the PPO explained: the bio-engineered viral phages MarsMicro brought to light up any bacteria we might find, using the Biolite technology. How could we assure those phages wouldn't create their own Martian pandemic?

"The phages remain wholly contained during every step of our tests," Shonstein said.

"No chance of spillage? No chance of escape?" the PPO asked.

"No. None."

"They've been integral to the mission from day one," Brando said. "Why worry about this now?"

"I don't think anyone expected to find a lake," the PPO said. "An accidental release of those phages on dry sand is a much different situation than their release in an aqueous setting."

"She's right, Mike. We thought we'd be looking for water in opals," Levitt said. "Or salt crystals."

"At most, we might find a pocket or two of liquid water," Cooper said. "And that's if we're really, really lucky."

"Why just a pocket and not an entire lake?" the PPO asked.

"Erratic freeze-thaw cycles," Cooper said. "Parts of the lake thaw, then refreeze, depending on the season. The thin atmosphere, all the dry ice from the carbon dioxide. The valley walls, how well they insulate the valley. Varying salt concentrations that affect the freezing point. Lots of variables means little pockets."

"But a virus could still contaminate a water pocket," the PPO said. "Still seems like too much risk."

"A virus would have no chance of surviving long term," Parada said unexpectedly. "They're fragile enough on Earth. In that kind of environment—"

"Our phages are designed to survive the trip there and a short stay, maybe a few months," Shonstein said. "We'll be fortunate to get that much out of them."

"Our sampling protocol is tightly regulated—temperature, salt concentration, moisture levels," Brando added. "But the environment in that lake—no way. Too harsh."

"Are you—" the PPO asked Parada.

"I'm a physician," Parada told her. "Visiting."

"An MD?"

"Yes."

"Is anyone else here an MD?" she asked.

We were a tentative go, pending a couple more perfunctory permissions. Parada, in my estimation, had swayed the day.

FOUR STABILIZERS ANCHORED THE MarsMicro rover against the bank on one side, the dirty-icy lake on the other. On a mission control monitor, we watched it unfurl the larger of two robotic arms, and spin a drill head into place, on what I'd describe as an interstellar Swiss Army Knife: drill, laser, vacuum, and other gear on a head that rotated to the tool of choice.

The spinning bit bored through the frozen ground, kicking up frost tufts and mud curls as it penetrated. We did hunt-and-peck explorations along the lake's perimeter for over a week. If not for my recording dissertation data, we'd have surely lost count of how many holes we drilled with zilch results. SHARAD—shallow radar—and spectrographic data suggested better places to drill. Dr. Marcum plugged the data into an algorithm he designed that narrowed down our choices even further.

But we were still back in Seattle before we got the news.

"They found water!" Dr. Shonstein yelled in the hallway, her head craned outside the conference room door.

And there it was on the 3D monitor, the rover's robotic pincer holding a small plastic vial with a few drops. Being the science nerd I am, I noticed the water at the top of the tube didn't have the traditional dip it does on Earth. Less gravity on Mars. It was also tightly capped, so it wouldn't evaporate. Above ground, Martian ice sublimes—turns directly to vapor. Liquid water doesn't stand a chance unless it's buried under layers of ice and dirt.

The rover's smaller robotic arm—for "fine motor skills" as Shonstein liked to quip—punctured the vial's sealed top with a slender syringe, injecting the phages. If bacteria were in the vial, the color-reading spectrometer on the rover would detect it. And if we were lucky enough to see through the murk, so would our eyes.

THE NEWS BROKE, HOT and colorful, on the fifth floor hallway of the PAB.

"They found something!" Dr. Shonstein yelled.

And for once, we were all in our offices, back in Seattle on one of many returns from JPL's frenetic environment. We ran out our doors and gathered around Shonstein's 3D monitor to watch history unfold.

"Oh wow oh wow oh wow," Levitt said, staring at the small plastic tube MarsMicro's steel fingers loaded into the bioluminescence detector. As always, MarsMicro started sending back Biolite readings a few minutes later. This time, the raw numbers were in line with what we were looking for.

Shonstein and Brando grabbed each other's shoulders and stared into each other's eyes with the most wondrous, wide-eyed amazement I'd ever seen.

"Watch the sample folks," a Mission Control specialist said.

The rover removed the test tube from the detector and held it steady as the onboard camera closed in on the water sample and everything around it started fading to black. Like the tip of a firefly, the bottom of the test tube glowed blue, our highly-trained Biolite phages in a cloudy tube of Martian water.

Then—*everything* faded to black.

"What just happened?" Dr. Cooper said.

Shonstein whacked the monitor.

"You have got to be kidding me."

Dr. Levitt feverishly texted; Dr. Marcum folded his arms.

"Some kind of glitch," Levitt said, looking at her phone.

"Glitch?" Brando said. "What kind of glitch kills a moment like that?"

"Bollocks," Marcum said. "They're messing with our minds again."

We spent the rest of the day trying to re-establish contact, while the clogosphere luminesced with its own explanations about why JPL had stopped reporting publicly shortly after MarsMicro's water discovery. Our corpora-government overseers rolled out a full press blackout on the third day, pointing to all the conspiracy theories as reason enough not to "create more hysteria."

In rebellion, "we found life," Shonstein started saying, in place of "good morning," "have a nice day," "have a great weekend."

"We found life. We found life. We found life!"

Seven

I can be dense, even when the answer to a question or puzzle is staring me in the face. So I was when I failed to understand why getting Crimsy back to Earth was so much more difficult than finding her in the first place.

It was all about rovers versus rockets.

"We have to get back into orbit," Dr. Marcum told me. "That's easier to do on Mars because the gravitational field is so much weaker than Earth, but it's still no mean feat."

There would be no more dropping from parachutes and bouncing along the planet surface in a cocoon of fancy air bags. Rocket maneuvers are precision personified, and in that spirit, the seeds for this journey were planted years earlier.

"Pre-Odysseus, SpaceTek, NASA, and JPL landed a small fuel production plant on the planet," Dr. Levitt told me. It captured, made, and stored methane—natural gas—a cleaner burning, low-hassle rocket fuel to which everyone eventually switched.

The Mars Refueling Depot, on the planet surface, pumped enough methane into a rocket to get it into orbit. There, an Orbital Refueling Depot regularly replenished with methane from Earth topped off the tanks for the long trip home. These dual Martian gas stations tanked up the *Odysseus* Return Craft for its voyage home, with the rocks and sand that almost brought Earth to the brink.

Rocket complications, I've learned, start with landing them, as this understated observation of a science journalist named Neel Patel suggests: "A fourteen-story piece of tube made of aluminum-lithium alloy, with fire bursting out the end, doesn't just make a smooth perch for itself in a giant empty field."

Mars is pockmarked with volcanic craters and to land sequential rockets, starting with the Mars Refueling Depot and now the Big Retriever Rocket (BRR) that would bring MarsMicro home, JPL's engineers had to find a site that was instead "smooth, flat, and boring"—the so-called Golombek Criteria, named for a JPL landing site specialist.

That smooth, flat, boring site, aka the return trip or takeoff site, had to be close enough to Coprates Chasma and its shaded frozen lakes in Valles Marineris that the rover could get to it in a reasonable time.

JPL found a good takeoff site in the Capris Chasma next door (all these Chasmas are confusing, I know). It would take just over a week for the rover to climb out of the Coprates Chasma, drive to Capris Chasma, and arrive at the BRR loading dock, where it was lightweight enough, at 1800 lbs (800 kg) to be the first Martian rover to drive aboard, seatbelt itself in, and return to Earth.

Our team was at JPL for the sequence, which began, as it always did, in the calm, climate-controlled utopia known as the simulation theater. Not only our team, but Dr. Hale, a handful of JPL engineers and SpaceTek execs, Senator Scherr, and lo-and-behold, Alexander Sparks sat in the theater-in-the-round, a souped-up version of an IMAX.

"So, first-time welcomes to a few of you, including our own Senator Scherr and Mr. Alexander Sparks," our frequent host, Argosy Reed, began at center stage. "May we have a round of applause for their steadfast support."

What a showman. Reed, I later learned, acted on Broadway before returning to Pasadena to care for his aging parents. He had a degree in aerospace engineering he never used, he told me. He wouldn't confess to using it now, but it "obviously comes in handy."

"And another round of applause," he continued, "for the masterminds behind this mission, Dr. Marcia Levitt and Dr. Harold Hale."

You bet we stood. We all stood and clapped and woot-wooted. This new class of large, long-range rockets capable of picking up and delivering fifty ton payloads had never been used before and might still be idle if not for the persistence of Levitt and Hale.

The original plan had been as it always was, to study whatever we found on the planet surface. Levitt fought for the *Odysseus* mission to actually *bring back* rocks and dust. Levitt and Hale fought even harder—and each other, until his surprise Congressional testimony—for MarsMicro to bring back Crimsy.

We all figured Levitt's success with *Odysseus* helped bring Hale around, though she was too humble—or too diplomatic—to admit it. I remember the months of back-and-forth in Washington State, Cambridge, Mass., and here in Pasadena, the stress it put on Dr. Levitt, and as I think about it, the toll it must have taken on her relationship with Parada.

I walked into her office during the intense middle period of the BRR negotiations to find her doing something she never did: crying, albeit muffled, with her head on her desk. I slipped back out.

She was so classy: here she was now, turning to Dr. Hale and encouraging applause his way. He reciprocated, pointing at her with both hands and beaming. Never seen him beam before, but he was now. Classy, classy.

"As you are all aware, this mission has been over a decade in the making," Reed continued.

Our other regular host, Pei Lin took it from there. "So—cool irony. The bacteria you're bringing home may, in fact, be a source of our rocket fuel," she said.

On the big screen around us, we saw a video of the Martian refueling plant and an animated rendering of the processes behind it.

"We have two ways to get the methane we need: the well-known Sabatier reaction that creates it from the abundant carbon dioxide in Mars' atmosphere; and a capture and storage mechanism using two common absorbent materials: aluminum-silica zeolite, and good ol' activated charcoal," Dr. Lin explained.

"Good time for a shout-out to our friends at Lawrence

Livermore and Berkeley for discovering the zeolite process," Reed interrupted.

"Zeolite captures and stores small amounts of methane already in the atmosphere before harsh solar rays can break the molecules apart," Lin said. "Though there are almost certainly others, your critter is the only living source we have yet identified—obviously—of Mars atmospheric methane."

"Making her a methanogen," Shonstein said loud enough for a few, but not all, to hear. From the Archaea domain, methanogens are bacteria that make methane from carbon dioxide.

"Making her a methanogen," Lin repeated.

"We've teamed up with Disney/LucasFilm to create your simulation today," Reed said. "You will dock the rover, and enjoy the experience of planetary liftoff with a stop at the gas station just before heading home, in this case, Deep Space Gateway.

"The simulation begins shortly before the Mars launch, as Dr. Shonstein and Dr. Brando secure the samples and board BRR's payload docking system.

"We now begin The Return of MarsMicro."

THE NEXT DAY'S ANNOUNCEMENT that we faced at least a week of Martian bad weather—blowing dust, electrical storms —before the return trip launch came with the option to go home until it cleared, or stay in Pasadena.

Drs. Levitt, Marcum, and Cooper stayed. I went back to Seattle with Mike Brando and Rebecca Shonstein. We spent three weeks in expectation limbo. The day we returned to JPL was equally inauspicious: Lexi Brando clinging to her dad, mom in the airport wings; Malachi Shonstein clinging to his mom, dad in the airport wings. Lexi buried her face in her father's arms; Malachi buried his face in his mother's neck. Lexi teared and sniffled; Malachi teared and sniffled.

TSSEA agents buzzed around, giving us the evil eye.

"We have a pair of Klingons today," Shonstein said, kissing Malachi's forehead and trying to rouse him to that infectious giggle we'd heard before, guaranteed to cheer up the other Klingon.

"You may have to take them," Martin Shonstein told us. "I hear Klingons love Mars this time of year."

"Flight 2765 to Hollywood Hope Airport now boarding," the intercom announced.

"There's hope for Hollywood?" Martin quipped.

"We probably need to get going," Melissa Brando said. "Lexi, sweetie." She reached out to take her daughter's hand, prompting Lexi to grip her father even tighter.

"I don't want Mommy go!" Malachi announced, using his words with astonishing clarity.

"Mommy has to go," Dr. Shonstein said. "She'll be back real soon." She kissed him again and with her free hand, tickled his side. He squirmed with a frown. She looked imploringly at her husband.

"C'mon buddy." Martin reached for his son, who swatted

back his father's hand. Melissa Brando was almost down on one knee, looking all the businesswoman in temporary repose, heels just high enough to be feminine yet appropriate, skirt the perfect length, jacket flattering, not an unnatural wrinkle in her uniform.

"I wanna stay with Dad," Lexi said.

"You can't stay with Dad," her mom replied. "Mike: help me here."

He leaned down and was about to whisper something when Malachi Shonstein let out a wail I was certain would bring the TSSEA. His mom was kissing him and his dad grasping him, gently trying to relinquish his grip on his mother's neck. The diplomatic approach wasn't working any better, with Lexi tearing up and on the verge of crying herself.

"Sweetie. Lex," I heard Dr. Brando say. "I'll be back and then we'll do a couple weeks. K?"

His wife frowned. "We'll see," she said.

"We'll *do*," he said.

"I don't think you should be promising that," Melissa said.

The looks they exchanged were discomforting to watch, let alone, I was certain, be a party to. I walked closer and stood, hinting I might be available for some girl talk. I was ten years Melissa's junior and thought Lexi and I had a pretty good thing going. I at least caught her eye.

"You goin' to Mars with me someday?" I asked Lexi.

Not having it.

"How 'bout the space station? That's easier."

Still not having it. But Dr. Brando looked hopeful and Melissa backed away.

"I know I'll have to train like crazy," I said. "They don't just let anybody aboard."

"They won't let me on board," Lexi said. "I'm a kid."

I bent down. "All the more reason they might," I said. "Kids are durable, and learn fast. You learn faster than most."

Her face relaxed.

"I gotta get on that flight, though. If I don't show up, they'll think I don't wanna go."

"I wanna go," she said. She looked over at Malachi, still crying. People walking by, talking, intercoms, security, announcements, the sound of rolling luggage wheels, someone yelling across the expanse of tile floor and fluorescent light.

"Hope they don't tow me," I heard Martin say.

"Your mom loves you more than anything," I whispered to Lexi. "It really hurts her when you act like you don't love her, too."

I don't know where that came from, but it felt right. I knew Melissa, in a way. She was like my brother David, stiff upper lip, all mission, no fuzzy, who showed her love by fulfilling her duties and fighting for what she thought was right. So I said it and I meant it.

"I love my mom," Lexi said. I felt a presence behind us, Martin now holding Malachi, who had quieted. I turned around and looked up.

"He wants to say goodbye," Martin said.

I babysat for Malachi, sometimes in small office spurts, one time at their house. I stood and he pouted but put out his hands. I looked at his dad, who acquiesced, and I took his son and kissed him and tossed him into the air. The pout vanished and he giggled, at first nervously, then infectiously. I kissed his cheek again.

"I have to say goodbye to Lexi," I said. "Do you want to say goodbye to her?" I landed Malachi on his feet and he hugged Lexi, who reflexively hugged him back, releasing her father. I hugged them both—group hug kinda thing.

The tension subsided.

"Last call for Flight 2765 to Hollywood Hope Airport. Now boarding, Gate C3."

"We're gonna need to run," Dr. Shonstein said.

We made our escape through light security. I looked back at the two kids and the parents. Lexi waved at me. Malachi was crying again. We were the last passengers to board.

Eight

The camera on the MarsMicro rover shook. The larger robotic arm jiggled free of its moorings and slid off the rover and bounced on the Martian ground.

"What the heck was that?" Dr. Cooper said. Our team was again gathered around engineers, monitors, touchscreens and joysticks at Mission Control, Pasadena.

The rover stopped momentarily, while a JPL engineer raised the arm and locked it back into place. "Hit a rock, maybe," the ground navigator (GN) said.

"I don't see any rocks," Cooper said. "And there's no wind strong enough to gust that hard."

The rover rolled onward, less than two kilometers, a little over a mile, from the awaiting Big Retriever Rocket, parked on the same flat Capris Chasma liftoff pad *Odysseus* used. The rover's camera offered a jittery view of the sandy-brown Valles walls as it approached a narrow, sloped ravine that connected the two Valles chasms, Coprates and Capris.

Everyone looked dizzy from watching the rover cam.

"Can you pan the area with the drone?" Dr. Levitt asked.

"Don't know," the GN said. "Batteries are low and its solar collectors are dusty."

"How'd that happen?" Brando asked. "I thought it was covered."

"It is, but the dust figures out a way to get in."

The rover's electrostatic repellent system didn't include the drone; a core-sample extraction drill; and a couple of smaller solar-powered tools stored under covers, designed to resist the dust with special coatings. The rover's robotic arms covered these tools after each use.

"I always tell people who want to 'colonize' the place—" The GN air-quoted "colonize." "—women are gonna hate it. Trying to keep a house clean with that kinda dust."

Standing behind him, Dr. Shonstein made a WTF face.

"We could charge the drone with the rover's batteries maybe, but under the circumstances—" the GN continued.

"We've got seismic activity," another engineer said from three stations away. "*Insight* readings translate to about a two Richter."

"Explains some things," the ground navigator said.

Insight landed on the planet with a seismograph and other measuring tools years ago. The seismograph still worked, sending a stream of readings to Earth, albeit with a four to twenty-four minute time delay (no EPR quantum bridge back then).

Marsquakes, it turns out, are like everything else on the planet: undramatic compared to their counterparts on Earth. They average less than one to four on our Richter scale, mainly because the planet has none of the tectonic plates that put the shake in earthquake. Its surface rather quivers, like a dog's flesh when you tickle it.

"Good news. I've got power left in the drone batteries," the GN said. "Let's give this baby a whirl."

The helidrone rose shakily, hovered then dropped, then rose again.

"C'mon," the ground navigator prodded. "Come on!"

It ascended high enough that we had a decent overhead view of the rover and something we had never seen—at least, I had never seen. Rocks, large and small, not looking like they'd been sitting in the same place for a gazillion years, but rolling across the sand.

"Whoa!" The ground navigator jammed the joystick, almost tilting the rover on two wheels as it swerved to avoid one.

"If a rolling stone gathers no moss on Earth, what does it *not* gather on Mars?" Dr. Marcum said.

"Dust," Shonstein quipped.

The rover shook so hard it stopped on its own.

"What's wrong?" Dr. Levitt said.

"Lost drive power," the GN said.

"Are we stuck?" Dr. Shonstein said.

"I hope not," the GN said.

The rover shook again, and we heard rumbling from the audio.

"These aftershocks aren't weakening," Shonstein said. "Isn't it just the opposite on Earth?"

"Usually," Levitt said. "But without tectonic plates, one marsquake is just like another."

After the *Insight* mission, we knew Mars had quakes, ascertaining they were an important source of the hydrogen

Crimsy needed to survive. A study published in our home-team journal, *Astrobiology*, found that a marsquake "could produce enough hydrogen to support small populations of microorganisms." The paper said something else Levitt the geologist repeated over and over in our search for mission funding: "The best way to find evidence of life on Mars may be to examine rocks and minerals that formed deep underground around faults and fractures."

Ironically, the force that had helped the barren planet support life now threatened to kill our painstakingly preserved samples.

"I'm no engineer," Marcum said, as we watched our quaking rover sit idle beneath the drone. "But is there any way to divert power to the drives? Say, from the cameras, the incubation chambers, anything else?"

"Divert power from the incupods?" Shonstein said. "What are you talking about?"

"They use power."

Crimsy would make the trip in these temperature-controlled incubators that rotated to reproduce Mars' 0.38 G gravitational field.

"We don't even know if more power would help," Cooper said. "Something may be broken."

"Nope," the ground navigator said. "Just finished a systems check. We just lost power to the drive. The incubators, the cameras, onboard computer, drone launch, the robotics are all a go."

"Back to my question," Marcum said.

"Are you out of your mind?" Shonstein said. "We can't cut power to the incupods."

"Why not?" he responded. "Just long enough to board the rocket."

"Can we divert power? Would that even work?" Brando said.

"We can send power from any system on the rover to any other system on the rover,' the GN said. "It's a key fail-safe."

"I say we try it," Brando said. "Our Martian bacteria should be good to go for a couple hours, at least."

"No way," Shonstein said.

"They'll die like this, Bex," Brando said. "What choice do we have?"

"This is not a choice," Shonstein said. "It's not worth the risk."

"We have no drive power, ma'am," the GN said. "We need to get power from somewhere."

"Do it," Levitt said.

"Marcia!" Shonstein said.

"Brandy?"

"I see where Rebecca's coming from, but—"

"You *see* where I'm coming from?"

"Do it!" Levitt said. "We'll debate the merits later."

The GN pressed two touchscreen controls, then stopped. "Tell you what. Let me try turning off everything *but* the incubators," he said. "Let's unfold the rover's backup solar collectors, too."

"Solar and nuke are on different drive networks, so it's worth a shot," Cooper said.

"A sitting duck with wings," Marcum said. "Excellent idea."

"The ground is still shaking, professor," the GN said. "We're sitting ducks, regardless."

We watched from the drone cam as the rover's small solar panels unfurled on both sides, while all *but* the incupods' power was diverted to the drive motors. The ground navigator pushed the joystick forward and held it.

"Hopefully, she'll move," he said.

The rover did move, prompting a mission control cheer stymied by the biggest shake yet. The large robotic arm slipped from its moorings again, sliding across and breaking one of the solar panels. We were a moving-but-motley sight: rover dragging its arm and a broken wing, creeping across a godforsaken ground, swerving around sliding rocks and swirling dust.

"Is that the next problem? The dust shields go up and we lose control?" Shonstein said.

"Shields are off, ma'am," the GN said. "We don't need them this late in the mission."

"How come you call me ma'am and him professor?" she said sternly, indicating Marcum. The two men looked at her. "I'm just kidding," she said. "Thanks for saving the greatest discovery in human history."

"Don't thank me yet," the GN replied.

The rover started into the ravine out of Coprates Chasma, robotic arm swaying over the right-side solar panel, which was gradually breaking up.

"Gonna need to stop when we have enough power to put the arm back," the ground navigator said. "Drone's got good power though. Air flow must have blown the dust off the collectors."

The rover stopped shaking and accelerated into the ravine. Then it stopped.

"Well damn," the GN said. "What now?"

He swung the drone around for a picture of a good-sized rock in our path. He pressed the touchscreen power controls and the robotic arm rose.

"That gonna kill our power supply?" Brando asked.

"We've picked up a little solar," the GN said. "Still running on fumes, but more fumes than before."

The GN swung the big robotic arm around to the rock, opened its claw, and tried lifting it. The rover went up instead. He also engaged the smaller arm, but to little effect.

"This ain't gonna work," he said.

He lowered the arms, retracted the working solar panel, and tried pushing the rock to the side with the rover itself. It bucked against the ravine wall, but the rock gradually slid.

"We gonna have enough room to pass?" Levitt asked.

The ravine was less than a meter wider than the rover. With the rock, I couldn't see much leeway.

"We're gonna try, ma'am—professor," the ground navigator said.

"I'm good with Dr. Levitt," she said.

"I'd settle for Doc," Shonstein said.

The arm pushed the rock over as much as it could. Dexterous driving and a side wheelie maneuver took the rover up and over the rock's edge and we continued up the passage.

Though we had every camera angle on a giant monitor all of Mission Control could see, I peered down at one of the desktop monitors to view the most awesome sight yet, coming into view as the drone topped the ravine's crest: the Big Retriever Rocket, dock door down, ready to accept our hobbled habitué. Mission control CHEER as everyone saw it.

Then we got stuck at the ravine's crest, right in view of the BRR. The tires spun, the rover slid backward. Only one tire had traction. The other three dug deeper ruts.

"Okay. Let's back it down the hill," the GN said.

"Careful," Shonstein said. "Incupods' on that side," where the rover was almost touching the ravine's jagged wall.

The helidrone hovered closer, like an impish tagalong watching and tattling on every move.

"Well I'll be," Levitt said.

"What?" Cooper asked.

"Look at the ground under the rover," Levitt said. "It's alluvial. This was once a stream or river."

Then I spoke, with a flash of what I hoped was brilliance. "There should be rockier soil beneath the sand at the crest," I said. "Let the front tires gradually dig in there while the rear tires stay idle."

"Makes sense," Levitt said. "If water flowed over and down, the crest would be the most-eroded, rockiest part. Maybe."

"We're on solid ground now," the GN said, stopping the rover a couple meters from the crest. "Your move."

"What do we do here, Bill?" Levitt asked. "We have four wheels, individually controlled."

"Try them in sequence," Marcum said. "Test each tire for grip."

The GN rotated each wheel, one by one. The front left and lower right wheels spun the least.

"Jennifer?" Marcum deferred.

Faith (in me). So cool. "Okay—give those two tires the most gas, the other two nothing—yet," I said. "Test again the minute anything changes." I spoke from the experience of helping my dad get Manny Tranny the non-self-driving vintage pickup unstuck on back roads.

The ground navigator crawled the rover up the ravine toward the crest, stopping every couple minutes to test each wheel. On one leg of the short trek, the two back wheels had the most traction. Minutes later, the left front wheel had the most traction and got the most gas. And so on, until we were at the crest again.

"Now, leave the rear wheels in neutral," I said. "Gradually accelerate the front wheels."

The front wheels dug into the sand, hitting rockier ground. The rear tires tagged along, not digging, not slowing us up. It was like treading water, arms only, not much leg work. We gradually crested.

"Nobody cheer," the GN said into his mic. "Don't want to

jinx anything."

"Not bad for an ABD," Brando said. "I'm taking *you* skiing with me next time."

Couple winters ago, Brando got stuck in a blizzard on I-90 near Snoqualmie Pass. It was Jack London-level scary until first responders rescued him.

The rover rolled into the landing area, at the smooth, flat, boring bottom of a small crater in Capris Chasma. The BRR launch site was a minimalist steel contraption positioned by past rover arms over the dry stream or river bed that became the ravine we were traveling.

The crater and stream bed acted in tandem as a flame trap, or in NASA lingo, a "flame trench deflector system" that swept the rocket's blasting takeoff fire away from the ship. With Mars' lighter atmosphere and lower gravity, it didn't have to be as elaborate a flame trench as on Earth. It worked well, but had to be completely free of rocks.

Now, it wasn't.

As we might have expected, the quaking surface had littered the launch pad with stones that could fly up during launch and hit the rising rocket.

"Well damn," the GN said. "Gotta clear the launch pad now."

"Launch delay, people," the chief flight engineer announced as he sauntered into the control room.

"How long?" Levitt asked.

"A day, maybe couple days," the GN said. "Gotta clear the site, run a bunch of systems checks. You know the drill."

"We do," Levitt said.

We saw a poignant image from behind a tent-like structure: the *Curiosity, Perseverance, Foresight,* and *Odysseus* rovers, left behind when samples but not rovers were all our rockets could shuttle home.

SpaceTek built its business on adaptive reuse of everything from "rockets to rovers" CEO Leon Telos liked to say. The grounded rovers and their robotic arms still worked fine, albeit slowly without EPR technology. Mission Control rallied them to pick up all the rocks.

THOUGH THE DELAY WAS an antithetical let-down, the launch more than made up for it. The leftover rovers cleared the site in less than two days. The securely-mounted BRR hadn't moved or experienced any damage.

The GN docked the drone and used the surfeit of robotic arms to remove the damaged solar panel. The semi-retired rovers back in their tent and the landing site clear, all systems were a go.

In a ceremony of faux flourish, the GN handed the joystick to Dr. Shonstein.

"Will you do the honors, doc?" he said.

"Dr. Levitt?" she deferred.

"Please," Levitt replied.

"I would be honored." Shonstein took the joystick and positioned our rover like we'd done in simulation. Up the ramp it went, into the BRR, where a flight engineer locked its wheels —and its precious, history-making passenger—securely into place.

"Docking request granted," he quipped.

It was time.

"Why all the long faces?" the chief flight engineer told his team. "Dock door up. Cue music. Let's get home."

From the drone and rover cameras, we watched the dock door rise and the Martian landscape disappear to those first notes from Strauss' *Blue Danube*. I was tearing up, sentimental fool, but my hurricane remained offshore.

UW

Nine

"Jennifer!" Dr. Levitt waved me into her office. Shonstein, Marcum, and Brando were gathered around the monitor on her desk. We looked at the live video with *Deep Space Gateway, August 7* flickering at the bottom. A gloved, hazmat-suited space station crew member with "Cpt. Rhonda Gillory" stamped below a pair of wings over her left pocket handled one of our vials—*our* vials—with heavy-duty latex gloves in a sealed acrylic, ultra-clean glove box.

We were awaiting the first test aboard the space station's lab: Did Crimsy survive the months-long journey into our orbit? She was sturdier than any life form known to science, but did she (and by "she" I mean the plurality of bugs we hoped to soon see under a microscope) return alive, sick, hanging on by a thread, or dead?

"I'm blaming you if she's passed on to that great agar dish in the sky, Bill," Levitt said to Dr. Marcum. Her tone sounded only half in jest.

"I made no predictions about survivability," Marcum said.

"What *did* you predict?" Shonstein said.

"About living or dying? Out of the realm of mathematics, I'm afraid."

"The suspense is killing me," Levitt said.

"Same," I said.

"Assuming she's alive, what's next?" Marcum asked.

"Can she reproduce? Grow?" Shonstein replied. "Then we determine if Crimsy is a Martian original or an impostor, maybe from Earth."

"Hale won't let up until that's put to bed," Brando said. His phone vibrated. He looked at it.

"Lawyer. Gotta take this." He slipped through the group and out of Levitt's office.

"Madam Principal Investigator," came from the monitor. Space station crewman "Cpt. Rob Hightower" looked at Dr. Levitt. "Drum roll please. Introducing *Crimsococcus halocryophilus* (say that three times fast)."

"So our alien visitor is alive?" Levitt said.

"Appears so," Hightower said.

Quiet "yays" and thumbs up circled our group.

"We took some pix under the microscope," Gillory said. And there she was: a few dozen oval-shaped bacteria with a red hue.

"You haven't stained anything, right?" Shonstein asked.

"Right," Gillory said. "Per your instructions."

"So *Crimsococcus* has some sort of native coloring," Dr. Marcum said.

"Seems so, though it could be just the way it reflects our onboard lighting," Hightower said. "We'll know more later."

"This is so awesome," Shonstein said, staring at the screen. "Somebody pinch me."

"I'll need smelling salts if she turns out to be a Mars Unique," Levitt said.

I WAS AT LUNCH when Dr. Levitt texted the team her big announcement of the Big Announcement: Whether or not Crimsy had reproduced, which meant we could study her in much greater detail.

"If Crimsy's viable, it's all Brandy," Levitt said. "I hate like hell for him to miss this."

"I hear ya," Dr. Shonstein said.

"So who came up with Crimsy?" Dr. Cooper asked. I thought about answering, but remembered how Dr. Hale felt about nicknames, a laboratory staple usually reserved for instruments.

"I believe that was Dr. Jen—"

But before Levitt could finish my honorary title, I meekly raised my hand.

"Love it," Cooper said.

Oh, validation. This was going to be a good day. The station-to-shore monitor buzzed.

"Everyone ready?" Levitt asked. She switched it on and the face of Deep Space Gateway (DSG) crew member Gillory appeared onscreen, in such high definition I felt like we were standing alongside her. I started parsing her facial expression.

"Dr. Levitt?" she asked.

"On pins and needles," Levitt responded.

"*Crimsococcus halocryophilus* is—" She indicated a robotic arm holding a stoppered glass test tube in the clean box. Ice dappled the metal arm and the glass. "Ready for your inspection," Gillory said.

Levitt leaned forward. "How?" she asked. "We're in a conference room. Should we move to Lecture A?"

"Just use an app. Put your cell on the table, screen up and unobstructed."

Dr. Levitt looked around. "Anyone have the app?"

"3D for Me?" I asked, cell phone poised.

"That'll work," Gillory said. "Sync it using the code DSG20350814XYZ."

On Z, a 3D image of the test tube in the robot's grasp hovered about a foot above my cell phone.

"What next?" Levitt asked.

"Whatever you want," Gillory said off camera. "Take the image. Turn it over. Bring it in for a closer look."

Levitt grasped the image and turned the tube. The robotic hand turned as she did. As she next pulled it forward, the image enlarged, and we could see the reddish bacteria covering the nutrient agar in the tube.

"Is Brando there?" Captain Gillory asked. "This is his specially-concocted Martian gourmet growth medium."

Shonstein leaned over and whispered to Levitt.

"He is not," Levitt said. "But we'll make sure he gets the news."

"WE'VE GOT MORE GOOD news," Dr. Shonstein said at our weekly staff meeting in Lecture A, with better projectors and bigger screens. "*Crimsococcus* appears to have qualities of both Archaeon and Bacterium."

"Are you kidding?" Levitt said.

"It does suggest a Mars Unique," Captain Gillory said from DSG.

"Unless past forward contaminants have evolved into something this unusual in the, what—seventy years—since our first probe landed, I have to agree. Crimsy is not a contaminant's grandchild," Shonstein said.

"So do we have a new Domain on our hands?" Dr. Cooper asked. "Or some kind of hybrid?"

"That's Brandy's bailiwick," Levitt said. "I can't believe he's missing this."

On "this," the most beautiful image in biology appeared in glorious high def on the screen in back of Dr. Levitt. Crimsy had undergone some staining tests. Her red-red coloring had given way to a brownish-red that resembled a Martian dust devil.

"She looks to be gram negative, boys and girls," Captain Hightower said, as we stared at Crimsy—millions of Crimsys, actually—under a microscope. "Kind of fitting, that reddish tint."

Dr. Shonstein approached the screen. I'd never seen the look on her face: She was a classic stoic, rarely breaking a smile unless Malachi was on her lap or that time her husband had the biggest spring bouquet I've ever seen delivered to her post-doc seminar.

"That is one unusual-looking bug," Shonstein said. "How can that not be a Mars Unique?" She turned to Dr. Levitt. "Marcia, can you believe this?"

"I can't believe it," she said in a breaking voice. "I'm trying to. This can't be happening. It's all a fluke. There's no way we discovered life on Mars. Life on Mars? Life on Mars? It's just an elaborate contamination."

"Unlikely," Dr. Marcum said.

"I agree with Dr. Shonstein," Cooper said, staring at the screen. "That's one weird-looking germ."

"What about pathogenicity?" Dr. Shonstein asked. "Any progress?"

Pathogenicity—as in would Crimsy start a deadly pandemic or turn us into zombies? But before I could catch the answer, my cell vibrated with a text message.

"Mom's missing." It was David, and this was a new thing.

I typed under the table. "Wat u mean mom's missin?"

"Call me. ASAP."

I excused myself and stepped into the hallway.

I WALKED AWAY FROM Lecture A dialing David. "What's going on?" I whispered.

"Last night. Mrs. Lukins stopped by to return some dishes and said the door was open and the lights were on in the living room and kitchen but no Mom. She called around, went upstairs, into the garage, back yard, everywhere."

"That's definitely not Mom," I said. "Her car there?"

"Yeah."

"You call the cops?"

"They won't do anything until it's been forty eight hours. No sign of a crime, no sign of a struggle. It's like she just walked away."

A knot tied itself in my stomach. "Do you need me to come home?"

"No," he said. "Of course not. Aunt Marjorie, Uncle Ron and several friends are looking for her. I've got a sub for tomorrow."

"Are you sure you don't want me there? I can get a flight quick. I finally got chipped."

"No, really," David said. "We've got this. If it's any consolation, cops don't think Mom was the victim of any crime."

"How do they know?"

"Hey—I'm over at Marjorie's. I'll call you later. K?"

"K," I reluctantly agreed.

I slipped back into the meeting. But I was anxious, distracted, and couldn't focus, feelings made all the more trying as Lecture A was awash in complicated emotions, Crimsy looming on screen.

SO—NOMENCLATURE, THE NAME we scientists give to the way we name things. Crimsy was named the scientific way—by committee—but not without the rules of our name game, aka nomenclature.

Crimso comes from "crimson," the color of Mars, better known as the Red Planet. "A *coccus* is any bacterium that has a spherical, ovoid, or generally round shape." (I got that from Wikipedia, which I "shall never cite," according to the Ten Commandments of Academic Research).

The second part of Crimsy's name is two names combined: *halocryophilus*. "Halophiles" love salt. "Cryophiles" love cold. Halocryophiles are ready-made for salty, icy Martian water. *Crimsococcus halocryophilus* is, therefore, an oval-shaped bacteria found on Mars that thrives in frozen saltwater.

Not very exotic, I know. But that's part of Crimsy's ironic charm: she's boring. In fact, if we had found her on Earth, she probably wouldn't even merit an article in a mid-tier microbiology journal.

But hailing from Mars makes Crimsy special, an exotic foreigner like her Earthling cousins in all ways except her hometown. The details of her drab existence in a pool of frozen saltwater on a cold and lifeless planet (if you define "life" as "lively") have prompted me to ponder just how exotic she is. Or even how foreign.

I gave Crimsy a simple, fun nickname and got in the habit of calling it *her* or *she* for the kids in my brother David's third grade science class, where he persuaded me to give guest lectures on the exciting life of a scientist in a field with a cool name—astrobiology—who just happened to be on the team that discovered Life on Mars.

We weren't allowed to talk to the media, but as far as I knew, it was okay to talk about Crimsy absent reporters or recorders. I asked the class to turn off any recording devices. I guess if a student went to the press, I could say "a third grader told you that?"

I put a slide on David's 3D whiteboard, which projected a three-dimensional image I could manipulate with my fingers a lot like my 3D for Me app. Except these images were magnificent. Discovered in that treasure trove of lost Steve Jobs papers, this breed of 3D whiteboard didn't display mere holograms, but images you could barely tell apart from the real things, in this case, blue spots photographed after Biolite infected the microbes with the colored reporter phages.

"Introducing *Crimsococcus halocryophilus*," I told the class. "Crimsy, for short."

"How do you know it's a real germ?" a boy asked.

"We've done lots of tests."

"Why is Crimsy a she?" another boy asked.

"She's really an it," I said. "But she's tough. How many of you have a really tough sister or aunt or mom?"

Lots of hands went up.

"What if she attacks us?"

"Could she kill us?"

"My grandpa said Martians invaded Earth when his grandpa was a kid."

"That was just a radio show," I explained. "By a man named Orson Welles. It scared the whole country, but it wasn't real."

"The first fake news, guys," my brother interjected.

"We're not that worried about Crimsy because we think she's like other bacteria found on Earth," I said. I put up another image, *Planococcus halocryophilus OR1.* "This guy was discovered in the Arctic. *Planococcus* lives in frozen saltwater, just like *Crimsococcus.*"

I called on a girl with her hand up.

"Orson Welles was born here," she said. "My mom says he lived just down the street from us."

"WHEN DID YOU GUYS finally land those white boards?" I asked David as he locked the door to the classroom.

"I don't know if we've landed them yet. They're on loan. School board is having a cow about paying for them."

"So you're not getting them?"

"I think the idea is to get us used to having them—at least, on the manufacturer's part—then reel in the board later. The kids love 'em. Parents at Westwood already bought one with PTA donations."

"You guys don't have that kind of money."

"No," he said. "Our parents are lucky if they can make it to an after-school night after second shift or third job."

We were outside now, standing next to my rental car.

"I'm sorry about what happened with Mom last night," he said.

"It's okay," I said.

"You've busted your ass. You have nothing to apologize to her or anyone else about."

I didn't want to talk about Mom, not now, not when there was nothing I could do except sulk on the flight back to Seattle. So I looked at the time hovering above my wrist.

"Gotta get back to the lab," I said. "Crimsy's here."

David stepped back and his lips parted for an indiscernible moment of awe. "You mean here? As in, Earth?"

"Yep."

"I haven't read or seen anything."

"News blackout," I said. "JPL wants to make sure everything's safe on the space station before we do the grand entrance." My car door opened and I kissed my brother on his cheek. "Thanks for being so supportive," I said.

"WE FOUND HER," DAVID told me, after Mom's daylong disappearance. He sounded exhausted.

"Where?"

"Leeward. Just sitting there, staring at the lake."

A beloved cafe on Lake Michigan. Mom had good taste in local ambience.

"Why did she leave the doors open and the lights on?"

"She doesn't remember," David said.

"Really?"

"That's what she said."

"How can she not remember? Mom's sharp as a tack."

"That's what I wanted to talk to you about," David said. "Remember what happened last Christmas? Mom got confused and no one knew what was going on."

"So?"

"It's happened a couple times since," David said. "It started getting worse not long after Brian died."

"She was grieving," I said.

"I thought that. But this long?"

"I spent a week in bed, staring at the ceiling comatose or dangling my arm over the floor in tears. You took family sick leave. But we're young. We recover sooner."

"This doesn't feel like grieving to me," David said. "She gets agitated at the least little thing, like when she flew off the handle with you. She'll call me thinking we made plans for dinner or to see Ron and Marjorie a couple days after we just did those things."

"Has she seen a doctor?"

"You know how she feels about docs."

"That was a pill pusher. She needs a neurologist, it sounds like."

"I know," David said. "But she doesn't listen to me, won't listen to her brother or her friends. Funny thing: if Brian or Dad were here, she'd probably listen to them."

"The two men who broke her heart," I said. "Isn't that poetically typical?"

David let some moments pass between us before mercifully changing the subject.

"How's little miss Crimsy?"

"Alive and well," I said.

"Yay," he said, with the passion of an emoji.

"Our team is pretty excited. I'm coming home."

"What do you mean?"

"Just what I said. You can't deal with this on your own."

"I most certainly can," David said. "And you are most certainly not coming home. You have one more year. You can't screw it up."

"I can take family leave, too, ya know."

"No," David said. "We have plenty of support. Come home when you have that Nobel Prize."

My voice broke. "I love you," I said.

"I love you, too," he said. "We'll work this out. I'm formulating a plan, and we'll work this out."

I went to bed with that knot in my stomach, stared at the ceiling, then cough-cried myself to sleep.

Ten

No news is good news until it's not. After no updates from Deep Space Gateway about the pathogenicity tests that would clear Crimsy's entry visa, Dr. Levitt emailed the crew.

"Any word? Everything okay?"

"Seems to be," Hightower emailed back a few hours later.

"Seems?" Levitt asked.

"Still running tests. Hope to have results soon."

"Should it take this long?" Levitt asked Dr. Shonstein at our partially-attended staff meeting later (Marcum and Cooper were out).

"It might," Shonstein said. "You figure they're running PCR and the genetics suite to check for virulence genes and disease markers. Then lab mice. Inoculation, airborne, oral transmission. And in double quadruple triplicate. *Exhaustive* is the operable word."

"Guess I'm just nervous," Levitt said. "What if we can't bring our little darlin' home?"

"Then we study her up there, I guess," Dr. Brando said, walking into Levitt's office with an armload of books.

"Howdy stranger," Shonstein said.

"Don't remind me," he said.

"That doesn't sound good."

He set the books on a table. "Melissa wants sole custody. I'm thinking of firing my lawyer. This is my family law reading material for the week."

"Ah, Mike. I'm so sorry," Dr. Levitt said. "How's your daughter?"

"I don't know, honestly," he said. "The other night, I walked by her room. It sounded like she was having trouble breathing. I went in and she had the sheet pulled up so tightly over her head, I almost had to pry it off." He put his hand on his forehead. "She is fearless. My Lexi is fearless. You should see her on the soccer field."

Levitt took his hand and squeezed. "Hang in there."

"We're here if you need us," Shonstein said. "You know that, right?"

"I might need character witnesses," he said.

"You? Character witnesses?" Shonstein said.

Levitt's cell buzzed with a message from Deep Space Gateway. She switched on speaker phone.

"Good news?" she said.

"Turn on your projector app," Hightower replied. She touched the app and set the phone on her desk. A white mouse sniffing the air in the space station's containment lab hovered above the phone.

"This is one of the mice we inoculated with *Crimsococcus*," Hightower said. "This," his voice cracked, "is what happened."

A pile of white salt replaced the mouse. We looked at it in horror.

"That's all." Hightower stammered and hesitated. "That was left. Of Roxy."

"The mouse?" Brando asked.

We heard some odd noises, like someone trying to restrain a sneeze.

"My esteemed partner in science is trying his best not to burst out laughing," Captain Gillory said. "Roxy's fine. I wish I could say as much for our supply of table salt."

Shonstein snickered. Stoic Shonstein. Then she laughed. We all laughed. Even Brando.

"So are we to conclude non-pathogenicity?" Levitt asked.

"Couple more tests," Gillory said. "But so far, *Crimsococcus halocryophilus* is a complete disappointment on the global pandemic excitement scale."

"If only we could say the same for some germs we know," Shonstein said.

I LOVE USING THE Intuitype keyboard. They've added a bunch of new features including Cloud-based grammar and composition checks so sophisticated, you can be barely literate and still churn out *War and Peace*. I'm a terrible typist but I just put my fingers on the touchscreen keyboard in typical QWERTY fashion and start typing. The keyboard does the rest, which this morning means tabulating salt dosage data from our successful creation of the extremophile phage that infected and lit up Crimsy on Mars.

I heard a noise in the hallway and checked it out. Cute, strange guy, which could mean a few things: a subpoena for Dr. Brando. A reporter who either sneaked into the building or was sent by our guileless Public Information Officer (PIO) on the mistaken notion we were finally ready to talk to the press. Or, as I was about to learn, University Legal Counsel, Intellectual Property Division.

"Dr. Levitt?" he asked me.

"Uh, no. Flattery will get you lost around here."

"They told me—"

"I don't think she's in," I said. "Can I help you?"

He handed me an old-school, tangible, non-ghost card. "Nathaniel Hawthorn, JD, MBA."

I looked at it and smiled.

"Different spelling," he said.

"You get that a lot, do you?" I said.

"Like a scarlet letter."

Another Keeper of Obscure Literary Knowledge. I was liking this guy already. But business before pleasure.

"I will get this to her," I said. "Do you want her to call you?"

"That's okay. I may just drop back by." He looked down at his briefcase. "When is she usually in?"

"Mornings. Early. You could call or text."

He smiled. "Six, seven?"

"Five."

"Five," he said reluctantly. "Okay." He started to walk away. "Oh—I never got your name."

"Jennifer," I said. "Dr. Jennifer, some day. But right now,

just Jennifer."

He smiled, I thought bashfully. So cute.

"THAT REMINDS ME," I said at our next staff meeting. I slid Nathaniel Hawthorn's old-fashioned, brick-and-mortar business card across the table to Dr. Levitt.

"University lawyer. He say what he wanted?"

"To meet you in person," I said.

"That can't be good," Brando said.

"I hate to be a Doctor Downer," Dr. Shonstein said. "But has anyone considered the shit show that will inevitably follow the love fest after the first stories break?"

"As in?" Dr. Levitt asked.

"You're kidding, right?"

"No, seriously," Levitt said. "I sometimes need to be slapped out of my reverie, naive as it sometimes is."

"As one who has received a major prize, I can attest that the glory of scientific discovery is not all blinding tidings," Dr. Marcum said. "When people asked how it felt to win a Fields, I used terms like 'gutted' and 'knackered.' When the press obsessed over the fact that I was the first and only Black recipient of such a prize, I reminded them that when he was alive, David Blackwell, the eminent Berkeley mathematician, had been far more deserving than I."

"Wait til you win the Abel Prize," Dr. Levitt said. "Rumor

has it you're a shoo-in."

"Oh, madam PI—be careful what you wish on I," Dr. Marcum said. "Besides—Sara Goode's the shoo-in, I hear."

"What does 'knackered' mean?" Dr. Cooper asked.

"Life sucked," Marcum said. "Then people started forgetting about it, I got some scrummy pay raises, and Dr. Levitt fell in love with my locks."

"Correction. I fell in love with your keys," Levitt said. She looked around the table. "Envy, jealousy, politics. What else?"

"Is there anything patentable about Crimsy?" Dr. Cooper asked. "I assume there must be."

"Like what?" Brando asked.

"Like your one-of-a-kind agar," Cooper said. "Like our Biolite adaptation. Like Marcum's algorithms."

"Patented. Held by Cambridge and me," he said. "Bollocks for earnings, however."

"What about Crimsy?" Cooper asked.

"Good question," Dr. Shonstein said. "They patent genes, clones, the Human Genome, vaccines, kittens."

"The cloned kitty controversy," Marcum said.

"There's certainly no prior art," Brando said.

"Haven't microbes been patented?"

"Supreme Court said so," Levitt noted, scrolling through her phone. "And I quote, 'The fact that micro-organisms are alive is without legal significance for the purpose of patent law.'"

"Chakrabarty case," Dr. Shonstein said. "He patented a bacteria. But only after genetically altering it so it could eat oil. Basically the modifications got the patent, not the germ."

"We won't be modifying Crimsy," Cooper said.

"But still," Dr. Shonstein said. "The minute our bug lands, whole new areas of interstellar law will spring up overnight. Who knows what kind of claims will arise. Finders keepers, so keep your grubby corporate mitts off. Mars Unique, so therefore worthy of protection. So huge for mankind, maybe a bunch of countries go to war over it."

"Remember what Jonas Salk said," Brando added. "You can't patent the Sun."

"Bad news for the rest of us if you could patent the Sun." Dr. Cooper threw up another quote on his cell phone projector app that hovered over our conference table.

"A patent on a product of Nature would authorize the patent holder to exclude everyone from observing, characterizing or analyzing, by any means whatsoever, the product of Nature. This barrier is inherently insurmountable: one cannot study a product of Nature if one cannot legally possess it." – Eric Lander, Harvard-MIT, Human Genome Project

"Chilling," Brando said. "Keep law out of science."

"Look what it's done to families, right?" Marcum said.

"You got it."

"Can you believe we've been able to keep the press out of this?" Levitt said.

"That's good and bad," Marcum said. "A wise Nobel laureate told me that if you win a big prize, but nobody hears the applause, did you really win anything?"

"I've never won anything," Shonstein said. "Never been close to winning anything. So I wouldn't know."

"Nonsense, Rebecca," Levitt said. "You've won so much grant funding I've lost count."

"Somehow," Shonstein said. "That never seems like a win. More like 'thank God, a reprieve for another year.' Relief my family won't be homeless. You know—basic needs kinda stuff."

"Grants are good. But credit is the coin of our realm and it's been no small worry to me that we haven't been able to build up much incremental credit via media, publication, or otherwise as MarsMicro has progressed," Marcum said. "We've done everything virtually in the dark."

"That's the way NASA and SpaceTek want it," Levitt said. "I've tried for a middle ground. Debated our Congressman for leeway. Stared down Hale to get off our case about making sure everything is perfect before publication. Listened to Rebecca arguing with JPL." She stretched her arms forward, glowered at the table. "Sorry. PTSD."

"I get it," Shonstein said. "I hate the politics, too."

The conversation paused, I thought uncomfortably.

"Well—we've beat this topic to death for the day," Levitt said. "I'll talk to that lawyer. Maybe he'll have some words of wisdom. Anyone have any specific questions for him?"

"Yes," Dr. Cooper said. "Will we have to own Crimsy to study it?"

Shonstein sighed and tapped the table with her pen.

"I'll be sure to ask," Levitt said.

I WAS SCRIBBLING NOTES and typing data in my studio apartment in a cool old building called The Mallory. "Hardwood floors and leaded glass doors" drew me immediately, and it wasn't far from the PAB.

David called with news about our mother.

"Ron thinks we should hire some kind of in-home, I don't know, caregiver."

"Caregiver? Has the forgetfulness gotten that bad?" I said.

"She forgot how to log into her computer. Forgot the key code on the office door. Then the fender bender."

"Fender bender?" I said. "Is she okay? How come you didn't tell me?"

"I'm telling you now," David said. "She's fine. But she calls Ron every time something happens. 'What's the key code? What's my password? Who's our insurance company?'"

"Just like she did with Brian."

"Yeah," David said. "And we saw where that ended up."

"I don't think Mom needs a caregiver. And I sure as hell know she wouldn't want one."

"It's not Ron's decision regardless," David said.

I tapped my pen on the table.

"Sometimes I wish she were here," I said. "I have this recurring dream of us living together, in like some separate, non-dystopian reality." I looked around my lovely little digs. "I'd have to get a bigger place, but—"

"Nice idea, sis, but alone, no friends, big, strange city?"

"Big, strange, *interesting* city. How much does she know about this caregiver idea?"

"Ron mentioned it. Sold the idea as kind of an extra set of hands. Housekeeping, shopping. Care giving, without the connotations."

"Sounds harmless enough."

"Yeah, I guess so."

"What can I do?"

David paused in thought. I looked over my glasses at my notes.

"When was the last time you and Mom talked?"

"It's been awhile. You know how it can get with us."

"Why don't you call her? She's in the office every day by eight thirty."

"Still?" I said. "Maybe that's the problem. She needs a vacay." I put down my pen and stretched, leaned back and looked at the ceiling. "I've got time I can take off."

"You mean go with her somewhere?"

"I mean have her out here," I said.

"Seriously?"

I looked at my sofa hide-a-bed, remembered my blow-up beds in the closet.

"Just you and Mom," David said. "Let me think about it."

I CALLED MOM THAT afternoon and left a message. The more I thought about it, the more I liked the idea of her getting away from Kenosha, from Ron and Marjorie, the memories of Dad and Brian, even David. I've been in school for as long as I can remember; Mom and I never had a girls-only vacation.

I've never felt settled. And the idea of Mom staying in my always-tiny apartments or the guest room my Cal Tech roomies maintained, usually for younger siblings but once for a hip dad, never appealed to me.

Truth be told, I'm also a little ashamed. I still can't report "I've made it!" Still can't present myself to my mother as a fully-formed, functional, success-suffused adult.

I'm in debt up to my ass if not my eyeballs; my chosen profession—astrobiology—has always seemed Quixotic, unrealistic, like the starving artist who puts herself through a $200,000 per year Master of Fine Arts program on little more than a government-guaranteed credit card.

While David is—David. And Mom is this debt-free pragmatist with the 820 credit scores, paid-off rental properties, home sans mortgage, no car loans, no school loans, and the proud title "Mother Who Helped Pay Tuition for Three Children," two of whom don't *yet* make enough money to return—or repay—the favor; and one of whom never will.

I've tried talking to Ron. He's all ears at first, sympathetic, wants to help. But then. Then, he goes into Ron mode and I go into Jen mode, a harmful remnant of my tempestuous teen years. We end up with listless agreement about vague plans based on illogical premises.

All I want to do is to connect with my beautiful mother. I want to hold her. I want to laugh with her. I want us to cry in each other's arms. I want to do more than tuck point the bricks of our misunderstanding.

"HEY." MY MOM CALLED me back with our usual terse greeting.

"Hey," I said. "How's Kenowhere?"

"Still here," she said. "How's Seattle?"

"The most brilliant sunny sky you've ever seen." And I wasn't lying just to get her to come out. "I can even see Mt. Rainier today."

"Sounds amazing," she said. She sounded fine, too, which led me to wonder if the men in our lives weren't over-reacting again.

"You need to come out. See for yourself." I said.

"I've never been to Seattle," she said. "You know, Hal almost landed there. Sent me the prettiest postcards."

"Dr. Hale?"

"Yes," she said.

"I thought—were you guys close or something?"

"Or something."

"What?" I said with a nervous laugh.

"There are things about me, darling daughter, you do not know."

"Ah. *Une intrigue.*"

"*Bien sûr! Et vous pensiez que votre mère vivait une existence aussi humble,*" my mother said.

"Don't try to talk your way out of it."

"*Parler de sortir de quelque chose? Bannissez la pensée!*"

"You win. My French will never rival yours."

"But what fun we could have stumbling our way across France, eh?"

I hadn't heard this tone in my mother's voice for a long time. It was charming, even a little seductive. This woman, thirty five years ago, standing on the shores of Lake Michigan, wind in her hair, chiseled cheeks ruddy and lovely, dashing off French elocution. Harold Hale wouldn't have stood a chance. Maybe that's why he left.

"How is Dr. Brando's little girl?" Mom asked.

"I just saw her," I said. "She's doing okay."

"What a little charmer."

"She sure took to you."

"I took to her. That was such a fun trip."

"It was. When was the last time we were all together like that?"

My mother was quiet, probably thinking. "The Christmas before Brian died," she said. "I guess it wasn't like that, though, was it?"

"No," I said. "It wasn't like Christmas at all."

"I need to get out of this cold. I love Wisconsin, but—"

"Remember how Dad talked about moving to Florida?"

I heard her sigh. "Have to do things in life before it's too late," she said.

"So can we plan on you coming out here? Staying with me? It's a little cramped, but—"

She didn't say anything.

"You never met the whole team."

Still nothing.

"Lexi Brando."

"All right," my mother chuckled. "You've convinced me. *J'aimerais venir te voir*." Which loosely translated means, "I would love to come see you."

I was on Cloud Ten for the rest of the night. We spent the next few weeks making plans.

Eleven

I walked past Dr. Levitt's office and her door was open. I could see her face in the reflection of the little window in the door. She stared at her computer monitor. I stood and watched, waiting for her to type something or move. But she was still. I peered in. Her face was uncharacteristically blank. I wanted to tap on the door but didn't want to startle her. No matter. She saw me.

"Jennifer."

"I heard a lot of noise in here, so I thought I'd check it out," I said.

She smiled. "Come in."

I did.

"I met with that attorney," she said.

"Nathaniel Hawthorn, with no 'e'?"

"The same."

"And?"

"And. He informs me Crimsy won't be coming home anytime soon."

"Something wrong with the pathogenicity tests?"

"We didn't get into that."

I felt a hollow, anxious feeling in my stomach. I didn't

know what to ask next.

"SpaceTek, it turns out, raised money for the mission from a number of sovereign countries and a slew of ultra high-worth investors," she said. "Legal is *suddenly* concerned that if we don't handle this properly, the university, the US government, maybe even us, could be deluged with patent claims and IP lawsuits. At least, that's what our lawyer says."

"Sounds like Dr. Shonstein's shit show," I said.

"Doesn't it, though."

"What do they mean by 'properly'?"

"You mean, how does legal define proper handling? Mr. Hawthorn didn't say. My guess is letting the lawyers handle everything."

"This why we haven't heard from the space station lately?"

"Could be," Levitt said. "I've fired off a few emails, but so far, no one up there's responded."

"This sucks," I said.

"Yeah," she said. "Really, really."

I sighed. I looked at her monitor, the stuff on her desk, her hands, the gray sky outside her window and hints of Portage Bay beyond.

"I better go," I said. "Got a meeting with Dr. Brando after lunch."

I stood and at the door, "Jennifer," Dr. Levitt said. "We'll figure it out."

"Of course," I said.

I SAW NATHANIEL HAWTHORN in the PAB parking garage.

"Hey!"

He was about to get into his car. I jogged.

"Hey—Nate!"

I don't know how "Nate" came out. But it felt good. He turned as I ran up to him, all button down and prim in his briefs and legals.

"Nate?" he said. "I didn't know we were on a nickname basis."

"Sorry," I said, a little out of breath. "Nathaniel Hawthorn's too long to yell."

"It's Jennifer, right?"

"Yes, right." I gathered myself. "I was wondering what was going on."

"I don't know. What?"

"Leaving the most amazing discovery in the history of science—undiscovered?"

"That," he said.

"Yeah."

"We have some things to work out."

"What things?"

"Legal things. Proprietary things. Ownership things."

"Who wants to own it," I said. "If I may ask."

He put his briefcase through the window of his used but fancy car and looked at me awkwardly.

"We, um, don't know yet. But rest assured, someone will. Like you said, the most amazing discovery in the history of science. Definitely not your grandma's Moon rock."

I resisted smiling at this quip. I played it cool. "Definitely not," I agreed.

He wasn't emotionally invested, and to me, he came across this side of cavalier. I felt the urge to slap him into our reality, but I also realized he was only doing his employer's bidding. And maybe his employer had a point. Dr. Shonstein apparently thought so.

"Shit show," I muttered.

"What?"

"Nothing."

"How'd your group take it?" he asked, putting his hands on the car top.

I looked at his tie, then his hands and fingernails. "Not everyone knows," I said.

"Is there any way you can do what you need to do aboard the space station?"

"Absolutely not," I said. "Its only set up for the basics. Is Crimsy real? Alive? Will she cause anyone to get sick."

"Crimsy?"

"Nickname."

"I see," he said. "Because you can't yell *Crimsococcus halocryophilus* in a crowded parking garage."

This time, I did smile.

"I wish I had better news," Nathaniel Hawthorn said. "Bad news is one of the things I hate about this job."

"Is there a resolution?" I asked. "All these people who want a piece of Crimsy won't get anything if she stays up there. Their investments lost, right?" I put sarcastic emphasis on the word "investments."

"I can't say at this point. I haven't seen the contracts," Nathaniel said. "I don't know what guarantees were made, who's supposed to get what, how or where they handle disputes. Mediation, arbitration, litigation, even venue. You've got the European Space Agency, NASA, Roscosmos, CNSA, ISRO, a few billionaires, and two of our three trillionaires."

The European Continent. The United States. Russia. China. India. And two people worth as much as a country. I caught a deep breath and released a long sigh.

"My sentiments exactly," Nathaniel said.

I waited while he got into his car. He started the engine and rolled down the window.

"Keep the faith," he said.

I watched him pull out and just as he was about to exit, I ran up to the driver's side. He stopped, rolled down the window.

"Where can *I* find all that stuff?"

"What stuff?"

"The contracts you were talking about. Names of all the players."

He hesitated.

"It's a public project, right?" I said.

"I can get them," he said.

I stepped back from the car. "Thanks," I said.

As he drove away, he stopped again and craned his head

out the window. "This the place to find you?"

"Yeah," I said. "I'm always here."

THE BAD NEWS FROM Dr. Levitt started with a team-wide email, Subject: Staff Meeting—Urgent! and the brief intro, "I want to update everyone on the status of MarsMicro and *Crimsococcus halocryophilus*." We gathered in the conference room with Dr. Cooper telaparting from Harvard, where he was back at the Hale Lab for a few weeks.

"I have someone who would like to join us," Coop said.

"Marcia." Dr. Hale—or more accurately, his image, all of him—materialized, seated next to Cooper's similarly-situated image, and across from Shonstein, Brando, and Marcum.

"Dr. Hale," came Dr. Levitt's strained reply. "What happened to the good ol' days of just Zoom?"

It was kind of creepy, having ultra-realistic, super-holograms beside us instead of the real deal. Telaparting (tell apart: get it) was supposed to be the new next-best-thing to being there, or so the higher ups told our office after the last pandemic. You got all the body language—this *was* the actual person, in real time, in their home, office, or wherever, but appearing in your conference room. Shonstein lobbied for a feature that would beam counterproductive participants back to the *Enterprise*.

"I came to offer support," Dr. Hale said. "Thanks for having me."

"I'm okay with it, if everyone else is," Dr. Levitt said.

The room was quiet. I could see the small bump on Dr.

Hale's cheek, snugged against his nose. TelaPart was that detailed.

"Where *are* the two of you, by the way?" Dr. Levitt asked.

"I'm in the lab," Cooper responded.

"On my deck drinking coffee," Hale said.

"Nice," Shonstein said. "Maybe we can all start telaparting it in?"

"As I recall, we've had that discussion," Levitt said. She grinned. "So—to the issue at hand. Legal tells me that, for the time being at least, we will be unable to perform further, in-depth studies on Crimsy."

"Crimsy?" Dr. Hale asked, though he had to know by now *that* was the official nickname.

"Crimsy," Dr. Levitt affirmed.

"What's the problem?" Dr. Brando asked.

"The problem, as I understand it, is that JPL and SpaceTek are concerned that if our Martian visitor lands on Earth, we'll be besieged with claims over who gets her, who gets to study her, which studies are performed, which patents get to emerge, which safety issues will become international incidents, and a whole lot of other legalese I neither understand nor appreciate," Dr. Levitt said.

"How do we know Crimsy's a *her*?" Marcum asked, feigning seriousness.

"Oh, it's a her," Shonstein said.

"Wanna bet?" Brando said.

"Are we to believe these legal issues weren't worked out well beforehand?" Dr. Cooper asked.

"I haven't seen all the contracts," Levitt said. "Nathaniel Hawthorn assures me they were, but he also makes an important point: Nobody ever expected this mission to bring back anything alive."

"Who is Nathaniel Hawthorn?" Dr. Hale said.

"Author of colonial witch hunt fiction," Dr. Marcum said. "Reincarnated as a university lawyer."

"So regardless what was previously agreed upon, all bets are off with a discovery of this magnitude," Dr. Brando suggested.

"Anything can be challenged, even the most airtight contract," Dr. Levitt said.

"Like the ironclad pre-nup that gets tossed out of court," Dr. Shonstein said.

"That's what they're afraid of," Dr. Levitt said. "Crimsy is too valuable a prize."

"She's not your grandma's Moon rock," I said. The group looked at me. Dr. Hale seemed to glare. "So Nathaniel Hawthorn says."

"You've talked to him?" Dr. Shonstein asked.

"Briefly," I said.

"Mr. Hawthorn is right," Marcum said. "Crimsy's not your grandmum's Moon rock. Or Mars rock, for that matter. We all saw what happened when *Odysseus* brought the first of those back."

Not quite the same, but I got the point. *Odysseus* didn't bring enough rocks back. Or dust. Every major Earthly power and most minor powers wanted their fair share—of rocks and dust. Corporations that provided money for the mission demanded their chunk of the Red Planet. Crimsy caught up in an even worse morass was as imaginable as her discovery was implausible.

"You helped resolve that fiasco," Shonstein said to Dr. Levitt. "So it can be done."

"I don't think what we did could happen with Crimsy," Dr. Levitt said.

"I was immersed back then," Dr. Cooper said. "I remember the disputes, but not much else."

"We worked with the United Nations," said Levitt, after the *Odysseus* mission. "Office for Outer Space Affairs, Committee on the Peaceful Uses of Outer Space. Five rocks are still traveling the world for public view."

"Which we can't very well expect a microbe to endure," Dr. Marcum said. "So what's the upshot? That we can't communicate with DSG? That we'll never have access to the science we've spent decades developing? That *Crimsococcus* will exist in some sort of interstellar limbo?"

I caught Dr. Levitt staring at Dr. Hale. I figure she wanted to form her words carefully.

"I don't know," she said. "Hawthorn says he's planning to dig into the contracts and follow up with me sometime in the next few weeks. But until then, I just don't know."

IRONIC, HAROLD HALE SITTING in on all this. He made his first scientific noise with an idea christened "Hale's Theorem," an interplanetary version of Occam's Razor: That in space, the simplest discovery is always the most likely.

We humans have failed to find life on other planets because we've spent too much money, time, and imagination seeking the exotic and romantic, i.e. the complex, Hale's Theorem claims.

"If we want to find life 'out there,' we're going to have to keep it simple, stupid," he said at age thirty three.

Now, we were watching one of the simplest life forms imaginable become unimaginably complicated.

Dr. Hale's later findings in microbial motility persuaded me toward his lab. He developed the first consistent model of how bacteria might move in recurring (or recurrent) slope lineae, dark, saltwater streaks that drip down Martian craters considered evidence of water, including ancient oceans that vanished with that planet's version of climate change.

I don't think Hale figured out who I was until about two months into my internship.

"You're Patrice's—?"

"Daughter. Yes. You went to high school with my mom, right?"

"I did. How is she?"

"Fine. Wonderful! She has her own business. Does really well."

"Please do tell her I said hello." Hale's voice was gentle. I wondered if he knew Mom more than in just passing, then didn't give the idea a second thought.

NATHANIEL HAWTHORN TOOK TWO OpenPad legal-sized, paper-thin computers from his briefcase, handed us one, and we scrolled together to relevant passages in The Contracts, passing said pad around the table.

"Here," Nathaniel said, running his finger back and forth down a paragraph, which action highlighted it on our screen. "They have a legal claim on whatever comes back. And they have a right to patent it. It may not fly. But there's enough legal precedent that could lead to appeals which could lead to years if not decades in court. If the patent's granted, game over. They own it. That could be challenged, too. It would just be more time and more expense."

"We'll all be dead by the time this is over," Shonstein said.

"Screw us, screw our work, to hell with knowing anymore than we already know?" Dr. Brando said.

"If that's what the patent holder wants, yes," Nathaniel said. "But in my way of thinking, I don't know why any person or corporation would want to stop you from studying your discovery. Just like owners of famous paintings hang them in museums for public view."

"I can think of a few reasons," Dr. Shonstein said.

"Uh oh. Here it comes."

"Brandy—don't start with me."

"Why is their money more important than our

provenance?" Dr. Marcum asked. "It was Levitt, Brando, and Shonstein who convinced NASA to fund us. Who developed the protocols. Who were sure, when no one else was, that what we saw from *Perseverance* and *Foresight* and *Odysseus* was the most convincing evidence of life we were ever going to get."

"Your investors wouldn't look at it that way," the attorney said. "They look it as taking all the risk, underwriting all the costs."

"They're not *our* investors," Shonstein said. "Dr. Levitt has staked her entire career on this. And we got lots of other financial help—NASA, JPL, ESA."

"I'm not denying any of that," Mr. Hawthorn said. "But all those players add more complexity, too."

He crinkled his nose and pushed up his glasses and his handsome face found a certain charm.

"Why can't we talk to DSG?"

"DSG?"

"The space station," Dr. Levitt said. "It's the least we should be able to do."

"I know," Hawthorn said. "I'm working on that."

"How? Is there some sort of court order? A gag order?"

"No," he said.

"Then what?"

"Could be a NASA directive. I don't know yet. My bosses are pretty tight-lipped."

"I don't understand that," Brando said. "Your bosses are our bosses. You'd think they'd support us."

"Yeah, well. That's not the way it works. Think of it this way: What if you won the billion dollar Powerball lottery? It's all yours, right? All that money."

But before anyone could agree or disagree, "Wrong," he said. "It's not all yours. The IRS would take a chunk. And every person you know would ask for a loan, or a gift. The guy you bought the ticket from would want his cut.

"The lady who once told you to bet on lucky sevens would want her cut, even though there was only one seven in the call out. The employees you used to pool a few bucks with to buy tickets might want a cut, even though you left that company six months ago.

"The sponsoring states would demand their piece, from income taxes to your forced consent that they could plaster your image on lottery ads for the next year.

"You'd have to hire a lawyer, maybe even a security guard, cutting into your winnings even more.

"You've won the lottery, you and your team. And have you thought about that? What each of your teammates is gonna want, what cut of the prize?"

He let his rant set in.

"Wow," Shonstein said. "I love that."

Nathaniel Hawthorn frowned. "Hmm?"

"Your passion. Clarity. I get it. I get that we have a good lawyer."

"Great lawyer," he said.

"We'll see."

Twelve

J ogging around Green Lake Park became one of my fave things to do. It's not as grand as Lake Michigan, where Brian and I jogged the Pike Bike Trail between Simmons Island and Alford Park, but it calms me just the same. I ride my e-bike down here, lock it with the app, and take off, for a blissful hour of solitude, twice around the lake, dodging walkers and joggers and cyclists and today, Rebecca Shonstein, rollerblading with Malachi.

"Dr. S." I ran up, a little out of breath.

"Dr. Z. Enjoying a rare day of sunshine?"

"Oh yeah."

Malachi was also rollerblading, but while holding onto some kind of steadying contraption.

"Never seen one of these," I said.

"Martin built it," Shonstein said. "Or rather, 'engineered' it. He made a prototype; put it through some tests; then took his final blueprint to work and they made it for him."

I jogged and they bladed. "What's it made of?"

"Fiberglass and stainless steel."

"Mars worthy."

"You had to bring that up," she quipped.

"I know." I reached out to help steady the contraption. "What do you think?"

"What do *I* think? If that only mattered, huh?"

We dodged some walkers.

"I still can't get over the shock of the thing," I said.

"*Shock* is right."

We pulled over to a vacant park bench. "I need to check someone's pull up," she said. She swung backward and glided both of them to a stop and sat. She pulled Malachi to her and set down the contraption. She squeezed his bottom.

"Potty?" she asked.

He shook his head.

"What about the other?" she said with a certain facetiousness.

"Nope," Malachi replied. He pointed to the paved trail, not busy on this weekday afternoon.

"Okay," she said. "But stay away from the water."

Malachi crawled on the grass then pushed himself up awkwardly at the trail and stumbled around in plain view.

"He's young for blades," I said.

"I've been blading out here with him since he was in his stroller," Dr. Shonstein said. "He's been relentless about trying it ever since he could walk." She looked up at the Sun, bright and cool. "Back to your question: What do I think?"

I waited.

"I think they could really screw this up," she said. "*They* being this cadre of unseen mansplainers who seem to think that they and they alone own our work. If there's an intellectual property claim to be made here, we should be at the top of legitimate claimants."

"I talked to that lawyer," I said.

"You mentioned that."

"Should I have?"

"I'm not your PI," she said. "That's between you and Marcia."

I looked at my hands.

"Malachi Shonstein," she called to her son. "Stay over here, please."

Some women jogged around him and one turned and smiled at us.

"You learn, you know, in this business, that we function in silos," Dr. Shonstein said. "People from Silo A can't interact with the aliens in Silo B unless they've been adequately inoculated. I know—the bacteriologist in me coming out. But that's how it is.

"You have to get the proper clearances and permissions. You must kiss the proper rings. You can royally screw a great career if you violate the silo protocols. You can screw up your career all kinds of ways, Jennifer. Being a woman, it's just that much easier."

"I get it," I said.

"I hope you do. Because you have a career to screw up. You know how many ABDs get to help find life on distant planets."

Malachi was headed toward a thicket near the lake's edge.

"No, nope," his mother said, struggling to stand in her blades. I ran to him and gently retrieved him. I started toward Mom with him, but he resisted and cried.

"He's fine," she said. "Just so long as I can see him. Right, sweet pea?"

He turned around defiantly. I went back to sit.

"Speaking of Dr. Levitt," I said, happy to brighten the subject. "I think she and Parada have finally set a date."

"Really? Do tell."

"She was talking to a florist."

"Any specifics?"

"Sounded like June."

"It's about time. I'm surprised someone hasn't stolen Parada away."

"Maybe someone tried," I said. "I heard them arguing."

"Think that's why Marcia popped the question?"

"I don't know who popped the question," I said. "But it sounded like the answer was 'yes'."

"EM DRIVE COMES UP** frequently in these contracts," Dr. Cooper said during our weekly staff meeting.

"You're actually reading them?" Shonstein said.

"I'm a frustrated climate lawyer," Cooper said. "Almost what I did, ya know. Til my dad got sick."

"Hope your dad's feeling better," Dr. Levitt said. "Maybe we have our own lawyer, after all."

"Not quite. But thanks," Cooper said.

"Arjan told me they were using a new prototype rocket," Shonstein said. "I figured that's why she was so uptight about payload weight."

"It seems to be the main reason all the deep pockets got on board," Cooper said. "It ain't cheap."

"I have to admit some astonishment that EM propulsion actually worked," Marcum said. "The idea has been around for about twenty, twenty five years, the miracle engine that wouldn't work because it violated the laws of physics. Which, I guess we are now learning, are no match for trillionaires."

I'd taken copious notes about electromagnetic propulsion for my dissertation. It was invented by a British engineer, Roger Shawyer. Because EM Drive doesn't use propellant, like a rocket, it seems to defy the laws of physics. To create forward momentum, a propellant has to come out the back.

"Every action has an equal and opposite reaction."

But EM engines use no propellant—no rocket fuel. Such a promising clean-burning, fuel-efficient idea, but for years it languished under the dread category "fringe science."

Second, third, and fourth generation EM Drives came from Italy, Britain, and China, with our final flight version known as the Shawyer-Cannae-Yang-Chen-McCulloch, or SCYCM propulsion system, named for inventors of various iterations.

"Mike McCulloch," Dr. Marcum said. "A fine mathematician. Some of his ideas about how galaxies rotate have proven both interesting and challenging."

"Prototypes of the SCYCM propulsion system are long perfected," Cooper said. "But the cost to build the real thing was prohibitive until SpaceTek and our cadre of deep pockets came along."

"The EM Drive saved our hover system," Shonstein said.

"Remember when we got stuck in the rocks?"

"So it saved our craft only to destroy our science," Brando said.

"GOOD NEWS, PEOPLE!" DR. Levitt's voice echoed in the hallway outside our offices.

I was bleary-eyed from dissertation writing all night, but still the second person to peek out my door—not *my* door, exactly, but the office all the post-docs use. Dr. Brando was first.

"Shall we?" he said to me. We walked to Levitt's office faster than usual.

"Well, well—what have we here?" Dr. Brando said, as we rounded the corner of a table to gaze upon Crimsy, in projected three-dimensional glory, hovering above Levitt's cell phone.

"We're talking again," Levitt said. "The gag order, or whatever it was, has been lifted."

"How did that happen?" I asked. She looked over my shoulder as Drs. Shonstein and Marcum filed in. Dr. Cooper was back East.

"Wha—?" Shonstein said.

"We're back online," Dr. Levitt repeated. "Gag order kaput."

"So if I say 'Gillory,' someone will hear me and respond?" Shonstein said.

"Yes," Captain Gillory said from Deep Space Gateway.

"And Hightower?"

"No," he replied. "I only respond to *Captain* Hightower. I've been having self-esteem issues."

"Big Brother does that to you," Gillory said.

"What about Ryong? Where do you guys keep him?" Levitt asked.

"He keeps us," Hightower said. "From falling to Earth. Commander Ryong?"

"I am hovering in your midst," another voice said, one I'd heard only once before. "But I don't know a thing about germs or aliens," Ryong said.

"Me, neither," Hightower said. "But that hasn't phased me."

"So is this *Crimsococcus*, in real time?" Dr. Marcum said.

"Slightly magnified, of course," Captain Hightower said.

"She's looking a bit dicky," Marcum said. "The King's English for green about the gills."

"She's perfectly healthy," Hightower said. "Don't know where the sickly green came from."

"Cyanobacteria can change color depending on lighting and other conditions," Dr. Brando said. "She may be a related species."

"Maybe she's part chameleon," Dr. Shonstein said.

"Or part *Prochlorococcus*," Brando said, referencing a majorly-important Earthling with a Crimsy-like pedigree: a green, round, photosynthetic cyanobacterium discovered by MIT biologist Penny Chisholm and her postdoc, Bob Olson.

"We have an idea," Gillory said. "We know how frustrating it must be to have us up here and you down there, so we were brainstorming and Robert found some old ISS research on antibiotics and *E. Coli*."

"Shape shifting?" Dr. Shonstein said. "In space?"

"Yep," Hightower replied. "It's simple and you'd get visible results, pretty quickly, if *Crimsococcus* responds."

"Shape-shifting," Marcum asked. "Sounds like paranormal fantasy. Who gets shifted?"

"Scientific term is *bacterial morphological plasticity*," Shonstein said. "Bacteria and most likely *Crimsococcus*, unless she's off-the-charts weird, have cell walls that give them their shapes. Antibiotics can break down those walls, causing bacteria to become amorphous blobs before they crash and burn. But if you wash the antibiotic out quickly enough, some bacteria have been shown to regain their shape. Hence, 'shape-shifting.'"

"One way bacteria become antibiotic resistant," Dr. Brando said.

"The research we read was fascinating," Gillory said.

"Videos, too. We watched a bunch of videos," Hightower added.

"I'm not opposed to trying some things up there. But this is Shonstein's bailiwick," Levitt said. "I'll leave it up to her."

"I plan to subject Crimsy to various antibiotics at various concentrations and under various conditions, but with our budget the way it is, hadn't planned to do anything more at the station than we've already done to clear her for Earth entry,"

Shonstein said. "Anti-gravity effects on bacteria are well-studied, and that's really the only thing we'd be looking at up there."

"We have no idea how long we're gonna be locked out," Brando said. "I say, why not?"

"Refresh my memory on the antibiotics you guys have," Shonstein said.

"One sec," Hightower replied. We could hear him prompt the onboard IT cloud to call up data. "Okay—in alphabetical order: Amoxicillin, azithromycin, cephalexin, ciprofloxacin. Cav Ulan Ate?" He paused. "Cal Vulcan Ate?"

"Clavulanate" Shonstein corrected.

"Clindamycin, doxycycline, levofloxacin, metronidazole, sulfameth. . . sulfamethamphetamine?"

"Methoxazole," Shonstein corrected again, "Sulfamethoxazole."

"Sulfamethoxazole, streptomycin, trimethoprim," Gillory interrupted and concluded. "Say all that three times fast. Oh, and minoxidil."

Dr. Shonstein folded her arms.

"Minox—" Brando said.

"Minoxidil is not on the list," Gillory said. "At least that list."

"Someone must be going bald."

"I heard that," Hightower said.

"Nothing else by slender chance?" Shonstein said.

"Not that I can see," Hightower said. "But we do have every disinfectant known to man."

"Would have been nice to have had trexomycin or

orthonizole," Shonstein said after the meeting broke up. "I don't see us learning anything new from what they've got on board."

"It's still a substantial list," Brando said.

"No big deal, I guess," Shonstein said. "I plan to study the exotic antibiotics down here, but still. Who knows when—or if —that's gonna happen?"

"If and when," Dr. Levitt said. "If and when," she continued in song.

"What if they cut us off again?" Dr. Brando asked.

"Agreed," Marcum said. "Hate to see us get started on something only to have the plug pulled."

I FOLLOWED MARCUM OUT of Levitt's office, and in the hall I heard her voice.

"Jennifer?" Levitt waved me back with a nod.

"Close that, would you?" She indicated her door. The "uh oh" reflex roiled my stomach as I complied.

"Our lawyer friend came by here looking for you the other day."

"What?"

"My question was 'why'."

"He didn't say what he wanted?"

"No, and I didn't ask. What I did ask is if I could tell you he came by."

"I don't get it."

I never guessed Nathaniel Hawthorn would show up here looking for me. I could see him showing up to speak with Dr. Levitt and then asking if I was around—maybe. Or talking to Levitt then schlepping down the hall to peek into the post-doc office, if he even knows that's where I hang.

But dropping by and asking for me by name? That's bold.

"It's not a big deal," Dr. Levitt said. "How old do you think he is?"

"I dunno. Thirty?"

"He acts twenty nine."

"Really?" I chuckled. "There's a difference?"

"You see anyone announcing their twenty-ninth birthday party like it's the end of the world?"

I smiled.

"I don't know what he wanted and apparently you don't either, but do refer any official business *to me*," she said.

"Absolutely."

She looked down as though to say "dismissed," and I went to open the door.

"One other thing. He's in a different department and regardless, you're free to see who you want. Just keep in mind that anything you do in the close confines of this place affects you and could affect us. The workplace fraternization laws are also something to keep in mind."

"I'm not planning to see him," I said.

"Honestly, that's probably a good idea."

My face cooled when I got back to my desk. I was typing and notating and annotating when I heard Dr. Shonstein in the hall with Malachi and a voice I hadn't heard since the faculty picnic.

"I really need you to take him," she said.

"They want me at the board meeting," he—her husband Martin—said. "I don't think they'd understand."

"Why can't I ever use that argument?"

"Your boss is a woman," Martin said.

"Are you kidding?"

The voices faded as they apparently entered her office and closed the door. I approached a self-imposed stopping point— if I had to stare at one more temperature/salinity reading from Crimsy's home turf—pools of encapsulated brine on the Martian planet surface—I would collapse from tedium-driven exhaustion.

I went down the hall, passed Shonstein's door. I could hear voices, maybe arguing, maybe just stressed. I headed for the elevator, thanking my lucky red stars I was so uncommitted.

Thirteen

After pulling an all-nighter in her office with Malachi sleeping on a cot covered with blankets and stuffed animals; and alone, after Martin picked him up, Dr. Shonstein launched Operation Lederberg, named for the Nobel Prize-winning geneticist who first observed *E. Coli* bacteria changing their shapes in response to penicillin.

"It's also cool that Joshua Lederberg was first to suggest we needed to decontaminate everything we take to Mars," Shonstein told us in the weekly staff meeting. "He was totally into finding life there."

The plan was to grow Crimsy in Petri dishes treated with different antibiotics. We'd observe how she responded, barring any new gag orders. Dr. Brando checked to make sure his ultra-salty agar—*caviagar* we were calling it—wouldn't denature (render impotent) or otherwise interfere with the test drugs.

"Calcium is known for mucking up antibiotics, but the calcium salt we have in the agar shouldn't be a problem," he told me.

"I'm so stoked I'm thinking in paper titles," I said. "Is *Crimsococcus halocryophilus* antibiotic resistant? Susceptibility of Martian bacteria to antibiotics. Efficacy of common antibiotics on treatment of Martian bacterial infections."

"You realize, don't you, that we'll be killing our darlings?"

"In the name of science."

"So I've got Lexi this weekend," Dr. Brando said. "Would you be up for a day trip?"

"Day trip? Where to?"

"Olympics. Lexi's learning about rain forests and I told her we have one. She's dying to visit."

"The Hoh?"

"It's not exactly the Amazon, but there's probably more of it left."

"The Hoh is more than a day trip," I said. "You could try a different one, like the Quinault."

"Lexi's set on the Hoh. Marcum wants to go, too. I've never been. What's it like?"

"Stupendous," I said. "I plan to take my mom."

"When? She visiting?"

"She is! Next week." In accordance with my vacation days.

"Love to see her again," Brando said. "Lexi, too."

"LET ME REFER YOU all to the areas I've highlighted in the documents on OpenPad." Nathaniel Hawthorn stood at the head of our conference table, taking us through page after page of contracts NASA, JPL, and other space agencies signed with investors, including SpaceTek founder Leonardo Telos (pronounced "tell us") and our very own Cloud computing titan, Alexander Sparks.

"Looks like the investors were *sure* we'd find something,"

Levitt said. "And they took steps to protect their interests in it. What are our options?"

"Play along until all interested parties work things out," Hawthorn said. "That's one option."

"I don't understand," Brando said. "You keep talking about working things out. Work what out? Why doesn't everyone just follow the contracts and at least get *Crimsococcus* off the space station?"

"I understand your frustration," the lawyer said.

"You feel our pain, do you?" Marcum asked. "Let me suggest a way to feel it even more acutely: one of us shines a light on this infuriating press blackout and entertains an interview with, say, *60 Minutes* or *Buzzfeed*?"

"I wouldn't advise that," the lawyer said.

"How long do you think we can keep this a secret?" Levitt asked. "MarsMicro's been back for a month. We get questions every day—Science, Science News, Scientific American, the New York Times. And a new clog [cloud log] every day.

"'What did you find? There's a rumor going around you found something. Did you guys find life? We heard it's a deadly bacteria you can't let off the space station. An alien invader that killed the crew.' Someone somewhere is damned lucky an enterprising science journalist hasn't broken embargo."

"There is no embargo about the microbe," Hawthorn said. "Just a full-on media blackout."

An "embargo" is a kind of gag order on the honor system. We have a public relations office where public information officers issue press releases to reporters around the world. If a press release says "Embargoed" until such and so a date, the reporter can't write about the story until the embargo "lifts." Reporters risk getting fired, blackballed, and shunned if they break embargoes, as I understand it.

"The world's best-kept secret," Marcum said.

"I wouldn't call it a secret," Hawthorn said. "But it is controlled."

"Controlled how and by whom?" Levitt asked.

"Government agencies," Hawthorn said.

"Anyone else get this memo?" Shonstein said.

"So it *is* top secret," Brando said.

"This project is *controlled*, which is the lowest security level. It's not top secret. But it is officially barred from public disclosure," Hawthorn said.

"Seems hard to believe NASA would do this without telling any of us," Levitt said.

"I don't know if it was NASA," Hawthorn said.

"We need to go public," Marcum said.

"Going public could be tantamount to espionage," the lawyer retorted.

"Bollocks."

"Sorry—I don't know what that means."

"It's British for 'bullshit'," Marcum said.

"ESPIONAGE," DR. MARCUM SAID. "I've a mind to give it a try. Beats sitting at my desk wondering if Sara Goode's won the

Abel."

I turned away from the car window. We were heading south on I-5, on the four-hour drive to the Olympic Mountains and the Hoh Rain Forest.

"I thought mathematicians were above such things," Dr. Brando said.

"When I finally get to say—publicly—I'm on the team that discovered life on Mars, I'll be above such things," Marcum said.

I looked at Lexi, taking a virtual tour of the Hoh on the car's Cloud monitor.

"Amazing," Dr. Marcum said. "I still can't get over how lifelike our digital world has become. Why have the real thing?"

"To feel," I said.

"Logical mind, lyrical soul. Ever think of switching to math?" Marcum said.

I grinned.

"Many thanks for inviting me," he said. "I've been remiss about exploring this beautiful part of your country."

"Glad to have you," Brando said. "Not enough activities for us singles and quasi-singles."

"Doctor Levitt's Lonely Hearts Club Band," Marcum said. "So was the cloud package optional?" He was looking at an exquisitely-rendered visual of a tree covered in bright green moss hovering above Lexi's lap.

"Not on this model," Brando said. "I splurged. Figured I better before, well."

"You can say it, Dad."

"Speaking of The Cloud, anyone know why Alexander Sparks is one of our investors?" I asked.

"The COS guy, right? Of Sparks Hall nomenclature," Marcum said.

"Yeah."

"Isn't Sparks one of the world's three trillionaires?" Brando said.

"Aren't there four now?"

"Two, Dad," Lexi said.

"Back to just two?" Marcum said.

"We're learning about him in class," Lexi said. "Sparks is to The Cloud what Bill Gates and Steve Jobs were to the disk. 'The man who 'liberated software from hardware.' That's what my teacher says."

"Hadn't thought about it that way," Marcum said.

Alexander Sparks invented a kind of Windows or Mac known as COS, or Cloud Operating System, a way to instantly and intuitively access all the information that resides on every computer and server on the planet, collectively known as "The Cloud."

COS transforms computer code into three-dimensional images, words, moving pictures, whatever, with virtually no hardware—no screens, no monitors, no pads, no keyboards. All you need is a Cloud password and an antenna, receiver, or projector.

Lexi called up her virtual tour saying "Hoh Rainforest," and had her pick of possibilities in front of her, ranked in order of popularity the way Google did before Sparks bought it.

"I remember when the government wanted to swap out Social Security numbers for Cloud passwords," Brando said. "Sparks was caught red-handed promoting the idea after he got taxpayer subsidies."

"Michael." Another voice I recognized from the faculty picnic, but from last year, not this year.

"Speaker off," Dr. Brando said immediately. "Now's not a good time," he said to his wife. He went to a whisper. "We discussed this. No—we're on the way now." He must have had a cochlear chip implant because I couldn't hear what she was saying, I saw no headset, and no phone. "I know what the court commissioner said."

A truck swerved into our path and Brando grabbed the otherwise idle steering wheel and swung our car out of the way. We veered into the opposite lane briefly before self-drive took over again and corrected.

"Have to call you back," Brando told Melissa.

"He has to call you back," Lexi said loudly.

Brando looked back as the semi pulled to the side of road and stopped. "Looks like OnStart got it," he said.

Two Washington State Highway Patrol drones flew past, one stopping in front of the truck, the other stopping at the driver's side window.

"Why didn't my car swerve on its own?" Brando said.

"This is the Onstart operator," a voice said. "We've stopped the other vehicle and are filing a report. Was anyone injured in your vehicle?"

"No," Brando said. "But my auto-drive malfunctioned. If I hadn't grabbed the wheel—"

"We're analyzing that now," the operator said. "We'll download a patch as soon as the issue is identified."

"Thanks."

"What about the truck driver?" I asked.

"We don't know, but do know that he can't start or move his vehicle until the highway patrol drone releases it," the Onstart operator said. "It has been auto-parked in a safe location."

"You still have your old-school jalopy?" Marcum asked me.

"I do. Five speed manual everything."

"And I thought you were a woman of the future," he said.

"Only parts of it."

LEXI PASSED HER FATHER on the trail into the rain forest. He didn't see her, too busy staring at a curtain of green that was as bright and full as I had ever seen. I usually saw at least some brown—on tree trunks, limbs, branches—hints of the framework behind the curtain. But today, even the dirt on the trail was mossy green.

"You were right," Dr. Brando said. "Stupendous. I've never seen anything like this."

"C'mon you guys," Lexi yelled.

"It rains all the time here, right?" Dr. Marcum said.

"More than usual the past few years," I said.

"It's blinding," Marcum said. "And quiet. The vegetation must absorb all the sound."

"Dad—what's our cloudcam password?"

"Brandelion Wine," he said.

We approached Lexi, moving her eyes and blinking, from green scene to green scene.

"Almost bought a cloudcam subscription," Dr. Marcum said. "But the idea of an invisible camera following me around —"

"It's great," Lexi said. "All I have to do is look and blink. Twice for close up. Three times for really close up. Stare and stop for Distance Vision," which creates a panoramic shot you determine with the length of your stare.

A group of teens headed our way so we single-filed along this narrow part of the trail.

"What do you make of Crimsy looking green?" Brando said.

"Maybe she caught something," Marcum said.

"Dr. Marcum? William Marcum?" It was one of the teens after they passed us.

"Only if I'm not in trouble," Dr. Marcum said.

"And Michael Brando?"

Dr. Brando looked amused. The five-person group conferred in whispers, then walked up to us. They looked like the nerds I used to hang with—brilliant, fearless, self-effacing, non-threatening.

"I'm Kelsey Bridges. These are my friends. We go to Timberline High School."

"Is it true you guys discovered life on Mars?" one of the

other students asked.

"Where is Timberline High?" Marcum asked.

"Lacey," Bridges said. "We can't believe we're really meeting you."

"And Lacey is—?"

"Not far from here," I said. "Where did you hear we discovered life on Mars?"

"Our biology teacher. But there's stuff all over the Cloud about it."

I reached out and shook their hands. "Jennifer," I said.

"My daughter Lexi," Brando said. She smiled.

"What's it like to be the daughter of a famous scientist?"

"I don't know," Lexi said.

"What is it?" another student asked.

"What did you guys find?"

"It's classified," Marcum said. "So they tell us."

The group laughed.

"Our teacher swears we all evolved from little green men —"

"And women!"

"Little green men and women from Mars."

"I thought men were from Mars and women from Venus," Marcum said. He was quite the card today.

"He's just kidding. I mean, Mr. Sanders," Kelsey said.

"I don't think so. He always sounds serious."

"Mr. Sanders?" Brando asked

"Our biology teacher."

"He can't be that serious," Dr. Marcum said. "You haven't even asked for our autographs."

"Autographs?"

"What's that?" Kelsey asked.

"You don't know what an autograph is?"

And while Dr. Marcum was explaining the fine points of this ancient signature-gathering ritual, I watched Dr. Brando, staring at the greenest tree in our sight line.

WE TOOK HIGHWAY 101 around the Olympic National Forest and visited Hurricane Ridge. With its breathtaking views of the Olympic mountains, the Strait of Juan de Fuca, and Canada beyond, Dr. Marcum called it a "spiritual experience" and Dr. Brando retreated from his reverie long enough to label it "awesomeness personified." Lexi filled her cloudcam with pix of the water on one side and snow on the other.

We ate fast food and stayed the night in the town of Sequim, aka Sunny Sequim, at the base of the mountains sheltered from the rain. I walked to the room Lexi and I shared bearing Cokes and candy bars and smelled a familiar pungency. Marcum and Brando sat on deck chairs outside their room puffing joints dispensed from a converted cigarette machine near the front office.

"Jennifer," Dr. Marcum said. "On behalf of my illustrious colleague and myself, I must thank you for a wonderful tour of this magnificent place."

"My pleasure," I said.

"It was spiritual for me and inspirational for Brandy. He's mulling an astonishing idea."

"What is it?" I asked.

"Can't say just yet," Brando said. "It's not much more than a hypothesis. And if we can't get *Crimsococcus* here, that's what it will stay."

"Those kids were right," Marcum said. "Our classified discovery has to be the world's worst-kept secret. Prat cloggers have seeded the Cloud with it."

"Which clogs?"

"*Science Mysteries, Alien Life, Are We Alone?* Names like that."

"Those weren't reputable back when they were blogs."

"Background noise," Brando said.

"I'd ask you to join us, but I see you're on a mission," Marcum said.

"Story of my life," I said.

I ASKED LEXI TO dial back the brightness on the cloudbook hovering above her chest, and fell asleep. I awakened later and heard her sniffling. I listened.

"Lexi?" I said softly. She didn't respond. "Lexi?"

"Yes?"

"You're awake."

More sniffles.

"You okay?"

I leaned over to the edge of my bed.

"Lexi?"

"I'm okay."

"Sure?"

She was turned away from me so I got up and walked to the other side of her bed. She had the covers over her head. "Bath light," I said, and the light came on in the bathroom. I reached down and pulled back the cover until I could see Lexi's face.

"What's wrong, sweetie?" I asked.

She stared ahead.

"Lex?"

"Stuff," she said.

I sat on the edge of her bed. "What kind of stuff?"

"Just stuff."

"Mom and dad stuff?"

"Yeah."

"They both really love you."

"I know."

"But it still sucks, huh?"

"Yeah."

I brought my hand to her head and smoothed it through her hair.

"That feels nice," she said.

"Yeah?"

"Mom does it sometimes."

"Bet I don't do it as good," I said.

"Almost," she said.

"It'll be okay," I said. "I've had all kinds of crazy family stuff, too."

"You have?"

"Yes, some of it pretty bad." I didn't want to get emotional.

She reached out from the covers. "I'm really sorry," she said.

"No, no. It's okay. My mom's coming for a visit, in fact."

"I remember her."

"She remembers you. Maybe we can get together." I smoothed back her hair. "Think you can sleep?"

"Prob'ly."

I sat on the edge of her bed until she closed her eyes. "Lights out," I said, and the bathroom light extinguished itself. I went back to my bed.

"Jennifer."

"Yes?" I waited.

"Would you hold me?"

"Absolutely."

I started to get up but she beat me and came around and tucked herself beneath my sheet and blanket. I put my arm around her and before long, heard the rhythmic breathing of sleep.

"ARE WE AT LIBERTY to share your idea with our ABD?" Marcum asked Brando on the drive back. "Realizing, of course, that it could consign you to the scientific loony bin if—"

"If I'm wrong," Brando said. "And that's a big if."

"Now you've got me dying to know," I said.

"The First Universal Common Ancestor," Brando said. "Crimsy. She might be the First Universal Common Ancestor. The FUCA."

"There's no such thing," I said.

"There might be now."

I frowned, made a skeptical face, like it was indeed a crazy idea. The First Universal Common Ancestor, if it existed, would be like the Missing Link of Everything, that living thing from which all Earthen life originated and evolved. Biologists and evolutionary types have characterized several *Last* Universal Common Ancestors (LUCA), heat-loving extremophiles mostly, that come and go each time someone discovers another, older LUCA. FUCA would be the oldest LUCA, the ancestor that started it all.

"How can you prove this?" I said.

"I need to know why she turned green," Brando said. "She was not green on Mars; she was not green during the journey here; she was not green for the first three weeks on DSG. So what made her turn green?"

"She's not that green."

"She's green enough. I can't believe it's just a trick of the spectrum."

"Okay. So what's next?" The now-eternal question.

"I need to know what changed. Atmospheric variables, sunlight exposure, even cross contamination, however minuscule."

"OpenGro is replicating conditions on Mars," I said. "If you need me to, I can comb its logs. Maybe find out if anything's been altered."

OpenGro is an open source, artificial-intelligence, micro-climate box used to grow plants, bacteria, even lab animals in artificial but perfect conditions. A smart greenhouse—genius smart.

"Sounds like a start," Brando said. "Now, I've gotta figure out how to get this approved without looking like a kook."

Fourteen

Our one approved project, Operation Lederberg, was proving a disappointment. None of the antibiotics affected Crimsy in any observable way. She did not die, stop replicating, or shape-shift. If she was susceptible to an antibiotic, it wasn't aboard Deep Space Gateway.

"Now I'm worried," Hightower said on a conference call. "What if I get infected?"

"I, uh, have an idea," Dr. Brando said.

The room went on quiet pause while he considered how he was going to present. Dr. Marcum was out on other business today, so I was his sole assured moral supporter.

"Okay," Dr. Levitt said.

"Can we have Crimsy on the projector?" he asked. She appeared, the green hue noticeable but unchanged from our last viewing. "You've doubtless noticed this green color," Brando said, using a laser pointer.

"The way light hits the agar," Shonstein said. "I noticed it right after the rover returned."

"I didn't," Brando said.

"What about it?" Levitt said.

"I'm wondering if it's not chlorophyll, or some version of chlorophyll like bacteriochlorophyll," Brando said.

"Like plants use in photosynthesis," Levitt said.

"Not just plants," Dr. Brando said. "Cyanobacteria, too."

Previously known as "blue-green algae," he explained, cyanobacteria are the only germs on Earth that make food like plants, with sunlight, chlorophyll, and photosynthesis.

"Would a Martian bacteria even need chlorophyll?" Shonstein said. "What evolutionary pressures would give rise to that?"

"On Mars, it maybe didn't," Brando said. "But something may have changed since Crimsy left the planet to prompt its appearance. I'd like to find out what that something is."

"It's an interesting question," Levitt said. "First, we'd have to establish if chlorophyll is indeed responsible for Crimsy's new hue. But I'm not seeing how that can happen until we have access."

"Jennifer offered to comb OpenGro's atmospheric monitoring logs, looking for even the slightest changes that might have brought on this color," Brando said.

"DSG—thoughts?" Levitt asked.

"We're running about ninety five percent carbon dioxide," Captain Gillory said. "Argon, nitrogen, a little oxygen. As exact a replica of Mars atmosphere as OpenGro can make it."

"That's my point, though," Brando said. "A—we don't know the composition of Mars' atmosphere exactly. And B—even slight variations might prompt Crimsy toward some sort of adaptation, like making chlorophyll."

"Awfully fast evolution," Shonstein said.

"Not really," Dr. Brando said. "Not if we assume she was

already equipped with some dormant capability. Like dormant chloroplasts," the cellular machines that make chlorophyll. "It might be a form of bet hedging."

"We've seen no indication of bet hedging," Shonstein said.

"Bet hedging?" Levitt asked.

"It's a way bacteria adapt to environmental changes," Shonstein said. "They hedge their bets, dividing into two populations: one with an adaptive trait that was always there, just not expressed; and the original unchanged group. Whoever survives wins the bet. It's one way bugs develop antibiotic resistance so quickly."

"How do we know she wasn't bet hedging when we threw all those antibiotics at her?" Brando said. "Subtly slipping through our fingers?"

"We saw no changes in any of the colonies," Shonstein said. "None. With bet hedging, some colonies should have died while others survived."

"It's a totally alien bug, Bex. How do we know what it was doing?"

"We don't, exactly, I admit, but—"

"We could do something like the *Pseudomonas* experiments," Brando said.

Pseudomonas fluorescens, used to make yogurt, divides about once an hour, he explained. It's found in soil and water here on Earth. Research teams at Germany's Max Planck Institute and New Zealand's Institute for Advanced Study observed it bet hedging its way through "rapid and repeatable evolution." They decided they were watching "among the earliest evolutionary solutions to life."

"It's an interesting question to explore that could lead to some exciting speculations," Dr. Brando said.

"Like?" Dr. Shonstein asked.

"Like cyanobacteria maybe evolving from *Crimsococcus*," Brando said boldly. "Like *Crimsococcus* being a Universal Common Ancestor."

"From Mars?" Shonstein said. "You're kidding."

"Not at all. If she can make chlorophyll after surviving a deep-space journey, what's to say she didn't land here three or four billion years ago, when Earth's atmosphere was more like Mars?"

"So not just any Universal Common Ancestor, but the First Universal Common Ancestor," Levitt said.

"Exactly," Brando said. "FUCA."

Shonstein glared at him. "I'll agree, it's a novel idea," she said. "But I don't want to see us drifting too far off course."

"How is this drifting?" Brando said.

"It's another big, major, history-altering idea," she said. "We're barely coping with the first one—finding Crimsy."

"All I'm asking for is group consent to do some initial reviews of the OpenGro logs," Brando said. "Would that inconvenience you guys?" he asked the space station crew.

"Not at all," Gillory said.

"Captain Hightower?"

"As long as I get a Scooby snack," he said. "All is good."

"We'll be sure to send a bag with the next payload," Dr.

Levitt said.

"Rooby Rooby Roo!" Hightower said.

"Velma here. We'll email you the log files and the password for the onboard monitoring system," Gillory said. "You can follow it in real time."

"What if we want to vary some of the conditions?" Brando said.

"Wouldn't be hard," Hightower said. "Set it up similar to Dr. Shonstein's project."

"Rebecca?" Levitt asked.

Dr. Shonstein opened her hands in reluctant acquiescence. Project Little Green Women (with props to Louisa May Alcott) was approved.

"I do have one concern," Hightower said. "Will we have to change Crimsy's name, to say, Greeny? Or Shamrock?"

"Never!" Dr. Levitt said.

AS PART OF THE Little Green Women kickoff, Dr. Cooper, back from Harvard, gave a non-specialist's presentation on the differences between Earth and Mars atmospheres. Drs. Marcum *and* Shonstein were out this time.

"Forget about oxygen," Cooper said. "We know Mars basically has none, so let's forget all the sci-fi *what ifs* and focus on the big deals, like carbon dioxide and nitrogen."

"The OpenGro box keeps Crimsy in ninety five percent carbon dioxide, plus or minus a fraction of a percent, and one point nine to two point zero percent nitrogen," I said, having by now memorized these stats.

"Duplicating Mars. But how does Earth compare?"

"Eighty percent nitrogen, less than point-one percent carbon dioxide." Me again.

"You get the idea," Cooper said. "Nitrogen is huge on Earth. Carbon dioxide is huge on Mars."

"I figure we're looking for some kind of spark," Dr. Brando said. "Something that might be making Crimsy think she is on Earth circa three billion years ago."

"The late Archean Eon," Dr. Levitt said.

"About the time cyanobacteria started making oxygen," Brando said.

"Earth had maybe eight to ten percent max carbon dioxide back then," Cooper said.

"So if Crimsy somehow traveled from Mars to Earth, maybe the reduction in carbon dioxide was the evolutionary spark?" Me this time.

We tossed around ideas for some test protocols and after we wrapped, I caught Dr. Cooper in the hallway.

"I've been meaning to catch up a little," I said.

"I know, right? Seems like I can't stay in one place long enough."

"So—scuttle is Hale might be thinking retirement?" I said.

"Maybe. We're catching up to you guys in the astrobiology rankings," Cooper said. "He wants to go out on a high note."

"Last I looked, you were a distant third," I said.

"Close second, girl. And numero uno in astroclimatology,

thanks to you-know-who."

"Hale?" I joked.

"Naaahh. So how you been? How's ma? Bros?"

"Good," I said. "Everyone's good." I could tell he didn't believe me, so I fessed. "Brian—didn't make it."

"Ah, man." He smoothed his hand along my arm. "I'm so sorry, Jen. I remember—"

"It wasn't unexpected," I said. "How 'bout you? Mom, Dad, sis?"

"Baby sister is acing Hopkins Med."

"She got in? She got in! That's fantastic. I remember when she stayed with you that summer."

"Did she talk about anything else?" he said. "Top of her class. My old man can't decide who he's more proud of now."

"How's he doin'?" I asked.

"Not so good."

I stopped. "What—?"

"Stroke."

"Oh no!"

"It wasn't debilitating. But he's scared to death he's gonna be a burden to Mom. Us."

"Did he need rehab? How bad was it?"

"Weakness on one side. Some vision stuff. Mom took him to the ER. They knew what was wrong immediately. He's hatin' life. They gave him a diet. No salt, no beer, no game day gorging."

"I'm glad he's okay. Hate it you all have to go through this."

"Life, man." He paused. "So how did . . . Brian—?"

"How do you think?" I said.

"I am so sorry, Jen," Cooper said. "I know how close you guys were."

"Is the other scuttle true?" I asked. "You might be taking over—?"

"Taking over what?"

"You know."

"The Hale Lab? If I do, will you come with me?"

"We're number one," I said.

"Not for long," he said.

I WALKED BACK TO the post-doc office and jumped when a young woman stepped out of the doorway, landing squarely in front of me.

"Hi." she said. "Maybe you can help me. I'm a little lost."

"What are you looking for?"

"Crimsy."

"What?"

Did I just hear that right?

"Isn't that . . . Well, here."

She flashed her ghost card, which went to storage on my microchip. Molly something, Freelance Journalist.

"I'm on assignment for Cosmic American. Crimsy?"

"There's no Crimsy here." Technically, I wasn't lying.

"Your PIO said—"

"PIO?" The PIO assigned to our team knew nothing about

Crimsy, let alone her in-house nickname.

"Yes."

"What are you wanting, exactly?" I asked.

"I'm writing a story. Is there an embargo on this?"

"Embargo on *what*?"

"That's what I mean. I think I'm lost," Molly said. "You don't seem to be the right department."

"I'm not a department," I said. "I'm Jennifer." I stuck out my hand and we shook.

"I didn't mean it that way," she said. "I just meant, I was looking around, read the department directories downstairs, and took the elevator to this floor. But it doesn't look like astronomy."

"Well, technically, it's not. It's Astrobiology."

"Ahh. *Microscopes* instead of telescopes."

Boy was she warm. Too warm for my comfort.

I walked Molly over to Dr. Levitt's open door and pointed at the small telescope pointed out the window at Portage Bay.

"Thanks," she said. "I'll find my way out."

She was at the elevator when I realized I might blow another covert ops opportunity.

"Molly," I called to her, reading the card. I walked up to her. "So who's—Crimsy?"

"An astronaut who came back from Mars, maybe?" she said.

"An astronaut came back from Mars?"

"Pure, uninformed speculation. There's a total press blackout."

"How did you get this name?" I asked.

"Clogosphere. I pitched it to an editor and he bought it."

She stepped into the elevator and smiled at me as the door closed.

"Good luck," I said.

I had seen clogospheric chatter insisting we found life, but nothing actually *naming* Crimsy, and I read the top clogs religiously. *That* would have been alarming enough. I wheeled around to Dr. Levitt's office, almost slipping and breaking my head on our newly-shined floor. I skidded to a stop when I heard raised voices. Her door was ajar.

"That's not fair." Dr. Levitt.

"It's perfectly fair." Sounded like Parada. "How else would you put it?"

"Not like that. No one here feels like that."

I leaned against the wall but didn't go away. I was freaking out and needed Dr. Levitt *now*. To knock or not to knock?

"How do you know? Have you asked?" Parada again.

"Asked what? 'Do you look down on my future wife because she didn't graduate from'—where, Para—Princeton? Harvard? Cal Tech?"

"I didn't say I thought anyone looked down on me."

"You implied it."

"You spend a lot of time with these people, Marsh. Most of your time. Marry me, marry my family. And they're your family, basically."

"I can't believe you'd give up on *us* over something this trivial."

"I'm not—"

I caved and knocked. This was just too urgent.

"Come," Dr. Levitt said. "Jennifer."

"Oh, sorry. Am I interrupting?"

"No, no. You remember Parada."

"Of course." Believe me, you don't forget Parada, even if you walked by her one time on the street.

"Jennifer. Nice to see you again."

"You, too." We shook hands. She was shaking.

"I, well—I thought this was urgent," I said. "A reporter just showed up here looking for Crimsy—by name."

"What?" Dr. Levitt said. "A reporter from where?"

"She gave me her card," which I produced from my microchip.

"How in the world did she know about Crimsy?"

"She didn't, exactly." I turned to Parada. "I'm really sorry." Back to Levitt. "She heard the name, claimed she saw it on a clog. Thought it was the name of an astronaut who'd come back from Mars."

They both smiled.

"That *is* funny," Parada said.

"In the words of a former professor, it would seem our firewall is rather porous," Dr. Levitt said.

"Perhaps you have a leaker," Parada said.

I looked at Dr. Levitt and knew what—or rather whom— she was considering.

LEXI LOOKED AT HER school-issue notebook. I was in her

dad's office studying atmospheric readings from Crimsy's containment pod before heading out to pick up my mother.

"What's another name for the Krebs Cycle?" she asked.

"You should know that," Dr. Brando said brusquely as he walked into the office. He went over to his book wall and took down a volume.

"How was the meeting?" I asked.

"Consider yourself fortunate not to be faculty."

"That bad."

"I don't need anyone else," he lowered his voice, "scolding me."

"Who scolded you?"

"Marcia. She was outta line, and I told her so."

I didn't want to pry and didn't have to. He kept venting.

"As much as accused one of us of leaking the *Crimsococcus* discovery. One of us with an emphasis on Marcum."

"Oh wow. I feel terrible."

"It's not your fault."

"I told her one of our PIOs sent that reporter," I said. "That's what the reporter told me. She wasn't here on a tip."

"But who tipped off the press office? That was today's big question. Marcia suggested Marcum made good on his threat to go to the media. He was *not* happy. Then she got all worried I might want to jump the PR gun about FUCA."

"It could have come from somewhere else," I said.

"Not Crimsy. How this woman got the name Crimsy—I

have to admit, I had my doubts. Still do. But Marcia's behavior has made me basically," he lowered his voice way low this time, "not give a damn."

"She's pretty stressed," I said. "I don't know what happened, but I wouldn't be too hard on her."

"We're all stressed. It's no excuse."

He sighed. I looked over at Lexi.

"Figure it out?"

"Nope," she said. "I could look it up, but that would be cheating."

I slid my chair next to her. "Actually, there are *two* other names for the Krebs Cycle," I said. "One starts with a 'c'."

"Citric Acid Cycle," she said.

"And?"

"Gimme another hint," she said.

"Try," I said.

"I am trying," she said.

"That's the hint," I said. "Try, try, again. Try me a river."

She screwed up her face and looked at me. "I'm trying. See me trying. Citric Acid Cycle and—"

"Keep trying," I said.

"Isn't this mom day?" Brando asked.

"She's in the air now."

"Your mom's coming?" Lexi asked.

"Just like we discussed. She's excited to see you again."

"Me, too. She's cool."

"By the way," I said to Brando. "I started the download. The readings are second by second. I thought they'd be hourly."

"That's a lotta data."

As in second-by-second atmospheric condition readings in the OpenGro box housing Crimsy. Thirty six hundred times more temperature, pressure, carbon dioxide, and nitrogen percentages than I had planned to review. Yikes!

"Tricarboxylic acid cycle," Lexi blurted out.

"You looked that up," I said.

"Did not." She looked at me. "You give great clues," she said.

I turned to the sound of soft knocking. "Mom!"

My mother smiled and walked in. She looked great. I stood up and hugged her and kissed her. We hadn't seen each other since Brian's funeral.

"I was supposed to pick you up at Sea-Tac," our airport.

"I hate the anti-climax of baggage claim," Mom said. She looked at Lexi and Dr. Brando. "I haven't seen this young lady or her father since the day you all landed on Mars."

"Hi!" Lexi said.

Mom shook Brando's hand and gave Lexi a cheek-to-cheek snuzzle.

"Jennifer's been bursting with excitement ever since you planned to visit," Brando said.

My mom beamed. "I have never visited my darling daughter for more than a couple days since she left home."

"And you've never visited here," I said.

"Never been to Seattle?" Lexi said.

"No my dear," Mom said. "Have you ever visited Kenosha?"

"No," Lexi said. "But I have been to Madison."

"Then you've saved the best of Wisconsin for last," Mom said. "When you come to visit me."

"Any dinner plans?" Brando asked.

"Thinking about Le Mer," I said.

"Woo—tasty *and* classy."

"I'd love to spend some time with this young lady," Mom said, looking at Lexi.

"That can be arranged," Dr. Brando said. "Right?"

His daughter smiled.

"*WHAT* IS THIS?" I asked my mother, looking at her rental car in our visitor parking. I left my e-bike in the building.

"What they gave me," she said.

Toyida *Flyby*, I read on the trunk. I touched the body, pressed it in. It felt like the rubber they use in those CPR mannequins.

"Weird."

"It's dent-proof," she said. "Hit it."

"Hit it? Why?"

She kicked the driver side door. The rubber absorbed the blow and the door moved in, like it was inhaling, to cushion it even more.

"I declined collision damage waiver," she said.

"Where to? We can grab something light, if you're hungry."

"I'd love to freshen up," she said.

The car's interior was a trip in itself, the first I'd seen with no steering wheel to manually correct auto-drive. It was voice and motion controlled. Lean left or say "turn left" and it turned left. It also read sign language, displayed Braille maps, and was at one with the Cloud. Mom and I viewed restaurant choices, menus, even meals on the way to my place.

The car parked and I went around to the trunk. "Open," I said, and it did—to nothing.

"Um, Mom." I looked at her. "Where's your luggage?"

"It's not there?" She walked around, looked in. "Well, darn. I must have left it at the airport."

"You really *don't* like the anti-climax of baggage claim," I said.

"It's okay. I'll go back and get it," Mom said. "Probably still on the conveyor."

I doubted that. Mom doesn't fly much, and so may have missed the signs and rules. "Bags left unclaimed for more than ten minutes will be searched and stored," warns every baggage claim. "Bags left stored for more than 48 hours will be disposed of," by bomb squad, I imagined. I convinced her to let me retrieve it.

"A brown suitcase and a blue one—the one your dad got us for the cruise," she told me.

"I'll need your ID and boarding code," I said.

She put her wrist out.

"You got chipped," I said.

"Finally. They wouldn't renew my driver's license without the damn thing."

I scanned her microchip with mine. In protest of the new chip mandates, Wisconsin and some other states passed ten-year driver's license renewal periods, hoping to stave off the Feds and make political points with angry constituents.

I had my old license for eleven years, driving a year after it expired, resisting as long as I could. Mom did same. But in the end, resistance was futile. It always is, isn't it? And of course, the State loves the Chip. Try to drive on an expired or revoked license, and your chip will stop the car from starting (unless you drive an old jalopy you have conveniently failed to retrofit, like I do).

The Flyby drove me to the airport in the devil-may-care style you might expect of a dent-proof car. We cut in and out of freeway traffic, exceeded the speed limit, then slowed to just under it when the car detected highway patrol drones, displayed as flying avatars on its traffic monitor.

It dropped me at the Sea-Tac Departures entrance, then drove around and parked itself at the Arrivals exit, where I had about twenty minutes before TSSEA agents would order it towed. I hurried to baggage claim and searched the conveyor islands.

Not a bag nor suitcase in sight.

I looked for locked doors with hard-to-read signs that might point me to the baggage claim office. I found a cart piled with unclaimed luggage next to one of these doors. I knocked.

"Come in."

"I'm looking for my mom's bags," I told the attendant.

"She here?" he said.

"No."

"Gotta scan her chip," he said. "Can't release bags without the claim code."

"Got all that on mine," I said. I upped my sleeve and tried to show him.

"Unfortunately, we can't accept that," he said. "Gotta scan the actual chip."

"Really?" I said.

"Sorry," he said.

"It's all here. I can even call her if you want."

"Regs," he said. "Only the chip holder may claim the bag. Turnstiles won't even let you out of baggage claim."

"I never noticed," I said.

"Chips are read automatically."

"Can you at least confirm you have the bags?"

"Only to the chip holder, ma'am."

I walked out of the office. I felt like screaming, but instead sat on a bench and took a deep breath. Go back, get Mom, bring back to airport, not even knowing if her bags made it.

I put my head in my hands and stared. I glanced over at the cart with the luggage. Idea. I walked over for a closer look on my way to get a drink from the fountain outside the restrooms. The door was open to the baggage claim office but I couldn't see the attendant. I reconnoitered around the cart. My heart started racing.

Dad's blue bag from the cruise and its brown companion were one atop the other about halfway along the cart, with one layer of smaller bags atop them. I passed a couple more times, checking the baggage tags and sizing up my strike.

I looked around for turnstiles or security guards or other impediments to my escape. But it was quiet down here post-flight. I looked at the time. Had a few more minutes before Mom's rental car was towed.

I hurried toward the luggage cart, stopped, looked around, then ran up and grabbed both bags with two hard jerks.

I raced across the shiny floors, keeping my face down as much as possible, away from the gauntlet of cameras watching my every move. They couldn't read microchips from their perches, or I'd have been arrested.

I looked back once, dashed into a cubby, smoothed the musses in my hair, took each bag by its handles, and calmly walked out.

"That was fast," Mom said when I got back. "I thought for sure there'd be some hassle."

We ate Italian delivery by candlelight, virtual fireplace (with real heat), and small-talk that tapered as Mom relaxed.

"Honey," she said. "Your place is adorable. I love it."

I did, too, but now a little more.

Fifteen

"Hey," David said from Kenosha. I was back in my office, typing and collating. "Hey," I said. "Mom tells me she lost her luggage."

"She's good. I picked it up at baggage claim."

"Everything okay?"

"So far, so good," I said. "Thanks for going with the visit idea."

"Sure. Absolutely. How are you?"

"Okay, too," I said.

"Just okay?"

"Yeah." I sighed. "Academic politics. Sucks."

"So I've always heard," David said. "How's it going otherwise? How's Mom?"

"Great. Downtown shopping as we speak."

"Alone?"

"She wanted some me-time."

"I'm not sure her being alone in a strange city is such a good idea," David said.

"You sound like Ron."

"Ron would be one hundred percent sure it's not a good idea," he said. "I'm at ninety nine percent."

"Mom's a big girl. She can take care of herself."

"That's the subject of the family debate you've been missing."

"Ron still pushing that caregiver idea?"

"Shoving it down our throats is more like it," David said.

"He must be going ape that she's out here."

"He tried to talk her out of it," David said.

"She looks great, David. Relieved. Relaxed. Her old witty, Dorothy Parker self. She just needs some space and understanding."

"Which is why she's out there with you, baby sister," David said. "Give her a kiss for me, but don't tell her I miss her—yet."

I figured Mom was okay. She knew how to contact me. And as she liked to say, "I'm chipped, just like Charlie," our canine companion who expired one snowy evening in front of the fireplace, a contented old hound. Any cops or first responders could access everything they needed to know about Mom—including David, Ron, and me—with a scan of her forearm.

I saw Nathaniel Hawthorn pass my door and for a welcome distraction, I got up to look. I heard the heavy steel door to the stairs thud closed. I thought about following him, then took the elevator to the parking garage.

"Uh!" He jumped when I appeared on the other side of his car.

"Mr. Hawthorn," I said. "I understand you wanted to see me."

"Not—"

"My boss said you came by."

"Oh, that. Could have been to warn you about a certain reporter."

"Molly Something? She came by."

"You shut her down, right?"

"I doubt it. She seemed pretty determined."

"What did you tell her?"

"Nothing."

"Nothing may not be good enough. What you guys found is class-i-fied. That means the US Government wants it kept hush hush."

"I get it," I said. "No need to mansplain."

"I'm not mansplaining," the lawyer said. "I'm just—"

I heard the cool glide of the most unusual car in the PAB garage at that moment, the Flyby. It parked in the visitor section and mother emerged.

"Mom," I hollered. I waved her over. She smiled and walked our way.

"That's your mother?" the lawyer asked.

"Yeah," I said. "That gorgeous woman is my mother."

"Not interrupting, am I?" she asked.

"Mom—you look amazing."

"Thank you, thank you. New do. Little gussying. Does wonders."

"Oh—this is our lawyer, Nathaniel Hawthorn," I said. He came around the car to shake her hand. Mom took it warmly and smiled.

"Relation or reincarnation?" she asked.

"I haven't heard that one before," he said. "No 'e' in my

family tree."

"Aren't you a charmer?" Mom said. She looked at me. "I came to pick you up for a late lunch. I'm over-shopped and underfed. I found a place called Cutters, on the water over by that fish market you wanted to show me."

"You'll love it," Hawthorn said, ducking into his car. "And thanks for the kind words."

"Were they?" Mom asked, coyly smiling.

DR. MARCUM WAS THE last person into the conference room for our weekly meeting. He sat down, put his fingers across his mouth, and assumed a thoughtful frown.

"By now, you've all doubtless heard," Dr. Levitt began. "The higher ups want us to lie, if necessary, to keep Crimsy's discovery a secret."

"Bloody prats," Marcum said. "The way they're going, the only humane thing to do will be to cut Crimsy loose. Return her from whence she came."

"It is discouraging," Shonstein said.

"I have asked and asked and asked, until I'm blue in the face, why the big secret, what the hell is going on," Dr. Levitt said. "I may as well be emailing a black hole."

"We need a Nobel laureate," Dr. Shonstein said. "Someone with enough gravitas to appear before Congress and the UN and the media and blow this puppy wide open without getting tried for treason."

"Why are we obligated to keep our mouths shut?" Brando said.

"If not treason charges, then our jobs?" Shonstein said.

"There are laws that protect whistle blowers," Dr. Cooper said. "Going public would be like whistle blowing."

"*Like* whistle blowing?" Marcum said. "It *would be* whistle blowing."

I looked at Dr. Levitt. She sighed. "Going public may be the only way," she said. "The deadlock only seems to be getting more rigid."

"Too bad Wikileaks folded," Cooper said.

"We have anything like that anymore?" Brando asked. "Global watchdog, central repository for stuff The Man doesn't want out?"

"Ten thousand clogs that run ten thousand stories a day," Marcum said. "But all is lost in such cacophony."

"What we need is singularity," Shonstein said. "One voice to rise above the noise."

MOM AND I ATE an early dinner with a view of Elliott Bay. The seafood in Seattle was a shock to me at first; I was used to walleye and blue gill and other freshwater lake fish. I thought Mom would experience the same shock, but instead she made a meal out of oceanic appetizers—oysters on the half shell, mussels, clams, calamari, wild salmon—exclaiming her passion with each different species.

"I'm in heaven, Jennifer," she said. "The only thing missing is Lake Mish."

"You miss Mish already?" I said.

"That's a saltwater bay," she said, staring out the window. "I'm a freshwater babe."

"I'll have to remember that," I said. "Especially when my Midwestern nature rubs someone here the wrong way."

"Has it done that?" she said.

"Oh yeah."

She looked at me questioningly.

"David says hi and wants me to reassure him you're doing okay."

"I'm doing great," she said, pausing. "I won't lie—I didn't think I'd ever recover. But I have, or at least, I'm well on the way."

"I wouldn't blame you if you never recovered."

"Ron thinks I won't," she said. "He thinks it's time to call in the cavalry."

"You're doing great. We're doing great, and you raised us. The business is doing great, and you run it."

"Thanks for noticing," she said. "But I have a lot of help. Great staff. Brandon my new office manager is going gangbusters."

The check appeared, a glowing memorandum of our evening, hovering hologram-style in the Cloud on the table next to my wrist. I touched it with my wrist for a chip scan. The check glowed red. Touched it again. Red again.

"Hmm. Payment declined."

"You using Ethereum or Bitcoin?" Mom asked.

"Both and more," I said. "Sign on the door says they take all blockchain currencies."

"Let me try. Check, please."

The virtual check appeared next to Mom. She touched it with her wrist. Green.

"What are you using?"

"Dogecoin," she said.

"THIS LOBBY IS SPECTACULAR," Mom said, as we walked into The Mallory from our dinner date. "They've done a wonderful job restoring it."

I went for the elevator, but Mom insisted on taking the stairs.

"And your place is adorbs," she said with a deep breath, taking in my apartment again. I closed the door as she walked to the front window and looked at the night.

"It's a little tight, but I love living here." I paused as something occurred to me. "So Mom—how come we're getting along?"

She didn't say anything and didn't turn around.

"I've been thinking about that since we started talking again," I said.

Just stared out the window.

"We haven't fought, haven't even argued."

"Maybe it's because," she began.

"Because what?"

"I can't say. It'll sound corny. I hate corny."

"I'm cool with corny," I said.

She looked at her feet.

"C'mon. Out with it."

"Oh good grief. Maybe it's because . . . we're falling in love," she said. She turned to me. "All over again. We're not the same people we were, the first time."

I wasn't sure I heard that right. "Mom," I stammered. I tried to walk to her, but faltered and caught myself on the back of a chair. "What?"

"Falling in love. Again. That doesn't mean I haven't always loved you, with all my heart. It's just . . . Corny, right?" she said.

"Sweetest corn I've ever tasted." I glowed. I felt it on my face, in my head.

"You mind if I turn in?" she said. "I didn't think I'd be this tired on day five."

"Jet-lag lag," I said. "Be right behind you. Got some reading first."

She took my double-sized hide-a-bed and I went for the fancy air mattress I placed next to my slender galley kitchen. I read for a while, but gave it up. I couldn't stop thinking about what she said.

I had wondered if we would ever get past the fight last summer after Brian's funeral. David thought it was over between Mom and me the winter before, after we retreated into our respective corners when I got in Ron's face about being a callous prick about Brian's then-failing second rehab stint.

BridgeWaters wasn't acknowledging its collapse—Ron was right. But I didn't want to hear how right Ron was again. And Mom didn't want to hear me arguing with her brother. It was adolescence all over and it was my fault. I should have kept my mouth shut, learned some tact (as David had long advised). But I charged ahead and damaged us, again.

Now, Mom and I were falling in love. With each other. Again. I fell asleep with that sweet on my pillow.

MOM WAS SLEEPING WHEN I slipped out to work. Despite vacay days. Dr. Brando needed me, I could tell. "Exciting news," he texted. "But you don't need to come in."

I hated to leave, but I planned to call Mom in a couple of hours, pop back in over lunch, and leave work early.

"Wait. Coming in," I texted back.

"It's nitrogen," Brando said the minute I arrived. "The OpenGro box has been running a little high on nitrogen."

"I wondered about nitrogen. But there's no ammonia. No nitrates. No nitrites in the containment atmosphere," I said. "So what's going on with the nitrogen?"

Bacteria, at least on Earth, convert nitrogen to all those things. Ammonia is what stinks when stuff decays. Crimsy didn't seem to be doing any converting. Just turning green.

"I can't explain it, at least not yet," Brando said. "But it makes intuitive sense. Throw a bunch of nitrogen-containing fertilizer in a pond, and what happens: a bright green algal bloom. Fertilize your lawn with nitrogen and what happens: brown to green."

There's comparatively little nitrogen in the Martian atmosphere, but lots of it in ours. Crimsy lands here a few billion years ago, evolves from a boring, methane-making red bug into an oxygen-making, food-manufacturing green dynamo.

"She's the earliest cyanobacteria!" He threw up his hands as I jumped. "We gotta get her off that space station."

"How?" I squeaked.

"I don't know." He looked crestfallen.

"Then—"

"Maybe subject Crimsy to varying nitrogen levels. We can do that from here."

"Makes sense," I said. "But what about carbon dioxide? Temperature, pressure?"

"Those, too. Basic idea will be to gradually make her environment more like Earth. But first, I want to see if we can rule in or out one factor at a time, starting with nitrogen. I've gotta be in court today. Can you let the gang know at our lunch meeting?"

"It's at lunch?"

"Marcia changed it last minute."

"Would it be okay if I left around eleven? I promised my mom I'd come by my place. Be back in time for lunch."

"Of course. Of course. You really shouldn't even be here. How's the visit going?"

"We're having a great time."

"Two weeks with my mom in a little apartment? They'd have to canonize me."

"Mom's dying to see Lexi. I was thinking the ferry, to Bainbridge or maybe Vashon."

"Vashon, definitely. Bainbridge is over-developed. Put Lexi down for it—if I still have custody of her after today."

"Is that really in question?" I asked.

"Every day."

MOM ATE A NICE breakfast at a cafe up the street. Caught up on the news. Spiffily dressed and waiting for me.

"I know we were planning to do lunch, but you wouldn't be interested in a lunch meeting with a bunch of cool scientists, would you?" I asked.

"Sure," she said. "If I won't be in the way."

"I asked Dr. Levitt. She'd love to see you again."

Caterers were dropping box lunches in our conference room when Mom and I got off the elevator. Dr. Levitt stepped into the hallway.

"Patrice, right?" she said to Mom, taking her arm and hand.

"Yes. Marcia?"

"That's me. And we have plenty of box lunches, so grab one and make yourself at home."

I walked in and heard Mom gasp behind me. She stopped at the doorway.

"Mom?"

"Is that—?" She stared at Dr. Hale's telaparted image.

"It is," I said. "I didn't think he'd be here. You wanna leave? You could go down to the post-doc office or the faculty lounge."

She gathered herself. "What is— that doesn't—"

"Latest in social distancing technology," I said.

"TelaPart?" she asked. "We were thinking about getting it for the office."

"Creeps me out," I said.

"I can see why." She walked in. "I'll be fine. I doubt he'd recognize me anyway." She sat.

"Patrice?" Hale said immediately.

"Hal?" she replied.

"Oh . . . boy," he said.

"I'm visiting," Mom said.

She smiled. Introductions went around the table. Dr. Cooper slid over a box lunch. Then the inquiries started.

"You guys know each other?"

"High school."

"Get out!" Shonstein said.

"Co-valedictorians," I said.

"You're joking?" Dr. Marcum said.

"So—how long has it been?" Mom asked Hale.

His image turned toward the sound of her voice. "Too long," he said, I thought somewhat suggestively.

And that's how the first couple minutes of our lunch meeting went. Despite her discomfort, Mom hung in. It was actually kind of fun watching her stare incredulously at 3D-

Hale. Also funny how quickly they recognized each other after all these years.

"Jennifer, I want to yield the floor to you," Levitt started after confirming the Deep Space Gateway crew was within earshot. "Dr. Brando couldn't be here, but has some exciting news he asked Jennifer to convey."

"We think nitrogen may be what's making Crimsy turn green—or greenish," I began. "Dr. Brando wants team approval to test this hypothesis."

"That nitrogen turns things green?" Dr. Shonstein asked.

"*Crimsococcus*, specifically," I said.

"I gathered we weren't talking lawns," she said. "What are you—Brandy—proposing?"

"Varying nitrogen levels with different sub-colonies," I said. "Raise it. Lower it. See if the coloring increases, decreases, or vanishes. See how rapidly it happens."

"Sounds reasonable," Dr. Cooper said.

"I continue having concerns about dividing the colony," Shonstein said. "We just don't know enough to know what impact this might have."

We'd divide the colony into multiple agar dishes, just like Dr. Shonstein did with her antibiotic tests, something I was dying to bring up until someone with a lot more pull did it for me.

"Seems a bit like the pot worrying about the kettle," Dr. Marcum said.

"How so?" Shonstein said.

"Your antibiotic tests."

"That was different."

"How so?"

"For one thing, we weren't poisoning the atmosphere," she said.

"No, you were poisoning the colonies."

"That's not fair, Bill."

"I don't see how changing nitrogen levels is tantamount to poisoning," Dr. Cooper chimed in. "You're not talking about crazy levels, right?"

"Reb—"

"Tell that to our choking neighbors in the Third World," Shonstein shot back.

"Okay. Okay," Levitt said. "Brandy's not here to defend the idea and I don't think he intended to hang Jennifer out to dry. Maybe we should just table it."

"We're okay with whatever," Captain Gillory said from the space station. Mom looked around the room. I leaned over to whisper.

"In orbit," I said, pointing upward. "Space station crew."

She nodded with an "ahh."

"I understand tabling the idea, but are we losing our urgency?" Marcum said. "The 'we never know when they'll cut us off again' urgency."

Dr. Levitt looked at 3D Hale. "Hal?" He turned to her. "What do you think?"

"Your team, your game," he said.

"C'mon. You *always* have an opinion."

I watched Mom watch him rub the back of his head in thought.

"I think you gotta do what you can as soon as you can," Hale said. "I don't know what's going on anymore than you do, but recent history suggests this project could get shut down at the stroke of a bureaucrat's pen."

"He always did have a way with words," Mom said after the meeting.

But even Hale's eloquence couldn't save Project Little Green Women from a delay. Dr. Shonstein's opinion carried massive sway with Dr. Levitt. Plus, there was Levitt's own prickly relationship with Dr. Hale.

"WHY DID YOU SANDBAG me?" Dr. Brando said as I walked into his office.

"I didn't sandbag you," Dr. Shonstein answered.

"Yes. You did," he said. "And when I wasn't even around to defend myself."

"There was nothing to defend. I brought up some concerns. We discussed them. Marcia made a decision."

"Are you angry we might be onto something?" he said.

"Why would I be angry?"

"Why, indeed."

"Don't gaslight me, Brandy."

"Because your project failed."

"What—the antibiotic tests?"

He looked at his palms grinding into his desk.

"What an unfair, bullshit thing to say," Shonstein said.

"What's unfair is how you've pushed back on every idea I've had while I always support you," Brando said.

"If you don't know me well enough to know by now that I don't play those kind of petty games, then I don't know what else to say," Shonstein said.

"Look—I saw something everyone else saw, too," Brando said. "The color green. You wrote it off to a trick of the light. Others probably thought, weird little Martian critter. Might turn purple next. But I saw it and I thought about it and we've just now started investigating it. And if we don't keep going we stand a good chance of having the rug pulled out from under us again, maybe permanently. That's all I'm saying."

"Spare me the 'I'm a martyr for my science' speech'," Shonstein said. "You're not Galileo," who pissed off The Catholic Church with his "heretical" cosmic contemplations.

"And you're not the Pope," Brando said. "You're not even the PI."

"But the PI has validated my concerns. We kill *Crimsococcus* with all this tinkering and then where are we?"

"Are you serious? She grows like dandelions on my agar. Or is that another hangup? That I solved the agar problem?"

"Hangup?" She dropped her voice. "Fuck you."

"What did you say?" Brando asked, I think gritting his teeth.

I had *heard* Shonstein and Brando—the two people on our team who study small things—didn't always agree, so I took their periodic bickering in stride. Now, it seemed on a whole new level.

"Look who I found." Lexi waltzed in with Mom at the door. Saved from another F-bomb.

"So—looks like everything went okay," Shonstein said, with her tone of voice dropping in a choppy, flustered sort of way.

"I won *that* argument," Dr. Brando said. His latest custody hearing was yesterday.

"Jennifer's mom wants to take me to the Space Needle," Lexi said.

"Correction," Mom said. "I want her to take me."

"What did *your* mom say?" Brando asked.

"Nothing," Lexi said. "I didn't even know until after she dropped me here."

Sixteen

One Space Needle trip and some much-needed alone time (for me) later, and we were on the Fauntleroy ferry crossing Puget Sound toward Vashon Island, aka Vashon-Maury Island, one of few nearby places I had yet to explore. We planned some antique and Americana hunting —Mom and I shared a fondness for crystal door knobs, tin ceilings, and vintage footwear—and Lexi had been with us off and on for the better part of two days.

"What does this remind you of?" Mom asked me, watching the water pass along the hull. I hadn't a clue. "You always got really excited."

"AP Calculus with Mrs. Ronaldo?" I said.

"Think road trip across the ocean."

"The Badger," I said. Instant recall. "It's a ferry back home," I told Lexi.

"You guys crossed the ocean in a ferry?"

"A ferry that looks like a cruise ship," Mom said.

"When we were little, my brothers and I thought Lake Michigan was the ocean," I said. "You can't see across it."

"You can't see across a lake?" Lexi asked.

"Not that lake," Mom said. "Hundred eighteen miles wide. On a good day, you can see maybe two to three miles."

"I have *got* to see this lake," Lexi said.

Lexi's mother called to "check on her." Probably twenty

years Melissa Brando's senior, Mom handled this latest inquiry with grandmotherly aplomb.

"I have to compliment you," she said, during their voice-to-voice encounter as we waited in the vehicle line at the Vashon-Maury dock.

"Is this Jennifer's mother?"

"Yes. And one mother to another, Lexi is just the most polite and charming young woman."

I gave Lexi a thumbs up.

"Why—thank you," Mrs. Brando said. "Parenting isn't easy, as you know. It's always nice to hear when we might be doing it right."

"We're delighted to have Lexi as our tour guide today," Mom said. "We'll be sure to have her back at the appointed time."

"Very good, Mother," I said after they concluded.

"She's been generous with Lexi's time," Mom said. "She could have objected."

"I begged and pleaded," Lexi said.

The Flyby drove us toward downtown Vashon.

"The number of persons driving under the influence, also known as driving while intoxicated, has declined precipitously in recent years. A discussion with automobile and law enforcement experts on the impact of self-driving cars, next on NPR."

"Radio off," Mom said. "I just want to enjoy the drive."

"I GOT QUITE A scare this morning after you went to work," Mom said on the phone.

"What? Are you okay?" I was in the post-doc office prepping for Project Little Green Women's nitrogen decision.

"So I'm stepping out of the shower." Her voice lightened. "And I hear this loud thud. I grabbed a towel, my comb, and ran into your main room. A drone was hovering over a package it apparently dropped inside your door."

"Oops—sorry Mom. It's supposed to ring first. And set the package down gently."

"I didn't hear any ring. This package is pretty heavy, too."

"You okay?"

"Fine."

"Why did you grab a comb?"

"Handy sharp end."

"What's in the package?"

"Don't know," she said. "Want me to open it?"

"Shake it first. Make sure nothing rattles."

I heard her unwrapping it.

"It's a big pile of papers. No—make that a huge pile of papers."

"What kind of papers?" I asked.

"I'm reading. Bunch of it's folded, legal size. Oh—here's a note. 'I know you probably don't think so, but I'm a man of my word.' Doesn't say who wrote it."

It didn't have to.

"I'll see you for lunch," I said.

I walked down the hallway to Dr. Levitt's office and stopped short when I heard her voice and Captain Gillory from the space station. I rapped lightly.

"Jennifer. Good morning."

"Morning."

"We were just talking about our next vicarious research project," Dr. Levitt said.

Vicarious research, the perfect oxymoron for a post-pandemic age.

"We're ready if you guys are," Gillory said. "We'll have to hook our nitrogen tanks up to the hyperbaric oxygen chamber to make another containment box, but Commander Ryong assures me it won't be a problem."

"Sure you want to sacrifice your main defense against the bends?" Dr. Levitt asked.

"Not planning any space walks," Gillory said. "Enough fail safes on the station to prevent decompression if we breach. Chamber shouldn't be out of service that long anyway."

"Not if Brandy's right," Levitt said.

"So the plan is, we only vary the nitrogen levels in the chamber," Gillory said. "The OpenGro box will be our control."

"That should make Dr. Shonstein happy," Hightower said from the background. "Shouldn't impact the original colony at all."

"Rebecca understands all that," Levitt said. "She's just feeling the stress. We all are."

"Tell her—" Gillory said. But a loud scream, or a yell, or some kind of resounding exclamation in our building cut her off.

"What was that?" Levitt said.

"I heard it," Gillory said.

I went into the hall. Dr. Cooper was outside his office. He shrugged. I went from door to door, peering in. Shonstein gone. Brando gone. Marcum's door was cracked open. I knocked.

"My apologies," he said. I opened the door. "I'm sitting here rather chuffed at the moment," he said. He turned from his cloud monitor. "I won," he said. "I bloody well won."

WILLIAM MARCUM, DPHIL, FRS, NAS had made history: one of a few mathematicians ever to win both the Fields Medal and the Abel Prize, and the only Black mathematician to win either award.

Everyone was chuckling and shaking hands as we settled in for our faculty meeting, where a congratulatory bouquet from the UW math department took center stage at our conference table. A card that said "Congratulations!" in over-sized symbols from different branches of math—geometry, algebra, group theory, tensor calculus, all-purpose Greek—peaked over the flowers. Marcum and Levitt hugged.

"Bill. We are so, so proud of you."

Dr. Shonstein was teary eyed. "I just—" she said as they hugged. "This is so awesome. Bill—I'm just." She waved her hand in front of her face. "I'm verklempt."

"Always love it when a brother's killin' it," Dr. Cooper said.

I just stood there with awe on my face. Dr. Marcum smiled and squeezed my shoulder.

"Thank you," Marcum said to us. "I'm entirely too happy, being part of this team and sharing this now."

"Ahh," Dr. Levitt said.

Dr. Brando dashed out, then returned with a box of Kleenex.

"Don't encourage us," Levitt said, grabbing one and dabbing her dry eyes. "So as we now formally acknowledge, congratulations are due to our very own William Marcum, winner of the Abel Prize in Mathematics for his work on—Dr. Marcum, would you do the honors?"

"Ricci-Hamilton Flow Solutions to the Navier-Stokes Existence and Smoothness Problem, or for the biologists in my midst, how living things like *Crimsococcus* wiggle around, and how we might track them in turbulent terrains," Marcum said.

"Your citation better say all that," Cooper said.

"Of course," Marcum said. "We mathematicians are practical to a fault."

Everyone laughed.

"I make a motion we move along to more important topics, and I thank everyone, from the bottom of my heart, for your wonderful support."

"Motion seconded," Dr. Levitt said. "Congratulations again, Bill." She paused. "You all have the hyperbaric chamber plan we've devised to see what's making Crimsy turn green."

"I see you want to use bleach to remove cross-contaminants from the chamber," Shonstein said. "It's not the preferred method—"

"No choice. Chamber has acrylic components," Brando said.

"Which is a problem why?" Dr. Marcum asked.

"Acrylic reacts badly with other disinfectants like alcohol," Dr. Brando said.

"I dunno," Shonstein said.

"Don't know what?"

"Bleach lingers. It could kill *Crimsococcus*."

"Bex," Brando lowered his voice and leaned across the table. "We've been over this how many times?"

"Sorry, Mike. This feels really Jerry-rigged. A hyperbaric chamber, for Chrissake?"

"I think it's pretty clever," Cooper said.

"Thank you," Brando said.

"It's transparent, portable," Cooper said. "They can put it near windows, wherever sunlight comes in. Sounds like it'll be free of cross-contamination. Not a bad place for an artificial climate."

"What other option do we have?" Marcum said.

"Fuck," Shonstein said.

"Dr. Shonstein?" Levitt said.

"Here we go again," Brando said.

"Don't you see how this is playing into their hands?" Shonstein said. "We do all these experiments, get all these projects done, and what happens to our argument that we *have* to have Crimsy on Earth, in our labs, to do meaningful studies?"

"Our argument?" Brando said. "I didn't think we had anyone to argue with, except each other."

"Just wait til we get hauled in front of Congress again, to justify how we basically wasted a few billion tax dollars, dicking around in the weeds," Shonstein said. "Since when have any of us ever settled for seat-of-your-pants science?"

"Since a few weeks ago," Brando said.

"I regret that," she replied. "There's a part of me that feels like boycotting this entire charade. Going on strike. You hear that, Big Brother," she said to the Cloud.

"Stop being so dramatic," Brando said.

"How's this for dramatic?" She pushed away from the table. "I quit."

"You don't mean that," Marcum said.

"Yeah." She stood up. "I do." She grabbed her note pad and went for the door.

"Rebecca," Levitt said.

But she was gone.

I WAS PENSIVE AFTER work, but other than stress-eating Beecher's Curds—a luxuriant local cheese snack I bought for Mom—I tried not to let it show.

"I have *got* to get a video of this," Mom said, as we watched two guys throwing a fish back and forth across a counter at Pike Place Market.

"There's no Cloud access here. You'll have to use your cell," I said.

"No Cloud?"

I pointed to one of the signs popping up around town. "No Cloud Allowed," aka Big Brother barred from these premises. "Cloud-blocking technology is making the rounds."

"Seems like just yesterday every cafe, bar, restaurant, and people nook had to have Wi-Fi," Mom said.

"No one counted on Wi-Fi morphing into the Cloud," I said.

"Good excuse to drop my cloudcam subscription." Mom took out her cell, ordered me to stand near the flying fish, and started filming. "Say hello to the folks back home."

"Hello Keno!" I said.

"Step right up! Step right up," one of the fish-creants behind the counter announced. "In this corner, halibut."

He raised a fish in his left hand.

"In this corner, salmon." Right hand went up with a different fish.

Mom filmed the dual-species duel, as each fish flew back and forth across the counter. They almost dropped the salmon a couple times; the halibut seemed easier to catch.

Assured the fish were never dropped and that both men always wore gloves, Mom intervened and had a sal-ibut combo cleaned, cut, and wrapped.

We sat down to eat lunch on an outdoor bench and I told her about the Shonstein drama. She was sanguine.

"She'll get over it," Mom said. "Didn't you guys have someone else threaten to quit?"

Not threaten to quit. But Dr. Cooper did get pretty pissed during the Great Dust Storm Dust Up.

Seventeen

Project Little Green Women commenced the following morning and I was lying on my air mattress texting Dr. Levitt. Everything was ready on the space station. Dr. Brando had to be in court by 9 a.m. Dr. Shonstein had not answered calls or texts or emails all weekend.

"Mom says she'll get over it," I texted, about Shonstein.

"At least someone's optimistic," Levitt replied. "How was your weekend, btw?"

"Awesome! Did the fan girl tour."

"Fan girl?"

"Cherry pie at Twede's, selfies in front of the Roslyn sign."

"She like Snoqualmie Falls?"

"LOVED it!"

"I was too young to watch *Twin Peaks*," Levitt texted. "Too young to understand *Northern Exposure*."

"Way before my time."

I fell asleep perusing the contract stack Nathaniel Hawthorn drone-delivered, to all of us, though probably only Dr. Cooper and I would actually read it all.

WE WATCHED CAPTAIN GILLORY on the space station monitor stringing some gift-wrapping ribbon across the hyperbaric chamber, positioned near a small window that let in sunshine.

"Mother always kept the ribbons," she said. "With all the birthdays in our family. Would you do the honors?" She handed the scissors to Captain Hightower.

"Hard to believe you guys have been up there since Christmas," Dr. Levitt said.

"Since Thanksgiving," Hightower said. He stuck his face into the monitor. "But who's counting. Where's Doc Shonstein?"

"Home sick," Levitt said. "I messaged her to watch online."

"Of all the days. She's always welcome to TelePart up here. Y'all are."

"We're good," we said at once.

He cut the ribbon.

"Congratulations," Gillory said. "Project Little Green Women is now underway."

The Crimsy colony in the hyperbaric chamber was immersed in Martian-type air with one difference: three percent nitrogen, four tenths more than on Mars. After waiting and observing, the space station crew would increase or decrease nitrogen by small amounts until we saw or measured some kind of change, like getting any greener or producing oxygen.

"YOU'RE WELCOME," NATHANIEL HAWTHORN texted me in the post-doc office.

"I am SO sorry," I replied. "We got the contracts and I meant to thank you. Personally."

"Apology accepted. Any questions?"

"Jotting down as I read."

"I'm free after work."

"Lots of reading left."

"Might be good to go over in stages."

"Lotta trees died for all that," I said. "Could've just emailed it."

"I tried. Email servers kept rejecting. File size too big. So, no questions?"

Though Nathaniel probably didn't think so, I liked him. But I also remembered Dr. Levitt's admonition and the Workplace Fraternization and Anti-Harassment Act, aka WFAHA.

"None so far," I responded tactfully.

Our floor was crazy quiet now.

Dr. Marcum drove to Olympia to address a "Governor's Science Committee."

Dr. Brando wasn't back from court.

Dr. Shonstein was still on her quit.

Dr. Cooper was in Cambridge for one of his regular visits.

Dr. Levitt hadn't returned from lunch.

"Anybody home?" Captain Hightower said through the cloudspeaker.

"Just me," I said.

"No one else?"

"Nope."

"Good enough. Meet us in your conference room."

When I got there, the 3D monitor had a magnified view of a familiar object looking a little less familiar.

"See anything?" Gillory said.

"Yeah," I said. "The colonies look—clumpier."

"Clumpier. As in more clumps instead of spread out?"

"Yes. More closely packed. Clusty."

"Shame on them," Hightower said.

"Clustier, clustery."

"We noticed it, too," Gillory said. "Wanted to make sure we weren't imagining things."

"This is with the three percent nitrogen?" I asked.

"A tiny bit more like Earth," she said.

I examined the colonies on the agar plates. "Don't seem any greener," I said.

"Nope."

"We need to know next steps," Gillory said.

"I'll text everybody," I said.

But an email from Molly Cukor with Cosmic American distracted me.

"Jennifer: We met a few weeks ago in your offices. I came by to see if I could catch you, but they've installed a fingerprint ID keypad system for building access."

News to me. But I never used the public entrance and so far, neither had Mom. Faculty and staff used a code to get through a gated entry into the PAB parking garage, then old-fashioned card keys to the back stairwell and garage-level elevator.

"Should have emailed FIRST," I replied.

Molly got back to me a few minutes later. "I just found your email. I can't get contact information for anyone else in your group. Would you mind answering a few questions?"

Delete.

"Did your team find some kind of microbe on Mars?" she began.

Delete.

"Has it harmed anyone on the space station?"

Delete.

"Does this suggestive silence mean yes to one or both?"

Bait taken. "It means I'm not authorized to speak to the press," I wrote.

"Is anyone authorized? My editor says NASA put its people under some kind of gag order. SpaceTek isn't saying anything. Your PIO won't return my messages."

Welcome to the club, sis.

"So I'm reaching out to you."

"Reaching out." I hate it when people say that.

"Were you threatened with espionage charges?" she asked.

"No!" I could have written "not yet," but decided precision was not the better part of valor. "How'd you find me?" I asked.

"Story in your local paper from a couple years ago," she wrote. She sent the link.

"What is it about Kenoshans and Martians?" it began. I remembered that story. Reporter interviewed my fifth grade science teacher and of course, Mrs. Ronaldo. "Hometown Girl

Made Good," that story. I wish Dad had been alive to read it.

NO ONE ELSE CAME in for the rest of the afternoon. I called Mom to check in—she was lounging around at my place, enjoying the nothingness time—then I used the quiet to work on my thesis, which I'm guessing is destined to become a top secret dossier sealed in a crate stored deep in the bowels of Area 51 next to the Lost Ark.

I was too worked up to concentrate on anything really deep, so I continued compiling my bibliography page, a growing list of sources we'd referenced, adopted, and adapted, science's version of not reinventing the wheel. I was assembling the "how to find water on Mars" portion, tripping down memory lane reading the abstracts—short summaries at the top of each paper.

Some ideas were prescient. A team from the Lunar and Planetary Institute in Houston said an EZ (short for "exploration zone") in the Valles Marineris would offer "unique potential for geologic, hydrologic, and astrobiologic investigations . . . an ideal target for future robotic and human investigations . . . exposure and accessibility un-equalled by any other location on the planet."

Other ideas ended up aboard *Odysseus*: "Refining The Search For Water On Mars Using Balloon-Borne Neutron Spectrometers." A team from the US Department of Science, Los Alamos National Lab envisioned high-tech divining rods floating just above the planet surface on balloons. Six balloons on the *Odysseus* mission flew around Valles Marineris shooting neutrons—parts of atoms—at places we expected to find water. The spectrometer recorded the way the neutrons scattered when they hit the ground, giving a thumbs up or thumbs down on possible H_2O. MarsMicro found Crimsy in a thumbs-up region.

This paper from the Johnson Space Center suggested why we found Crimsy in extremely salty water: "Martian Halite: Potential For Both Long-Term Preservation Of Organics And A Source Of Water." Halite is a fancy name for rock salt.

I texted Dr. Shonstein, figuring she was just as lonely as me. Texted again. And again. "Need direction. Brando in court."

"Hey Jennifer," she finally responded. "You contact Dr. Levitt?"

"No."

"Ynot?"

"Need your input."

No response.

"This is a totally bacti thing," I wrote.

"Dr. Brando."

"He's microbiology."

"It's his project."

"Space station crew said need bacteriologist," I replied.

"OK," she texted, five minutes of consideration later.

"JENNIFER." IT WAS DR. Shonstein on the office cloudspeaker.

"Here. Post-doc office."

"I'm downstairs. Outside. What's going on?"

"Some changes in Crimsy."

"No, I mean—we're locked out. Front entrance. Looks like they did away with the key cards."

"I heard. Is there a place to put your finger?"

"Um, let me look."

"A little screen, maybe."

"Here's something. What did they do?"

"I never use the front. I heard it's a fingerprint lock."

"Tried forefinger, thumb. No go."

"I'll come down and let you in."

"We can go around to the garage."

"No. Hang on. Two seconds."

I dashed down the stairs to the lobby and ran to the door. Dr. Shonstein and Malachi, a little wet from a sprinkle, walked in. She folded her umbrella.

"When they change the locks, they oughta tell us," she said.

"Hey, Jen." Malachi looked up at me with these luscious brown eyes.

"Hey, big guy. I'm impressed."

"He's using his words. We've been working on that."

Malachi put out his arms and I picked him up. He kissed my cheek.

"He's been so lovey lately," his mother said.

We stepped into the elevator and he put his palm on a

touchscreen I'd never seen. It didn't do anything, but still.

"What's that?" Dr. Shonstein said.

"No idea."

"Gotta love science," she said.

We got out on our floor and walked to the conference room.

"Projector on," I said, putting Malachi down. "DSG hyperbaric chamber."

The clustier, clumpier image of Crimsy appeared. Shonstein peered at it. "When did this happen?"

"Saw it today, doc," Hightower said, startling us both.

"Hey Rob. So, like when today?"

"First thing this morning. Hey to you, too."

"Any changes in the control colonies?"

"Nada. As I keep telling my partner, we couldn't be babysitting a more boring being."

"I've got a less boring being, when you guys get back," she said, eyeing her son. "Can you increase the magnification?"

The image enlarged. Shonstein looked closer.

"Let's see the control."

The control—Crimsy in her native environment, or at least, as native as we could make it aboard DSG—appeared. Shonstein moved the experimental and control images closer, so they overlapped.

"Hard to tell what's going on," she said. "The colony has changed, but without an accurate colony count, I can't tell if it's reproducing or these are entirely new colony forming units," she said. "You guys wouldn't happen to have an automated colony counter up there?"

"No, ma'am," Hightower said. "Forgot to pack that."

Shonstein circled the two 3D images in highlighter yellow with her finger.

Malachi took my hand and we approached.

"What's that?" he asked.

"Is that Sir Malachi the Magnificent?" Hightower said.

"One in the same," Shonstein said. "Those are bacteria from Mars," she told her son.

"Back from Mars?"

"That, too."

"What's next?" Gillory said.

"Captain Rhonda," Malachi said.

"Hey buddy. Ask your mom what she wants us to do."

"Store these 3D images," Shonstein said. "It's not as precise as I'd like, but there's an open source colony counter we can use on digital images to take a closer look." She turned to me. "The variable still just nitrogen?"

"Yes. Tenth of a percent increases after the three percent benchmark."

"Still can't reach Brandy?" Dr. Shonstein asked me.

"I've been trying all day," I said.

"Call Mike Brando," she told the Cloud. We heard the ring on speaker and his answer message.

"Mike—pick up if you're home."

Nothing.

"*Crimsococcus*' colonies appear to be clumping," Shonstein

continued. "I'm telling DSG to raise the nitrogen another tenth percent. If that's a problem, let us know immediately. Hope everything's okay. End call." She looked at me. "He ever get back from court?"

"I HAD THE NICEST day," Mom told me when I got home. "Went to the gym around the corner, ate a light and lovely lunch, walked around the neighborhood. Very low stress."

I probably seemed distracted. I certainly felt distracted.

"How was your day?" she asked.

"Something cool happened," I said, pulling my thoughts together. "Crimsy changed—sort of. We're doing some tests and thought something like this might happen."

"We should celebrate."

I looked at my mother and thought, celebrate. *I want to hold her. I want to laugh with her. I want us to cry in each other's arms.*

"Mom?" My voice sounded like it was fixing to crack.

"Jennifer?" She came closer.

"Mom, I—"

I heard faint notes in my head from this song we used to listen to when I was growing up, just Mom and me. Stevie Nicks, her favorite singer. *Landslide,* our favorite song.

I took her in my arms, she was close enough now, and pulled her close. She seemed a little awkward at first, but then the first tears came, my tears.

"Jennifer? What's wrong, sweetie?"

"Nothing," I whispered.

And I smiled, and we cried, in each other's arms.

DR. LEVITT WAS SEATED when Dr. Marcum and I entered the conference room for our rundown of the week's activities.

"Just us this morning?" he asked.

"Just us," she said. "How was your trip to the capital?"

"Capital," he said. "I felt positively feted."

"Love that feeling."

"It wasn't all roses at my feet, however. I did have to correct a couple of introductions. I'm not African-American. And though flattering, the title 'greatest mathematician of our time,' rightly belongs to Sara Goode."

"I beg to differ," Levitt said.

"Not after you find out how unprepared I am today," Marcum said. "I just now got a look at the images Jennifer sent."

"Thank you for handling that, by the way," Levitt said to me. "I'm glad you got a hold of Dr. Shonstein."

"She just emailed her notes," I said. "She increased the nitrogen and wants me to get three or four images before we up it again. Dr. Brando emailed late last night and said that was fine."

"Duly noted," Dr. Levitt said. "Speaking of Dr. Brando, he's asked me to convey his sincerest apologies. He won't be in for a while."

"Everything okay?" Marcum said.

"He lost custody of his daughter."

"Oh no," I said.

"Dear lord."

"I don't know if it's permanent or just temporary," Levitt said. "We didn't get that far."

"I can't believe they'd do that," I said. "He's an amazing dad."

"I know."

"Poor chap," Marcum said. "I can barely a remember a time when he hasn't been in magistrate's court over this bloody split."

"Magistrate's court," with all its Dickensian connotations.

"Anything we can do?" I asked. "Does he need anything?"

"He asked to be kept in the loop as much as possible," Levitt said. "If anything remarkable happens, I'm sure he'll be available."

"Such sad news," Marcum said. "I'll give it a few days and touch bases with him. I take it our other astro-microbiologist hasn't made good on her threat, I hope?"

"We talked over the weekend," Levitt said. "She's frustrated, like we all are, but she's not resigning and I wouldn't let her if she did."

I BROKE THE NEWS about Mike and Lexi Brando to Mom over croissants and espresso. She looked at me aghast.

"He's been worried about this for a while," I said.

"Does he at least have visitation?"

"I don't know."

"I so wanted to see Lexi again before I left," she said. "I wouldn't wish divorce on my worst enemy. Your father and I barely avoided it."

"I remember."

"It was awful, Jennifer. Those were some of my darkest days. But I was fortunate to have a few close friends—and my brother and his wife—who let me cry on their shoulders."

"Ron?"

"Ron of Gibraltar," she said. "We drifted apart when we were younger, but our shared marital problems went a long way toward bringing us back."

"Ron and Marjorie always seem like the perfect couple."

"No such thing," she said. "You and David were real troopers, too." She reached across the table and set her hand on mine.

"So—I've been meaning to ask you. Did you actually date Harold Hale?"

"Yes," she said, without hesitation.

I must admit to being a little flabbergasted. But I tried not to show it.

"How serious?"

"Serious enough?"

"Well, why—"

"Did we break up?" She sighed. "Different directions beckoned. He wanted out of Kenosha. I wasn't interested in following him out. At least, not then."

"It was that basic?"

"Pretty much. His dad and mom split years before we met. She raised two kids alone. His sister had some kind of neuromuscular disease. His mom took care of her at home and couldn't work much. Child support, government help, he started working at thirteen. Hal dreamed of the day he'd make enough money to support them." She sipped her coffee. "What a small world, that you worked for him. I still can't get over that." She seemed lost in thought. "Hal was the first person I ever told about how my mom and your aunt Lucy died. Not first boyfriend. First person."

Our conversation gave way to soft chatter, bean grinder, milk steamer, door opening and closing, sunshine through the long, streetside window.

PART OF ME WENT to Cal Tech to avoid Harvard and the man whose reputation preceded him on two levels: as the vicar preeminence of the Harvard-Smithsonian Center for Astrobiology; and as the geeky kid with the homemade haircut who stood on the high school plaudit stage with my mother so many years ago.

The other part of me went to Cal Tech to be exactly like this man, the one who got away, who escaped, the suffocating forces—hardly unique to Kenosha—I'm convinced killed Brian, and might have killed me.

David didn't share the pessimism Brian and I inherited from our dad, and so was better able to see and breathe when the fishbowl got cloudy. Had Brian left, he might still be alive. Had Harold Hale not left, he would never have become the force of nature he was in my scientific circles. Something about the escape seemed essential to his evolution and maybe, mine.

I spent a year courting astrobiology with Cal Tech's Motility Group, a research team whose work MarsMicro referenced many times: vast databases of microbes in motion, from teaspoon ballets in tepid tap water to stultified skittering in pores of deep sea ice. But I ultimately decided on an internship with Harvard for the Hale Lab's work designing "deep space micro-visualization" techniques, of which Biolite would become the most famous.

I knew almost nothing about Hale's years-ago relationship with my mother, just that they knew each other, I assumed casually. I figured it didn't hurt on my application that I was a Red Devil, too (as in Rowdy the Red Devil, Kenosha's Bradford High mascot). But since Hale and my mother had lost touch long ago, he had no idea I was the daughter they never had.

Eighteen

Crimsy continued her clumpy cell division routine without any marked change despite our edging up the nitrogen levels little by little every forty eight hours. I captured images, emailed them to the team, got feedback.

"Maybe we need bigger nitrogen increases," Shonstein emailed.

"Dial down the carbon dioxide?" Brando replied.

"What's methane measuring?" Shonstein asked. "Maybe increase oxygen."

Then, nothing. No decisions, just a repetitious limbo as our two key decision-makers sat it out in their respective corners. I wanted to scream some days, demand they return, fully engaged; turn their backs on hurt egos and other distractions that had nothing to do with logic or science.

But in retrospect, it was remarkable we'd been together this long. Even the unflappable Dr. Marcum hit some bumps, showing us a congratulatory letter from the White House in one hand, a warning letter from ICE (about overstaying his worker visa) in the other.

"Bloody prats," he said. "I've spent a good six months trying to get this fixed." It still wasn't fixed when I asked him about an upcoming Presidential honor.

"Any decision on the gas balance?" I emailed Shonstein and

Brando.

No response.

"One percent nitrogen increase?" I suggested. "You suggested dropping the carbon dioxide, too. Maybe increasing oxygen."

"If Brandy's okay with it, just do the first two," Dr. Shonstein finally emailed. "We wanna see if Crimsy produces oxygen, so my bad on number three."

"Good plan," Dr. Brando got back about ten minutes later. "Thx!"

"Livin' large now, baby," Hightower told the Crimsy colony in the hyperbaric chamber, as Dr. Levitt and I watched Captain Gillory make the adjustments.

"Carbon dioxide to ninety four percent. Nitrogen to four percent. Be back in two Earth days," Gillory said. "Sooner if something Earth-shattering happens."

But nothing unusual happened two days later, or two days after that. Crimsy seemed to get a little greener, but not much else. Mom and I, meanwhile, took a day trip on the ferry to Bainbridge Island.

I FINALLY HAD QUESTIONS about the stack of contracts Nathaniel Hawthorn delivered to all of us, and I asked Dr. Levitt if a question-answer session was on the calendar.

"Not presently," she said, the two of us standing in her

office. "You and Dr. Cooper are probably the only two who've given this thing the kind of thorough read it needs. It's a time issue for faculty. What good's a Q&A if no one knows what to ask?"

"What if I met with him? He suggested it."

"He did?"

"I haven't responded."

"I'm not overwhelmed by the idea," she said. "I don't want a repeat of what happened a couple years ago."

"I understand," I said.

"Do you?" she said. "You swore then you'd always come to me, or one of us, when something like that happened."

"I know, Dr. Levitt."

"When you met Mr. Hawthorn in the parking garage, the opportunity for mouth to engage before brain presented itself, did it not?"

My face was beet red, I could feel it. I wondered if she could see it, too.

"Um."

She looked down at her desk, considering. "I did say you could see who you wanted. We're all adults. But if it affects the team—"

"I understand," I said. I moved to leave.

"This might affect the team positively," she said. "Maybe if you meet with Mr. Hawthorn, he'll feel more predisposed to consider himself a member of the team."

She gave me a few questions of her own and asked that I take careful notes.

"WHAT'S THE 'CONSORTIUM'?" I asked, over coffee at Grounded, our newest entrant into the crowded Seattle klatsch space.

"Off hand—"

I turned a few of the pages I'd highlighted around to him. He picked them up, then slipped a pair of reading glasses out of his vest pocket.

"Funny what happens to your eyes when you never read paper," Nathaniel said. He started reading, mouthing some of the words. "How's your mother?"

"Great. Best time we've ever had together."

"This city is magic, I tell ya." He kept reading. "Okay, so the Consortium refers to the various private entities that financed the mission. Businesses, individuals—anyone who put in money."

"Like Alexander Sparks."

"Yes."

"And this Consortium owns all the rights to whatever we find," I asserted.

"Yes. There are some caveats, however. They cannot interfere, for instance, with our right—if you can call it that—to study what's been found."

"So who's keeping Crimsy in space?" I asked.

"I honestly don't know. At first, I thought it might have been the CDC over pandemic concerns. But now my odds are on the Department of Science. Back when they were the

Department of Energy, they had control over all the national lab stuff."

"I still don't understand the logic behind the media blackout."

"It's known as withholding material information."

"Whatever."

"You found stromatolites, right?" he said.

"The *Odysseus* mission found stromatolites," I said. "Other than Dr. Levitt, we had nothing to do with that."

"So why aren't the stromatolites *Odysseus* found on display with the rocks and sand?"

"No idea."

"Withholding material information. In fact, you'll only find a tiny handful of stories about finding Martian stromatolites, mostly after Dr. Levitt's Congressional testimony. I can't even find any old press releases about it. Rocks and sand are the only things the public knows much about."

He had a point. I could only recall reading a couple of academic papers, one written by Dr. Levitt, about this second-most stupendous discovery in the history of science. I knew about the stromatolite findings because I'd been working with Dr. Levitt for so long.

I had done something unscientific: I took the knowledge for granted, figuring everyone else knew, too. The only thing that *was* widely reported about *Odysseus*—the return of rocks and dust—now seemed like an elegantly-choreographed distraction.

"Are you suggesting this is the fate that awaits Crimsy?" I asked. "She gets buried as deeply as her fossils?"

"I don't know what the plan is," Hawthorn said. "I do know no one wants a custody battle."

MOM WANTED TO DO laundry, so I took the Flyby to work. I bicycled everywhere, so it was a treat to travel under power other than my own. The car stopped at the PAB garage entrance and I swiped my employee key card as always, but the gate didn't rise.

I swiped again. No go.

I got out of the car and checked the gate. I never paid much attention to it before, but it looked new—sharp blue paint, heavy rubber bumper, even the steel hydraulic lift arms shined. It also looked larger, thicker, sturdier. No plastic, no wood, all metal.

I decided to pull around to the front entrance, but as I backed up, the gate went up. "Cool," I said to myself, figuring security saw me through one of the cameras that watch the garage from every conceivable angle.

The Flyby parked a few spots from the elevator. Instead of the key card reader next to the stairway door I usually use, I saw electrical wires protruding from a hole in the concrete wall. I instead swiped my key card at the glass door to the elevator lobby, but it didn't unlock. I turned and saw a new security camera. But before I could hold up my card and yell "hey, I'm legit" I heard the door's electronic lock click. I pushed it and went to the elevator, whose doors opened before I could swipe my key card for a third time.

It started ascending before I touched the floor-five button. I looked at the oddly-shaped round touchscreen Malachi playfully palmed a few days ago, then got off on the fifth floor.

"You made it. Good," Dr. Levitt said. "Conference room."

We hurried, and on entering, saw the interior of one of the space station's two labs on the big screen monitor. Unpacked boxes, other containers, and equipment I didn't recognize sat beside the hyperbaric chamber housing our latest Crimsy experiment.

"What's up?" I asked Dr. Marcum.

"A Deep Space Gateway Christmas," he said. "Someone has come bearing gifts."

"We still have a couple stragglers," Levitt said.

"What's with the gauntlet?" Dr. Shonstein said as she walked in.

My eyes lit up. "You're back."

"For now," she said coyly. "The building isn't making me feel very wanted."

"They've assured me—" Dr. Levitt said.

"Garage gate wouldn't open," Shonstein said. "Had to go around front. But that fingerprint thing still doesn't recognize me so I'm standing there knocking and waving. Jill from Astropaleo let me in."

Dr. Cooper walked in. "Hey!" He fist bumped Dr. Marcum and waved at me and Dr. Levitt. He opened his arms and went toward Dr. Shonstein like he was going to hug her, but instead hugged the air. She reciprocated.

"Virtual hug," Cooper said. The latest satire going around about the Workplace Fraternization and Anti-Harassment Act.

"We're only missing one Mike Brando," Levitt said.

"Dr. Brando's back, too?" I asked.

"He better be," Captain Hightower said from the station. "We need to know what to do with all this stuff."

We mulled around, then Dr. Levitt went to the head of the table. "I texted Dr. Brando," she said. "Let's get started."

We were all seated when he appeared at the door.

"Mike!" Levitt said. She stood up and I could tell she stopped herself from going further. She smiled and held out her hand to the table. "Please."

He smiled, we exchanged waves and nods, then he sat, I thought a little awkwardly, next to Dr. Shonstein. They whispered to each other.

"Captain Hightower," Dr. Levitt said. "You have the floor."

"Dearly beloved," Hightower began. "We are gathered here today to thank whomever sent all this new equipment we have no idea what the hell to do with."

"Two state-of-the-art glove boxes with pre-loaded OpenGro software, an automatic colony counter, fresh supplies of nitrogen and carbon dioxide, a new autoclave, and more of Brando's caviagar," Captain Gillory added. "CRS delivered a couple days ago."

"CRS?" I whispered.

"Commercial Resupply," Levitt said.

"Ryong didn't get a bill of lading," Hightower said. "When has that ever happened?"

And for the first time, I saw their third crew member, who very matter-of-factly said, "Never."

"I don't believe everyone's been properly introduced," Gillory said. "Flight Engineer Ryong," and she went around our table, introducing and reintroducing.

Ryong, I learned, was from North Korea.

"You with NASA?" Cooper said, squinting at the DSG monitor.

"NADA," Ryong replied. He approached the camera so we could read the fine print on his jacket patch: National Aerospace Development Agency. He handed Hightower a box and concluded with a Korean greeting, *Annyeong-hasimnikka.*

"Forgot to mention these vials," Hightower said. He took one from the box Ryong gave him, held it up and read it. "Teixobactin. If I'm reading it right." And another. "Tetrodecamycin." Yet another. "Dihydrotetro—"

Dr. Shonstein leaned in, staring at Hightower reading the labels on the monitor.

"Rob—hang on a sec," she said. "Anything in there labeled trexomycin?"

He pawed through the packaging, took out another vial, and held it close to the camera where we could all see the label. *"Trexomycin."*

"How about orthonizole?" Shonstein asked.

"Right here," he said.

"I asked if those antibiotics were aboard DSG," Shonstein said. "And suddenly, they are?"

"The missing exotics," Brando said, the first time I'd heard his voice in two weeks.

"How many more vials are in that box?" Shonstein asked.

"Fifteen, twenty," Gillory said, taking the box from her partner.

"Are we being watched?" Shonstein asked.

"All the time," Hightower said. "Lotsa cameras up here."

"But none down here," Levitt said.

"Audio bugs then?" Shonstein said.

"Sure as hell better not be," Levitt said.

"Could JPL have overheard during a conference call?" Gillory said.

"Are they listening to our calls?" Shonstein said. "Not only shouldn't they be, but I don't think I mentioned wanting to test exotic antibiotics during a call."

"Testing exotics is in our original grant proposals," Brando said.

"Well they're a mite late, dontcha think?" Shonstein surveyed the room. "Why didn't anyone contact us before shipping that stuff?"

"Anyone contact us about the staff garage?" Cooper asked.

"Should be finished next week," Levitt said. "So they keep telling me."

"What's the plan for this stuff?" Hightower asked.

Levitt looked at Brando and Shonstein.

"I say we finish what we started," Shonstein said. "We can

use the colony counter. Refrigerate the antibiotics until further notice." She looked at Brando.

"How about until right after Little Green Women?" he said. "Fire Operation Lederberg back up."

"That suggestion pleases me," Shonstein said. She smiled. A thaw. "I'd rather do it here, but—"

"Any news on our favorite Martian?" Levitt asked.

"Tad greener," Hightower said. Crimsy appeared on the 3D projector. Brando moved in for a closer look. He bent down, eyeing the sides of the Petri dishes.

"Bex."

Shonstein joined him. "Errant agar?" she asked.

Gillory looked too. "Hmm," she said. "That shouldn't be happening."

"What's so interesting?" Cooper asked.

We gathered around. I bent down, circling the Petri dishes. Crimsy was growing on the sides of the glass while the only agar I could see was spread along the bottom of the dish as always.

Our colony protocol used three techniques called "plating methods"—spread, pour, streak—to spread agar and bacteria in each dish. "Avoid splashing the melted soft agar onto the sides of the Petri dish" so bugs grow in the right place is standard operating procedure.

"What's she growing on?" I asked.

"Any chance you might have gotten agar on the sides of these dishes?" Brando asked.

"Nope," Gillory said.

"Contamination?"

"On sterile glass? How?" Shonstein looked at Brando. "Should we take one of the plates out for a closer look?"

"Might be too disruptive," he said. "What about culturing Crimsy on a blank dish?"

"We have the equipment," Hightower reminded.

After the meeting broke up, I performed the daily ritual of taking Crimsy pix before DSG adjusted the gas again. We were at ninety percent carbon dioxide and six percent nitrogen, approaching Earth's atmosphere as it was four to five billion years ago.

Maybe Crimsy hitched a ride from Mars, on a chunk of volcanic gunk blasted from the planet surface that brushed against a passing asteroid headed toward Earth, or disintegrated into a bevy of interstellar dust bunnies. If she could grow on sterile glass, she could probably grow anywhere.

I WANTED TO CATCH Dr. Brando before he left and in the hall I saw a smartly-dressed woman enter his office. I softly rapped at his open door and peered in.

"Jennifer," he said. We hugged with quick discretion.

"Welcome back," I said.

"Jennifer—I'd like you to meet my court-appointed custody evaluator. Jennifer is finishing her PhD in our department."

We shook hands.

"Penelope," she said.

"The court wants to know if I'm a fit father."

I wanted to say something snarky to her, but thought it best to hold my fire.

"Would you mind if I asked you a couple of questions?" she said.

I looked at Dr. Brando. He shrugged in assent.

"Fine," I said.

We stepped into the hall and she asked how long I'd known "Mister Brando," ("Dr. Brando," I corrected); what we worked on together; if I'd observed him around his daughter and if so, what had I observed; if I'd observed him around his wife ("a couple of times, at faculty gatherings"); what were his work hours, generally; if anything we worked on was contagious or hazardous; how often we were together and if we were ever together alone.

"What's that supposed to mean?" I asked.

"Nothing. These are just routine questions."

"He's always a perfect gentleman," I said, as she followed me back into his office. Now seemed a good time to introduce another ally. "Mom wanted to know if you'd come to dinner with us," I asked Brando. "She's bummed about not seeing Lexi again."

"Sure," he said. "When's she leaving?"

"Sunday."

"I get Lexi every other weekend. It's not my weekend, but if we can do Friday night or Saturday, I'll see if I can get her."

"You gonna be around?" I asked.

"For awhile," he said.

I left his office but heard Penelope ask him about my

mother. I popped my head into every open door and knocked on all the closed doors, delivering a simple pitch. "There's this woman in Dr. Brando's office who wants to know if he's a good dad," I said. "She's a court-appointed custody evaluator."

"You're kidding."

"Da fuck?"

"Shouldn't they have figured that out *before* he lost custody?"

"Jarndyce and Jarndyce continues. Lead the way."

Which I did, delivering Dr. Marcum to a line at Brando's door. Cooper, Shonstein, and leaving her office, Dr. Levitt. Cooper knocked, I heard voices, and everybody filed in. I looked through the little crowd, at Brando making introductions, and Penelope the court-appointed custody evaluator, looking slightly off balance.

Nineteen

You'd have thought Mike Brando was her long-lost son, the way Mom hugged and made over him when we met up at One Luv, an amazing Caribbean sandwich shop he suggested.

Lexi was not with him.

"No go," he said. "I tried."

"I don't understand," Mom said.

"It's temporary," he said.

"So what? It still sucks."

"We had shared custody. It was working fine. Melissa's lawyers want other things from me—"

"More money?" I said.

"Partly. They tried a gambit. The Court Commissioner awarded temporary full custody to Melissa pending reports from the custody evaluator Jennifer met today. Thank you, by the way."

"I hope Penny got an earful," I said.

"Penny is—?" Mom asked.

"The custody evaluator," Brando said. "She's just doing her job, I guess."

"You're taking this pretty well," Mom said.

He cast his eyes down and looked at his clasped hands, then at the people lining up for a taste of whatever smelled so wonderfully.

"You've missed all the crying," he told Mom. "Punching walls, cursing Melissa, damning the lawyers, private tirades over straight shots, curled up in the dark." He sighed. "How do you like Seattle?"

Mom chuckled at the abrupt segue. She loved it, she said; most beautiful city; and couldn't understand all the fuss about rain, clouds, and "seasonal affective disorder."

"You lucked out. We're in our annual sunny streak," he said.

We talked about Seattle's "down years," before my time, when Boeing the aircraft giant shuttered factories, prompting "Will the Last Person to Leave Please Turn Out the Lights" billboards and the city's headlong push to diversify. A terrible homelessness crisis followed decades later, as housing costs soared, drugs became du jour, and policies harmful until, finally, they weren't. Mom and I understood these social crises better than most, and we sat enthralled as Dr. Brando fluidly portrayed this City of Second Chances.

We talked about my nascent career, how much everyone in the office "admires and respects your daughter," the whole Crimsy-secrecy thing.

"Jennifer *is* somewhat coy about what you all are working on," Mom said. "Whenever I ask for details, details, she talks about 'attorney-science' privilege."

Brian came up and Brando recalled my angst. "But Jen is pretty stoic," he said. "She didn't let on."

"Brian," Mom said. "Remind me to call him."

My facial expression made light of the comment. Dr. Brando was mid-chew, and I don't think he heard it. Mom talked about her sister like she was still alive, too. "Lucy would love Seattle," she said. It was close enough to "would have loved" not to raise eyebrows. But then, "I bought some smoked salmon for her."

Don't say anything, don't let on, just keep the conversation moving.

"We used to have a lot of salmon in Lake Michigan," I said. "Dad loved it."

After we said our goodbyes, with Mom promising a return visit and Brando promising to visit Kenosha, she got turned around when we crossed the street. The car was a few meters away, in clear view under street lights.

"Car's over there, Mom."

"Got it." She looked at me. She looked around. "Where?"

"Right there," I said. "In back of the red truck."

"That isn't our car."

"Yeah it is. You've been driving it."

I went to take her arm but she withdrew. "Don't. Please."

"Don't what, Mom?"

"Don't touch me." She turned and looked behind her.

"Everything okay?" a guy called out to us.

"Fine," I called back. "Just looking for our car."

Mom was frozen, in the middle of the street, thankfully empty this time of night. I went for her arm again.

"Don't" she said. "I can see the car." She started walking.

"Wait here, Mom. I'll bring the car around."

"Are you leaving?"

"No. Just getting the car."

I could bring the car remotely, but had never done that before. I was nervous enough being driven around by a bunch of invisible computers. But remote drive beat standing here. I pulled out my cell and scrolled to the app.

"Everything okay?" That guy again. And I recognized his voice. I looked up to see Nathaniel Hawthorn.

"Yes. Hey! Yeah. My mom and I—"

"Your car's right over—"

"Mom—look who's here. Remember Nathaniel?"

She looked at him. "You're Jen's friend."

"Yes," he said. "We met in the parking garage."

"He found our car."

"I recognized it." He pointed. "Up the street."

She hesitated. He extended his hand. "I'm, uh, happy to—" he said.

She took his hand. I followed them.

"This is it, right?" he said, beside the Flyby.

Mom looked at me. I nodded.

"Yes," she said. "It's an unusual looking car, isn't it?"

I unlocked the doors with the app and he opened the passenger side. Mom got in, auto buckled, and turned to him. I could see from the street light her bewilderment was fading.

"Thank you," she said. "Jennifer, I am *so* impressed with your friends."

He looked at me across the top of the car.

"Me too." I meant to say thank you, but that came out instead. "So what brings you out here?"

"Hoping to catch you guys," Nathaniel said. "Brando told me your mom was leaving tomorrow."

"You came to say goodbye? How sweet."

"And—hungry." He held up a takeout One Luv sandwich. He leaned in to Mom. "Almost missed you," he said. "Hope you enjoyed your visit."

"I most certainly did," she said. "My daughter has found her tribe."

I AWAKENED IN THE wee hours with a feeling of light on my face. It took my brain and eyes a second to adjust, but when they did I saw my front door open to the hallway. I raised up on my air mattress and looked around. Door must not have latched completely, though I thought I remembered locking it. I went to close it. I looked at my bed. I couldn't make Mom out, so I moved closer.

"Mom?"

I tossed the sheets and blanket. No Mom. Two twenty-seven AM. Don't panic, I thought, but still I felt my heart creeping into my throat. I threw on some pants and a flannel shirt that belonged to Dad and some slip-on leather boots and a light jacket and went into the hallway.

"Mom?" I whispered.

I hurried to the elevator, scanned the lobby, rushed outside, to the dying traffic on Fifteenth Avenue. Should I call

David? Not yet. It was probably fine. The nights here this time of year were tender and easy. She probably just went for a walk, more me time, and the door didn't latch.

I walked up and down my side of the street, around the corner to Forty Fifth, down and across and back and forth, then back to Fifteenth, where I crossed to the side opposite The Mallory, and ran past the Burke Museum, then beyond it to Parrington Lawn, a park-like part of the UW campus, letting the street lights guide my eyes beneath the trees.

I went up four more blocks, then turned around and started back. I detoured onto the bike path into Parrington Lawn. I felt my legs cold and shaky, felt the light leave my eyes, saw through the fog. I had to keep it together.

"Mom!" I yelled as loud as I could and ran, to a figure lying against a tree in a nightgown. I took off my jacket and brought it around her shoulders and kissed her cheek.

"Mom. Are you all right? Are you okay?" I patted her cheek, looked into her eyes.

"Nine," I gasped. "Nine One One."

"What's your emergency?" said a voice from the Cloud.

"My—something's wrong."

"We have you at Parrington Lawn, on Fifteenth," the operator said.

"Mom!"

"Jennifer?"

"We're sending a responder drone now."

Mom grasped my hand strongly. I could tell she wanted to get up.

"Cancel it. Cancel it. I'm okay," I said. "We're okay."

"Are you sure, ma'am?" the operator said.

"Yes. Yes, I'm sure."

"I'll still send the drone, but it won't descend. Is there a reason you're in the park?"

"My—a relative. I'm taking her home. Just up the street."

"Okay. I'll have the drone follow you until you're safe."

"Thank you," I said.

My mom looked at me. "A drone? What good will that do?" She said it so earnestly, globally, and knowingly, her question sounded rhetorically funny.

"It's a precaution, ma'am," the operator said. It was like she was standing next to me.

I helped my mother to her feet and we walked back to my apartment. She remembered to put on slippers, otherwise I would have carried her.

We walked into the lobby and stood. I looked at her, picked leaf and grass from her hair and nightgown. An old but brilliant grandfather clock began its chiming ritual. Gong, gong, gong, it concluded.

Thank you, thank you, I said to myself. The scientist, talking to her God.

RONALD GULLIVER—UNCLE RON—is my mother's only surviving sibling, only surviving blood relative, other than us kids. I say "surviving" because Mom's little sister was killed in a freak accident.

Grandma was changing her diaper in the front seat of a car called a "compact SUV." Guess they were popular for family vacays forty years ago because that's what they were on. Mom, Ron, Grandma Jennifer (for whom I was named) and Grandpa Max.

Mom and Ron were playing a board game—I think Monopoly, but because Mom never talks about it, I'm not sure. The backs of these SUVs were large enough for kids to spread out on a blanket, chow down on snacks, nap, and play games to wile away the mileage.

Grandma Jen was changing my aunt Lucy's diaper, door open, in the front seat, at a rest stop. A car plowed into them. Grandpa Max ran out of the men's room. He found Mom and Uncle Ron huddled in the back of the bashed-up car, covered with blood and inches from death, but otherwise unscathed. Ron was holding my mother, shielding her eyes.

Grandpa Max never recovered. He never remarried. Uncle Ron has trouble recalling any times after the accident that his dad laughed. The happy-go-lucky man who had been afraid of nothing, the pragmatic doer who had worked since age fifteen, and who grew up learning patience and resilience on the road while his mother searched for work after his father died a young man—that easygoing, fearless guy became afraid of his own proverbial shadow.

Which may be why when his decline began, we at first

attributed it to grief rather than the well-characterized disease that may now plague my mother.

Alzheimer's was actually a mercy in Grandpa Max's life. It made him forget his grief. He couldn't even remember how to walk toward the end, and while I cannot say he was happy, he was no longer in realizable pain.

I GAVE IT A couple days. I did not call David. I wanted to talk with Mom first, without angst on the other end of a phone line.

"I have to talk to you about something." As I whet my resolve, my mouth got dry. "You remember what happened the other night?"

"What other night?" Mom said.

"You were in the park," I said. "Across the street."

"I don't follow."

"I've been wanting to say something about it, but I kept hoping you would."

"I would what? Jennifer, the only time I've been in a park here was today."

"You don't remember? A few nights ago, I found you in the park across the street. It's called Parrington Lawn."

"At night?"

"In your nightgown."

"Oh, Jennifer. What?"

"Last weekend, you got really turned around in Roslyn. You didn't know where you were. You wanted to know if I was Dr. Hale's kid."

She looked hopelessly befuddled.

"I thought maybe seeing him freaked you out, but then One Luv, with Dr. Brando—"

"I don't have any idea what you're talking about. Honest."

"I'd like you to see someone," I said.

"What do you mean? A doctor?"

"Yes."

"I don't need to."

"You do."

"I'm in excellent health. And I don't need my life under somebody else's microscope."

"You're not in perfect health, Mom."

"I don't know what happened the other night, nights, whatever. But I am not interested in seeing a doctor."

Mom looked out the window.

"You might have been hurt or killed the other night," I said.

"Please. Spare me the melodrama."

"All right," I said.

IN SCIENCE, MY PESSIMISM has served me well. I question everything, argue with everyone, and try not to come across as that "clueless chick" archetype many, but certainly not all, of my male peers see lurking within every woman in a lab coat.

Some of the most amazingly brilliant genius people I've met, at conferences, in classrooms, seminars, and the scroll of authors on the greatest new papers, are women.

In high school, I was enamored of Maryam Mirzakhani, the only woman until Sara Goode last year to win the "Nobel Prize" in Mathematics, aka the Fields Medal (there is no Nobel Prize for Math, hence a void the Fields Medal fills with forty-and-under geniuses like Goode and Mirzakhani and a whole lot of guys, including our own William Marcum).

Young and male describes all but two of the Fields Prize winners, reflecting, I think, academe's age and gender biases. Dr. Marcum likes to argue this observation with me, but I merely need recite my litany of women overlooked to win our cafe debates.

Every occupation, every human endeavor, every geographic place has its own unique suffocating forces, maybe reflecting how, in the end, all humanity tends toward small town thinking.

I didn't want my own small-town thinking to again jeopardize a relationship this awesome visit had done much to restore. I was hard on my mom growing up, a real heel as a teen, to the woman who taught me, by example, to admire people like Mirzakhani, Goode, Levitt, Shonstein, and Parada.

I had escaped real introspection by using my talents to flee. Now, I had to step back, think, and plan, as carefully as any plan we'd made for Crimsy. And though I didn't recognize it at the time, I had to stop being the Mary Sue in the room. That person, I was learning, lacked sufficient empathy to provide real strength, was too shortsighted to see the road ahead.

"YOU GET A HOLD of Para?" Dr. Levitt asked me after everyone left the conference room.

"She can meet with us Thursday morning," I said. "Is that

time okay here?"

"Absolutely."

"She's been great. I really appreciate this," I told my mentor.

I TOOK DAVID'S CALL in the Mallory lobby after Mom and I got back from dinner.

"I still can't believe it," he said. "You actually got her to see someone."

"You have to promise that when she gets home, you'll make sure she follows up."

"Think it'll be serious?"

"She's had a couple episodes."

"There? With you?"

"Yes."

"Why didn't you tell me?"

"I didn't want to worry you. Not with Mom out here."

PARADA PRACTICED ENDOCRINOLOGY FROM a well-appointed office overlooking downtown Seattle. She was as warm and gracious as she seemed from a distance, taking Mom's hand in both of hers, explaining what she could and could not do, then asking if it was okay with Mom if I explained what prompted me to request her intercession.

I detailed only what had happened at Parrington Lawn and Roslyn. I didn't want Mom to think David and I were spying on her and commiserating behind her back.

I squeezed Mom's hand.

"I want to spend some time with Patrice," Parada said. "Then offer some suggestions about who she might see and what questions she might ask back home."

I sat in the waiting room. Mom emerged an hour later, trying to smile through red, moist eyes. Parada was behind her.

"You will let me know how everything turns out?" Parada asked. Mom nodded and said "yes" almost breathlessly.

SO HERE'S A COINCIDENCE: Bradford High students from Kenosha designed part of the hyperloop now streaking toward SeaTac Airport. Mom and I dropped the Flyby at a downtown rental car return and boarded the friction-free, electromagnetic bus, which plunged underground for about half the short trip, emerged in a long vacuum tube that paralleled 99 Highway, then—mysteriously until you understood the politics of it— stopped about two miles shy of the terminal.

From there, we hoofed it to a shuttle.

People rode the hyperloop for the novelty of it. It was supposed to cross the freeway and stop in a bunch of cities along I-5—Kent, Renton, Federal Way, Tacoma, Olympia—but the devil in those details halted its progress well short of the planned route, Portland, Oregon to Vancouver, British Columbia.

From downtown to the shuttle (twelve miles) took two

minutes on the hyperloop; the last two miles via shuttle, ten or more minutes in traffic.

"I hear they're building one of these from Milwaukee-to-Chicago," I said.

"And we have the honor of hosting the first section," Mom said. "They eventually wanna run it under the lake. Connect to Michigan."

"Rowdy the Red Devil is blushing with pride," I said.

We checked Mom's luggage outside and passed the metal detectors with a couple of carry-on bags into the terminal lobby. We went through the security checklist.

"Wrist, please," I said. I scanned her microchip with my cell. "Ticket, boarding pass, Real ID, VaxPass, reasonable facsimile photo. You're good. Just don't forget your luggage this time."

"I won't. I won't. Speaking of forgetting, I'm making an appointment with a neurologist next week," Mom said.

I took her hands in mine and looked at her. She was so pretty. "I love you," I said. "You can't believe how much."

"To pieces and beyond?" she said. She took me in her arms and we hugged and she kissed my cheek. Her face felt cold and fresh and alive.

"I'm proud of you," she said, in almost a whisper. "You amaze me."

Wow. That felt so good, you cannot imagine.

I watched her walk toward the boarding sections, missing

the days family and friends could wait until the very last minute to say their final farewells. It was noisy out here in the lobby and there was no place to sit and TSSEA agents passed every few minutes, scowling as though we humans were cars parked in the five-minute, terror-proof, tow-away zones.

Mom blew me a kiss and waved and I waved back, watching her pass through the first set of body scanners and disappear, into the crowd of passengers and carry-ons, scurrying toward their final identification ritual.

Twenty

"Jennifer, right?" Molly Somebody from Cosmic Something startled me as I slipped off my bike at the PAB parking garage looking all the fit, ruddy, backpacking student.

"Hi," I said, walking my bike to the rack next to the elevator doors.

"Hi! I wanted to talk if you had a minute. I'd wait to meet you inside, but as you can see—"

The same fingerprint-readers at the front door were now here, at the doors to the stairwell and elevator lobby. Hoped they worked. I placed my forefinger on the stairwell door scanner. No good. Tried again. Still no good.

"You've been unfriended," Molly said.

I went to the elevator lobby door with the same fingerprint routine. The lock clicked. I opened the door.

"I'd invite you in, but it looks like we don't want visitors," I said.

"That's okay, really. Just—can you? We're running a story about you guys. I just needed to confirm a few details."

I stuck my foot in door. "Story about what?"

"What else?" She looked at her phone. "*Crimsococcus*

halocryophilus. The most amazing discovery in the history of Earthling science."

I felt my face go white.

"I can't comment," I said. "Not my place. I do, I get fired."

"But I mention you in the article."

"I can't talk to you," I said, restraining myself and my mouth. "All press inquiries have to go through our PIO. That's the same policy for the entire campus, not just here."

"All they've done, Jennifer, is stonewall. In fact, all anyone has done is stonewall. NASA won't talk; SpaceTek declines comment; JPL won't return calls or emails. I've tried reaching your bosses, even followed Dr. Brando and staked out his house."

"Are you kidding me? You stalked Dr. Brando?"

"'Staked. Staked out. I went to the door. His neighbor stopped me."

"Neighbor? Like next door?"

"She yelled at me. 'Why don't you people leave him the hell alone?' She thought I was a process server."

"Good for her," I said.

"She was sweet. She apologized."

"Why would that stop you?"

"She said he was going through a terrible divorce and a custody battle over his little girl. He'd been home for a few weeks trying to get his head together. His little girl used to live with him. She didn't anymore."

I felt the red returning to my face. "I appreciate that you left him alone. We all do."

"I keep coming back to you," Molly said. "Or getting sent

back to you. I figure it must be kismet or karma or some other 'k' word for fate."

She had me at her mercy on Dr. Brando. Toss in the clever "k word for fate" and I was starting to soften. But still.

"The best I can do is let Dr. Levitt know you came by again."

"That's all? You don't mind forcing us to write, 'Unconfirmed sources tell Cosmic American that—'?"

"That's a stupid question," I said. "I don't mind a story that might be riddled with errors about my work? Of course I mind. But if I can't help you, I can't help you. Capiche?"

She looked at me. "Yeah. Okay."

"What unconfirmed sources?"

"Now you want *me* to talk," she said. "Have a nice day."

I let the lobby door close and did the new voice recognition check at the elevator. Door opened. I stepped in. No buttons. The door started to close and I stuck my foot in it.

"Please close door," a soothingly malicious voice announced from an overhead speaker. Okay. I'll play. The doors closed. "Floor please?" the voice asked.

"Five," I said.

The touch pad screen that had fascinated Malachi glowed green. "Please face screen for iris scan."

A fingerprint, voice recognition, and iris scan? And if a car had driven me in, a fourth identification at the gate? Our weekly faculty meeting promised fireworks for sure.

"Iris not recognized." The elevator doors opened. "Please contact campus security."

I saw Dr. Marcum's car parking. He got out and walked to the elevator lobby door. I opened and held it for him.

"No, no, Jen. Let's do this the *right* way," he said, gently pulling back the door. I let it close.

He placed his forefinger into the scanner. Nothing. He tried again. Nothing.

"Perfect," he said.

I opened the door.

"And you're waiting here because—"

"The elevator doesn't recognize my eyeball," I said.

"Of course not," he said. "Shall we?" He led us to the elevator. "Your turn."

The elevator voice printed me again. Doors opened. Disembodied voice spoke.

"Five," we said together. Dr. Marcum turned to the iris scanner this time.

"Please show faculty ID card," the voice said after the scan.

He slipped his ID card from his vest pocket and held it to the screen. We went up.

"Whom the gods would destroy," he said, "they must first identify."

As we got off the elevator, I saw Shonstein, Levitt, and Cooper heading into the conference room. But our staff meeting wasn't for another hour.

"Looks like they're starting the revolution without us," Marcum said.

We walked in and everyone was gathered around the 3D

monitor. I peered forward for a closer look.

"What happened?" I said.

Crimsy filled the sides, bottoms, and tops of four Petri dishes with faint green colonies.

"Sudden development," Captain Gillory said. "Like overnight."

Crimsy had grown like a lawn weed in our makeshift hyperbaric chamber box, while the original colonies in the OpenGro box hadn't changed much. The two new glove boxes were empty and awaiting an assignment.

"Where's Brandy?" Shonstein said.

"Running late," Levitt said. "Getting his daughter to school, I think?"

"Huh?" Shonstein said. "I thought he lost—"

"You'll have to ask him," Levitt said. "Okay gang. Ideas on the table: We transfer some or all of these colonies out of the hyperbaric chamber and into the new glove boxes, where we program OpenGro to accelerate the atmospheric changes. Or we leave well enough alone."

"How fast?" Dr. Cooper said. "I mean, like ten percent a day, twenty percent?"

"I'm thinking we up CO_2 ten percent a day, drop nitrogen by the same amount," Shonstein said.

"Earth's troposphere, circa what—three billion years ago?" Cooper said. "Give or take five hundred million."

"We should keep a few colonies in the hyperbaric chamber

undergoing more gradual change," Shonstein said. "Otherwise, how do we know where the trigger lay?"

"How do we know there is a trigger?" Cooper said.

"By the looks of things, there's a trigger," Shonstein said. "I'm contemplating the day our DSG crew wakes up to bright green Crimsy colonies pumping out massive amounts of oxygen."

"I'll settle for measurable amounts," Cooper said.

"Our own Great Oxygenation Event," Marcum said.

"Can you imagine?" Shonstein said. "What that would mean?"

"*Crimsococcus halocryophilus:* The First Universal Common Ancestor," Gillory said.

"Would go a long way to confirming Mike Brando," Levitt said. "What else would explain that kind of evolution? Any concerns, Rebecca? You were dead set against repeatedly tapping the original colony."

"Which is doing fine, by the way," Gillory said.

"We could just get it over with," Shonstein said. "Drop Crimsy into eighty to ninety percent nitrogen, ten to twenty percent carbon dioxide? Hydrogen, some ammonia, methane. Earth's atmosphere circa three point five billion years ago. See what happens."

"I still want Mike's imprimatur," Levitt said.

"Of course," Shonstein said. "Brandy: Where the hell are you?"

"One other item for the agenda," Marcum said. "What's going on with ingress into this building? Fingerprints, retinal scans, that monstrosity called a garage gate?"

"Thank you," Shonstein said.

"I couldn't get in this morning," I said. "Fingerprint and voice print worked, retinal scan didn't."

"Go down to campus security," Levitt said. "Make sure they have a scan file for you. They're at least supposed to have everybody's fingerprints, from our security clearances."

"Mine didn't work," Marcum said.

"I let him in," I said. "He borrowed my fingers, I borrowed his eyes."

"The very definition of teamwork," Marcum said. "I'm going to have a word with the President about all this."

"I'm sure he already knows," Levitt said. "I get an admin email a week."

"Not *our* president, madam," Marcum said. "*The* President."

"That's right," Cooper said. "You have an audience."

"We'd all have an audience if it weren't for this bloody secrecy campaign," Marcum said.

"Oh, yes. Speaking of that," I said. "They're running a story about us."

"Who?"

"That astronomy magazine. Reporter came by this morning."

"So, what—they're running with this?" Shonstein said. "How?"

"Sounds like the UK Sun," Marcum said.

"What did you say to her?" Levitt asked.

"Referred her to the press office."

"Good," she said, drawing out the word as though she recognized I was listening. "I guess we better—"

Dr. Brando walked in looking rushed and flushed.

"Sorry, sorry, sorry," he said.

"Mike, I thought you lost—"

"Yeah," he said. "Long story. Long, effed-up story. But *you* try turning down the chance of a cheek kiss with coffee."

Dr. Levitt reached across the table and grasped the top of his hand. "Understood. Talk to Rebecca." She turned to the rest of us. "I will speak with our attorney about the pending media circus."

SPEAKING OF NATHANIEL HAWTHORN, I texted him, totally personal stuff. "Can I call you later?"

"Sure!" he replied.

At lunch, "I wanted to thank you for helping with my mother the other night," I told him.

"You did."

"No. I think I told you I was impressed."

"No big deal. I like your mom."

"She likes you."

"I take it you had a good visit. She was here for a while. I don't know if I could have had my mother visit that long."

"We couldn't have done it even a year ago," I said.

"You're too much alike, probably," Nathaniel said. "A law professor once told me that whenever two people are too much alike, they don't get along. Want a successful marriage, partnership, whatever, pair up with your opposite."

I GATHERED DRS. BRANDO and Shonstein for my daily activity report in the conference room, with special guest Rob Hightower.

"I killed it," Hightower announced, as we gazed at four Petri dishes inside one of the new glove boxes.

"This is our primordial Earth replica colony?" Shonstein said.

"I told Rhonda. Give me a plant. I kill it. Even a cactus."

"Close up?" Brando said.

We watched the projection scale up, as the camera zoomed in. Marks from the inoculating loop that crisscrossed the cavi-agar were all that remained of the attempt to grow Crimsy in an atmosphere that matched the Earth billions of years ago.

"Well hell," Shonstein said, pushing her hands through her hair.

We still had three "successful" cultures: the original in the old glove box (Box One), maintained in its Mars-like atmosphere; our first experiment in the hyperbaric chamber, changing atmospheric gases by about a tenth percent per day; and our second experiment in one of the new glove boxes (Box Two), changing the air composition to make it more like ancient Earth ten times more rapidly, one percent per day.

Our fourth and most radical experiment—dropping Crimsy

into an atmosphere we surmised was most like ancient Earth without the gradual change—flopped in Glove Box Three.

"Rob may be a plant murderer, but I actually have some good news," Gillory said. She zoomed in on the one percent-change culture in Box Two.

Brando and Shonstein leaned down. "Are you seeing this?"

"I am," Shonstein said.

Crimsy was marginally—but definitely—greener.

"Oh, would I love to stick you under an electron microscope," Shonstein said, rising and stretching her back.

"Don't say that so loud, doc," Hightower said. "We don't have room for no electron microscope up here."

"Up there, up there!" Shonstein opened her arms to the sky. "Please L-rd, either get her down here or get us up there."

"If I could sneak out some cultures under my space suit, you know I would," Hightower said.

"She is growing chloroplasts," Shonstein said.

"The little green machines plants use for photosynthesis, if my high school memory is still intact after all that partying," Hightower said.

"You can only see them under an electron microscope, about the only thing technology hasn't shrunk," Shonstein said. "Chloroplasts have evolved up there, and in short order. I'd stake my reputation on it."

"I hope you're right, Bex," Brando said. "My lawyer bills hope you're right."

"It was your idea. If it weren't for you, we wouldn't be seeing this," she said.

THE NEXT FEW DAYS went similarly, with me reporting incremental changes in Crimsy's green coloration. Between thesis writing, experiment monitoring, and meetings with different team members, I also found time to visit campus security for a retinal scan, and call my brother David. I was relaxed at my place now, gazing out the window at the bustle below.

"I don't know what happened with you guys, but whatever it was, good on ya," David said. "Mom seems like a new woman."

"Has she made plans to see anyone yet?"

"Yeah. Neurologist. Dr. Bowcan, something like that."

"How's she doing?" I asked.

"Still forgets stuff, gets turned around. But doesn't seem as anxious. And hey—you'll never believe this."

"What?"

"She's getting together with that guy she dated in high school. The guy you worked for."

"Dr. Hale? When did this happen?"

"They hooked up," he said. "I don't mean literally, but you know, phone, text, email, dock.io. Sounds like they still kind of have the hots for each other."

"Get out! Mom and Dr. Hale? You know, she saw him here. Well, not him exactly. His telapart. But she didn't say much."

"They must have had something good, the way she's been

chattering."

"I don't wanna spoil the romance or anything, but what does Ron think?"

"You know Ron," David said. "He loves it! It's like this Hale guy was the man he always wanted as a brother-in-law."

"Un. Be. Leevable," I said.

"Her guy's not even here, and Mom's a little more put together, a little better dressed, hair just a little more perfect."

"Mom the hottie."

So wasn't this some interesting news? I couldn't wait to tell Dr. Levitt. And Parada. I have to think that whatever Parada told Mom was playing some role in this rekindling. I just hoped Dr. Hale would be good to her. I guess he must have been, hard as that is for me to believe.

"HE CALLED US LAB girls," a fellow HaleyBop told me. "Can you believe that?"

She gripped the counter top next to a scintillation counter, a device we used to detect fluorescent light in radioactive phages mixed with *E. Coli* bacteria. It was one inspiration for the method we used to find Crimsy, and I credit Hale in my thesis.

"To your face?" I asked.

"No, but right in front of me. He was talking to Kevin," a post-doc, "like I wasn't even there." She started programming the machine. "He just kind of blurted it out."

"Rarely talks to me," I said.

"I'm so done with this, Jen. Hale's like a god around here.

The guys worship him. He's creating whole new generations of dissy male HaleyBops."

"Imperious, abrasive, chauvinist, snob." I'd heard it all about Dr. Hale over the years, like a caricature from a bad movie. Some of his more memorable lines (to women):

"Take the heels out of my lab."

"Cut your hair or cover it."

"Power-dressing is a distraction."

"This is why women don't get credit," Hale said during a heated discussion about Henrietta Leavitt, who received little credit or recognition for her work on the brightness of stars, which revolutionized astronomy and made a lot of male careers. Hale's cognitively-dissonant conclusion: "Women aren't forceful enough."

Long skirts, loose pants, tops that hung languidly rather than perched. I never once heard him tell one of the guys with long hair to cut it or cover it, or what kind of pants to wear, or the value of forceful presentation.

When he dressed down the male students, which all of us overheard or heard about a time or three, it was about intellectual, not physical, quality. Which, with guys my age especially, engenders respect. Prompts phrases like "god of astrobio" and dreams of being him someday.

To have Hale tell you no way were you cut out for the kind of grueling, thankless lab hours—and hours—and hours that make Nobel laureates because you were basically too stupid, was a badge of guy honor greeted with meekness, humility, and deference.

But to have him tell you the same thing because you might get pregnant someday or you were thinking of getting married and by golly, what might that mean for your career or something that had nothing to do with your intellect. Well—that kind of criticism was just offensive.

And now Mom was—maybe—what?

Seeing the guy?

Dating the guy?

Thinking of rekindling some old flame and maybe—gasp—marrying the guy?

And just when I started wondering what I should do, in walks Alonzo Cooper, PhD, Hale's polar opposite in every conceivable way. Not only thriving at the Hale Lab, but succeeding, as in Hale's successor.

Which seemed to suggest that Hale was a changed man, or a changing man, or that if I talked to Mom, warned Mom, said anything negative about him, I could jeopardize a potentially transformative relationship.

And if their relationship was hastening his exit and Cooper's taking of the reins, might I also be jeopardizing the Hale's Lab's entrance into the Twenty First Century?

So my deliberations went: canceled-out arguments that kept me silent—for the time being, at least.

Twenty One

So here I am, standing in the most uncomfortable place imaginable, a room with a growing crowd of people I don't know.

But what a room!

From what I had seen so far, Parada had the most amazing house I'd ever seen, in a part of Seattle called Lower Queen Anne. It was historic, like I like, elegant but spare, spacious but warm, the perfect place to do what we were doing, feting Dr. Marcum for his Abel Prize win and seeing him off with all kinds of things, I'm sure, to tell the President.

The White House was celebrating the winners of all the big science prizes this year: Abel, Nobel, Wolf, Vetlesen, Fields Medal, the Fundamental Physics Prize, MacArthur Genius Grant, the Templeton Prize (which mixes in religion, and is hence controversial), the Breakthrough Prize, the Lasker Award, and of course the Sparks Prize, aka "The Great Alexander," which lavishes recipients with one more dollar than the other prizes—combined.

People I'd seen in the parking garage, elevators, and hallways of the PAB were here, joining the university president and his wife; the Mayor of Seattle; most of the math and physics departments; our team; and plenty of strangers.

"Parada knows half the town, if not all of it," Dr. Levitt said, as I scavenged the nosh pit. I picked up a shrimp lacquered with a delicate orange sauce.

"This is so nice of you guys to do this for Dr. Marcum," I said.

"And likewise," she said.

"Hmm?"

"You'll see." Dr. Levitt smiled and plunged into the crowd.

I navigated toward one of the bars, smiling but trying to avoid eye contact. I'm a hopeless INTP in an office where the only other "I" (for introvert) was probably Dr. Brando.

"INTJ here," I heard a low voice say. I jumped and turned.

"Hey, what? Did I—"

"Just tell me your Myers-Briggs?" Nathaniel Hawthorn smiled. "You find it difficult to introduce yourself to other people," he said. "You often get so lost in thought, you ignore or forget your surroundings. You do not usually initiate conversations."

"I can't believe you overheard me."

"Who were you talking to?"

I looked away. "Who else would an INTP be talking to in a room full of strangers?"

"An INTJ," he said. "Better yet if he's not a stranger."

"You're good," I said. We were at the bar. "What are you having?"

"After you," Nathaniel said.

"Tonic water," I told the bartender.

"Same," Nathaniel said. "With a lemon."

"You don't drink?"

"Not tonight."

"Driving?"

"That's one reason," he said.

A gentle shock crept up the back of my neck.

"How's your mom?"

"Good," I said. "May even have a new guy in her life."

"Really? You know this guy?"

"Yeah." I directed my glass of tonic water toward him. "He's right over there."

"Him?"

I watched Dr. Hale hand his black rain coat to a party staffer.

"Harold Hale," I said. Cool of him to fly out here for our celebration. Maybe he really was mellowing. "I used to work for him. Dr. Levitt used to work with him. And Dr. Cooper works with him now."

"Your mom—" Nathaniel said.

"High school sweethearts."

He jerked his head back and opened his eyes.

"Jennifer." Dr. Brando held up a beer and moved between some people. He swapped the beer with his other hand and shook Nathaniel's hand.

"Our lawyer," Brando said. "Getting used to you guys."

"Doesn't sound good," Nathaniel said.

"Divorce."

"That sucks," Nathaniel said.

"You said you had Lexi the other day," I said.

"Took her to school," Brando said. "I take what I can get."

"How's the custody evaluation going?" I asked.

"Still evaluating."

"No way I'd ever do family law," Nathaniel interjected.

I saw Dr. Cooper, Dr. Shonstein and her husband Martin, and Dr. Marcum shaking hands and photo-opping with cloudcams around the room.

"Can you excuse us?" I said to Brando. I took Nathaniel's wrist. "I might need a lawyer." I led him toward Dr. Hale before co-workers and admirers devoured his attention. Nate almost flew off his feet.

"Whoa!" he said.

"Dr. Hale." I jutted out my hand. He took it. His hand was surprisingly soft. I don't know what I expected. Tough guy, rough hands, though I doubt he worked outside a day in his life.

"Jennifer, right?" he said. "You work for Dr. Levitt."

"With Dr. Levitt," I said. "This is Nathaniel Hawthorn, our IP attorney."

They shook hands. "Saw you at the staff meeting," Hale said.

"So—my mom." I worked up my gumption, always hard in a chattering crowd, but often necessary. "My mom says you two have reconnected?"

"Your mom? Patrice—that's right," he said. "I knew that."

I leaned in so he could hear me better. "She really likes you, I hear."

"I like her." His face softened in a way I hadn't seen before. "Who did you hear that from?"

"My brother."

"And of course, the family wants to be sure you treat her right," Nathaniel broke in. He was grinning so it came across as only half-serious. There's not an astrobio grad student, post-doc, HaleyBop, or ex-HaleyBop on the planet who would have had the courage to say that, let alone me.

"Your mother and I almost got married," Hale said. "We would have, too, if my mother hadn't been so against it."

I leaned way in. "Your mom?" I said.

"Yes."

As always, just when the conversation was getting good, a server appeared. I took an hors d'oeuvre and thanked him. Another server was close behind. Dr. Hale took a glass of champagne.

"It was nothing against Patrice," he said.

"Handle with care," I heard Dr. Shonstein whisper in my ear. She extended her hand to Hale.

"Harold—good to see you again," she said. "My husband, Martin."

"We may have met—AbSciCon, a couple years ago?" Hale said, about the annual astrobiology conference.

"You're from Harvard, right?" Martin said. "Work with Dr. Cooper?"

"Yes. Is he here? We've hardly had any time to talk since he picked me up at the airport."

"Somewhere," Dr. Shonstein said. "If I see—"

Ding, ding, ding. Ding, ding, ding. Someone was ringing a glass. The chatter tapered.

"Welcome," Parada said. "Welcome, everyone. We have a very special guest and a very special announcement. Mar, would you do the honors?"

"Thank you, Par," Dr. Levitt said. "As you all know, a member of our University of Washington team recently made history by becoming one of only a few people to win the two biggest awards in mathematics.

"William Marcum, on generous loan to us from Oxford University, is this year's recipient of the Abel Prize. Five years ago, he won the Fields Medal.

"If it weren't for him, we'd have never gone to Mars or returned with such exci—" She caught herself. "The first humans will step foot on Mars sooner rather than later, thanks to Bill Marcum's beautiful equations."

She motioned him from the crowd and he stood next to her.

"Speech," people said, after the applause.

"Thank you, Marcia. Thank you, everyone," he said. "I'm humbled and honored to be in such incredible company, working for such an amazing team. I'd like to especially thank you and Parada for hosting us tonight in this wonderful abode."

He looked around the room, back and forth, a couple of times. His voice drifted into a rhythmic cadence, part Jamaican, part Marcum, that lent his words a passionate compassion.

He came from nomads, he said, missionary grandparents and foreign service parents whose work took them from Spanish Town, Jamaica around the globe and finally, to London.

"There is nothing more important to the son of nomads than the embrace of strangers, the love of friends, and the feel of home. With that in mind, we have an even more important announcement this evening. If you'll all step back, make some room. 'Small up yuhselves,' as they say in my hometown."

We were gussied and looked amazing. But Parada, at six feet and an inch, was on a different plane. She strode into the center of the room with something in her hand, reached out, took Dr. Levitt's hand, and led her into the center of the room. They stood for a moment, then Parada went down on bended knee.

"Oh my god," I whispered.

"Didn't see this coming." Dr. Cooper was standing behind me now.

"Marcia Levitt," Parada began.

"Louder," I heard someone say.

"Yes," Marcum said. "Bos out!"

Parada seemed uncharacteristically nervous. I couldn't see Dr. Levitt's face, but I gathered from her body language that she felt same.

"Marcia Levitt," Parada said. "Will you marry me?"

My eyes assumed cry posture and I felt my sinuses congest and my face warm. But that's where my emotions got totally confused.

Instead of proclaiming "yes" and leaping into her lover's arms, or coyly grinning between a few profound tears and taking Parada into her arms and accepting the ring with an extended finger and saying "I will," Dr. Levitt just stood.

I moved to the side to look at her face and she looked like I did at my first school play, paralyzed with stage fright, lost in the lights and anticipations.

"Marcia?" Parada said.

That feeling like a sink draining was coming over me, when I'm so mortified for someone else I need to look away. It's so much worse than being embarrassed for yourself because when that happens, you're so caught up in the embarrassing act and how to escape it, you barely have the wherewithal to consider the embarrassment itself.

You can't see yourself, either, like I could see this woman I loved and the woman she loved, whose grace had helped reopen my mother. I started feeling sick.

Just as I heard the first uncomfortable whispers making the rounds of the room, down I went. Nathaniel (mostly) caught me.

As he told me later, Parada darted over, murmuring "I'm a doctor" amidst a Babel of exclaimed concern. Dr. Levitt was over my shoulder and Dr. Cooper and Nathaniel at my head. Dr. Brando leaned down and said "anything I can do?" and Dr. Shonstein picked up the plastic cup I'd dropped, guiding people around the spill on the floor.

The university president's wife gently encouraged people to step back, give Parada some room, she might need CPR. The doctor took my pulse and listened for my breathing and felt my forehead. She put something cool on my face and waited.

I blinked my eyes and gasped and took Parada's arm and heard "she's okay," and "Jennifer," and "she's conscious," from Martin Shonstein. Nathaniel and Dr. Cooper helped raise me and I coughed and Dr. Marcum handed me a cup of water.

"I'm so—I don't know—got hot all of a sudden," and other confused-sounding things. I stood and heard a sort of muted mission control cheer appropriate for dinner parties. Dr. Levitt handed Parada a damp wash cloth and she dabbed my cheeks and forehead.

"You okay?" Parada asked. "An ER visit—"

"No," I said. "No, not necessary. Really. I'm okay. Thank you."

"How 'bout some fresh air?" Nathaniel said. "Would that be okay?" he asked Parada, who nodded.

Nathaniel helped me through the crowd toward the front door, as people placed their hands on my back and smiled encouragingly. I looked back, at the party returning to normal, and felt the heat and congestion recede. I felt a hand on my shoulder as Nathaniel opened the door.

"I hope that wasn't over the thought of me seeing your mom." Dr. Hale's mischievous grin caught me off guard.

"Oh, no," I said. "Room got, uh, really hot. I'm okay."

"Good," he said. He squeezed my shoulder and reflexively, I guess, I reached around and squeezed the top of his hand.

Parada came outside with us. "May I?" she asked. She felt around my head. "When you fell, did you hit your head?"

"I don't think so," I said. "I didn't feel anything."

She looked at my eyes with a pen-light. "You feel tired, or suddenly sleepy, you must get into the ER. We don't want a concussion."

"I'll make sure," Nathaniel said.

"I'm so sorry I screwed up your proposal," I said.

"You didn't," she said. "Not at all. In fact, you might have saved it."

I had taken Ryde—our self-driving taxi-slash-ride-sharing service—to the reception, but Nathaniel Hawthorn, who insists on driving his own car, took me home.

I took his hand. I looked at his eyes as that gentle shock on the back of my neck returned. "Thanks for catching me." I moved toward the elevator but he tightened his grip on my hand. The shock stayed on my neck.

"Thanks for falling," he said. He freed my hand and it was me who watched him depart.

Twenty Two

"FYI, Fw: University of Washington team leads Martian life discovery," read the subject line in Dr. Levitt's email. "Meet in conference room, 1 pm," she ordered, above a press release from Cosmic American "embargoed until 9/14," which meant we had a few days before the story itself went live.

News outlets are usually and exclusively on the receiving end of press releases. But this news was so big, Cosmic American apparently felt it needed to send an embargoed, preemptive, loud-and-clear message to its competitors: "We broke this. It's our scoop. And if our competitors have an ounce of journalistic integrity, their inevitable follow-up stories will read, 'as originally reported in Cosmic American.'"

Good luck with that.

Every space, science, and news clog on our planet had been running this story for months, albeit without the details Molly Cukor unearthed. All the clog coverage had made Crimsy's discovery like a smoldering fire. The embers never ignited and we had lulled ourselves into falsely believing they never would.

I went down the hall, clicked on the conference room lights, and called up the 3D projection from DSG for my morning report. I reviewed the appearance of the two experimental colonies. The green coloring was about the same.

"No discernible change," I noted.

I reviewed the gas concentrations. No increase in oxygen levels down to parts per billion, which meant if Crimsy was becoming photosynthetic, she was keeping that talent under wraps or hadn't developed it enough to show it off.

"YOU'RE NOT GONNA LIKE this," Nathaniel Hawthorn announced at our emergency staff meeting, short Dr. Brando, who was somewhere, and Dr. Marcum, who was on his way to the White House. "But the plan is to deny everything."

I looked right at him, but he avoided eye contact.

"What's in this for us?" Dr. Shonstein said. "We've kept our mouths shut for how long now, and Crimsy is still up there. Now we're supposed to say nothing ever happened?"

"It may be the only hope we have of bringing your discovery home," he said.

"You've said this before," Dr. Cooper said. "Why don't you stop being cryptic and explain what the hell you mean."

"I agree with Coop," Levitt said. "Cut the crap."

"I can't really say anything else," Nathaniel told us. "I'm trying to protect you guys, protect your work. That's what my bosses want. That's what I'm doing."

"Who *are* your bosses?" Shonstein said. "The university? I can't believe they'd support all this fact-fudging."

"Why can't we just refuse to comment, like we've been doing?" Cooper asked.

"At this juncture, refusing to comment is as much as an admission," Hawthorn said. "We call it a 'stipulation' in court."

I was barely out of the conference room and Nathaniel was already stepping aboard the elevator. Dr. Levitt stopped me on the way into the post-doc room.

"You gave us a scare," she said.

"I'm sorry. I felt like I ruined the evening."

"I got the jump on you there," she said. "I'm the one who should be apologizing."

"No worries. I had a great time. I know Dr. Marcum—"

"Poor Bill. I felt so bad. The public proposal was his idea."

"So—are you guys ever gonna tie the knot?"

She raised her eyebrows. "I don't know."

FINGERPRINT, VOICE RECOGNITION, RETINAL scan. I had the whole security thing down and was first on our floor this fine, bright Saturday morning. Dropped into the post-doc office to log the week's Crimsy observations, add some sources to my thesis bibliography, and squeak out another couple pages of scientific prose.

Then down the hall to the conference room, where I clicked on the lights, turned on the projector, and watched the image aboard the space station resolve.

"Holy cow," I said. I looked at the oxygen measurements. "Double holy cow." I texted the team. "A very green Crimsy is producing oxygen!"

And doing all these great things in the second set of cultures, where we were *gradually* changing carbon dioxide and nitrogen, originally in the hyperbaric chamber, but which we had since transferred into Glove Box Three.

Crimsy was growing beyond the agar again, too, making each Petri dish look like a St. Patrick's Day cookie or a wee Leprechaun's front lawn. I wouldn't have predicted this result: both gases were off what we thought was a best match for Earth's atmosphere billions of years ago.

But science is as science does, and what I may have been witnessing was the first scientific evidence that everything we thought we knew about Earth's atmosphere back then was wrong. The first set of cultures in the other glove box looked about the same, even a little pekid, producing methane with no measurable oxygen.

"Pix please!" Dr. Shonstein replied to my announcement.

"Absolutely," Dr. Brando said.

Levitt, Marcum, and Cooper replied with variations and please-look-sees, as I sent images of Crimsy and the oxygen readings via forwarding links randomly generated for security reasons. The links allowed each cell phone to display its own 3D image on any decent projection app.

"This is fantastic," Brando wrote, the first time he seemed truly enthused about his science in months.

"For Mike's a jolly good Fellow,

For Mike's a jolly good Fellow,

For Mike's a jolly good Feeelllow

No Academy can deny."

That was Dr. Marcum from DC, referencing all the scientific academies that would doubtless line up to grant Mike Brando the honorable title "Fellow."

"Brandy, you're a shoo-in," Levitt added.

"For what?" he asked.

"Anything you bloody well want," Marcum texted.

"Congrats, Mike. This is huge!" Cooper.

"Yay Mike. Go Mike. Woot woot!" Shonstein.

I walked over and bent down, staring right at the green cultures in the glove box.

"Hey, Miss Jennifer," Captain Gillory said. "Oh wow. Oh wow!" She moved toward the glove box. "When did this happen?"

"Hang on," I said. "I need to get a pic for posterity."

"Five two seven A B nine four," I said, logging onto the faculty cloudcam.

Then the image vanished.

"What? Captain Gillory?" I said. Texts from my team piled up.

"Link not working."

"Image link no go."

"???"

"*&^%$#!"

"Captain Hightower?" I said. "Commander Ryong, come in please. Deep Space Gateway. Come in please. Over."

But they were gone, too.

BETWEEN DR. LEVITT CALLING everyone she could think of, Dr. Shonstein cursing in Yiddish, and Dr. Brando lambasting the muckety-mucks and their lawyers, the office was chaos for the rest of the day. Only Dr. Cooper seemed calm, even after breaking the news to Dr. Hale. I expressed my admiration.

"I grew up in what you might call a chaotic environment," Cooper told me, raising his eyebrow in a way he had that put the *fine* on a *point*. "Dad always said, 'stay calm, stay alive.'" We ended up talking for an hour about our parents' wisdom, and how long it had taken us to appreciate it.

Dr. Marcum's science prize group was due at the White House tomorrow, and he assured us the President would get an earful about Crimsy's vanishing acts.

"If the Secret Service lets you talk to her long enough," Shonstein said.

Meanwhile, I became the girl who might have cried wolf. "You're sure *Crimsococcus* was green?" Brando said.

"One hundred percent."

"Not greenish?"

"Not greenish," I said.

"And producing oxygen?"

"That's what the readouts said."

"Hey." Dr. Cooper leaned his head into the post-doc office. "My boss wanted me to convey a message." I sat up. "He's visiting your mom."

"He is? I had—nobody's said anything. He say when?"

"With all this excitement, that's all I know."

About "this excitement," Dr. Levitt texted Nathaniel Hawthorn throughout the day. I went home unsure if he'd responded.

I THOUGHT I HEARD someone say "miss" as I walked through the Mallory lobby to my elevator.

"Miss." It was a man's voice, twice.

I turned. A man in a dark suit stood, with another man in another dark suit seated nearby. They looked right at me. I stopped.

"It's Jennifer, right?" standing man said, approaching me. He showed me his ghost card. Paul Malone, Agent, Federal Bureau of Investigation. "ID's on your phone."

Two official-looking, government-stamped identification badges appeared on my cell. The second agent didn't show me a business card and I was too nervous to pay attention to his name. Just Paul Malone.

"We'd like to talk to you, ma'am," said the second agent.

"What about?" I asked.

"Maybe somewhere more private?"

"Shouldn't you tell me what you want to talk to me about?"

"Rather not here," Agent Malone said.

"Where, then?"

"How about your apartment?"

"I'm not in the habit of having strange guys up to my apartment," I said.

"We're not strange guys, ma'am," the second agent said.

"Well, sometimes we are," Agent Malone said.

I wasn't smiling.

"Okay," Malone said. "We understand. We're here about the ISA. We'll be visiting everyone on your team."

"What's the ISA?" I asked.

"The Invention Secrecy Act," Malone said.

"Of 1951," agent two said.

"What's that?" I asked.

"Most people haven't heard of it," Malone said. He looked back at the lobby couches and chairs. "Can we sit?"

I had an idea. "Just a sec," I said. I texted Nathaniel Hawthorn. "We meet? At my place? Half hour or so?"

We sat in the lobby and Malone opened a slender laptop.

"Tied up," Nathaniel wrote back.

"Urgent," I replied. "FBI here."

"Be right there."

I looked at the two agents, spreading out down here in the lobby. Some cramped quarters might mix things up a bit, especially when Nathaniel walked in.

"Can I see your ID's again? Like, hard copies?" I asked. Both agents opened their wallets. I acted like I was looking at every detail. "I guess it's okay."

"What's okay?" Malone said.

"If you guys come up. Might be better. More private."

THEY LOOKED OVER-SIZED IN my cramped apartment, I thought to good effect.

"What's this Invention Secrecy Act have to do with me?" I asked.

"Look on your phone," the second agent said. He sat on the couch. Malone stood near the window.

I saw the download alert and opened the document. "Office of Licensing and Review. US Patent and Trademark Office," I read to myself. "SECRECY ORDER. 35 U.S.C. 181-188. NOTICE: To the applicant, legal representatives of the applicant—"

The patent applicant's name was blacked out. But the "invention" was spelled out in detailed patent-ese: "A microbial life form returned from the planet Mars otherwise known as *Crimsococcus halocryophilus—*"

"The appropriate Government agency has notified the Commissioner for Patents that an affirmative determination has been made by the Government agency, identified below, that the national interest requires this Secrecy ORDER," I continued reading. I glanced at my guests, number two watching me from where he sat on my hide-a-bed couch, Malone standing and looking out the window like a real G-man.

"Whoever shall . . . with knowledge of this ORDER and without due authorization, willfully publish or disclose or authorize or cause to be published or disclosed the INVENTION . . . shall, upon conviction, be fined not more than

$10,000 or imprisoned for not more than two years, or both."

"Consider yourself served," agent two said.

"What's this even supposed to mean?" I asked. "We haven't been allowed to talk about Crimsy since she docked at Deep Space Gateway."

"Who's Crimsy?" Malone asked.

"The *Invention*," I said.

"We don't know anything about that," agent two said. "All we know is that some person or business tried to patent whatever you guys found, and the government agency checked off on that secrecy order thinks a patent could adversely affect national security."

"Which government agency?" I asked. Each one listed on the order—Army, Navy, Air Force, Department of Science, Department of Justice, Department of Defense, Homeland Security, NASA, and Other—had a checked box next to its name.

"Looks like all of 'em," said Malone, looking at his phone. "Haven't seen that before."

"I still don't understand," I said. "Our lawyer said Crimsy was already classified. Top secret or something. Is this why?"

"Couldn't be," agent two said. "We just got that order."

"Don't know what your lawyer's talking about," Malone said, settling in next to his partner on my spring-challenged couch. "The Patent Commissioner doesn't have authority to classify something unless someone tries to patent it first."

"Then who—" My phone vibrated. Nathaniel Hawthorn's bright face greeted me. I buzzed him onto the elevator. "525," I texted. "Down hall to right."

"You were asking," Malone said.

"If Crimsy's not classified, why does anyone care if someone patents her?"

"The patent's the trigger," the second agent said. "The ISA authorizes a secrecy order on any patent application deemed sensitive to national security."

"Maybe Crimsy—is that what you call it— maybe Crimsy is a biohazard," Malone said.

"How?"

"Could be used as a bioweapon. Pandemic portal. Always a big concern."

"How?" I asked. "Crimsy's non-pathogenic."

Door buzzer. Then a firm, old-fashioned knock.

"Ma'am, if that's—"

I opened the door to Nathaniel. He stepped in, gallantly in my opinion. Nothing more dashing than a Seattle man in an Aquascutum trench coat, belt askew, hair mussed. The two men on my couch, their knees riding high, watched him. He stared at them. They sat (sank was more like it); he stood. And while my place was cramped before, it was downright claustrophobic now.

"This is my—our lawyer," I said. "Nathaniel Hawthorn."

"Who—" Nathaniel asked, as Malone leaned forward with his ghost card again.

"Check your phone," the second agent said.

"FBI?" Nathaniel said, looking at the IDs on his cell. "Let

me guess. ISA."

"Just a friendly visit," agent two said. "We have to notify everyone."

"So you knew about this?" I asked.

"Who's applied for a patent?" Nathaniel said.

"Someone," agent two said. "Or some entity. We just served your client a secrecy order which bars her from disclosing any information about the Invention."

"Who applied for a patent?" Nathaniel said.

"We don't have that information," Malone said.

"Sparks? SpaceTek? Someone from the Consortium?"

"No idea."

"We'll challenge it," Nathaniel said boldly. "First Amendment. Fourth Amendment. Unlawful seizure. Wrongful taking."

"We just work here," Malone said. The two agents pushed themselves up from my couch.

Then I remembered Molly Cukor. "It's not gonna matter," I said. "There's a story coming out."

"Not about this," agent two said.

"They've already announced it," I said. "Cosmic American."

"There won't be any stories," Malone said. "You two have a good day." They let themselves out.

"Did you lie to us?" I asked Nathaniel. He walked over and indicated one of my two dining room chairs. I nodded. He sat.

"No," he said. "I predicted." He stood up. "Mind if I take off my coat?"

I held out my hand and he gave it to me. I tossed it on the couch.

"We were trying to head this off," he said. "We predicted, rightly it looks like, that if word got out about what you found, there'd be a patent stampede."

"Who's 'we'?"

"My bosses. ERC. The Executive Research Committee."

"A committee? Who's on it?"

He looked at the wall.

"Who's on it? Don't we have a right to know?"

"Yeah. Okay. You wanna know?"

"You owe us that much."

"Ask Dr. Levitt."

"She knows? I've never heard her mention this committee."

"Why would she?"

"If it's so important that it can direct you to lie to us."

"That's where you and I see things differently. I've been trying to protect you. And since my efforts—ERC's efforts [sounded like irk]—have apparently failed, you and your team could be hopelessly screwed."

"I thought you said you were going to challenge the order."

"And I will. But it could take a year. Years. Meanwhile, you're down here and the thing you're researching is up there. And up there is where it's gonna stay until this is resolved."

I sat in the other dining room chair. "She turned green," I said. "Full-on, photosynthetic, oxygen-making green."

"Hmm?"

"Crimsy is probably the progenitor of all life on Earth."

"What turned green?"

"The cultures. The colonies. Aboard DSG. They were green and we were detecting oxygen, until your Committee or whoever cut us off. Again."

Nathaniel's gaze went blank.

"Cut communication with the space station. Like flipping a switch."

Stayed blank.

"They cut us off. Again."

He came around.

"Don't know anything about that," Nathaniel said. "ERC doesn't control what goes on up there." He stood and retrieved his rain coat. "You hungry?" he said.

I wasn't, but we went to dinner anyway, at a cramped Thai place down the street in the rain.

Twenty Three

The Invention Secrecy Act would have been the only thing we discussed at the weekly faculty meeting, if not for Dr. Marcum's visit with the President and their unusual exchange. Malone and his partner had served the gag order on everyone *but* Marcum, who was making the rounds back East: Washington, then New York, then Boston and the Hale Lab. He was under no legal obligation to keep his mouth shut—yet.

"Don't answer your hotel door for anyone," Shonstein told him on our conference call.

"I feel like a wanted man, furtively darting about, looking over my shoulder," Marcum said. "Bloody hell."

"Just remember: You have plausible deniability until you actually receive the gag order," Shonstein said. "Isn't that what our lawyer said?"

"In so many words," Dr. Levitt said. "Though it's best that none of us violates it regardless."

"I probably already have," Marcum said. "I told the President what a mistake it was, to treat the greatest discovery in scientific history as a state secret."

"What did she say to that?" Dr. Cooper asked.

"Two words: world peace," Marcum replied. "'How can we *ever* share this?' she asked me, hopefully rhetorically."

"What's she talking about?" Brando said. "Can't share this. It replicates, like any bacteria. Plenty to go around."

"She did bring up the Mars rocks," Marcum said. "The fighting at the UN. The sanctions imposed when North Korea wouldn't return the traveling exhibit."

"Which led to a good result," Levitt said. "Commander Kim Ryong."

"Originally a bargaining chip in that diplomatic dust storm, as I recall," Marcum said.

"He played a huge role calming the winds," Levitt said.

I'd heard this story, too. Ryong turned out to be one of NASA's best-ever joint venture gets, a mechanical genius with the mind of a bureaucrat, the heart of a diplomat, and the soul of an entrepreneur. In other words, the very embodiment of contemporary astronautics.

"I can't believe you got to talk to the Prez for so long," Shonstein continued. "Who'd you have to bribe?"

"Where others were shy, I was bold," Marcum said. "She knows all about Miss Crimsy and is not as sympathetic to our cause as we might have expected. But I made sure to be overheard, and have wrangled a couple of extracurricular invitations, including to the National Press Club."

"The National Press Club?" Levitt asked.

"Science journalist covering our event invited me," Marcum said.

"They don't want you to talk, do they?"

"I gather they do."

"About Crimsy?"

"That remains to be seen."

"I don't think that's a good idea," Levitt said.

"Why not, Marcia?" Brando said. "We've been good little boys and girls and where has it gotten us?"

"We've worked damned hard just to see all this end up crated in some secret government warehouse," Cooper said. "I say go for it."

"They're right," Shonstein said. "We said we needed a singular voice, and for all kinds of reasons, Bill might be that voice."

I CAUGHT UP WITH Dr. Levitt in her office after the meeting.

"Jennifer. I've been meaning to meet with you," she said. "I'm sorry this has been so screwed up. But you've been a trooper and I really appreciate it."

"Thank you," I said. "What did you want to meet with me about?"

"Just sort of a check in. I feel like we've been running in a million different directions, putting out fires, dealing with craziness. I just thought . . . And here you are."

"So, I wanted to ask you something. Is this a good time?"

"Absolutely," she said.

I wasn't sure how I was going to put it tactfully, but I'd been tossing it around since Nathaniel Hawthorn hinted that my mentor and adviser might know more than she's been letting on.

"Shoot," she said.

"What's the Executive Research Committee?"

She looked at her desk, then at me.

"It's a group charged with oversight of research projects that involve more than just this institution."

"Are you on it?"

"Yes."

"What does it do?"

"Well—we—it's—ERC supervises inter-institutional research, from planning to implementation. Quality control, ethical considerations, legal issues, politics. That's probably the biggie. Politics."

"Who else is on it?"

"From our project, just me, Dr. Hale, and Davi Chandrasekhar from Cambridge." She pushed back from her desk and leaned back in her chair. "If it weren't for our committee service, Hal and I probably wouldn't be speaking." She moved up to her desk again. "How'd you hear about the ERC?"

"The FBI guys who came to my house. They said Crimsy wasn't classified until now."

"So?"

"Why did Nathaniel Hawthorn tell us it *was* classified, over a month ago?" I beat around the bush in search of tact.

"You'd have to ask him," she said, boxing me in.

If I said I already asked Nathaniel, then she'd ask what he told me, and I'd say he said the Executive Research Committee basically told him to lie about Crimsy being "classified." Which means Dr. Levitt knew about said lie, maybe even had a vote in ordering it, and that by obfuscating now, she perpetuated said lie.

I was pissed. Or was I disappointed? Disappointed and pissed. And hurt. I so wanted to blurt out that I knew we'd been duped for the past month, but my nascent diplomatic side was tactfully asking what I thought such blurting would accomplish. "Getting something off my chest" wasn't good enough. Opening my emotional relief valve wasn't worth the damage pressing the issue might cause.

Nevertheless, I plunged ahead.

"I did ask him," I said.

"Oh?"

"He explained it. And I understood. It was a gambit and it didn't pay off. Someone has still filed for a patent."

"A gambit. That's a good way to put it," she said. "You try things. Sometimes they work. Most times, they fail. You wanna keep everybody in the loop, but unforeseen circumstances prevail."

"Yeah," I said. "Science and politics."

"Science *is* politics," Dr. Levitt said.

Then—I backed down. Wimped out. Left my feelings unspoken for and felt the worse for it. Pretended that I understood why the leaders of our team felt they needed to lie to us.

I didn't feel as badly about *why* I wimped, however. I hadn't done it to "protect my career" so much as I didn't have the heart, guts, whatever to confront Dr. Levitt about her interpretation of what it meant to do the right thing. I had no doubt her intentions were sound. I'd grown up loving the well-intended, even when they failed spectacularly. Whether or not Dr. Marcum's well-intended gambit would succeed or fail—and how spectacularly—we were about to find out. He texted us a note to tune in, as he ascended a podium against a familiar blue backdrop.

"I'd like to thank the National Press Club for—" he began.

"He's *not*—" Dr. Levitt said, walking into Brando's office, where we were gathered around his monitor.

"Looks like it," Shonstein said.

"And here's our attorney now." Levitt took Nathaniel's call. "Yes. Yep. Let me call you back."

Brando cut the lights, leaving us in cloud-filtered Sun through his office window, hallway fluorescence through his door, and the glow of truth from his monitor.

" . . . that as hard as this is to believe, the greatest discovery in scientific history has remained unknown to all but a select group of scientists, bureaucrats, and cloggers for reasons none of us—my team at the University of Washington, specifically—understands," Dr. Marcum continued.

"I can't believe he's doing this," Dr. Shonstein said. "Go Bill!"

"I was asked here to take questions, not make a speech, so if there are any," Marcum said.

The camera panned the room and every hand was up. He

looked to his side, like he was asking someone off stage a question. "Anyone?" I could make out him saying. "So I just pick—" He turned back to the audience. "Yes. The young woman in the turquoise cardigan."

"Can you clarify just exactly what you found?" she asked.

"I can. But first thing to clarify is that it wasn't just me who found it. Not hardly. It was a team of hundreds, from NASA, several universities, the Jet Propulsion Lab, SpaceTek, and a consortium of private investors. Now—what was your question again?"

The audience laughed.

"What did you find?" the reporter asked.

Dr. Marcum looked around the room, it seemed to me feeling the weight of what he was about to announce. This trim, finely-tuned man with the most beautifully-coiffed, defiantly-situated dreadlocks, was about to tell the world we found—

"Life," he said, to audible gasps and then a stirring hush. "We found life."

Hands, noise, clamor. So cool.

"We found life," Marcum said again. "And like all the best science, the life we found is elegantly simple. Not an alien threat. Not a sentient being with the intelligence of a god. Just a simple, archaic bacteria with a fancy-sounding name, *Crimsococcus halocryophilus*. One of my teammates nicknamed it Crimsy, as simple and perfect a name as it gets."

I felt myself blushing and congesting, like I was about to tear up. I glanced at my team mates and could see similar emotions in their faces, feel their feelings in the room: pride, exhaustion, exhilaration, relief.

We watched, gripped, for little over an hour, I think each of us wondering when the FBI or some other shadowy law enforcement agency was going to cut the power, storm the room, and haul Marcum off the stage.

But our worries were for naught. He couldn't have picked a better place to make such a controversial and momentous play. In government quarters, even a church was less sacrosanct than the blue-and-white stage he stood upon. The only question he couldn't answer was: Why the big cover up?

"I have it on good authority that world peace is at issue," he said. We heard the audience chuckle over the hyperbole.

"I am so proud of Bill," Shonstein said. She turned away from the monitor and though the room was dark, I could tell she was, in her lexicon, verklempt.

"I second that," Cooper said. "Good—no, great work, team."

"Marcia?" Brando said.

But I saw her shadow in the hallway, just beyond his door. I stood and peered around. She was on her cell, it sounded like with Nathaniel Hawthorn again.

"WTF?" MOLLY CUKOR EMAILED. "They killed my story and I see Dr. Marcum breaking it at the press club? Unbelievable!"

"I feel your pain," I replied. I was in the post-doc office.

"We all got served gag orders. Marcum would have too, but he's out of town. And probably in serious trouble."

"My editors are seriously reconsidering *their* decision to kill this piece," she emailed back. "It's like our version of the Pentagon Papers. If we don't stand for Free Speech, what the hell *do* we stand for?"

I understood, but from where we sat, Free Speech wasn't an issue. We were employees, functionaries, just like any functionaries at any national lab, "entrusted" with a state secret that could impact national security.

Of course, we considered it all BS, but BS came with the territory. We signed contracts, security clearance permissions, and agreed to all kinds of handcuffs to finance our big expedition. Marcum was exercising his right of Free Speech on a mere technicality. The rest of us would continue groping along in silence.

"You heard from your mom?"

I almost jumped out of my chair.

"Sorry," Dr. Cooper said. "Didn't mean to startle you."

The only thing startling about Alonzo Cooper was how good-looking he was. I sometimes caught myself staring, drifting off between the whys and the wherefores that had come to dominate our faculty meetings. He was one of those guys that's so good looking he's hard to fall for, if that makes sense, which made him the perfect object of my attentiveness when I felt like dozing off or screaming. Dr. Shonstein apparently agreed. She once leaned over and whispered to me when I was staring at him.

"Oh yeah," she said.

"I haven't called Mom," I told Dr. Cooper. "She's on my list."

"After a—what was it, three weeks—visit, you can probably be forgiven."

"You don't know my mother. So, hey: I've got a question for you."

He walked in and sat. "Sounds serious."

"I don't know," I said. "Ever heard of the Executive Research Committee?"

"ERC? Yeah. Hale's on it."

"Has everyone heard of this committee but me?"

"I don't know," he said.

"I heard they oversee all our research."

"Where'd you hear that?"

"Our lawyer."

"I read all those contracts Hawthorn gave us," Cooper said. "ERC's mentioned, but that's about all."

"So they don't have any power? They don't make decisions?"

"I don't know—I mean, maybe. I don't run with the executive crowd. At least, not yet." He paused. "I do seem to recall that ERC had to approve, sign off on, or something about our landing coordinates in Valles Marineris. At least for the return trip. Had to do with the fact that we were bringing back living things."

I thought about what he said. "*Should* you know more

about this committee?" I asked.

"Maybe. But I gotta tell you, a project of this size—I just try to keep my head down and my nose to my own grindstone. It's impossible to keep track of who's doing what all the time. And you know how Hale can be."

"Impossible?" I blurted.

"Oh yeah." He chuckled. "Funny about him and your mom."

"Yeah," I said. "Definitely. So how do you know ERC had to approve where to land the Retriever rocket?"

"As astro-climatologist in chief, I had to review all that. Trickiest part of the entire mission. Never want to go through it again."

True, that. Docking the rover during an earthquake—or more accurately, a marsquake, its own peculiar brand of tectonic shake—was the worst kind of antithesis to the other promise of our project: that soon a first human mission would fly there and return. After what we went through getting off the planet, that prospect looked remote, at least in the near term, probably in the middle term, maybe even in the far term —a decade or more away.

Twenty Four

Life on Mars.
Life found on Red Planet.
Martian microbe makes human history.
Crimsy: Discovery of the Century. *Any* Century.
And those were just the mainstream headlines.

I scrolled through the news sites hovering over my lap in the Cloud, reclining on the post-doc couch, waiting for our weekly meeting. I read the best of breed, the *Cosmic American* piece, "University of Washington Team Discovers Life on Mars," which I'm sure Molly Cukor was delighted to have finally seeing daylight.

And all because of William Marcum, our wonderful loose cannon, wandering unfettered in the land of politics and policy, like a scientific D. B. Cooper, one step ahead of the authorities, but with a far more precious loot. Dr. Marcum was on the fifth day of a two-day excursion. At the invitation (and expense) of the United Nations Office for Outer Space Affairs, he'd flown from Washington to New York for a meeting with the United Nations Committee on the Peaceful Uses of Outer Space.

Alexander Sparks was reportedly furious about something, and Nathaniel Hawthorn was doing figurative somersaults: calling, emailing, popping in for updates, unable to reach Dr. Marcum.

We, however, were able to reach him just fine.

"Still no word from the space station, I presume," Marcum telaparted this morning.

"No," Dr. Levitt said.

"Want to have my facts straight when I make my pitch."

"Of course," Shonstein said. "So, um, what pitch are you making?"

"What do we want?" Marcum asked. "I have some ideas, but—"

"I don't know if you should be making demands," Levitt said. "That's not really our place, is it?"

"Keeping one's place keeps one *in* place," Marcum said.

Dr. Brando walked in with guess who: Lexi!

"Hey," I whispered to her.

"Hey," she said. I motioned her over and hugged her, cheek to cheek.

"What am I missing?" Brando asked.

"Bill is meeting with the U.N.," Shonstein said. "I still can't believe it."

"Your opportunity to take a stand," Marcum said.

Dr. Cooper came in next. "Fight the Man," he added.

"Nice of everyone to be on time today," Levitt said.

"Apologies. Totally," Cooper said. "Hale is heading out of town and he's got me wrapping a grant app."

"Okay—so." Levitt said. "What do we want Bill to say to the United Nations on our behalf?"

"Get Crimsy a green card," Brando said.

"Or at least a temporary worker's visa," Shonstein said.

"An easy, simple ask," Marcum said. "Speaking from experience, of course."

"Demand that they tell us why she's being kept up there," Cooper said.

"What if they say no? Or that they can't help with any of that?" I asked.

"There is no 'no,'" Dr. Shonstein said. "There is only no project, no meaning, a wholesale descent into complete insanity. We need to be done fu—" She looked at Lexi. "Messing around, and stand up for the integrity of our work."

"I'd like to think we haven't been messing around," Levitt said.

"I didn't mean us, per se. More like our lawyer," Shonstein said. "And whomever he answers to. I had such high hopes for him. Where is he, by the way? Isn't he supposed to be here?"

"Scheduling conflict," Dr. Levitt said. "Mine."

"I wish I had the same luxury with my lawyer," Brando said.

"So, it's bring Crimsy back, or here, or to Earth, or some variation on that theme, or—" Marcum said.

"Bring her here, to the Levitt Lab, University of Washington, Department of Astrobiology, Physics-Astronomy Building, Seattle, Washington," Shonstein said. "We'll even spring for postage."

"This all still quasi-legal, right?" Levitt asked. "You've still managed to avoid the cease and desist order muzzling the rest of us?"

"So far," Marcum said. "Fingers crossed."

"Before we wrap, has anyone here *not* seen the Mars sand and rock exhibit?" Levitt asked. "It's opening at the Pacific Science Center."

"I read that, or heard it, or something," Shonstein said. "But I saw it last year in New York."

Cooper saw it too, in Boston. Levitt was part of the *Odysseus* mission that brought the samples back.

"I haven't seen it," Marcum said.

"I haven't seen it, either," I said.

"I need to take Lexi," Brando said.

"Mom wants to take me," Lexi replied.

"It'll be here a while and I have tickets," Levitt said. "Compliments of Alexander Sparks."

DOWN THE HALL, I heard Dr. Levitt tell Dr. Brando something like "it's okay, fine, understand." I also saw Lexi peak out of his office in their direction. It seemed like a good cue.

"Hey, girlfriend," I said, walking up to her.

"Hey," she said. We went into her dad's office. "Wanna go somewhere?"

I wasn't sure what to say. "If it's okay—I guess, I mean, okay with your dad."

"How 'bout even if it's not."

"Hmm," I said.

Dr. Brando walked in. "Good morning again," he said. "I read your abstract, got about twenty pages in." He was referring to the first draft of my dissertation. He looked at me in the most quizzical way. "Wanna know something that really sucks? It's not gonna work, not one page of it, unless *we get Crimsy here*. You need hands on her as much as we do, maybe more."

"I know," I admitted.

Painful truth. I was spinning my wheels. Sure. We all were. But I gathered what Brando was trying to say was that everyone else could move on. They had their doctorates, their reputations, their grants, their titles, their awards and accolades. I had six years work hanging on a microscopic thread. If that thread broke, I had nothing.

"You think about another approach?" he asked.

"How? My diss is our compendium. Our hypothesis. Our tests. Our theories. Our proof."

"Yeah," Brando said. "I get it. Lex—you are witnessing science inaction. Inaction. One word."

"Can Jennifer and I go somewhere?" she asked. "Maybe Gas Works Park?"

Brando looked out the window. "Little drizzly for that, isn't it? Jennifer?"

"I told her it was up to you."

Brando looked at the door. "I wish you could take her down the hall and show her our magnificent find. I've never done that. I can't believe it. We could have come in here over the weekend, whenever. Flip on the projector and voila! Now—too late."

"I'd love to see Crimsy," Lexi said. "Let's do that."

"We can't," I said.

"Why not?"

"They won't let us."

"Who won't let you?"

"We don't know."

Brando laughed. "So absurd."

"So can we, Dad? Go somewhere?"

"Yeah." He caught himself. "Hold it. This is a teacher work day and you don't have any homework?"

"Nope."

"Just a sec." He made a phone call to a woman named Janie —they sounded like friends. And about an hour later, Lexi and I were at the Pacific Science Center staring at their just-arrived traveling exhibit, which wasn't open yet: *The Red Planet: Will Humans One Day Inhabit It?*

Before us was a large round glass-enclosed diorama of sorts. Sand and rocks from the *Odysseus* mission in transparent, hermetically-sealed glass containers helped recreate the planet surface in strategic positions—this kind of rock here, that kind of sand there, complete with miniatures of the various rovers, the Capris Chasma launch pad, and a frozen lake lightly covered with Martian sand.

I looked at the sand and swore I saw individual grains I somehow knew were finer than talc. Finer than any Earthly powder, in fact.

"How's things with your dad?" I asked Lexi.

"Effed up," she said.

"You're with him a lot."

"So's the custody lady."

"She's still evaluating?"

Lexi rolled her eyes. "Yes. Dad says if she weren't, I wouldn't even see him."

"Jennifer." I turned to see a woman in a lab coat with a name tag I read walking toward us. "Lexi." She extended her hand. "Janie Sawyer."

We thanked her for hosting us.

"Your dad and I have known each other since grade school," she told Lexi.

"This is amazing," I said. "I've never seen any of it."

"It's taken this long to get to Seattle," she said. "And it isn't even the *pièce de résistance*," she said. "Come with me."

She led us through a door, down a hallway, and into a room marked Curation Preparation. I saw an empty Styrofoam container marked "Astromaterials Acquisition and Curation, NASA" on the floor. Then I saw *it*, under a glass enclosure on a stainless steel table. We walked up to it: A delicately-layered rock with feathery fans of faded bluish-green in red sandstone.

"A stromatolite?" I said.

"From *Odysseus*."

"But I thought—"

"We've never been allowed to display them," Janie said. "They're here for VIP eyes only."

Lexi looked at the alien fossil. "What is it?" she asked.

"It's a rock formed over billions of years from layers of dead bacteria," I explained.

"From Mars?" Lexi asked.

"From Mars," Sawyer said. "Too bad we only have the fossils, huh?"

Unbelievable. As in, thanks, unidentified muckety mucks. Thanks for getting the dead off the planet, but not the living off the space station, Thanks for lying about it, covering it up, these last few years.

"Is it okay if I tell my team I saw these?" I asked.

"Sure," Janie said. "By the way, we're having our opening gala next Saturday. You're coming right?"

I saw another piece of the planet, more dust, in vials. I walked to it and instinctively, like the lab rat I am, picked up a vial.

"Careful," Sawyer said. "That stuff is nasty. It's so fine, it acts like a gas. But once it gets into your lungs, it doesn't get out like gas."

I carefully put the vial back.

SPEAKING OF THE PROVERBIAL devil, I saw Alexander Sparks entering our elevator with a large man I assumed was a bodyguard. I had the snap thought it'd be fun to catch up with them and ran through the parking garage and landed beside them. Bodyguard guy eyed me.

"Jennifer, isn't it?" Sparks said.

"Yes."

Bodyguard guy leaned into the retina scan, got cleared, and up we went. I looked up at him warily, wondering why *his* biometric features were in our system.

"He couldn't hurt you if he wanted to," Sparks told me. What an odd thing to say. They let me out ahead of them, and seemed to disappear in the vicinity of Dr. Levitt's office.

"CONFIRMS WHAT WE HAVE long suspected," I overheard Dr. Levitt say, in the hallway on my way to the restroom. "Now the question becomes: How do we protect it? We humans aren't exactly the best stewards of endangered species."

"Who said it's endangered?" Sparks asked, at the door to Levitt's office. "Anyone here think it's endangered?"

"Maybe not now," Levitt said. "But if we thought forward contamination was a problem with the rovers, we ain't seen nothing yet."

"If you mean, when we send humans to Mars, I couldn't disagree more," Sparks said.

"That's exactly what I mean," Levitt said.

"We have more than enough technology to prevent such a thing, if you're worried about *that* harmless bug," Sparks said. "What are you calling it? Crimsy?"

And there she stood, Dr. Levitt arguing with the world's richest man. We would all live to see humans on Mars, he insisted. Not if we couldn't prevent forward contamination, she insisted. Environmentalism on Mars. The Endangered *Alien* Species Act.

"We'll send androids. Best of both worlds," Sparks said.

I waited discreetly behind a corner until he and bodyguard guy left.

"Our benefactor had nice things to say about you," Levitt told me a few hours later. "He came by to thank me—us—for not 'feeding the lies' about Crimsy."

"I don't like him," I said.

"Join the club."

"Haven't some of us fed the lie?" I asked. "Nathaniel Hawthorn told me the Executive Research Committee encouraged him to claim Crimsy was classified."

"We never told him any such thing," Dr. Levitt said. She ran her hand through her hair. "Why didn't you tell me this earlier?"

"I didn't think—" I searched for the right words. "I didn't think it was my place."

She put her hand on her hip, all serious like. "You don't have a *place*," she said. "Not when you're part of a team."

"I'm not an equal part," I said.

"You're equal in every way but the degree after your name. But you have to act like it. I know, you're still learning."

I nodded.

"I'll be talking to Mr. Hawthorn about this," Dr. Levitt said. "If he was my lawyer, I'd fire him."

I AWAKENED WITH BEATING in my chest. My heart's raced before, but this didn't feel like what I remembered. I called David.

"You okay? It's four in the morning," he said.

"I don't know."

"You sound out of breath. You been out running at, what is it, two your time?"

"No," I said. "I just wanted to call. Remember when I was in the hospital?"

"Of course."

"I remember Mom. How she handled it. She got all orderly and businesslike."

"That's a good description," David said. He yawned.

"Brian freaked out."

"They didn't expect—" David said.

"I remember you. Steady Eddie. Sitting with me, holding my hand."

"I did?"

"You told me everything was gonna be fine. Doctors said I was going to live."

David didn't say anything. I heard him yawn again. Then a little cough.

"You there?" I said.

"I'm here," he said.

"What's wrong?"

"Nothing, I guess."

"You guess?"

"I don't want to take credit for something I didn't do," he said. "I was the biggest mess of all."

"When I got hurt?"

"Yeah. I couldn't go to the hospital. I mean, for the first over, like a week, they wouldn't allow visitors. Then when Mom told us how you looked, what was broken, I don't know. I just couldn't—"

"You were right there," I said. "Either that, or I was hallucinating on pain meds."

"Had to be the latter," he said. "I was there when you got out, and the one time Mom and Brian came by with a bouquet. But that's"—yawn—"it."

"Wouldn't you know it," I said. "I remember you holding my hand, but I don't remember any flowers."

"They were in the room, I mean, I guess they were. That's where the nurse told us to leave them. She let us come in and personally deliver them. You weren't awake."

I went to my apartment window and looked out at the street. The rain had lifted, leaving the clean wetness that brightens the street lights, glimmers on the asphalt, and cloaks the night in her shadowy finest. A few cars passed.

"I remember Ron being like, totally shocked when he saw me."

"When you went in or when you got out?" David said.

"Day before I got out. He couldn't believe it. He touched my face, my head, took my hands and held them up and looked at them. 'This is unbelievable,' he said. Marjorie and Caroline just stared."

"Docs did great work, Jen. I don't understand Mom hating on them so much."

"Has she seen the neurologist yet?" I asked.

"She has," David said. "But she asked me not to say anything."

"About what?"

"She doesn't know anything, or at least, says she doesn't know anything, and she wants to be the one to tell you if there is anything," he said.

I saw a woman in a long coat walking with an open umbrella across the street. It must have been drizzling. Yes, I could see them now. The finest rain mist drops imperceptible to all but discerning Seattle eyes.

"All right. Okay. I get it," I said. "I need to call her anyway. I've been avoiding it."

"She still slips," David said. "I think it's gotten worse, but it's hard to tell. Sharp as a tack one day, forgets my name the next. Totally lights up about this Hale guy, though. He's coming out next week."

"Thanks for keeping me so well-informed, big brother."

"I don't want to—I know—your plate's pretty full, Jen. I figured you needed a break from Mom drama for a while."

"Steady Eddie," I said. "Even as a hallucination."

Twenty Five

In the media, Dr. Marcum's UN presentation displaced the discovery it referenced. Diplomats from nations with space agencies spoke to the press about the "international deception" of keeping Crimsy on Deep Space Gateway. Diplomats from other member nations condemned their First-World counterparts for the extraterrestrial version of business as usual.

"I regret to say that what has happened with this mission, and the discovery of *Crimsococcus halocryophilus* represents an arrogance we cannot abide," the Cambodian ambassador explained, leaning toward an aide who was whispering in her ear.

"We have an astronaut on that space station," the ambassador from the Democratic People's Republic of Korea— aka North Korea—said to the cameras. "And still, we've received only the sketchiest of details."

"We are awaiting a formal report from the Committee on the Peaceful Uses of Outer Space," the UN Secretary General said, in diplomatic deflection speak. "At that time, we will make further recommendations."

I didn't know what was more exciting: Marcum's bravado

on the world stage, or learning my mother had apparently run off with Dr. Hale (though I think it was more like driving to the airport and flying off, since they were nowhere to be found in Kenosha or Cambridge.)

"I heard," Dr. Cooper told me. "Hal called me."

"Tell me!" I said. "Mom won't answer anything. Where are they?"

"They're fine. She's fine. He's fine. In fact, he hasn't sounded better."

"You have got to be kidding."

"His voice usually has an edge. No edge. No joke."

"Where are they?"

"He wouldn't say, but said you'd be okay with it."

"He mentioned me?"

"And your bro." Cooper paused and smiled. "Hal's a good guy, Jen. If I had to choose a guy for my mom to run away with, Harold Hale would be top of my list."

Quite a recommendation. Reservations about Dr. Hale dispelled again. Still, I wanted to scold my mother for making us worry, just like she scolded me, David, and Brian for staying out too late, not calling, not "keeping your father and I informed of your whereabouts."

Instead, I waved my hand in front of my face to shoo the emotions away.

THE *ODYSSEUS* EXHIBIT OPENED at long last tonight, and I raced around gussying for the gala—if you can call frenetic getting-ready activity in my small apartment a race. It was a tuxedos-and-ties-and-evening-gowns affair complete with red carpet and local paparazzi, on a clear evening where the Sun shown low, befitting and brilliant; Mt. Rainier transcended a cloudless horizon; and the temperature was hovering between warm and cool, a perfect outdoor showcase for suits and capes and frocks and shawls, and gown-framed arms and shoulders.

I spent some time trying to look magnificent, trying to find just the right red accouterments (I settled on earrings and a brooch my grandmother gave me) and before you hate on me for going with Nathaniel Hawthorn, do know everything we were doing these days was in the name of diplomacy.

And I didn't dislike Nathaniel. In fact, much the opposite. He frustrated me. Angered me so much, in fact, that sometimes I wanted to throw a shoe at his head. But this was me in hyperbole-think, forgetting the tightrope I knew he walked to keep more than one master happy.

"Our second social event," he said when I invited him in. "We should celebrate."

"I fainted at the last one," I said.

He looked me up and down. "You look—"

"Magnificent?"

THE EVENT WAS OUTSIDE beneath the science center's five white Arches, in Seattle lore and renown second only to the Space Needle, both built for the 1962 World's Fair. Lighted for events and holidays—St. Patrick's Day green, Halloween orange, Fourth of July red, white, and blue—the Arches, rising one hundred feet, bathed in a dusky crimson tonight, so uncannily like the planet's actual colors I got goosebumps. Wouldn't it be grand if we were announcing the arrival of Crimsy this evening?

Wouldn't it be?

"You'll appreciate this," Nathaniel said. "The same Seattle architect who designed the World Trade Center, designed these arches," he said.

"Minoru Yamasaki," I said. He also designed everything beneath the arches, including the reflecting pools.

"Bet you can't second-guess *this* question," he said. "How long am I gonna live?" We were making our way to the red carpet. "When am I gonna die? What year?"

"I have no idea." I smiled. I've always had a soft spot for nerdy flirting, if indeed that was what this was. I mean, he couldn't be serious, right?

"Take a guess."

"Twenty ninety," I said.

"Wow. Twenty ninety four," he said. "Bummed I'll miss the turn of the century."

"How could you know when you'll die?" I asked.

"DLA test. Deep Learning Algorithm lifespan prediction," he said.

"Right. A test that predicts your lifespan."

"Fill out an online form. Give 'em access to all your medical records, DNA tests, etcetera etcetera," he said. "They give you the year of your death in about two weeks."

So I kissed him. I stopped. I stopped him. I took his face. And I went for it, right there about two meters from the red carpet, in full view of God-knew-who, knowing full well the consequences, and with a lawyer no less.

When I released him, he stood looking at me, lips pursed in the most charming way, confused, off guard, speechless, kinda open, kinda not, like a fish between breaths. Nathaniel was recovering, about to speak, when I took his arm.

"Is that your mom?" he asked.

And then I saw my mother and Dr. Hale. And my brother and a woman I didn't recognize. We marched up to the quartet.

"Mom—what—David—?"

"Jen!" Mom almost leaped into my arms.

"We wanted to surprise you," Dr. Hale said. Dr. Hale. Said this. To me.

"You guys look incredible," I said.

My brother smiled, deferring to his date.

"You know Hal," Mom said. We shook. He actually pulled me in for a gentle hug.

"Jeri—my lovely sister, Jennifer. Jennifer, my lovely date Jeri," David said.

We did the cheek-to-cheek thing.

"I teach with David," she said.

"Nathaniel Hawthorn," I said to everyone. "*My* dashing date."

"We've met," Mom said, taking his hand. "And I agree."

"David kinda sprung this on me," Jeri said.

"I took a well-earned liberty," David said.

"I am so thrilled to be here," Jeri said. "David talks about you all the time."

I kissed my brother's cheek, glanced over at my mother. She looked so good. So fit, bright, happy.

"Thank you," I said to Dr. Hale.

We stepped onto the red carpet, our place in a line of formally—and some outlandishly—attired guests, each with his or her own version of a crimson accessory or elegant, Martian-themed cosplay (that incorporated more than a little green). The traditional men stuck with red handkerchiefs peaking over pockets or green vests and ties; the women with red gowns, scarves, and jewels. I saw more than a few rubies I knew were genuine. The emeralds were fewer, but larger and just as real. Discreet security guards that reminded of Secret Service agents stood watch at key spots.

I turned and saw Dr. Levitt and Parada, several people down the line. Dr. Levitt extended her hand to greet someone, and all I could see was her arm. I saw all of Parada. I think every eye was upon her. She must have been six four in heels.

"Miss?" A TV reporter with a camera-mic. "Do you have a second?"

Before I could answer, she stuck it in my face. Nathaniel put his palm up to nudge it away, but I looked at him then back at her, and he lowered his hand.

"Isn't this thrilling?" she said.

"It is," I said.

She pulled us aside. "Everyone thought we'd never be able to bring anything back from Mars," she said.

"That was before my time," I said. "My team always knew we could."

"Your team?"

Nathaniel squeezed my arm suggestively.

"Yep," I said. "University of Washington."

"Are you—are you part of the group that found Crimsy?"

"I don't know—" Nathaniel interjected.

I deferred to him. I wanted to talk, but not disrespect him.

"She is," he said finally.

She lowered the camera-microphone. "You have a huge fan here," she said. Then she raised it again. "Can you tell us—will Crimsy be here tonight? Is it some big surprise reveal?"

"Uh, no," I said. "She's still aboard the space station."

"We're working on that," Nathaniel said.

I saw Molly Cukor. We waved to each other. She came over.

"Hey—fancy meeting you here," she said.

"This is Molly Cukor, who wrote the best story about Crimsy," I told the reporter.

"Really?"

We excused ourselves, stopped for a photo-op against a backdrop branded with SpaceTek and several companies Alexander Sparks owns, then made our way around servers with drinks and nosh and through the hubbub to the center of the event.

"Thanks for taking my cues," Nathaniel said.

"Sorry about earlier," I said.

"Earlier?"

"You know."

"The kiss?" he asked.

"Yes."

"I'm not," he said.

Someone tapped a wine glass, quaint when accessing a cloud speaker would have silenced the crowd immediately. Ding, ding, ding. Talk, talk, talk. Ding, ding, ding. Chatter, ruckus, shuffling, coughing, less chatter, lower voices. Ding, ding, ding. A few coughs, then silence. I looked around. I couldn't see any of my team. It was standing room only out here.

Janie Sawyer stood on a chair.

"Welcome to the Pacific Science Center's—"

The microphone wasn't working.

"Use the Cloud," someone called out from audience.

"Welcome to the Pacific Science Center's opening night reception," Sawyer said with cloudspeaker amplification and resounding applause. "We've all been hearing about the discovery of life on Mars. Eight years ago, humanity began that amazing journey with an amazing feat: *Odysseus* brought back rocks and sand."

Definite applause line. Would've been better with "and stromatolites."

"The *Odysseus* mission paved the way for MarsMicro, which as we have all recently but belatedly learned . . . "

Laughter. They got it. ". . . discovered a simple, harmless bacteria—a germ, basically—living deep beneath the ice, where the water wasn't frozen."

More applause.

"Living!" Janie exclaimed. "Although Crimsy—that's the germ's official nickname—can't be with us this evening, a part of her planet is. The Pacific Science Center is proud to present 'The Red Planet: Will Humans One Day Inhabit It?,' the maiden leg of a West Coast exhibition."

Thunderous applause.

"I'm proud to introduce the exhibit's chief sponsors," Alexander Sparks (knew him); a high-ranking NASA official; and "Leonardo Telos, the founder and chief executive officer of SpaceTek."

Leon Telos? The world's third (or was it second) trillionaire *never* appears in public. I tugged Nathaniel to get us through the crowd so we could see him, an appearance almost as historical as the exhibit itself.

Sparks stood, but not on the chair.

"I'd like to give a round of applause to the scientist behind tonight's exhibit, Dr. Marcia Levitt," Sparks told the crowd. "Marcia, if you're out there—"

"Here," Parada said, holding up Dr. Levitt's hand.

"If it weren't for Marcia's persistence, persuasiveness, and uncanny ability to predict what else we were about to find . . ."

Laughter, applause, woots.

" . . . NASA, Leon, and I would have been hopelessly lost . . . in . . . space," Sparks said.

A few laughs, probably polite laughs. He needed more enthusiasm.

"I'd like to turn the dais over to our official government sponsor," Sparks concluded.

The NASA official, a forty-something woman, spoke highly of the DSG crew, JPL, our team, and the world community gathered for MarsMicro. "If it weren't for *Odysseus*, MarsMicro would never have materialized," she said. "*Odysseus* galvanized the world, bringing back small parts of the planet surface."

And an actual fossil, made of bacteria. *You will be the first people to view that fossil, known as a 'stromatolite,' this evening.* Yeah, right. Fat chance. In my dreams.

"Now I'd like to turn the evening over to another very special guest, SpaceTek founder and aerospace engineering genius Leon Telos."

The applause died down, as everyone watched in wonder, curiosity, and awe as the notoriously-reclusive Telos—stood on a chair.

"Like an old-timey stump speech," Nathaniel said, capturing the glam-but-quaint feel I really liked. I figure Janie Sawyer could have had her choice of over-the-top stagings, but instead settled for intimate simplicity.

"Dr. Levitt," Telos opened, scanning the crowd. "Would you do me the honor?"

He extended his hand. The crowd parted, Nathaniel and I stepping aside with it, as my boss and mentor walked to center stage.

"I am sure Dr. Levitt has a lot of people she'd like to thank this evening, and some things she'd like to say," Telos said. "So I give you now, Marcia Levitt."

I raised my hands overhead and beat them together and cheered. Nathaniel clapped and whistled. I was shaking, so excited.

"Hey everybody. Good evening," Dr. Levitt said.

"Speakers," came the replies. "Louder."

"Good evening," she repeated, with the cloudspeakers engaged. "Mr. Telos is right. I do have a lot of people to thank, starting with—Leon Telos." She paused for applause throughout. "And Alexander Sparks. And NASA and the wonderful engineers at the Jet Propulsion Laboratory. The crew of the Deep Space Gateway space station has been enormously supportive and helpful. They've given ingenuity a whole new meaning. So Kim Ryong, Rhonda Gillory, Rob Hightower: a huge shout-out from planet Earth.

"But most of all, I want to thank my amazing team and their families, the greatest group of people a simple scientist like me could ever hope to work with. They're almost all in the audience, so please raise your hand or hands so I can point you out."

She went down the list, starting with Dr. Rebecca Shonstein, "our bacteriologist," Harold Hale, "one of my mentors and a key supporter," and ending with "Dr. William Marcum—"

The crowd burst into spontaneous applause and cheers. It was unseemly, but in a good way.

"I see you've heard of Bill Marcum," Levitt said. "As you all probably know, he's been unavoidably detained—by the United Nations." Bada bing! "If it weren't for Bill, for his courage, his willingness to stick his neck out in the name of science and truth, we might never know about the next discovery I sincerely hope arrives here soon. Her name is *Crimsococcus halocryophilus*, Crimsy for short." Dr. Levitt scanned the crowd. "And I would really love it if the young woman who made up that wonderful nickname would say a few words."

Her smiling eyes settled on me. "Jennifer," she said, waving me up. Nathaniel whispered "go for it," intimately close to my ear.

The crowd parted. I took a good look at Leon Telos, knowing I'd probably never see him again. We shook hands. Janie Sawyer whispered "nice to see you again," and I ascended the chair.

"Three four seven one five." I whispered my cloudspeaker password. And when I looked at the sea of eager faces, I froze. No, no, no, no, no. Don't do this to me. Heart and soul, don't fail me now.

Then I heard a soft, encouraging voice.

"You'll be fine, Jennifer. Just phase out the visuals and tell them what we're thinking."

I . . . who was this? I recognized the voice, but . . . .

"About going to Mars."

Sparks. I looked down and saw his lips moving. But how

could I hear him up here? Another hallucination, like the one about David at the hospital?

"About what Crimsy proves," the voice said. I mean, Sparks said. Or maybe the auditory hallucination said.

"Good evening," I began. "Thank you all for being here." I remembered a shout-out to my family. My mom waved. I thanked Nathaniel Hawthorn for his legal guidance, something Dr. Levitt forgot (probably deliberately). But I figured she wouldn't mind. Then I talked about my "terrific team" and what an incredible experience I'd had. Dr. Levitt hired me only six months after an accident that almost killed me. I didn't get into that, but did say I was grateful for the opportunity "in more ways than you will ever know."

"People on Mars," I heard the voice say. "Humans to Mars."

I didn't get the voice. There was no way it could have been Sparks, and I wasn't prepared to address the much vaster issue of humans on Mars during a talk about dust and rocks and bacteria.

So I talked about the humans I knew already in space: Captain Gillory, Captain Hightower, and Flight Engineer Ryong.

"We need to get Crimsy home," I concluded. "Her new home. Otherwise, everything will be a total waste."

I caught a glimpse of Sparks as I stepped down from the chair. He looked away. I bumped into him—literally—on the way to the restroom inside the lobby.

"Wow," he said, stepping back. "You pack quite a punch, Jennifer."

We shook hands, I think for the third time now. I glanced around, surprised to see him alone. No bodyguards. No entourage. Just this man who was about an inch shorter than I am. Awkward, that.

"Are you in a hurry?"

"No," I said.

He smiled. We stood there in the lobby.

"I was surprised nobody spoke about humans on Mars," Sparks said. "Don't you think that's important?"

"Of course," I said. "I used to tell my little brother we'd fly to Mars together someday."

"I know," he said.

"You do?"

"I try to keep up with my invest—people."

A couple walked behind us and stared at Sparks. The woman smiled.

"I don't think there's a more important human endeavor," he said. "Not at this juncture of human history, anyway."

A man swooped in and grabbed Sparks' shoulders affectionately and smiled. "Alex." He flashed a thumbs up. Sparks barely acknowledged him.

"I'd settle for getting Crimsy home," I said.

"Mars *is* home," he said.

"I realize that—"

"It could be home for all of us," he continued, in a soft, cajoling tone. "Someday. Imagine that. Look around you. What do we have here?"

I couldn't tell if he was angry, sad, ironic, or psycho. I wanted to respond—I mean, Earth *is* pretty messed up. The Cloud, Big Brother, so many people barely getting by while we spend billions testing nukes on the Moon.

"How many more coastal cities do we have to lose?" Sparks asked. "We're on life support, Jennifer. I was disappointed no one bothered to acknowledge that."

I clasped my hands and fidgeted. Had he actually been talking to me while I was standing on the chair?

More people came and went. I tried to resist a giggle when I saw a strand of toilet paper trailing behind a high heel. She must have caught a glimpse of it because she stopped, raised her foot, took it off, looked around furtively, stuffed it into her jewel-encrusted handbag, and headed back to the gala.

"I probably should get back. My date—" I said.

"Leon doesn't think we should go to Mars," Sparks said. "Doesn't think we're ready. Doesn't think humans can handle it." He looked at me, bored his eyes into me actually. "Why didn't you say anything? I asked you to. I know you heard me."

Okay. Time for me to slip away. "Mr. Sparks, I really appreciate your—"

I moved, but he blocked me. Subtly, but he blocked me.

"Appreciate this," he said. "I made you. And I'm still making you."

"We are all very grateful for your financial support," I said. Diplomacy, diplomacy. "Everyone knows we couldn't have done this without you."

"Why you? Why do you think *you* were selected for this team? Some flyover-country bumpkin."

I raised my hand and grabbed his arm and gently squeezed.

"Would you please get out of my way?" I said. I could tell my grip was starting to hurt.

"Let me go," he said. "You'll tear it off."

My hand unsnapped. He stepped aside and I walked passed him. My face was hot. But I gathered myself and moved through the crowd until I found Dr. Shonstein and Martin and Dr. Brando and Lexi, dressed in the cutest red dress I've ever seen.

MOM AND DR. HALE met David and Jeri and I for breakfast the morning after the Red Planet gala. I wondered if they were planning "the big announcement." Dr. Hale took Mom's hand when she spoke.

"This is hard to say, hard to put into words," Mom said, after we bantered about last night and things in Kenosha and David's new lady. "I did see a doctor, a neurologist. And he thinks I could have Alzheimer's, the early onset variety, but isn't sure. It could be something else."

"Oh, Mom." I felt a terrible pang in my stomach and my body got cold. David took my hand.

"I wanted to tell you here," Mom continued, "away from home. Maybe it feels—less real, that way."

"I'm . . . I'm—" I teared up, and she placed her palm on the top of my hand.

"Your mom and I aren't planning on letting this slow us down," Dr. Hale said. "We're gonna do what we planned to do in high school."

"You're getting married?" David said.

"We are," Hale said. Mom smiled and looked up at him. I teared up a lot.

"Jennifer," Mom said.

"It's okay," I said. "I'm smiling too."

"They have amazing medicines these days," Hale said. "So, if it's true—"

I didn't know what to say, how to feel. Terrible disease, great meds, they're getting married, Mom happy, Hale my father-in-law.

"How's Ron taking all this?" I asked.

"Better," Mom said. "Really, better than I thought he would. He takes great comfort in the idea that I'm under a doctor's care. He likes Hal, too."

"Maybe he likes me," Dr. Hale said. "I still haven't quite figured him out."

"What's this all gonna look like?" David asked. "After you guys get hitched."

"Travel," Mom said. "Coming and going from Kenosha and Cambridge."

"I've got to get MarsMicro finished. I'd been thinking about retiring, or at least cutting back," Hale said. "Can't do any of that yet."

"I thought I detected some rivalry between the two guys that financed everything—Sparks and—" David couldn't think of the name.

"Telos," I said.

"Could that be part of what's screwing things up?"

"Hard to tell," Hale said. "Telos and Sparks are so intertwined, it's hard to separate them sometimes. Telos is the hardware guy; Sparks is the software guy. Telos builds the space ships; Sparks designs the AI. The operating systems. They both have a lot of power, but I give Sparks a slight edge."

"They didn't seem to much like each other," Mom said. "Why do they work together?"

"Money," David said. "Money and power."

"They're beyond that now," Hale said. "They're legacy building. What people like them do when they finally realize they're not immortal."

"So when's the big date?" David asked.

Mom looked at Hale. "We haven't set one," she said.

WE WERE SAYING OUR so-long, farewells when David and I hugged next to his rental car, another self-driving Flyby.

"What do you think of that thing?" I said about the car, trying to take my mind off Mom.

"Not bad," he said. "Mom recommended it."

On hearing her name, I pulled David close and buried my face in his shoulder.

Twenty Six

Dr. Marcum made his triumphant return, old-fashioned paper gag order in hand, on the same Monday Dr. Brando kidnapped Lexi, old-fashioned paper custody order in hand.

It was going to be one of those weeks.

"Found it on my door," Marcum told us after he stuck his head into the first floor faculty lounge, accepting hugs, fist bumps, and handshakes.

"Guess they gave up," Dr. Shonstein said. "Hawthorn told us it meant nothing unless they personally served it."

"They may still try," Dr. Marcum said. "I'm keeping a low profile."

Marcum timed his return right after the UN Security Council's majority resolution—that every member nation, every nation on Earth, in fact, had a new right: A fair share of "scientific discoveries which promise to impact, either positively or negatively, planet Earth and the life upon it."

Wasn't hard to gauge Crimsy's impact. What *was* hard was defining "fair share." The United States, one of ten permanent members of the UN Security Council, voted against the resolution, thereby putting it in limbo until the United Nations

General Assembly—every member nation—could vote on it. The term "compromise" was floating around meanwhile, as member states continued expressing outrage and disbelief the American Ambassador admonished "not turn into saber rattling."

Dr. Brando timed his decision to kidnap—or rather, dadnap, Lexi—after my mother, in sweet ignorance, invited them to Kenosha "any time you'd like, to stay as long you like."

"This is such . . . crap," he exclaimed, throwing the custody order across his office. I stood at his door and I don't think he saw me at first.

"Hey," he said. "Can you close that?"

I started to, backing out.

"No. Stay."

I walked in and closed the door behind me.

"They're taking her away from me, Jen." His voice started cracking. "They're taking her away."

I didn't know what to do, what to say. I just stood there.

"I'm not gonna let 'em do it. I'm not."

I got a little closer. "What happened?"

"You tell me. You saw her. You saw us." He could tell I wasn't comprehending. "The custody evaluator. Based on her report, the Court Commissioner found it 'in the best interest of the minor child that sole custody be granted to the mother,' one Melissa Mills-Brando. She never hyphenated before."

"I can't believe they'd do that," I said. "On what grounds?"

"As asinine as this sounds, the way I read the report, it's mainly because I live too much like a bachelor. Which I just happened to be."

"You're a fantastic dad. Didn't that lady talk to anyone?"

"Melissa. Our group, here. My neighbors."

"They like you."

"Yeah, but Mrs. McFall made the unforgivable mistake, apparently, of telling Penelope about all the people who come to my door with papers to serve. Except for our government-issue gag order, most of the papers come from Melissa." He sat at his desk. "Made it sound like I'm some kinda dead beat."

"None of this sounds like any reason to take Lexi away," I said.

"It's not about reason," he said. "It's about money and the power money buys. Melissa makes great money. Her family is rich. They have the best lawyers with the best connections money can buy."

I pulled up a chair. "You think they paid off the judge?"

"Who knows?" He paused. "We can't have anything anymore. Our children don't belong to us. Our privacy doesn't belong to us. Our identities don't belong to us. Our careers, our reputations, our memories—they all belong to someone else." He spun in his chair. "I'm not letting it happen."

Back to that again. "Your lawyers can't stop it?"

"Lexi and I are leaving."

"Mike—I mean, Dr.—"

"What else am I supposed to do?" He thrummed his fingers on his desk.

"You can't kidnap her. You'll be in all kinds of trouble."

"What do I have to lose? They put me in prison? Like I'm not in prison already?"

I placed my palm over the top of his right hand and squeezed.

"You can't kidnap her," I said. I heard an odd noise, like quick inhaling. It didn't register that it was Dr. Brando until I saw him grimace, like he was having a heart attack. I pushed the chair back and stood. "Are you okay?"

He relaxed and rubbed his right hand.

"You okay?"

He rubbed his wrist, too. "It's—I'm fine."

"Please don't kidnap Lexi."

"Your mom said we could stay with her. Til the dust clears."

"Mom would never go along with something like this."

"She doesn't know," he said.

"Then you need to tell her."

He looked away, dodging the question.

"If you don't tell her, I will."

"You'd betray me, too."

"It's not a betrayal. I don't want my mother involved." Then something I didn't regret at the moment but knew I probably would. "You guys can stay with me. Til the dust clears."

"**FACULTY MEETING AGENDA:** My Favorite Marcum! The return of—audio? Jennifer's Close Encounter. Some important news from our attorney."

I'd asked for a few minutes to tell the team about my unusual meeting with Alexander Sparks. I mentioned it to

Nathaniel, without going into detail, on the way home from our gala date night, from which he politely, with a sweet-but-shallow kiss on the lips, delivered me to my door. The "return of audio" was evident the minute we took our seats.

"Boo!" Everybody jumped. Captain Hightower snickered from somewhere in the Cloud. "That was Ryong's idea," he said. "You guys miss us?"

"Absolutely," Dr. Cooper said. "So where are you? Home? Back here with Crimsy?"

"Not quite," Captain Gillory said. "We were told to be at this meeting."

"How is fair Crimsy?" Dr. Marcum asked.

"Growing like a weed," Gillory said. "The new strain, if that's what you'd call it, does quite nicely in our artificial air."

"You mean, no more controlled containment?" Brando asked.

"You got it," Hightower said.

Dr. Shonstein smiled giddily. "Yippee!" she said. "Brandy, you were right. You were right!"

"All signs point to *Crimsococcus halocryophilus* being the First Universal Common Ancestor," Gillory said. "Of course, nothing can be confirmed until you have her there."

"Major, major congratulations," Dr. Levitt said to Brando. "And not only major congrats, but also welcome back, Bill Marcum."

"Good to be back," he said.

We had a round of applause and everyone, except Marcum, stood. It was sweet, looking down at him smiling and a little weepy-eyed and hearing the space station crew cheer on audio.

"Total ballsy move. Loved it," Shonstein said after we sat back down.

"Jennifer has asked for a couple minutes," Dr. Levitt said. All eyes turned to me.

"So I had a strange encounter with Alexander Sparks at the Red Planet gala," I began.

"Strange and Alexander Sparks in the same sentence?" Shonstein said. "Tell me it ain't so."

"He cornered me. He was bummed nobody brought up sending humans to Mars. He thought it should have been our focus. Like *Odysseus* and Crimsy were just . . . preliminaries."

"So we can't get a microbe from Mars to Earth, but we're ready to send humans from Earth to Mars?" Dr. Cooper said. "That's some logic."

"Ain't it though," Hightower said from the space station. "And Sparks, if you're out there listening, I didn't mean it, buddy."

"Did he say anything about our present dilemma?" Levitt asked.

"Well . . . I mean, honestly—he sounded like he didn't really want Crimsy here," I said. "Something about Mars being home."

"I know he wants to be the guy who got us there," Marcum said. "Us humans."

He pulled up a Cosmic American article in the Cloud. "The Red King's Dream." It showed Sparks, standing as tall as he could, arms folded, before a backdrop of Mars. I read the subtitle: "Alexander Sparks' Final Frontier. By Molly Cukor."

Interesting.

"How much real control does he have over this mission?" Cooper asked. He looked around the table. "Anyone know?"

"Dr. Hale said he made all the software. The artificial intelligence," I said. "Telos made all the hardware."

"Our onboard computer software is all Sparksware," Hightower said. "It's cloud-based, and since he controls the Cloud—"

"Funny," Levitt said. "How you think of an investment as money when it's also stuff."

"So could *he* be the one hampering our ability to get Crimsy here?" Brando asked. "Is that possible?"

Nathaniel Hawthorn rapped on the door frame. Dr. Levitt waved him in.

"Good morning, everyone," he said.

"Long time, no see," Captain Hightower said. "Still no see."

"I see," Nathaniel said. "Hopefully, we're getting close to remedying all that." He stood straight, took a breath, and smiled at Dr. Marcum. "Welcome back." They shook hands.

"Glad to be back."

"You've made work for me," Nathaniel said.

"For which you are happily well-compensated, I presume," Marcum said.

"Keep hoping," Nathaniel said. He was in a mood today.

"Anyway, I come with an interesting proposition. It may seem outlandish at first. But our hope—my bosses, NASA, the US government, and so forth—is that we can work something out."

He took another deep breath.

"Would anyone here be amenable to working on the space station?"

Eyes went around the table.

"Rhonda—" Levitt said.

"Captain Gillory knows all about it. Same, Captain Hightower. And Commander Ryong," Nathaniel said.

"I'm not clear what you're asking," Levitt said. "That one of us, what—go up there and, do what, exactly?"

"Work on your discovery," Nathaniel said. "Do your tests. Do what you've been wanting to do down here."

"If it were that easy, we'd have set it up before the mission," Shonstein said.

"It would be temporary," Nathaniel said. "Just until we can resolve the ins and outs of getting Crimsy Earth bound."

"What ins and outs?" Brando asked.

"That's what none of us understands," Shonstein said. "Why all the nonsense? Crimsy is not pathogenic. There's no reason any of us can fathom why she's still up there."

"I'm just presenting what I was asked to present," Nathaniel said.

Dr. Levitt cleared her throat and leaned forward. "I think you owe us better than this," she said. "You say you represent us, but every time you come here, you represent them, whoever them is."

"Here, here," said Dr. Marcum.

Nathaniel straightened his posture, almost like he was rearing up.

"Why don't you go?" he said to her. "Step up. If I'm so ineffective—"

"We don't need to go there," Levitt responded. "None of us are astronauts. Honestly, this sounds like a stupid idea."

"Actually—it's not," Hightower said. "We're short one crew member, maybe by design, wink, wink. Someone who's reasonably fit, not tied down to family—so single, probably."

"You need to come up here and see this thing," Gillory said. "It's gonna blow your mind."

Everyone sort of looked at their hands, around, uncomfortable.

"By 'you,' she means someone on the team," Hightower said. "Our appreciation for all this is very high, but it can't match yours. So I agree. You need to get up here and see this thing."

Our eyes darted around the table.

"Don't look at me," Shonstein said. "I have a very demanding child at home. And Malachi, too."

"I might be able to do it," Cooper said. "If Jennifer hadn't brought her mom here, which set off a chain reaction that now has me running the Hale Lab."

We chuckled at these good-natured remarks, but the implication was clear as we went around the room. Marcum was "a significant means of support for some of my family back in Jamaica." Brando—no way. Levitt ran the show ("besides, Parada would kill me"). Which left—.

"No," Levitt said. "Out of the question. Too risky, too much liability, way beyond my pay grade. If anything happened to Jennifer or anyone else, I—Jesus, I can't believe we're even discussing this."

"Shouldn't this be Jennifer's call?" Shonstein said.

"No," Levitt replied. "It shouldn't."

Twenty Seven

L ike everyone for ages, I "grew up" with boxes—boxes that broadcast radio, television, Web pages, email, texts, even the Cloud before Alexander Sparks "liberated" it. I was coming to think of the Sparks/Telos rivalry as software battling hardware, brains against brawn, ethereal subverting corporeal, box versus out-of-the-box.

"I still can't get used to watching TV on nothing," Mom said when we watched Antiques Road Show during her visit.

But with the exception of cell phones, for when we wanted a rare modicum of privacy, and paper-thin pads when we felt the urge to touch and hold the written word, the ether was everywhere and "nothing" was everything. Classic movies like *One Flew Over the Cuckoo's Nest* I used to watch on a digital monitor were on CloudCast or SkyFlick or Trimensional now, playing out on a vivid, three-dimensional, hi-def hologram— aka a cloudscreen that formed next to the furniture every time we said "on TV".

McMurphy, *Cuckoo's* hero, was positioning the Chief—his six foot, nine inch ally—for a basketball game between the patients and the orderlies.

"All right, let's have a little ball from you nuts in here," he said. "Here" was an old-school insane asylum, a cuckoo's nest, where brawn triumphs by killing brain.

I heard voices and rustling outside my door. Dr. Brando and Lexi appeared at the lower right of my cloudscreen. "Pause film," I said, and opened the door before they rang.

"Jennifer," Dr. Brando said.

"Come in. Come in."

They entered with luggage. I grabbed the last bag outside the door.

"More in the car," Brando said. "Don't need it."

"You're really doing this."

"Yes," he said.

Lexi looked downcast.

"She's a little sad," her dad said.

"I totally get it," I said.

"I like to think it's because she left her cat, but, you know —"

"You have a kitty?" I asked. "I'd love to have one, but they're not allowed here. What's his name?"

"It's a her," Lexi said. "Galico."

"Cool. I take it she's a calico."

"A galactic calico," Lexi said.

"A feline Galileo," Brando said.

She almost smiled.

"Has there ever been a cat in space?" Brando asked.

"Félicette, Dad," Lexi said. "You know that."

"What a ball club," Brando said, looking at McMurphy and his team, frozen mid-basket.

"So, what are you guys doing for money?" I asked.

"Have my own accounts. Separate. Set 'em up a year ago."

"School?"

"Home schooling. Where would you like us?" he asked.

"I've got air mattresses. Bags—over there, along the wall."

He came up to me and spoke softly. "Jennifer, I—You don't need to do this. It might even be better—" I took him around to the kitchen.

"Lex," I said to her, peering around the narrow wall. "Make yourself at home." I turned to her dad. "I hope you'll be here a while and reconsider. Does your wife know?"

"She'll know when she gets home and Lexi doesn't," he said. "I left a detailed note. I don't want her to worry."

"You kidnapped her—your—child," I said, keeping my voice way low. "She's not gonna worry?"

"It's known as 'custodial interference'," he said. "First or second degree. First degree is a felony."

"And I'm aiding and abetting."

"Not if you don't know about it. Anyone asks, we're just visiting." He stopped and looked around in obvious frustration. "You don't need to do this. We can stay at a hotel. I've got friends."

I stood there looking at him and thinking what to say.

"I can't not do this, Mike," I said.

"You threw the goddamn ball into the fence. Christ almighty!" McMurphy was yelling at his team, dribbling and passing on my living room hardwoods again.

"Lex, no way. Can't watch that," Brando said.

"Dad!"

"It's too old for you."

"Defense. For Chrissake!" McMurphy cried. "Yeah, baby! Put it in. Put it in."

The Chief made a basket and turned the tide and as he strutted across the court, I turned it off. I dragged out the air mattresses and of course the pump didn't work. Brando took a mattress; Lexi and I took the other. She huffed and puffed then handed it to me, winded. I took a couple deep breaths and forced it in and the mattress rose firm. Brando's mattress was slumping.

"Christ almighty," he said, staring at me.

"Used to swim," I said.

I made microwave popcorn and Lexi and I cuddled on the couch watching something harmless and forgettable. She zoned out against me and Brando moved her to the mattress and covered her. I almost overslept.

THE ASTROBIO 115 CLASS was joining the 500-level grad seminar our group team-taught in Sparks Hall, for a presentation this morning by none other than Mike Brando. Until now, only Dr. Levitt and I knew for sure what was going on with him. In a departure from office norms, however, Dr. Levitt did *not* want to hear about his temporary accommodations, only that everything was kept out of the office.

"At least he's safe," she said.

I walked down the center aisle toward Dr. Shonstein, reviewing PowerPoint slides on stage.

"I heard," she said. "That poor man. That poor, crazy, sweet, lovable man." She lowered her voice. "What is Brandy thinking?"

"He's staying with me," I said.

"Jennifer."

"I asked him. He was planning to stay with my mom in Kenosha."

"Jeez. I feel so bad for him. We all talked to that stupid custody evaluator. Did she not listen?"

Students started filing in, so we cut the chit-chat. The auditorium gradually filled, with the Freshman class of fifty five, the fifteen-person grad seminar, other Astrobio grad students, our team sans Brando, faculty from other offices, staff, and a handful of people dressed like vice president, provost, and dean types.

"Mike Brando couldn't be here today," Shonstein began. "I'm Rebecca Shonstein, for those who don't know me. So without violating a Federal gag order that may still be in effect and could get me fined or jailed, you all probably know by now we found something important on a planet known for its red color that on a good day is thirty four million miles, or fifty five million kilometers, from Earth."

And so it went, with Dr. Shonstein never mentioning Crimsy or Mars or our mission by name, marshaling every euphemism she could think of to describe anything that might run afoul of the Feds—and getting a lot of laughs. Her cynical delivery hit an academic nerve.

I heard her cell phone vibrate on the podium, where she used it to control the PowerPoint. She looked at it.

"Hmm," she said. "The space station sent me a message." The PowerPoint slide vanished. "Watch the stage, it says."

She seemed as befuddled as we were. The lights went down, the room got dark, only low aisle lights remaining. Gradually it appeared, an ebullient green something, hovering above the 3D projector. It wasn't clear what we were seeing until the cloud camera aboard DSG pulled back and we made out Petri dishes. I heard a questioning hum from the audience.

"Greetings from Mars, ladies and gentlemen." It was Commander Ryong, speaking pretty fair English. "Permit me introduce *Crimsococcus halocryophilus*, better known by nickname, Crimsy."

The hum gave way to gasps and talk. I stared. Crimsy filled each Petri dish, bottom, sides, lid, thick as a velvety mold, growing on agar and bare, cold glass.

"Anyone who wants to come up for a closer look is more than welcome," Dr. Shonstein announced.

The line began with me.

"HOW DID *THAT* HAPPEN?" Levitt said. Our team was milling around in the lecture hall after the seminar.

"North Korea's not subject to our patent laws."

"You *know* Sparks had something to do with it."

"Let's see if we still have visuals," Shonstein said, firing up the projector. "Nada. Audio looks like it's off again, too."

"A cruel tease," Marcum said.

That was my day at work. At first when I got home, I didn't think much of it when Brando and Lexi weren't there. Just out somewhere, shopping or eating or something. The air mattresses were propped against the wall. Sheets and blankets neatly folded. But there was no luggage. I heard a knock at my door and saw Nathaniel Hawthorn on security cam.

"Jennifer!" He had something in his hand. "I felt—I wanted to—"

"Come in," I said. He did.

"I felt bad about yesterday," he said. "So when Alexander Sparks was asking for your address—"

"He what?"

"He wanted your address."

"You didn't give it to him."

"No, no, no. We don't give out student addresses. I'm sure he already has it, anyway. Just an excuse to check on me and get me to give this to you." He held out a small white box, about the right size for a ring.

"For moi?" I said. "How strange."

"Is it?"

I looked at him like, yeah—it's *very* strange. Everything about that guy is strange. I undid the ribbon, opened the box, and took out a tiny glass vial filled with what I immediately knew was Martian dust.

"How is this legal?" I asked.

"What is it?"

"Dust from Mars. How can he give it away?"

"How do you know it's from Mars? Is it marked?" Nathaniel asked.

I gave him the vial. "Look at it. It's obvious."

"I can't tell," Nathaniel said. "Sure it's not fake Martian dust, like they sell in museum shops?"

"It's not fake." I felt discouraged all of a sudden. I put the priceless trinket into its box and set the box aside with red-level care. "Know anything about family law?"

"I run when I hear those words."

"Mike Brando kidnapped his daughter."

"I don't follow."

"He lost custody of her. So he took her. It's not kidnapping, legally speaking. Parental something."

"Custodial interference," Nathaniel said. "It's serious stuff, legally speaking."

"Hey, so. Sit down. I'm being rude."

"I can't stay," he said. "I just came by to drop that off. Figured you wouldn't want Sparks doing it."

Nathaniel had his gallant moments, and I appreciated them. I also didn't want him to leave. My takeout order arrived and the delivery drone handed it over and scanned my wrist chip for payment. I closed the door and took the food into the kitchen.

"Smells awesome," Nathaniel said.

"New North Korean place. Ryong sent me a list of

suggested dishes: raengmyŏn, gimchi, and this must be," I said as I opened the seafood dish, "tongyeong-bibimbap. You hungry?"

"I wasn't," Nathaniel said, walking in and eyeing the food.

I don't drink but I keep wine for guests and Nathaniel had a glass for dinner, another glass when we sat on the couch.

"I heard about Ryong," he said. "Bet I know who cooked up that little demonstration."

"We're betting on Alexander Sparks," I said. "But why?"

"For you."

"No, seriously. Why?"

"Seriously. He wants you on that space station," Nathaniel said. "All this stuff is mere foreplay."

I didn't want to get into the whole space station thing and redirected the conversation. About halfway through a third glass of wine, Nathaniel joked about being too drunk to drive home. I joked about how self-driving technology had deprived him of that ploy. He examined the Martian dust vial.

"How can you tell this is real?"

His body language suggested I get closer to him, and I cupped his hand in mine, moved my face next to his, and looked at the vial.

"Crystalline structure," I said. "It's not like Earth dust."

"You'd have to have a microscope to see that small," he said. "Even I know that."

He smelled good and I reached over and touched his cheek.

He looked at me and I'm not sure who was first to the kiss. We kissed for a while.

"Where's this going?" he asked finally.

"Where?" I said.

"Probably not a good idea. Right?"

"Right," I said. Kiss, kiss. Didn't want Lexi and her dad interrupting us, so I kept one eye on the hall cam.

"Don't need the aftermath," he said.

"No we don't. Plus, I'd never be rid of you."

He pulled back. "Is that right?"

"Yes."

He came back to me, closer this time, and I caressed his cheek and looked at him.

"You're making me regret."

"What?" I asked.

"Saying you should go to the space station."

"So you'd miss me?" I kissed him.

"I might. If this goes any farther."

"If this goes any farther," I said, "you'll be doing more than missing me."

"That again. Is it self-confidence or cockiness?"

Neither, actually. I was just stating a fact.

"You think I'm hopelessly ineffective, ineffectual, unmanly, whatever you want to call it," Nathaniel said. "Don't you?"

"No." I sat up. "I don't think that at all."

"I know it probably seems that way at times."

"I get frustrated," I said. "Everybody's frustrated. Limbo is a frustrating place."

"I'm a handmaiden of the powerful," he said. "I know it. I'm also committed to your welfare. You and your team."

I touched his cheek again, wanting to bring him back to me. But he took my hand. "I saw the note," he said. "I really don't wanna say so, but I agree."

"What note?"

"Over there. On your kitchen counter."

"I didn't see—" I got up to check.

"It says you should go to the space station."

"I'm not an astronaut."

"You'd be trained," Nathaniel said. "They wouldn't just send you up there."

On my kitchen counter I read an old-fashioned, handwritten note: "GO! And bring Crimsy home. We'll be fine."

I panicked. I grabbed my phone and started texting Mom. "Mike Brando has—" Then I stopped. Should I tell Mom? Make her an accomplice, since I knew she wouldn't turn them away? But then Dr. Hale would know. It would get out, everyone would know. Kiss of death for Brando's career, even if Hale tried to help him. Who could I tell? Who would I not compromise? We'd done a good job so far of keeping everything off the record.

"Anything wrong?"

"I think Brandy took off. Left town."

"Well, yeah—"

"He was staying here til things calmed down."

"Jesus, Jennifer. Not smart."

To hell with smart. I called my brother.

"My lovely sister." David's voice was always so calming, even when he wasn't calm.

"Dr. Brando and his daughter may be headed your way," I said. "Mom invited them. He took her. They gave sole custody to his almost-ex."

"Sorry to hear that," David said. "Isn't that kidnapping?"

"It's custodial interference," Nathaniel said loudly. "And it's a felony."

"Who's that?" David asked.

"Nathaniel. You met him the other night. My date."

"So Mom's gonna be an accessory?"

"Yes," Nathaniel said from afar.

I turned and put my hand over the phone. "Shut up!" Then I felt bad. "I mean, please hush."

"Does Mom know?" David asked.

"I have no idea. They were staying here."

"Hiding out," Nathaniel said in a loud whisper.

"Just for a while," I said.

"Mom's not in town. What if they show up?"

Nathaniel took the phone from behind me. "Hey, David. Just lay low. Check on your mom's house, see what happens. But don't get directly involved."

"Easier said than done," I heard David reply.

"I'm gonna try something on this end," Nathaniel said. "Maybe Jennifer can help."

"What's the plan?" I asked after signing off with David.

"Get Sparks to intervene. He doesn't get involved with personal matters, but this isn't your average personal matter."

"And I help how?"

"If he knows how upsetting this is to you," Nathaniel said. "If he thinks resolving it might get you on the space station." Nathaniel rubbed his forehead. His eyes looked tired. "I need to get going," he said. "Don't worry. Just bought a Flyby."

Twenty Eight

Brian and I were going to be the first brother and sister in space and the idea of making that trip without him had me thinking about why I lost him, the way I lost him, and how powerless I was to do a damn thing about it.

An otherwise minor boating accident sent Brian home with a bottle of large white pills engraved with lines that split them in half. Mom and he didn't think anything of it—take the pills for ten days and the pain will subside—until he started acting jittery and out-of-sorts after the pills ran out.

"Did he take too many of them?" I asked Mom at Thanksgiving.

"I don't think so," she said. "He just took them until they were gone."

"Was he weaned off them?"

"Weaned? What do you mean?"

"Like, did the doctor gradually decrease the dose? One pill every hour, one pill every three hours, one pill a day, until no more pills."

"I don't know," Mom said. "I don't think so."

I asked Brian. He slouched in the porch swing with a dying cigarette hanging between his fingers, barely bundled against the November chill, staring at damp fallen leaves and newly-barren branches. The Sun peaked through like it only did in fall: bright, clean, shadow-less, illuminating.

"I don't know," he answered. "They gave me the pills, I took them."

Prickly.

"When'd you start smoking?"

"Why the third degree?"

"You always hated smoking."

"Coaches hated it."

"So?"

"Calms my nerves," he said.

"You were always my mellow," I said.

"You're not here anymore. There's just Mom. Davey boy on Saturdays. Sometimes."

Contrast this with the two of us lying on the grass at Eichelman Park during Spring Break, listening to Lake Michigan lap the shoreline, eyes closed behind shades in the light of an unseasonably warm March day.

"I'm really proud of you," Brian said. "It's so cool, what you're doing. Sometimes I can't even believe it."

"Gonna join me? Be the first astronauts on Mars?"

"Get out."

"I'd go with you."

"Wouldn't that be wild," he said. "Brother and sister the first humans on Mars. We could lie on the sand next to what used to be a lake and stare at a sky that used to be blue." His poetry turned reality just as I was imagining it. "The pictures you send are pretty dull, honestly," Brian said. "Looks like a boring place."

"Gonna prove you wrong," I said.

"Yeah," he said.

"Already looks like we found something."

He raised up on his arm and turned to me. I looked at his face and saw my own. We could have been twins, lots of people said. David was the odd man out.

"What?" Brian asked.

"Something."

"C'mon."

"I'm not supposed to say anything."

"Are you kidding? That big?"

"Yeah," I said. "That big."

"I always knew you were destined for greatness, but major greatness? This is major greatness."

"I haven't said what."

Brian sat up. "Little green men. Alien invaders. Martian monsters. What else could it be?"

"Lots of things."

"They already brought back rocks," Brian said. "What else could it be—but life?"

I broke out in goosebumps. I turned and looked at him and he would have seen the acknowledgment but for my sunglasses. I felt emotions coming on like afflicted Dr. Levitt and Dr. Brando, our "mission wimps," as Dr. Levitt liked to joke.

"Jen?" my brother said. He leaned over.

"What?"

He scooted next to me and when he parted my hair from

my face, I smiled behind tears.

"It's that big," he said.

I couldn't speak at first. "Yeah," I said finally.

"Now *I'm* gonna cry."

It was surreal, my brother and I there, laughing and weeping, embarrassment and realization, in the Sun, on the grass, near the wide water and such horizons beyond.

BRIAN AND I THE first humans on Mars? What if there were humans or someones there millions or billions of years ago, and Crimsy was all that remained?

What had reduced the planet to such desolation only the hardiest of tiny things could survive? (Maybe there were other types of life, but I doubted it).

I daydreamed about Brian and our first voyage toward a new horizon together, just us, on the SS Badger where we decided we were crossing the ocean instead of a Great Lake. It was during that interlude after David moved out, leaving our sibling dynamic stuck in the stills, like a tricycle without its third, big wheel. Two little tires, supporting the rest of the apparatus. If one toppled, so too the other.

We made the crossing on a warm spring day, a short sojourn to get away from parental drama and all that David Copperfield kind of crap.

Caller ID Block rescued me from my bittersweet reverie.

Should I pick up? Brandy was still out there somewhere—he and Lexi never showed up at Mom's. Maybe it was him.

"Jennifer," the soft voice said.

And only a voice. No video. No cloud projection. I hesitated.

"Leo Telos," he said.

At first, I didn't make the connection. Leo who?

"We met at the science center. The *Odysseus* exhibition."

"Leon Telos," I said. "Yes. Yes, sir. I remember."

"Friends call me Leo or sometimes just Lee."

"Okay."

"Alex—Mr. Sparks, as he prefers to be known—informs me that your team would like a berth aboard DSG. I'm not in on every conversation, but is that what you understand?"

"Yes. Absolutely."

"He also tells me you are the presumptive nominee for such a spot."

"I am, well, kinda. I mean, nothing's been decided."

"I believe, as Alex does, that you are the right choice."

"Thank you," I said. "Your vote of confidence means a lot."

"It's no mere vote of confidence," he said.

This was news. I rarely flew, even on commercial airlines. After the intercity rocket explosion that took out Telos' biggest competitor, I vowed to stay off rockets, too. So how in the hell I was "the right choice" was a mystery to me.

"We have an excellent training program," Telos said.

I think he could feel my hesitation, especially since I could barely breathe.

"Dr. Brando's custody case will be settled in his favor at the end of this month," Telos said. "We should get that out of the way right off, don't you agree?"

What?

"Mr. Hawthorn insisted."

Double what?

"So what does that mean?" I asked. "Mike gets Lexi?"

"He and his former bride, with admittedly some gentle persuasion, have crafted a much more equitable custody arrangement. They will share their daughter, of course. We aren't in the business of breaking up families. But Dr. Brando will enjoy a larger share than he presently does, or to date in their proceedings, ever has."

"Are you serious?" I asked.

"Never more so."

I stared at my wall, as this kindly, non-threatening voice laid down the law. *This* was what real power sounded like.

"Thank you," I said.

"Mr. Hawthorn deserves any thanks," Telos explained. "Frankly, I was a bit surprised Dr. Brando and his daughter meant so much to you. Alex assured me you would not be unpredictable before we brought you aboard."

"Dr. Levitt hired me," I said. "And I really don't know Mr. Sparks."

"It wasn't just Dr. Levitt who hired you. The Executive Research Committee, Alex, myself."

"I don't know anything about aeronautics, astronautics,

whatever it's called," I said. "Nothing."

"You're a fast learner," Telos said. "SpaceTek has expedited mission training programs for commercial crew and payload specialists, as you will be classified, and space tourists, whose presence has greatly expedited the training timeline. Virgin, Disney, Blue Orbit, LunAir—we work with all of them. Perhaps you've seen the list of unlikely space travelers who've completed our program over the years. The King of England. And more than one octogenarian, including Donald—"

"I've seen that list, yes," I said.

"The commercial crew payload program is three months long," Telos said.

"How do you know I—I could totally blow it. Wash out."

A long pause. Given how much money he earns in one second, a pause that probably cost Telos two billion bucks.

"You won't," he said.

"JENNIFER." DR LEVITT STEPPED into the post-doc office. She looked concerned and I immediately worried if I should be, too.

"I've been thinking—" she said.

I looked at her. She pulled up and straddled a chair.

"I seem to be the sole holdout on the idea of you going to the space station," she said. "Normally, I'm all in on expeditions in the name of science."

"Of course," I said. Talk about stating the obvious.

"I just—it's asking you to put your life and your future in considerable harm's way. You're not trained," she said.

"None of us is. It's not your life's dream to go into space—is it?"

"No. Well, I mean—my brother and I fantasized about going to Mars together. But being an astronaut: I've always thought of it as a calling, a total life devotion kind of thing."

"Like anything you love. Like this," she said.

"Yes. But like you said, it's a lot more dangerous."

"That's right. Which is why I can't ask you to do it. It seems like the ultimate in asking a person to do way more than they ever signed up for. If anything happened to you —"

"What if you didn't have to ask?" I interrupted. "What if I said I wanted to do it because it felt, well—right?"

"Does it?"

I thought. I considered. I had been thinking, considering. Each time someone encouraged the idea—me on DSG, doing whatever it took to get there, maybe, hopefully, bringing Crimsy home, or at least, doing something meaningful—I thought even harder.

But since it was the kind of choice that could kill me, I'm not sure I had made up my mind until now, right this minute, sitting as close as I've ever sat to my scientific and professional mentor.

"Yes," I said finally. "It feels right."

"WE HAVE SOME EXCITING news," Dr. Levitt began our

faculty meeting. "Jennifer."

"I—" I couldn't find the words and looked at everyone. I thought about Telos, my family. David was super excited. But Mom was the one who floored me.

"I don't want you to go," she said. "I *insist* you go." She was back home, with Dr. Hale flying in shortly. "I'm doing great, honey," she said. "Meds leave me a little foggy, light-headed, but a lot less forgetful."

Parada entered smiling like crazy and sat next to me.

"You want me to tell them?" Dr. Levitt asked.

"No," I said. "No." I mustered my courage. "I'm going . . . to Deep Space Gateway."

Parada shot out of her chair and motioned me up and hugged me. "We're so proud of you," she said.

Everyone rose—it felt like a standing ovation—smiling and grabbing my arms and shoulders and getting all touchy-feely and wonderful. I felt like dissolving in a pile of sentiment.

Whoever thought science could be so soulful?

"I'm involved in weather planning every step of the way," Dr. Cooper said. "You can count on the best day of the year to fly."

Dr. Marcum took my hand in a fierce grip and pulled me toward him. And with an American twang manufactured in the finest of allied traditions, "We're rootin' for ya, kiddo," he said.

"Hug, girl," Dr. Shonstein said. "We thought this might happen, so Malachi put our thousand hard-to-find words into a picture." She handed it to me.

In one frame, I flew toward a blue sky with darkness beyond, all stick-figure and crayon-yellow hair, in a simple rocket with orange flames, my team—and Malachi—waving goodbye.

"You can tell that's me, right?" Dr. Marcum said.

"Perfect weather," Cooper said. "And I wasn't even consulted."

In a second frame, I was coming home, in a different rocket now, with blue flames and a blunter nose cone. "Yeah, so, Martin and I tried to explain that rockets don't land that way," Shonstein said. "But you know artists."

My team, in the second frame, was waving again, but this time, hello. Malachi hadn't aged a day. Dr. Shonstein stared at the picture.

"Just noticed something," she said. "May I?"

She took the picture and added some green dots in my homecoming craft with her pen. She circled the dots like a Petri dish and handed it back to me.

MY TEAM HELD OFF on a going away party (that would come with my trip to the space station) and instead gathered for a paper plate potluck at Dr. Marcum's place in Columbia City. I'd never been to his house, but had been hearing about it since he joined our team. If Dr. Marcum liked you, your service, your product, whatever, he told everyone.

It's difficult to find anything to rent in Seattle, almost impossible in coveted neighborhoods like Columbia City. Dr.

Marcum prevailed, on "charm and good looks," he said. The owner was a retired math professor who had made it his life's work to solve the great mathematics problem Marcum ended up solving, an equation named for two scientists, Claude-Louis Navier and George Gabriel Stokes, about how fluids flow in space.

Marcum liked the neighborhood for its diversity and hard-times roots (once run down, it had long since thrived). Dr. Canberry, Marcum's landlord, was in fanboy awe.

I was piqued when I didn't see Dr. Brando at our potluck, and I let Nathaniel Hawthorn know it.

"I still haven't heard from him," I said. "Telos said you guys fixed everything."

He leaned over and in a way that disarmed me, whispered into my ear. "Chill."

I eyed food and poised to fill my plate when I felt a presence beside me. I turned, dropped my empty plate, and hugged him.

"Mike!"

"We wanted to surprise you," Dr. Levitt said.

"Got back a few days ago," Brando said.

"Mom said you were—"

"Got as far as Spokane," he interrupted.

"Why didn't you say anything? Call?"

"My lawyer said anyone who helped could be prosecuted. Then he called with amazing news." Brando's custody arrangement was much as it had been since he and Melissa split: PRN, medical lingo for "as needed, as required, as requested." But with a new rule: no rules, no schedules set in stone. No hard-and-fast time limits.

"Lexi's a different kid," he said.

"I'm so, so happy for you guys," I said.

"I'll second, third, fourth, fifth, and sixth that," Dr. Cooper said. "Seventh, if you include Hale."

Nathaniel Hawthorn and I said our "farewell-but-not-goodbyes" on the walkway outside Marcum's house. I peered around, then grabbed and kissed him just as I knew he planned to grab and kiss me.

It was a hot little moment.

JSC

Twenty Nine

I left Seattle at peace on the one hand—my team mates took turns keeping an eye on my place; family matters had calmed—but anxious on the other. WTH was I doing bound for Johnson Space Center (JSC)?

Years ago, it took a minimum two years to train for a space station journey. But with the demand for space tourism, evermore sophisticated flight automation, and so many private partners, different tracks opened and the time to qualify became subject to a kind of aeronautical Moore's Law.

Two years became two weeks for a tourist-centered sub-orbital flight; three months for the designation I would receive. Regular astronaut candidates (ASCANS) were the sole exception: Their training time *increased* by a few months, for Mars preparation.

On graduation, my official title would be "payload specialist," not pilot, so I was exempt from several requirements, like learning to fly a T-38 jet (which the seasoned hands called the "training wheels model").

Medical wouldn't need pre-qualification bloodwork. And my psychological testing was limited to simple stress prompts and an IQ test. My lung capacity was terrific (the medical technician who administered the test looked befuddled, even when I bragged on my championship swimming days) and I did better than the tech (so he said) on a grip strength test. For the broadest overview of my long-term well-being, Medical also got a Deep Learning Algorithm test, like the one Nathaniel Hawthorn took, that would tell me the day I would die.

"You guys, too?" I asked. "A friend did a DLA."

"It's pretty accurate," the technician said. "Had a master chief in my office, healthy as a horse, retiring from the Navy in a few weeks. But when his DLA came back, it said he had only a few weeks. He died before we could go over the results."

Chilling, that. But accidents would be my concerns over the next few months, not death by natural causes.

After the med tech, I visited an audiologist who did some tests, inserted a probe of some kind into my ears (it made an unusual clicking sound) and assured me everything would be "just fine" as I experienced gravity in all its simulated glory (in training, aboard a passenger jet).

I had ear trouble on a commercial jetliner after seeing a specialist at the Sparks-Mayo Clinic after my accident. I tried a Valsalva maneuver to relieve the pain, but it didn't help much. I went back and the same specialist fixed what ailed me (a post-surgical complication, so I was told).

"Obviously, let us know if you have any more problems," the audiologist told me.

After my physical, I joined fifteen other astronauts in

training—four space tourists from China, Mexico, Morocco, and Montana; and eleven full-fledged ASCANS—six women, five guys—from parts near and far. I occupied an unusual middle-ground in their midst. We gathered in a small classroom for a live greeting from DSG, a future way station for most of the astronauts and my next duty assignment.

"Long time, no see," Captain Hightower said to me, standing before us.

The 3D projectors they had here were even more amazing than ours (except for the one in Sparks Hall). One of the ASCANS reached out to shake hands with Hightower and the two smart-asses played like they just couldn't get a grip on each other's hands.

Our group asked questions about how to handle the unexpected; space walks; what it was like living without gravity ("Levity rules," Captain Gillory said) and our North Korean astronaut candidate thanked Commander Ryong "for inspiring our people."

"Learn how to fix everything and anything," Ryong advised. "And listen to everyone except when they tell you food is great."

A question about Crimsy came up and I was flattered (at first) when Hightower deferred to me. "We found *Crimsococcus* living beneath a sheet of ice," I explained. "We haven't been able to study her on Earth, so I'm going up there."

I said "flattered *at first*" because at JSC I became known as *Bugsy*. "A nickname is the heaviest stone the devil can throw." Or so I thought until now.

In a proud tradition dating to 1959 that included "The

Mercury Seven," "The Chumps," and last year's "Flying Sparks," we got our group nick: The Shock Diamonds, another name for a glowing wave pattern in the supersonic exhaust plume of a jet or rocket. Also known as "Mach Diamonds," after the physicist Ernst Mach (as in Mach, or supersonic, speed), the waves look like diamonds and appear when jet exhaust travels faster than the speed of sound.

Diamonds in the rough awaiting polish and shine: I loved everything our nickname implied.

WITHOUT GRAVITY, MUSCLES SHRINK, so we learned the resistance moves we'd be doing in orbit. Our exercise physiologist (EP) strapped each of us to a treadmill, which added about fifty pounds and aboard the space station, kept the jogger's feet on the treads.

The tourist-trainee preceding me grimaced as he plodded along. The Russian cosmonaut candidate smiled sheepishly as the device wore him down. The triathlete grinned and held up her hands in a Rocky Balboa victory pose when she stepped off. I jogged at first, then tried to sprint toward the end. I didn't feel that winded, but—swimmer. I exchanged a fist bump with one of the gals. A few of us matched the strongest guys on the "advanced resistive device," a high-tech barbell punctuated with calipers and calibers we squatted and bench pressed.

Sisters still doin' it for themselves.

The next test struck me as critical, and fortunately (I thought), a cinch.

"You're doing a space walk. You need to turn a valve or hook a line or dislodge something from a robotic arm. What's that gonna feel like?" our EP said.

One after the other, we stuck our hands into a glove box fitted with two space suit gloves. It was smaller but similar to the boxes Gillory and Hightower used to work with Crimsy.

"When we depressurize the box, it simulates what it feels like to move your hands and fingers in space," the EP explained, turning a valve that sucked out the air.

Two trainees couldn't get their fingers into the gloves. Others had a helluva time manipulating the tether hooks.

"This is like threading a needle in the dark," one of the guys said.

I got my hands in okay. I turned my wrists and wiggled my fingers, which felt really heavy. I picked up the two tether hooks but something was wrong.

"You're doing great," the EP said. "Just snap them together. This is your lifeline, folks. You lose it, you end up like—what was that movie?"

I saw people looking at each other out the corner of my eye. Now *I* thought, "which movie?"

Focus, focus.

"*Gravity*," the triathlete said. At least I think it was her.

Focus, please. Focus.

But I couldn't get those stupid, simple tethers snapped. They were just two hooks, like mountaineering carabiners.

"You're doing fine," triathlete said.

But I wasn't. And my vision was wacky. The more I tried to focus, the cloudier my eyesight became. Just a little more. Lift this up. Press against clip. Press. Presto! Success. I pulled my hands out and stood back, oddly exhausted. Everybody clapped. So embarrassing, but triathlete put her arm around me.

The ordeal bothered me through our space food lunch: Salisbury steak, cornbread, mashed potatoes, carrots, and chocolate cake out of envelopes we tore open like the military MREs—meals ready-to-eat—my dad ate and hated (our food wasn't *that* bad). We even drank Tang, which I had maybe twice as a kid.

Still brooding over the manual dexterity fail, I felt more like getting organized than socializing, so after our training day ended, I went back to our long-term stay hotel and browsed the class schedule on the in-room cloud monitor.

All space tourists, including me, took the FAA-approved National Aerospace Training and Research Center (NASTAR) basic "suborbital" track that got us from ground control to just above Earth's atmosphere at velocities eight times slower than it took to reach full orbit, where I would eventually end up. The astronauts called it "baby space" and the coursework was basic, from the history of space vehicles to life support systems and "Introduction to G-Forces."

The fun stuff, so they said, began with Advanced Space Flight: Altitude Physiology, Spatial Disorientation, Rapid

Decompression, Loss of Control In-flight, Emergency Preparedness, simulations and more simulations: vibrations, noise, and orbital views; rendezvous and payload operations; the micro-gravity virtual reality laboratory.

I was all by my lonesome on the payload specialist track, "designed to equip researchers and scientists with the knowledge and skills to design, plan, and conduct experiments on commercial orbital spaceflights." Courses included "science experiments in simulated orbital environments," and I guessed soon something like "Basics of Alien Life" or "Fundamentals of Martian Microbes," given the introductory note I read.

"The discovery of Life on Mars has opened up exciting new vistas in space exploration. STAY TUNED for relevant updates to our latest curricula."

It seemed like over half the curricula was how to survive mishaps: fires, toxic gases, life support failures, explosions, crashes, and crash landings. "Land and Water Survival: This course provides pilots, crew, and passengers with the knowledge and skills needed to survive unanticipated land or water landings and/or other episodes where rescue may be required."

Maybe it was the power of suggestion, but whatever was plaguing me during the manual dexterity test seemed to reappear when I got into the curricula about flight simulations and how G-forces and high altitudes can mess with your brain: "Spatial Disorientation during Launch and Reentry, Loss of Consciousness In-Flight, Recovery from Upsets (any kind of disaster), Hypoxia and Rapid Decompression, Recognition and Recovery from Visual Illusions."

I held up my hand and watched it tremble.

Finally, a course-long exercise I heard the ASCANS sardonically nicknamed "The Depression Sessions," which tasked us with writing something called a "Life Journal."

A trend in higher ed I barely missed, now making its way into high school, the Life Journal was like an assigned introspection, a diary in hindsight, the beginning of an autobiography few, if any, of us would ever complete. If the unexamined life wasn't worth living, as Socrates famously said, this course aimed for the examined life that was.

Though the course did not specify when and how the Life Journal was to be composed, and the space tourist trainees weren't required to write them (though a few did, mostly for the holistic experience), guidelines suggested we write in sections. If a training or other experience here prompted a so-called *life memory*, the guidelines urged writing as soon after the experience as possible. Regardless, I planned to "write at first light," as Hemingway advised.

The value of such an exercise seemed obvious, especially for the highly-trained: the astronauts, fighter pilots, doctors, soldiers, police, fire, lawyers, researchers, and others who needed clear heads and sound minds.

The Story of My Life would be the hardest, by far, of any course I had ever taken. I've included it as I wrote it.

Thirty

"We interrupt your regularly-scheduled classes for something awesome," was how our Space Flight Systems instructor started my Monday at five in the morning. The space tourists perked up; the ASCANS took a wait and see attitude. We boarded a hyperloop bus for a one-hour trip from Houston to San Antonio.

"You spent last week learning about G forces and today we'll be experiencing them," our instructor said, standing in the bus aisle. "Johnson used to have a centrifuge, but our G-force training is at Brook City now."

I fell asleep to the low hum of excited chatter, phone calls home, and triathlete sipping coffee next to me. We were just starting to get acquainted.

"Ali," she said.

"Jen," I said.

That's as far as we got between classes, tests and now, a field trip.

In a building at the former Brook Air Force Base, two technicians and our instructor gathered us around a giant blue- and-white mechanical arm with a passenger pod on the end that reminded me of a carnival ride at the Kenosha County Fair, which isn't in Kenosha but Wilmot, about twenty miles west. Brian had to drag me kicking and screaming to get on anything that spun or plunged, and I dreaded this gizmo.

"The centrifuge mimics gravitational, or G-forces," our instructor said. "We'll show you some maneuvers to keep from passing out, and gradually ramp you up to three Gs, about what you'll feel leaving Earth. Those of you who are pilot and crew trainees will experience a more robust excursion."

He told us what to expect with successive G increases: loss of color vision, aka a "gray out," then loss of peripheral vision, aka tunnel vision; and at ASCAN-level Gs (four to six), total black out while still conscious, aka "G-LOC" (gravity-induced loss of consciousness).

"Blood flow gets lost to the eyes before it's lost to the brain," cuz intraocular pressure, he explained. We'd be asked to recall each step of vision loss during our simulation.

An Air Force medic took everyone's blood pressure, checked our pupils, and made us say "ahh." The tourist I nicknamed "Mr. Montana" remarked it was all a good way to make sure no one was hungover.

Five ASCANS went first, then the four tourists, then the rest of the ASCANS, then me. We watched each other's faces on monitors in a room that overlooked the centrifuge bay. The arm circled slowly, so it was hard to imagine the person in the pod weighed three times his or her body weight at the full 3Gs. But that's the magic of circular motion. It creates a "centrifugal force" that mimics gravity, even at low speeds.

"One, two, *breathe*," the instructor told each rider as the centrifuge accelerated. Faces grimaced. "You okay, you okay? *Breathe*. Legs tight, calves clenched. *Breathe*."

Each ASCAN—and me—went to six Gs. Things got hairy with the last ASCAN before the tourists. Her face crumpled when the monitor read G = 05.17.

"Stay tight. Stay tight. Are you with me?" the instructor said.

But she slumped into G-LOC.

"Sit up, sit up."

The centrifuge slowed.

"You with me," the instructor asked again.

She staggered and her head swung as she tried to sit up in the seat. She woozily eyed the monitor. The centrifuge stopped. With some water and rest, she stepped off, dazed but revived.

Mr. Montana slumped into G-LOC, then stumbled around looking sick when he got off. Ms. Mexico was surprisingly giddy. Mr. China play acted like he could barely walk, then gave us a smiling thumbs up. Ms. Morocco's hijab framed a whimsical, playful smile that gave me hope as she emerged.

I was fourth, right before Ali. "Three Gs," I said. "I'll weigh like four hundred pounds."

"Wait til six," the instructor said.

I slipped on the anti-G suit—"it's like a whole body blood pressure cuff," the medic said—and they belted me into the passenger compartment, where I faced a control stick like I'd seen in a fighter jet at AirVenture Oshkosh, aka "The World's Greatest Aviation Celebration!"

"Curl your toes, clench your glutes and calves. Breathe up

here," the instructor said, indicating my diaphragm. "If we see you going into G-LOC, we'll slow it down."

The first two Gs were weird but okay. By G three, I could feel the weight on my hands. I breathed and clenched my entire lower body. I raised my hand and looked at it, showing off.

"Gonna start your next ride at five Gs," I heard.

"Okay." I nodded.

"I'll say 'legs, breathe, pull back on the stick,' and you're gonna wait for me to say 'breathe' then I'll have you back off—"

And blah blah blah. I was getting nervous and not paying as much attention as I should.

"When you lose your lights . . . I'll say 'terminate' . . . let go of the stick," I thought I heard the instructor say. "I'm gonna ask you where you're from."

Shouldn't be too hard.

"Ready? Legs, *breathe*, pull back," he said and off we went. I was now in ASCAN territory, higher G's than the tourists and I felt it.

"*Breathe*. Out and in."

I huffed and puffed.

"Keep the stick back. Where are you from?"

"Oshkosh," I said.

"Where?"

"Osh . . . no. Kenosha."

"Keep your eyes open. Eyes open. Crisper breaths. Breath

crisp and legs tight. Okay, let go of the stick. Stay tight."

And we were back to normal.

"What was your light loss?" the instructor asked.

"Huh?"

"When you started to black out? How did that happen?"

I couldn't remember. I don't think it did.

"I don't—"

"That's okay, that's okay. Most people lose their light from the sides. Gets gray. Can't see clearly. You remember that?"

"No."

"Okay. That's okay."

We went to six Gs.

"Butt tight, legs tight, *breathe, breathe,* keep the stick, keep the stick. Watch your light, *watch your light.*"

Something surprised the technician watching the monitors.

"Look at her face," he said. The speaker picked up his voice.

"Everything okay? You with us, Jen?"

I smiled.

"Never seen that," the technician said.

I survived, but again couldn't recall any vision loss. The instructor acted like I was trying to be a tough girl or maybe I was just lying or not paying attention. I ended up insisting I didn't lose any vision. No gray out, no tunnel, nothing. After everyone was finished, I asked the instructor what they saw on the monitor during my ride.

"Something on my face?" I asked.

They gave still photos to the tourists as souvenirs, and the technician showed me mine. Every capillary rippled in bold relief on my forehead and upper cheeks. Gross. I felt my face as it got warm and red. I didn't know what to say. I was glad it wasn't my chief souvenir.

"Probably just the light," the instructor said, staring at the photo over my shoulder. "Don't worry about it."

OUR INSTRUCTOR ADVISED WE eat light for tomorrow's "zero G" experience, but nothing would stop our group from a celebratory "no space food" dinner at a barbecue joint on the Riverwalk, downtown San Antonio's version of a Venetian waterway. We were lucky to find enough seats on the patio overlooking the water.

"Vomit Comet tomorrow, folks."

"Which is?" I asked.

"Premature," Ali said. "The real Vomit Comet comes later."

After rounds of ribs and beers, and water for us non-imbibers, the conversation turned to Crimsy. "What was it like being part of the team that made such a momentous discovery?" was the gist of the questions.

"A lot of us are training for Mars," AstroCan—the Canadian astronaut candidate—said.

"Not if they shut us down over her bug," a US ASCAN said, looking at me.

I'm sure I looked confused.

"Environmental concerns," he said. "Seriously."

Echoes of Alexander Sparks, but I still didn't really get it.

"There's talk we won't be able to go to Mars," Ali said. "They're worried about cross-contamination."

"Crimsy is harmless," I said.

"It's not about *us* getting sick," AstroCan said. "It's about us contaminating the planet and killing off, what did you call it?"

"*Crimsococcus*," I said. "I've heard that argument. But it's mostly been dismissed."

"We might not set foot on Mars in my lifetime," another US astrocan said. "They're actually talking about sending robots instead."

"They already do," I said. "We used one to find Crimsy."

"No, no," one of the other women said. "Human-like robots, Life-like."

"Androids,'" Ali said. "Mandroids. Womandroids. There's a big debate going on that since we found life on Mars, we have a duty to protect it. Part of protecting it means humans can't go there—at least, not until we can guarantee we won't bring contaminants from Earth."

"Which could be decades away, or never."

"War of the Worlds," Ms. Mexico said. "Only in reverse."

That mostly dismissed argument. Who knew the everyday germs Orson Welles imagined saving us from Martian invaders might save the Martians from us someday?

Talk about an ironic sort of revenge. Ali must have seen the look on my face, as I wondered how Alexander Sparks—Mr. Humans on Mars—was taking all this. She rubbed her shoulder against me and the low light out here caught her affectionate smile. The hairs stood on the back of my neck.

LIFE JOURNAL: FIRST ENTRY. So there I was and have been, in David's sixth grade science class, talking about our search for Crimsy, missing the teachable moment his third grade student suggested: Orson Welles, the man who made "Martian" a household fright, was born in Kenosha and lived here for the first five years of his life.

I've talked about his famous *War of the Worlds* radio broadcast. I've blamed him for casting Martians as murderous invaders. I've rescued our quest from the clutches of his century-old scare fest. But I've never visited his childhood home. Might have driven by it a few times. It was blue, I remember. And a duplex when I was growing up, I learned from one of *Kenosha News'* periodic retrospectives of Welles' life, work, and mixed feelings about his hometown.

I resolved to make the pilgrimage on my next trip home, and this was that trip. I wish Brian was with me. It would have been a good excuse to get him out of the house when any excuse would do.

After it rounded the Simmons Library, I got off the streetcar near Sixty First and Seventh Streets, and within half a block was in front of a faded bronze plaque on a rock in the front yard: *Birthplace of Orson Welles, Actor and Director.* I couldn't see much else: a street lamp in the yard cast a cloud of light against the falling snow.

Kenosha was "vital," "charming," and "terrible," Welles said, his contradictory sentiments years apart. "I'm not ashamed of being from Wisconsin. Just of being from Kenosha." He reportedly didn't like the bleakness of the day his mother was buried.

I can't think of a place where I've lived more contradictions, conflicts, and constrictions. But I have never stopped loving Kenosha.

I stared at the Welles house until my feet got cold, then wriggled my toes and walked back to Sixty First Street, where on a clear winter day, you can see Lake Michigan. I started toward Eichelman Park, two long blocks away.

The snow made everything soundless, and I walked with it against my cheeks and eyelashes, opening my mouth to catch an occasional flake, letting the chill air fill my lungs and sting my ears.

I pulled up the fur-lined hood and cinched it tight and patted my gloved hands and walked, in low lights from the houses along the street. I figured I'd walk to the trail, maybe down to the beach. The streetcars ran a couple hours later than they did when I was growing up, so I had about an hour before I needed to be back.

I crossed Third Avenue and started down a recent addition to the park: a concrete walkway painted with murals of Kenosha, including an homage to Welles: "Rosebud," Citizen Kane's last word, written across a sled in the snow.

I gazed into the great grayness that is Lake Michigan in winter, and saw what looked like a jacket and clothes someone had left on a park bench near a streetlight made to look like a gas lamp. I walked toward the lake and looked over. The clothes took on form and shape, looking more like a person, lying, maybe sleeping, on the bench. I stopped and stared as the falling flakes settled on the shape in the light. I walked over. The clothes told me it was a man.

I didn't want to write what I knew was coming next, so I went to bed. But I couldn't sleep. I didn't sleep, until I got it out.

LIFE JOURNAL. ENTRY TWO.

"Sir?"

He didn't stir.

"Mister? Sir?"

Nothing. I walked closer.

"Are you all right?"

The accumulated snow made it hard to tell, but I thought I recognized the coat.

"Sir?" I said. "You're gonna freeze out here."

I thought about shaking him, but I didn't know how he'd respond. With a knife? A gun? A heart attack? I got a few steps closer and turned on my phone's flashlight. I scanned his body with it, and as I came to his face, partly buried beneath the coat's collar, I sucked in my breath.

"Brian." I rushed to him. "Brian!"

I pulled back the collar and patted his face.

"Brian. It's me. Jen. Jennifer. It's me. Wake up."

His cheeks were freezing and I couldn't tell if he was

breathing so I just said it, reflexively.

"Nine one one."

My phone heard and connected. I heard the operator mumbling.

"Overdose," I yelled. "Doing CPR."

I heard her asking questions and giving advice. Their GPS would find us, she said.

I knew it was a bad idea to move my brother, but I needed to know if he was alive. I put my ear to his mouth and listened. Thank God for the silence of the snow. I heard him gurgling, like snoring, but maybe he was trying to breathe. I pinched his ears. Kissed his forehead.

"Brian," I said.

No response. Trying to keep him as immobile as possible, I unbuttoned and pulled back his coat and let the cool air circulate—he was hot—and took off my coat and put it under his head. I rested my ear on his chest and listened. I heard a soft, regular thumping I figured was his heart which set me more at ease.

I couldn't remember the CPR steps—breath first, chest first, clear airway first, what? So I did what he seemed to need most, opened his mouth and puffed my life into it. I was crying by now, between breaths begging my beautiful baby brother not to die, begging him, breathing into him, then remembering and pumping his chest.

I listened for his heart again and heard his struggled gurgling and kept giving him breaths until the gurgling receded. I kissed his cheeks and his hair, let my tears wash over him and melt the snow.

He lurched forward, his head colliding with mine, and threw up on both of us. He plunged his head over the bench, as if instinctively, as if he'd done this before, and vomited again.

I saw something orange in the snow—maybe a syringe cap. David told me about how finding these in Brian's room prompted a confrontation.

"Brian—do you have anything on you? Any drugs?" I said.

He didn't answer but for a guttural mumble.

I patted his jacket and pants. I reached into the pockets that lined the inside of his coat. He turned his head and I saw something sick—an uncapped syringe resting in his jacket hood, near his ear, like a fallen carpenter's pencil. I reached over and took it.

"Is this all you have?" I said. "Is this it? Just this syringe?"

He laughed languidly and stared up at the light.

"The cops are coming. You have to tell me. Is this all you have?"

"Kaww," he said.

I reached down and picked up the cap and covered the needle. Should I keep it? Show it to Mom? Show her and Uncle Ron what I found: hard evidence of how screwed up Brian's life had become, how their "solutions" hadn't worked?

What if the cops searched me, thinking I was Brian's shooter? Should I just throw it away in the snow? Or in the trash can across the trail?

I ran across, buried it in the can beneath the rubbish, ran

back. Enabler, but—my baby brother wasn't going to jail if I could help it. No way. Brian was bent over again, heaving and mumbling when paramedics and a police officer arrived.

Thirty One

If the effect of life journaling was supposed to be some kind of cleanse, I felt polluted when I woke up the next morning. Hung over. Weary. Glad today's exercise seemed relatively passive and according to reports, fun.

"We fly three types of what's called 'parabolic patterns'," the pilot explained.

We were in a corporate hangar at San Antonio International Airport, getting ready to board a jumbo jet that would mimic weightlessness. I'd seen Stephen Hawking do this in a documentary and it didn't strike me as particularly difficult.

"Climb forty five degrees, then level off, where for about thirty seconds, we're actually in a free fall," the pilot continued. "That's when you'll be weightless. Then we head down, level off, then up and down, up and down, like a car traveling over a bunch of hills."

"Vomit Comet," one of the tourists said. A bunch of us, including me, took Dramamine.

"You may experience mild nausea," our instructor said. "Which is why—" He held up the sick sack we'd each received. ("Only about three percent of Zero G passengers ever get sick,"

I had read.)

"This is not the real Vomit Comit," Ali reassured with a smirk. "Sheesh."

"First pattern is like on Mars, where you'll feel one third your body weight," the pilot said. "Second pattern is like on the Moon, where you'll feel one sixth your body weight. Most of the patterns will be total zeroes—you'll be completely weightless."

Ali sat next to me as we buckled into the passenger seats in back and lost our shoes to a collection bag. The front roughly three quarters of the jet was hollowed out and looked like a big padded room.

The jet made a wide turn and started down the runway. I must have looked pensive because Ali ribbed me.

"Gonna be magnifique," she said.

Once the plane was safely airborne and the seat belt sign went off, we unbuckled, then moved to the padded area, where we lay on the floor. So far, so good.

The plane began its first ascent and everything inside me felt unusually heavy. Then it leveled off and we got lighter and rose. It was the craziest feeling. People were oohing and ahhing and laughing nervously.

"First stop: Mars," the pilot said.

The ASCANS tried walking and moving around. The tourists watched and took selfies and videos. Up here in the clouds, there was no Cloud, so no cloud cams. We were tethered to the natural but not the technological, a welcome respite.

Lunar gravity was more dramatic. Butterflies roiled my

stomach with each pass. And though I thought I was fixed, the first signs of ear trouble just *had* to start during the highlight of the trip: twelve passes at Zero G.

"Gulp it," I heard, as an ASCAN opened her mouth around a shimmering globule of water, floating above the bottle she squeezed. Others spilled Skittles and M&Ms and Everlasting Gobstoppers.

"Anti-Gravity's Rainbow," Ali said.

"Pynchon," I said, pinching a Gobstopper.

"Munch on," she quipped back, grabbing a floating candy with her tongue and her lips and opening her perfect straight white teeth to display her colorful catch.

"Feet down," our instructor cried.

We fell back to Earth and my ears full on ached. I squeezed my nostrils and blew against them, for incomplete relief. So much for the audiologist's assurances.

"You okay?" Ms. Morocco asked, her hijab unflappable even up here.

I nodded and tried to smile.

Up we went again, people tucking in their legs and twirling in mid air. I gazed at the ceiling, squeezing my nostrils and expanding my eardrums. Ali took my wrist and pulled me toward her.

Then we settled back into normal gravity.

"May I have the next dance?" she asked.

Gravity lost again, she rose above me and looked upon me,

squeezing my nostrils. She did a kind of mid-air pirouette, then took my free hand and stretched out her other hand and leaned forward, as though taking a couples bow after a star turn on a dance show.

I felt ridiculous holding my nose and knowing the look on my face was hardly exhilarating. But she smiled anyway and when we were back on our backs on the padded floor, turned to me, held her nostrils, and breathed against them exaggeratedly, opening her eyes over-wide.

I smiled when she puffed her cheeks like a fish. As we went up the last couple times, I let my hands roam and in the charm of the moment, tried to forget my ears.

A SHUTTLE DROPPED US at our hotel back in Houston late that afternoon. I was spent and collapsed on the bed, drifting in and out of sleep as the Sun gradually withdrew. A light rapping at my door opened my eyes.

"Hey ya chickee." Ali held up a beer—and a Coke. "Thought I'd check on you." She waltzed in and set the drinks on a table.

"Thanks," I said. "You saved me from journaling."

She made a face. "Lucky you. I will have to journal about me in the dunk tank, an experience in fear, phobia, and panic unbecoming an officer."

"Not a water baby?"

"Not in a two-hundred-pound suit," she said. "I freak out in a crowded elevator. My dad thinks that's why I want to go to Mars. No crowds."

"What about getting there?" I asked.

"Flyin' first class, baby. No claustrophobic mind fucks for this freedom fighter."

She handed me the Coke. "I noticed you didn't drink last night, so I figured you—don't drink."

"Family history," I said.

"Opposite here," she said. "Our house is dry as a lifeless planet."

I inched my head and back against a pillow on the bed. She took a chair near the window.

"Everybody's talking about you guys," she said.

I eyed her over my Coke.

"Which guys?"

"Your group. You dub. MarsMicro."

"All good, I hope."

"I think," she said.

"I really don't—"

"Heard this shouting match, over in Building Two, ya know, where public affairs is. They were arguing about—you."

"How could you tell?"

"It was like reporters or something," Ali said. "Bugging a lady in the office about where you were staying. What you were doing."

"Were you eavesdropping?"

"Hard *not* to hear them."

"There's been some press—"

"*Some* press? There are entire news channels devoted to

you guys. Your team is every young scientist-astronaut-engineer-pilot kid with her eyes in the skies dream."

I looked at the Air Force patch on her open jacket. "You had your eyes in the skies long before we came along."

"True, that. But—MarsMicro is the best thing to happen to space exploration since we first landed on Mars. That critter you found, though. Starting to sound like a different story."

"Who'd a thunk it?" I said.

"Not me. Finding life means sending life, right? To look around, find more life. We can't do everything with robots." She sipped her beer. "Is it true what you guys discovered is the — what do you call it—common something?"

"The First Universal Common Ancestor," I said. "Maybe. We won't know until we can do more tests. Real tests in a real lab."

"Which is why you're going to DSG."

"Not for those kinds of tests. They have to be done here, in a controlled lab environment."

"Toast," she said, and raised her beer. I raised my Coke and tried to lean forward to clink bottles, but felt dizzy.

"Whoa," I said.

"You okay?"

I tried to raise my bottle again, but it slipped out of my hand and hit the floor.

"Jen?" She stood and hovered over me. "Jennifer?"

I DIDN'T REMEMBER ANYTHING else until I awakened in some kind of clinic or hospital room. A nurse walked in after I opened my eyes.

"Welcome back," she said. "Doctor will be in shortly." She walked out.

I reached for what I thought was my cell phone on the stainless steel bed table, but it was something else, so I left it.

"Time," I said.

A cloud clock appeared. I'd been unconscious, or whatever I was, for a day. The doctor came in and right behind her, Ali, grinning, with a vase of flowers topped with a card. She set them on the counter and gave me a piano wave, like when you tinkle the keys with four fingers. She was in a flight suit and I planned to tease her about how hot she looked.

Doc sat on a wheeled stool and slid over with a lighted scope—an otoscope, ENT scope, whatever you call it.

"Good morning."

"Hey."

"You've been out a while," she said. "How you feel?"

"Like an elephant stomped on me," I said.

"This ever happen before?"

"No. Where am I?"

"JSC Clinic. Building Forty Five N."

"Not the hospital?"

"No. Not serious enough for that, fortunately." She paused and scrolled through her cloud chart. "I see you had a pretty serious accident a few years ago. Recall anything from it?"

"I was on the passenger side and it was dark."

The doc probed my eyes and ears with the light.

"They said my ears wouldn't bother me," I explained.

"Who said?"

"During my physical. I had problems with them after the accident, but thought they were fixed."

"Ever try Earplanes?" the doc said.

"No. What's that?"

She rolled over and took a box of these "miracle ear plugs tested by U. S. Navy pilots" out of a drawer and handed them to me.

"Forgot about those," Ali said. "Good idea."

"Say ahh," the doctor said next.

I did.

"Great teeth."

She listened to my heart, had me breathe deeply, in and out.

"Sounds good."

She slipped on some gloves and pressed my ears forward and raised the back of my hair, examining my head. She took my hands.

"Grip," she said.

I did.

"Wow," she said. "Didn't expect that." She looked at my chin, my neck. "Didn't expect this, either," she said.

"What?"

"No scarring. I read your medical history."

"My brothers said it was bad."

"Your dad . . . was he—"

"Yes," I said.

"I'm so sorry," she said. She looked at my chart again. "We could do a CAT scan. But you appear to be in perfect health. Maybe it was just a stomach bug."

The doctor stood, made some notes on her cloud chart. "Anything else, don't hesitate," she said. "Keep an eye on her," she told Ali, smiled at me again, then walked out.

Ali took the card from the flowers.

"Gave us a scare there, chickee." She handed me the card. Everyone signed it. Mr. Montana sketched a cowboy hat above his signature, urging me "Back in the Saddle."

"How sweet," I said. "Thank you guys."

"Tourists took off today," she said, pulling up the wheeled stool. "You're stuck with us ass cans."

I laughed.

"That was gonna be our nickname, ya know. But Shock Diamonds was just too cool."

"Lookin' pretty hot in that flight suit," I said.

Ali stood and swept it with her hands. "You like?"

"I do."

She sat on the doc's stool and rested her chin affectionately on my hand and chest. She looked at me and grinned.

"What?" I asked.

"Just 'mirin."

"Stop." I gently swept the hair from her eye and forehead.

"I sing the body electric," she said, staring at something beyond me.

I turned.

"The armies of those I love engirth me and I engirth them." She slid around on the stool to the other side of the bed, reciting the Walt Whitman poem. "They will not let me off till I go with them, respond to them."

I joined her in the last line. "And dis-corrupt them, and charge them full with the charge of the soul."

She picked up the gadget on the hospital table. "Combo Ohm meter," she said. "Volt meter. And amp meter. Learned to use one in the Air Force." She stuck its two steel probes into the wall socket.

"Looks like a short," she said. She withdrew the probes, held them up, and turned the knob. "If you crank the sensitivity way high, it'll pick up the charge in the Cloud."

She showed me the meter. She moved closer and the reading jumped. Toward me the readings rose, away from me, they fell. "The force is obviously with you," she said.

"This force, maybe." I wiggled the pulse oximeter attached to my finger, which was sending electronic measurements of my heart rate to the Cloud and probably what the meter detected.

"Killjoy," she said.

I HAD A TON of emails and texts to answer back in the hotel room. I answered one.

"Totally missing you guys," I emailed Dr. Levitt, who had "heard I'd had a little mishap and everyone was worried and sending get-well wishes and love."

"Just a dizzy spell," I wrote. "Doctor thinks it was a stomach bug."

I called David. No answer. Called Mom. No answer, either. I was homesick. For Kenosha, especially, but I'd take Seattle. I also wanted to ask David what else he remembered about the accident. So many forces affected my recall. I couldn't remember ninety percent of what happened from a purely physiological basis—injury, concussion, loss of consciousness. The other ten percent I blocked out.

I remember Dad's face; I remember arguing with him; I remember watching *Papillon* with him the night before: Steve McQueen hugging Dustin Hoffman and jumping off the cliff into the sea. Another guy flick about friends in the throes of goodbyes. David wasn't answering. Neither was Mom. I wanted to hear their voices. I felt like crying. I didn't leave any messages.

LIFE JOURNAL. ENTRIES THREE, FOUR. David was always good about keeping in touch. But as I got older, the long-distance version of our relationship evolved in ways I never expected, as we became tethers in a fray.

"You last saw Brian in March, right?" David asked me as I looked across Seattle high atop the Space Needle.

"Yes. Spring Break. What's up?"

"He's lost like twenty pounds. I can see his chest bones."

"Brian? He's all muscle."

"Not anymore."

"When did this start?" I asked.

"I don't know. Summer, maybe. Seems like it was hot and humid. He'd fall asleep at dinner when I came over, then get irritable when Mom or I asked if he was okay. I chalked it up to his usual bouts of seasonal affective disorder."

"Is he trying to lose weight?"

"No. His hygiene sucks, too. Doesn't wash his hair. Dirty clothes. Mom says he gets pissed whenever she comes into his room to take the laundry downstairs."

"He should do his own damn laundry," I said.

"He might be on something," David said.

"Like what?" To this day, I'm hopelessly naive about the "somethings." They are the building blocks of a dark alternative universe. Atoms and quarks in my world, pills and powders in the other.

"I don't know," David said. "There's been a lot of that new synthetic opiate going around. Veranyl, I think it's called. Overdoses. Busts. Cops show up at my school. Kids don't return to class. Ever."

"In *elementary* school?"

"Yeah."

"Brian's nineteen, in college, doing great. Right?"

"Prime demographic. Young, upwardly mobile, male. Bright. Sensitive. Shy."

I slunk down against the wall as families with kids and cute, kissy-face couples passed me, gawking through the Needle's telescopes or looking wistfully at today's version of sky gray.

"What are we gonna do?" I asked.

David sighed. "I dunno."

I rested my head against the phone in my palm and stared at the wires on the suicide prevention enclosure in front of me. I shivered. Cloudy and fifty in Seattle.

I MISSED THE FIRST SIGN something was up with our mother—I suppose we all did—when David called with news Uncle Ron was suggesting Mom go on some kind of drugs "to keep her moods modulated."

"Drugs?" I said.

"I agree," David said. "It seems radical."

"Is this drug thing *Ron's* decision?"

"No," David said. "But you know that weird hold he has on her."

"Yeah, well—it was his bad advice that cost Brian his life."

"It was Brian's decision. Or lack of decision. Much as I'd like to blame Ron or anybody else, Brian was in charge of Brian."

"That's crap, David. How can you say that? Brian wasn't in charge of anyone, let alone himself. Screw Ron. If this comes up again, I want you to call me. Put me on speaker. And if my voice in the matter from here won't work, I'll come home."

"I know what you mean about Brian. I've just. I've just had

to. Learned to, I guess, learned to distance myself." He paused. "I gave up. We all did. What else were we supposed to do?"

"Save his life," I said.

"Nice guilt trip."

"I was left out of it. I had no say. He was my brother, too."

"You weren't here, Jennifer."

Those four calm, right words blew the wind out of my psyche.

"I didn't even get to say goodbye," I muttered.

Thirty Two

We spent the next week touring space vehicle mock-ups, mostly in Building Nine. It was surprisingly emotional (as if life journaling wasn't emotional enough) getting so close to the (albeit scale model) shoulders of giants: the International Space Station, *Curiosity, Orion, Perseverance, Foresight, Odysseus*, and Deep Space Gateway.

I now observed that DSG was laid out like my student apartment at Cal-Tech: four-to-six (depending on the mission) autonomous crew modules surrounding a central control and meeting area that broke up the claustrophobia I saw Ali experiencing as we roamed through these confined spaces.

DSG's center also rotated and like a centrifuge, created artificial gravity. Though my apartment didn't rotate, its center kitchen and living area was our center of gravity, four unrelated students living in autonomous bedroom/bathroom suites.

"Deep Space Gateway is an updated version of NASA's Nautilus-X Multi-Mission Space Exploration Vehicle from 2011," a recorded tour guide explained. "Designed and built by CloudSpark and TeloSky, DSG is the first gravity-wheel space station. It has admirably and economically proved a concept originally described by Konstantin Tsiolkovsky, the Father of Space Exploration, and Wernher von Braun, the Father of Rocketry. Gravity wheels are better known through the works of Arthur C. Clarke and others," e.g. *2001: A Space Odyssey*.

"Pretty roomy in here," Ali said about DSG's rotating hub. "I'm likin' it."

The crew modules seemed bigger to me here than during our DSG conference calls. They did not rotate with the wheel, however, and so were gravity free.

"I'm definitely cutting my hair," Ali said, watching a cloud video of an astronaut moving around a DSG crew module, hair in the air. The replay looped as she took off her baseball cap, smiled at the camera, hair flying up. It looked more funny than annoying.

The highlight of "Sim Week" which was actually ten days, started with bragging props for our Canadian trainee, CANASCAN.

"CanArm is *amazing*," he said. Without it, he explained, Telos, Sparks, and NASA could not have built the gravity wheel.

Designed by our neighbor to the north, CanArm was a dynamic trio of robotic arms and a hand, explained our robotics instructor, whose name tag read "Joshua Logan, Canadian Space Agency."

The first arm, CanArmPex, manipulated payloads and attached mission crew modules, things that require pushing and lifting strength ala your pectoral muscles.

Sibling CanArmDex performed maintenance tasks

requiring manual dexterity, such as cleaning and adjusting solar collectors and fixing stuff. It worked in tandem with a human-like titanium-alloy hand known as the *Dexterous Manipulator*, aka Dex, with right *and* left opposable thumbs that attached to the arm's end.   CanArms and hand could travel to any location on the space station, where crew members on the ground or in a glass-enclosed DSG cupola controlled them.

"Do we have a couple volunteers to take the simulation controls?" Logan asked.

Ali raised her hand and mine. We ducked into the glass cupola dome, cramped with screens and controllers. The rest of our group watched on monitors outside, awaiting their turns.

It seemed kinda unfair: the last people to do the simulations would have the benefit of watching everyone before them either get it right or screw it up. The pressure was on us guinea pigs.

"We have two sims," Logan explained. "Use Dex to un-stick the gravity wheel. We don't know how it got stuck. Maybe a bird hit it."

LOL.

"And use Pex to attach a crew module that has just arrived from Earth."

"Which one's harder?" Ali asked.

"Pex," Logan replied. "At least, that's what everyone says. I broke a hydraulic line on the Dex sim, so my experience was, shall we say, a bit different."

"I'll do Pex," I said. I figured after all the fuss and haze, I needed to prove something to myself. "Unless Ali—"

"I'm already hooked on the gravity wheel," she said.

"Okay, so," Logan began, "here we have rotational controllers that rotate the arms." He pointed at two joysticks, marked D and P. "These translational controllers move the arms up, down, and out. Pex also has a new telescopic feature, like the old car or radio antennas, where three ten-meter segments can extend for thirty meters, about one hundred feet total."

He pressed the top of a toggle switch to extend the arm, the bottom to retract it.

"Finally, these gloves control Dex," Logan said. "Put your hands in, watch Dex on the screen, do what you need to do."

Everything around and above us gradually went dark.

"This cupola rotates. The floor can do a three sixty. We can also tilt sixty degrees forward and back."

I heard servomotors spin, felt tilting and rotating, and broke out in goosebumps as simulated Momma Earth, in all her baby- blue, milky-white glory, gradually filled the glass dome around us.

"Gravity wheel repair simulation," Josh Logan said. "First, we need to find out what's wrong so we run a computer diagnosis."

The verdict: broken hydraulic line, Servo Bay Four, "code name Logan's Done," we read.

"Broken hydraulic line, huh? Very funny," he said. "Wait til

I find the wiseguy who programmed this sim."

"It wasn't a guy," a woman's voice said on a speaker. I heard laughter from our group outside.

"Watch and learn, Bren," Logan replied. "Watch and learn. First step: let's swing Dex into view."

He put Ali's hand on the joystick. She toggled it around and the giant arm (actually an elaborate 3D image) emblazoned with Canada's maple leaf flag appeared through the cupola.

"Next step: Attach Dex."

A couple touch screen commands attached the companion hand to the mighty arm.

"Let's have a look at the servo bay. It'll be on your left. Just follow the camera."

We saw a lid marked with the number four.

"Open sesame. You right or left handed?" Logan asked.

"Left," Ali said. A woman after my own rebel heart.

"Left hand glove. Put your hand in and open the bay."

So this glove control was cool. It took charge of both arm and hand, and with Ali's fingers and left thumb, Dex opened the small bay door.

"Freaky," she said. "I can actually feel it."

"What do we see?" Logan asked.

Ali shrugged.

"Let's take a closer look." A camera with a light moved into the bay, a cubby filled with tubing and hardware. "Put your hand in there and gently pull the tubing forward."

She did. It didn't look broken.

"So why don't we have hydraulic fluid spewing all over?" he asked.

"Automatic shut down with any pressure drop," Ali said.

"One hundred percent—correct," he said. Our group outside cheered.

"Lordy. I have an audience," Ali said.

"And a straightforward fix," Josh said. "Line isn't broken. Just unplugged. Take it, follow your flashlight into the bay, and plug it back in."

"Wow," she said. "My hand's getting tired."

"Why we have this." He swung an arm rest over. "One for each arm. It helps holding your hands steady. Dex can't do super complicated maneuvers because of controller fatigue, but it has eliminated the need for maybe, what, forty percent of space walks?"

Arm and wrist on the mobile rest, Ali took the tubing and plugged it into the socket, well inside the dark cubby.

"Now slowly twist to the left until you feel it lock."

She did.

"Okay—now the real test," Josh said. "Flight engineer: re-pressurize."

Some digital readings appeared but skittered around and fell back.

"Sim complication one: pressure not holding; hydraulics disengaged," said Bren, the woman's voice from our great beyond. "You sure the line locked?"

"I'll check," Ali said. She took the hand back into the bay, grabbed the line. "Feels loose," she said. "I can feel it in the glove. This is so wild."

"Turn it again, gently. Gently. Dex can break stuff as well as fix it, as I found out the hard way."

She turned her wrist and we saw the line turn in the plug.

"It locked? Feel it. Any slack?"

"No."

"Engineering: re-pressurize servo bay four hydraulic line."

The readings came back up and stayed up. We heard clapping and whistling outside.

"Nobody cheer yet," Josh said. "Okay—let's get Dex outta there. Take the joystick and fully retract."

We watched all the screens, every angle of the giant flywheel as its robotic helpmate moved along the hull and away.

"Engineering: start the Ferris Wheel."

"I'm sorry Josh," Bren said. "I'm afraid I can't do that."

"Don't argue with me, HAL," Josh jested back. "Now start that wheel."

The artificial gravity wheel started turning in space. Our team applauded. With her hand in the glove, Ali—and Dex, on one of the monitors—gave us an interstellar thumbs up.

My simulation was comparatively simple. I used CanArmPex's telescoping arm to corral and attach an Orion crew module that arrived by rocket to one of two vacant module bays. Parts of the module unfolded and unfurled, like a fancy tent. The arm attached it to form a vacuum seal at the bay, then our hypothetical crew members did the rest, attaching oxygen, waste, hydraulic, power, and communication lines, all from inside.

The most I got to do with the Dex gloves was put my hands into them, wiggle my fingers, and make Ali laugh when I flipped her off against the backdrop of CloudSpark's "lightning in a thunder cloud" corporate logo on the side of DSG.

I LEFT THE DOOR of my hotel room ajar to let some air in, hopefully sans bugs.

"Hey ya chickee." Ali peaked in. "Let's . . . " She hopped on the bed. " . . . go out."

"Where?"

She put up both feet and her skirt fell back.

"Cute dress," I said.

"It's not the dress I am displaying." She clicked her boots together. "Have you no sense of smell? No twinge of envy?"

I sniffed the aroma of new and expensive on her cowboy boots.

"Are these a hint?" I asked.

"Line dancing," she said. "Most of our group's going."

"I've never line danced in my life."

"Me, neither. But when in Texas." She slid off the bed, slipped out the door, and back in with two large square boxes. I picked up a different aroma before she took the first lid off and put the brimmed hat on her head.

"Gorgeous," I said.

She took out another hat and put it on my head.

"Ali—"

"Hush." She directed me to the mirror. "Hottie, absolutely," she said.

"This looks like it cost a fortune."

"Looks can be deceiving," she said. "But don't think for a minute that not spending a fortune means I value you one bit less."

She took her hat by its brim, swept it off her head, and bowed like a knight-errant. The cowboy hat, the boots, the skirt, the flight jacket all made a kind of weird-western-wonderful sense.

She unzipped the jacket to a shirt with fringes, turquoise, and rhinestones.

"I can't compete," I said.

"I've looked in your closet," she said. "You can try."

WE HAD THE BEST darn time boot scootin', toe tapping, heel clacking, and do-si-doing through what felt like every one, two, three, and four-wall line dancing classic—Brooks and Dunn, Alan Jackson, Shania Twain, and a few that caught my rhythm off guard. I'd never heard Britney Spears before, so when this song called "Toxic" came on, Ali had to step in.

"One two, one two, one two," she said, watching my not-exactly-cowboy-boots, then leading with hers. "Forget the lyrics. Go with the bass."

I finally got it. One two, one two, one two. Clack clack

clack! Every heel in the room hit the floor at once. Clack clack clack! The club's two fiddlers jumped in—the song had some rousing string riffs they attacked with C&W gusto. It was loud, boisterous, exhilarating. I'm not big into touchy-feely, so in pretty much every way, this was my kind of dance.

Alice Merton was next and since I knew her song (it was one of my tween anthems) I got the rhythm and the twist right off. Every time she said "no roots," we said "no *boots*," our boots hitting the floor in synchronized defiance.

I took Ali's "go with it advice" when I saw strangers recognizing me.

"Oh my god!" a woman who looked to be about twenty said, smiling and staring.

"Unbelievable. I can't believe I'm standing next to you!"

"So cool."

"Crimsy!"

Contrast this with a pretty drunk guy at the bar. He was put out I wouldn't let him buy me a Coke and . . . rum, vodka, tequila, Jack—he recited a list. He finally asked to arm wrestle "for the honor." I pursed my lips and tried to convey I wasn't interested. But he kept at it and I relented. I heard him call me a "bitch" when his hand was in mine, elbows on the bar, straining but not moving.

"What did you say?" I asked.

"I don't know why you're acting like this," he said. "I just wanted to buy a pretty lady a drink."

"I appreciate that," I said, holding his arm. "But I also politely said no."

"This ain't polite," he said.

"What?" Ali appeared behind him, nursing a beer.

"Problem?" The bartender swooped in with a rag.

I didn't want to cause a scene or be humiliated in losing to this guy in front of Ali, so I squeezed his hand, felt something give, let go. He slipped off the stool rubbing wrist and palm, scowled at me, and vanished into the low-lit crowd.

"What the hell?" Ali grinned.

I sipped my virgin Coke and gazed at her, innocently, over the straw.

LIFE JOURNAL. FIFTH ENTRY. Little victories on my mind.

There's nothing like watching the single headlight from one of our vintage electric streetcars gradually approach in the twilight snow. The Red Rocket (could it have been more appropriately named?) headed my way, signal bells clanging— ding ding ding—steel wheels squealing as it rounded the freezing track.

I'm a vixen of vintage, from my lead-glass flat in Seattle to my 70-year-old, fur-lined, knee-high boots, and I've always thought Kenosha's streetcars were some of the coolest things on more than four wheels. Mom's car drove me to the streetcars' north terminal, where I waited with the heater blowing until I could see the headlight.

Part of the old Lakota Plan, a downtown redevelopment scheme heavy on historic preservation, the north-south route expansion was the first major change since the streetcars returned to service after a long dormancy decades ago (Y2K). Kenosha had ten streetcars now, up from the original six from the 1950s. Some had memorable nicknames—the Green Hornet, Wings, and the Red Rocket—none of which I had ridden in years.

I remember going with Dad to the Common (City) Council meetings to expand what was then a small streetcar loop when I was in junior high. I wrote a report on the proceedings for a civics class, quoting Aldermen and public testimony. It was democracy in action, Dad said, and I was witnessing everything that made this country great.

Route expansion opponents claimed too many trees would get cut down and it would be too expensive. The pragmatic Midwest contingent called the streetcars little more than an elaborate amusement park ride. To die-hard supporters, however, they were "the gems in Kenosha's crown."

Never much of a civic cheerleader, Dad was nonetheless in this latter camp. We need to preserve our history for future generations, he testified. I was so proud of him. I could never speak like that in public, even though he urged me to give it a shot (I settled for standing by his side, close enough to worry that someone else might catch a whiff of the bourbon on his breath). The streetcar expansion won the evening with a super majority. We took the bus to City Hall and home.

Democracy cuts both ways, though, and the Kenosha Common Council scrapped the expansion a year after approving it, with an even larger majority. The cost of moving underground utilities was the reason they cited, but more trolley haters surfaced, most complaining that no one rode the damn things anyway.

Dad mobilized after the defeat. He stopped drinking, at least as much, and became a force in the trolley resurgence. He organized petition drives; had visiting tourism experts over for dinner; badgered state officials for extra money to move the underground utilities; became a booster right out of a Sinclair Lewis novel, Kenosha's Number One Fan.

What city on Earth could boast of such a magnificent lakeside setting, all within view of the streetcars? Dad argued. How could Kenoshans, living and working next to such a limitless horizon, impose such artificial limits on the city's potential? The Council came back a third time with near-unanimous approval of the north-south streetcar expansion. But dad was gone before the first track was laid.

Thirty Three

"The most important course you're ever gonna take," tempered our simulation exhilaration after breakfast the following Monday.

Mishaps: Their History and How to Avoid Them

The five-day, forty-hour course would take us through space tragedy in detail. Large, brilliant photos of the crews that suffered mishaps—Apollo, Challenger, Columbia—depicting their civilian and aeronautical lives greeted us each morning and bade farewell every afternoon, beneath a quote in raised pewter lettering on the wall outside the classroom.

The conquest of space is worth the risk of life. — Virgil "Gus" Grissom

NASA has had only three major mishaps. I say "only" because given the dangers of space travel, that's incredible. Our instructor, Commander Shara Myles, was the first female astronaut to survive a near-mishap that came within one wrong move of killing her and her crew.

"You never get over it," she told us. "They talk about survivors' guilt. You can still have it, even when everyone survived."

We watched grainy 2D video and vivid 3D projections about each calamity, starting Monday with Apollo One, the first manned mission in the Apollo series that would ultimately take us to the Moon. A routine "launch rehearsal test" of an

Apollo capsule killed Grissom, Edward White and Roger Chaffee over seventy years ago. A spark—a simple spark—ignited oxygen in their cabin. No one imagined something like that could happen.

"That's one reason mishaps are so important," Myles said. "They show us what we *need* to imagine." NASA wasn't prepared, she told us, for safety problems with an exit hatch and flammable clothing.

"We've got a bad fire," was one interpretation of Apollo's last garbled transmission.

I BROKE OUT IN chills and touched Ali's hand—she sat next to me—when Christa McAuliffe—beautiful, smiling, alive—appeared before us in a newly-rendered 3D projection Tuesday. There she was, sitting for an interview in a bright orange suit, wearing a pearl necklace you could reach out and touch.

"I would like to humanize the space age by giving a perspective from a non-astronaut, because I think the students will look at that and say, this is an ordinary person," she said, with a slight Bostonian brogue. "If they can make that connection, then they're gonna get excited about history, they're gonna get excited about the future, they're gonna get excited about space."

"Christa had six lessons planned," our instructor said. "Magnetism, Newton's Laws, things she could demonstrate up there." She motioned with a nod.

McAuliffe was a teacher, and the first American civilian to venture into space. We watched her and the rest of the Space Shuttle Challenger crew—Dick Scobee, Ron McNair, Mike Smith, Ellison Onizuka, Judy Resnik, and Greg Jarvis—get into a van, and into the shuttle, for a second try at launch.

"T minus six minutes, thirty seconds and counting . . . four, three, two, one," mission control counted down. "And we have liftoff! Liftoff of the twenty fifth space shuttle mission and it has cleared the tower." That sounded like a reporter.

"Challenger now heading . . . good roll program confirmed . . . engines throttling down . . . normal throttles . . . three engines running normally . . . three good fuel cells . . . velocity: twenty two hundred and fifty feet per second—"

Scary fast. But everything was normal. Everything looked fine. We heard a calming beep tone, like a steady heartbeat, pinging in the background.

Mission Control came on. "Challenger go with throttle up."

And then a blast. I jerked. Ali looked up. Smoke and debris littered the brilliant late-morning sky, and a white cloud that looked like a snail extending its antennae gradually ascended, the antennae separating, jellyfish-like smoke tentacles trickling to Earth, as the unimaginable gripped the sky. Another view showed us a crowd with children in viewing stands, every eye skyward.

"Picture you were just seeing is Christa McAuliffe's parents, watching in horror," a narrator said. "These are the students from her school. Just a huge fireball and a huge cloud of smoke. They may not realize yet what has happened."

"Obviously a major malfunction," said a mission control voice. "The vehicle has exploded. Awaiting word from any recovery forces."

But there was nothing to recover. We watched the families in the viewing stands, crying, hugging each other, flailing their hands, bowing their heads.

"That was an O-ring," Myles said. "The major malfunction that killed seven people just over a minute after launch was nothing more than a simple O-ring," a rubber seal that failed in the cold.

Engineers from a contractor named Morton Thiokol tried to warn NASA management about the potential for just such a failure. They *had* imagined the unimaginable, but couldn't get management to do the same.

We watched interviews with Bob Ebeling and Roger Boisjoly, who worried about too-cold temperatures the night before Challenger launched. Cold stiffens rubber. Stiff rubber allows heat and gases to meet in places they shouldn't and in this case, explode. But nobody with the power to stop the launch would listen.

"They were in such a 'go' mode," another Thiokol engineer, Allan McDonald, recalled.

"These engineers lived with a form of survivor's guilt," Commander Myles said. "Maybe the worst kind: surviving the tragedy you tried to prevent."

LIFE JOURNAL. ENTRIES SIX, seven, eight. The Christmas

before Brian died, David picked me up at the Amtrak terminal in Sturtevant, about twenty minutes north of Keno. He grabbed my bags and kissed my forehead. We walked to his car.

"Good trip?"

"They couldn't scan me," I said. "Or at least, they said they couldn't. Had to go full pat down."

"Merry Christmas, huh?"

"Yeah."

"You need a new chip?"

I looked at my forearm. I could barely see the little bulge. "I hope not. You saw how long it took me to get this one."

As Amtrak upgraded its routes with high-speed rail, security got an upgrade, too. Transportation Safety and Security Enforcement agents and increased wait times invaded that staple of bucolic travel, the train station.

"Home," David told his car. "Don't be surprised about Brian," he said, after we were on the highway.

"What do you mean?"

"How much weight he's lost."

"Like how much?"

"Just don't be surprised."

I thought about the implications of that admonition.

"Since we're on the subject, I've been finding it's best not to get into solutions," David said. "Fixes. Brian shuts down and Mom stresses out."

"Fixes? Like a drug fix?"

"No, no. Like suggesting another rehab stint. Like methadone. Like asking why Brian just sits around the house, between drug fixes."

"Mom's enabling?"

"Maybe. But what's the alternative? Getting a midnight call that her baby boy is dead in some back alley?"

On that note, Christmas vacation began.

We drove up to the house and Mom must have heard the car doors slam because she came down the steps without a coat and with hugs for me while David grabbed my always-travel-lite gear, plus presents, and went into the house. Mom looked worn in the Moon and porch lights.

"Good to see you, sweetie," she said.

I kissed her forehead. "You, too."

David took my bags upstairs to my old bedroom and came back down. "Let's get this fire started," he said, poking and prodding a hive of dying embers upon which he placed another log.

I looked at his strong, veiny hands in the firelight.

"Where's Bri?" I asked Mom.

"He *was* in his room," she said.

"Hey big sis."

"Speak of the devil," David said.

I gasped, audibly, then stopped myself, as Brian descended the stairs. He looked like a raggedy doll, clothes he used to fill out hanging on him, cheeks and eyes sunken. We hugged and I kissed him. He kissed me. He didn't smell good. But he was smiling.

"You guys get the gifts I shipped?" I asked.

"Voila!" Brian said, taking my hand and leading me to the Christmas tree. His hand was cold.

"I have a couple more things," I said.

"Are you hungry?" Mom asked. "I can warm some stuff up."

I looked at Brian. I was hungry, but didn't want to ask Mom to cook anything for just one. Brian looked hungry.

"I might have a bite, if anyone else would join me," I said.

"Stuffed," David said.

"Brian?" Mom asked.

"You asked me earlier," Brian said. He sniffed and coughed.

"I know, but I thought—"

"I wasn't hungry then. I'm not hungry now."

"Mom's not asking. I am," I said. "I would love it if at least one of the two most important men in my life would break bread with me." I took Brian's hand and ran my thumb along its veins. He sniffed again, like he had a cold.

"You make it sound like The Last Supper," he said. He looked at Mom. "Okay."

Mom presented Brian and I with ham and scalloped potatoes and the most out-of-this-world cranberry cobbler. I was ravenous, but seeing how Brian fiddled with his food, I nibbled.

"I'm surprised you got the time off to come home," Mom said. "They keep you so busy."

"I promised myself, no more missed Christmases," I said. "Dr. Levitt's very understanding. Unless we're on deadline. We've been on deadline with something forever, it seems like."

"I met her wife," Mom said. "Para something."

"Parada," I said. "And they aren't married. At least, not yet."

"She seemed very shy to me. Your boss is so outgoing."

"How's the project?" David asked.

"Great," I said. "The rover and samples are on their way back to Earth as we speak."

"I remember reading about that," Mom said. "The takeoff from Mars gotta little hairy."

"Everything on Mars has been hairy," I said. "Watching the rover get out of the canyon was just mind blowing. We almost lost it, like twice."

"Better than living in Kenowhere," Brian said. Sniff, sniff. Cough.

"How's classes?" I asked.

"Mine?" Brian said.

I nodded between bites.

"Dropped all but one."

I saw Mom turn away. "Why?" I said with my mouth full.

"Wasn't working out," Brian said. "I'll pick them up next semester." Sniff.

"You want a Kleenex?" I asked.

"There won't be a next semester pretty soon," Mom said. "They're not going to keep letting you re-enroll."

"It's fucking community college, Mom," Brian said. "It's not like Harvard or Cal-Tech or something."

David rolled his eyes at me from his stance poking the fire. He looked like he wanted to say something.

"It's been a godsend," Mom said. "You weren't ready for Carthage."

"I was absolutely ready," Brian said, puffing out his narrowed chest. "That's bullshit."

"Ya know," David walked over with the poker in his hand. "The profanity isn't necessary."

"You gonna hit me with that?" Brian asked. David looked at him.

"Why don't we go sit on the porch?" I asked.

"It's cold out there, Jenny," Brian said. The sniffles prompted me to drop it.

"Okay. Downstairs in the men cave."

"I have just as much right to be here as David does," Brian said.

I reached across the table to Brian and put my hand out. David receded. I heard Mom in the kitchen. Brian finally reached out and took my hand. His fingers and wrist bone were so prominent. And cold. His fingers were like ice.

"Okay," he said.

We went downstairs, Brian leading, to the big, comfy, plush couch that sat in front of the game consoles and 3D portals and the other indoor fantasies that had turned generations of Brians into pale, slender, addicted zombies. Dad didn't want to get all this stuff, but Brian worked on him relentlessly. Now, it just sat, like so many childhood memories rattling around in place of the children who created them.

Brian rested his head against my shoulder. "I'm sorry," he said, after a while. "I hate when I get like that."

"It's hard on Mom and David," I said.

"I know," he said.

"They love you."

"I know. It's not me talking. It's somebody else."

Brian took a Kleenex from a box and blew his nose. He wiped his face and around his nose with another few. I wanted to ask him if he was using again, but I knew the answer, so why get into it. Besides, it was too early. You return a stranger when you've been away, especially when you come home. I needed time to become big sister again.

"What about you?" he asked.

"Me?"

"Do you love me?"

"To pieces and beyond," I said.

"You used to say that to me when I was little," he said. "Like Buzz Lightyear."

"That's to infinity and beyond, baby brother. To pieces is way better."

I turned down the lights and clicked on the television and turned the sound down to watch the late news, *Fox6 News at 11*. David walked downstairs about an hour later. He slid up the dimmer switch, but slid it back down when he saw Brian, head against the couch, mouth open and snoring.

My big brother turned and walked back up the stairs.

YOU KNOW WHEN YOU'RE asleep and something is waking you but you don't know what it is and you think you're dreaming when real sounds are trying to penetrate your conscience? That's how I awakened on the second day home. The sounds were voices downstairs.

"I don't care, Mom. It was here. Now it's gone."

"Nobody stole your money."

"Yes, they did. It was two hundred dollars in small bills. You knew about it. You saw it."

"Who would steal your money? Me? David? Jennifer just got here."

"I fell asleep on the couch last night. When I woke up and went upstairs, it was gone."

"You probably just misplaced it."

"I wouldn't misplace money. I wouldn't do that. Somebody stole it."

I got up, bedhead and sleepy eyes, wrapped a robe around me, and started downstairs.

"What's up?" I said.

Mom looked at me. "Brian thinks someone stole his money."

"Here in the house?"

"Yes," Mom said. By this time, Brian was in the men cave, probably rummaging through the couch cushions.

I came down the stairs to Mom. "How could someone steal his money in the house?"

"It doesn't matter," she said. "It doesn't have to be logical."

"No?"

"Not even remotely," she said. She paused and lowered her voice. "I would really like it if he would just get the fuck out of here."

I wanted to hold my mother, but she was too agitated.

"Mom."

"I mean it, Jennifer. I can't—you have no idea. No idea."

"David tells me," I said.

"Tells you what, big sis?" Brian emerged from downstairs, disheveled and red-faced.

I didn't respond.

"Tells you what? What does David tell you?"

I turned to go back upstairs.

"Don't want to hear it, huh?" he chided.

I kept moving, one step at a time.

"Just like when Dad was alive. Just like how everybody tiptoed around."

"That's enough," Mom said.

"Tip toe upstairs, Jennifer. Tip toe into the kitchen, Mom. Tip toe to your car, David. Everybody better just *shut the fuck up*."

I stopped and watched. Brian moved toward Mom, apparently trying to intercept her before she went into the kitchen.

"Isn't that right?" He was in her face. "Right?"

She slapped him and my underweight little brother spun around. He was upon her before I could react.

"Don't you fucking hit me!" He pushed Mom against the wall. I leapt down the stairs and grabbed him and pulled him back and we crashed against the stairwell.

"What the hell is wrong with you?" I said. "That's our

mother. That's our mother!"

Brian panted in my arms.

"You see?" Mom said to me. "See how this is? See how life is with my junkie son?"

Brian tried to break free but I was strong enough to restrain him.

"Let me go," he said.

"No," I said.

"I'm gonna head butt you if you don't let me go," he said.

"You head butt me, I'll kick your nuts into your skull," I said.

I don't know where that came from—maybe the reserve of rage I call upon for acts of construction, my father's gift to me, the drive that twists through my life like a corkscrew. Or maybe it was just some spontaneous shit, something I figured Brian, with his druggie friends and hard living, would understand.

"Always the peacemaker," he said to me.

"You need help," I said. "You know how much it's killing me to see you like this?"

He smacked his tongue against his palate, in what I took as a display of disinterest.

"Do you?" I shook his body. "Do you?"

I couldn't see his face. His back was to me, but his head was motionless and it looked like he was just staring ahead, into the oblivious void he accesses between doses.

"I love you," I said. It sounded corny. I figured it went in one deaf ear and out the other.

"Me too you," my brother said finally, in almost a whisper.

"THINGS GOT REALLY BAD this morning," I told David on the phone. I was lying on my bed, still in my robe, reminded of the tweenager and teenager who used to lie in this exact spot, on her phone or staring at the ceiling, happy, joyous, dreamy, or destitute, depending on the day at school, the night with friends, or most of all, the voices downstairs. "I saw what you've been talking about," I told David.

"I'd have called the cops," he said. "And Brian knows it. He doesn't pull that crap when I'm around anymore."

"You haven't told me about this."

"We've had cops over several times. Always happens when he's coming down."

"What do they do? Arrest him?"

"If they can't get him to calm down."

"Jesus," I said.

"Tried Him, too."

"How can Mom go on? I mean, I could barely stand to be in the same room with him this morning."

"Same thing Uncle Ron keeps saying." He paused. "I'm coming over."

"No," I said. "Why don't you wait a while. Everything's quieted down. I might see if Brian wants to go somewhere— take a walk, go downtown, watch the snow fall on the lake."

"He hates the cold," David said. "But I like the idea of you spending some one-on-one with him."

But Brian was nowhere to be found after I showered and dressed. Not in his bedroom, where I'd have been lucky to find him in the mess anyway; nowhere indoors; and when I opened the front and back doors and called to him, nowhere around the yard.

"Where'd Brian go?" I asked Mom.

She was reading on the couch, looked like on an older Ember Blaze, in the low, winter light from outside.

"No idea," she said.

I walked over and sat across from her, reached and turned on a lamp next to her. "You'll ruin your eyes," I said.

"Not with this." She shook the Blaze. "Reverse lighting technology. It's even better in the new ones."

"Listen to you," I said. "Miss Tech Guru."

"You wouldn't believe the things I've had to learn," she said. She was quiet, reading or maybe just staring. "I'm sorry you had to see that."

"I'm sorry you had to experience it. That you have to experience it," I said.

"I didn't mean to call Brian a junkie."

"Why hasn't anything worked? David says you've tried everything."

Mom put her device down, sighed. "Dr. Russell says it's like so many diseases. You try a lot of maybe cures and they don't work. Then you wait."

"Wait?"

"Wait. Pray. Hope. But you don't keep trying failed cures."

"Are you saying you've given up? That Brian's basically

gonna die and there's nothing anyone can do about it?"

Mom hesitated. "It's not just what I'm saying. It's what everyone is saying."

I looked at her. Then I stood.

"Jennifer?"

"I have to get out for a while." I felt like crying, and I didn't want Mom to see.

"David's coming by later," she said.

I shook my head and almost ran to the front door. A few scattered snowflakes were falling and I breathed in the chill, dry air.

Thirty Four

Catastrophes come in threes, they say, and we learned NASA was no exception on Wednesday and part of Thursday.

"Columbia Houston, UHF, Comm Check. Columbia Houston, UHF, Comm Check. Columbia Houston, UHF, Comm Check. Columbia Houston, UHF, Comm Check."

Mission control's last words, repeated over and over without response, to the crew of the Space Shuttle Columbia: Rick Husband, Willie McCool, Michael Anderson, Kalpana Chawla, David Brown, and Laurel Clark from the United States; Ilan Ramon from Israel. I wrote their names fully, slowly, taking notes for a test I hoped I'd never have to take.

The video from Mission Control started the same way as Challenger, with a crew member documenting the day's normalcy. "Control's been stable, I see good trims. I don't see anything out of the ordinary."

About twenty minutes before touchdown, the first hint of a problem. "I've just lost four separate temperature transducers on the left side of the vehicle: the hydraulic return temperatures."

I squirmed in my seat. I knew what was coming, but not what form it would take, what unimaginable would swipe the sky this time. The calm before the storm set in after a final, "Roger, that," from the shuttle crew.

"Columbia Houston, Comm Check."

The flight director at Mission Control, a young guy, looked pensive. His body language was so telling, I couldn't take my eyes off him. He put his hand on his forehead and rubbed the distress with the tips of his fingers. He kept his hand in front of his face, and we couldn't see his expression. I saw his wedding band, his thumb against his cheek, and through a shadow around his eye, suggestions he was on the verge of tears. When he finally took his hand away, his eyes looked moist, his expression lost, his gaze searching. Every moment of the loss of this spacecraft and its crew played out in the way he looked and moved.

"No phone calls," he said into the microphone around his head. "Lock the doors."

At first, his index finger did not leave his lips. Then he rubbed his chin anxiously, touched his face, looked at screens and fellow controllers. He folded his arms, paced the floor, commanded calmly yet emotionally. His name, we learned in a subsequent video, was Leroy Cain, and even years after the Columbia disaster, he still looked devastated.

"The unimaginable here was almost as simple as a frozen O-ring," Myles said. "A piece of insulating foam had hit a wing during takeoff two weeks before. The gouge absorbed more heat than the rest of the wing as the shuttle re-entered Earth's atmosphere, and it broke apart."

Turns out NASA knew about problems with the foam insulation, too. It was applied to keep ice from forming and breaking off during launch, but had itself become the thing that broke off, often in well-documented particulate cascades that hit the shuttle's wings, thermal tiles, and other components. None of the particles had been large enough to do serious damage until Columbia.

Engineers had actually seen the deadly piece of the foam break off and hit the wing, eighty one seconds after liftoff, but not until a video replay the day after. The flying foam didn't look to have done anything, especially given how many times foam disintegration had been observed, without incident, before.

"Foam" was probably misleading, the word itself creating a false sense of soft. It wasn't like Styrofoam. It was hard, with fewer air pores. And when it broke off, it hit the wing with about one ton of force. We watched a film demonstrating the impact, on a scorching hot Texas day, when engineers and astronauts gathered to see a simple piece of foam fired at a reconstructed shuttle wing with the same force. It blew a big hole in the wing instantly.

After the crash, which looked strangely like E.T.'s glowing fingertips caressing the sky, twenty thousand people—ten people for every square mile of debris field—scoured the ground for Columbia and her human remains. They identified the foam culprit after re-assembling about forty percent of the downed craft, but it should have come as no surprise.

As with the Challenger, engineers had begged and pleaded for a better examination—using satellite cameras, telescopes, even a spacewalk—of the shuttle exterior before it returned from space. They'd seen the foam hit the wing. But management turned their pleas away. A "routine email" informed the crew, too. "There's absolutely no concern," it said.

"Our astronauts, our mission control, our managers: We're like a family," Myles said. "And part of the family, we all felt, had failed the rest."

The Columbia Accident Investigation Board "found that Mission Management decision-making *operated outside the rules*, even as it held its engineers to a stifling protocol. Management was not able to recognize that in unprecedented conditions, when lives are on the line, flexibility and democratic process should take priority over bureaucratic response."

"Amen," I heard our ASCANS say, as these official findings scrolled before us with voice-over narration.

"Amen," I whispered.

It was "bureaucratic response," after all, that had brought me here, kept Crimsy up there, and in a real way now dawning, was endangering me and the DSG crew by creating tensions and encouraging, if not forcing, unnecessary travel. Crimsy would be home without the risk of any lives, had she been permitted the entry she and everyone working this mission had fought so hard to secure. She had been found, collected, and returned by robots and other machines. Not one human life was jeopardized—yet.

"The great irony here is that without the Columbia disaster, none of you training for Mars would be here. Jennifer," and

Commander Myles looked at me, "wouldn't be here, either. NASA refocused, and decided to get serious about a program that had been drifting for years. If you're gonna risk lives, risk them for a purpose, right?"

Columbia and Challenger crew family and friends—survivors—spent the latter half of Thursday talking to us, answering our questions, reliving.

FRIDAY BROUGHT RESOLUTION—and exhaustion. We'd been running, lifting weights, doing emergency drills, surviving simulations, studying, taking notes and tests. But nothing had produced greater emotional fatigue than this past week. I'd forgotten to try home again. I still hadn't heard from anyone and I was still worried, but I just couldn't muster the emotional reserve. The Life Journal took its own toll, but as a reflection of things past, didn't have the power of these worrying stories.

Today we learned about all the fixes, from streamlined designs—like putting crew quarters on top of, instead of alongside—the launch vehicle, where they can't be hit by flying debris; and collaborations, under NASA contractors like SpaceTek, TeloSky and CloudSpark, that had gone farther than ever imagining the unimaginable.

"We've made a lot of mistakes," Shara Myles said. "Too many chefs in the kitchen, too many spices in the soup. We haven't had a mishap in decades because we cut out a lot of the complications." (NASA wasn't part of the Intercity Rocket explosion, a one hundred percent corporate disaster with its own strange history of mistakes, conflicts, and even skulduggery).

"As the crew looks back at our beautiful planet, and then outward to the unknown in space, we feel the importance, today more than any time, of space exploration to all those who are living on Earth." These were our parting thoughts, delivered by Shuttle Discovery Commander Eileen Collins decades ago, in orbit. "Our flight is the next flight of many in the human exploration of the Universe. Finally, we reflect on the last several missions, the great ship Columbia, and her inspiring crew: Rick, Willie, Mike, K. C., Dave, Laurel, and Ilan. We miss them. God Bless them. We are continuing their mission."

IF WE DIE, WE want people to accept it," Ali told me that Friday afternoon, quoting the rest of Gus Grissom's admonition. "We're in a risky business, and we hope that if anything happens to us, it will not delay the program."

I lay on my bed in the hotel room staring at the ceiling, wondering what on Earth I had gotten myself into. Would Mom, David, Mike Brando, Nathaniel Hawthorn, the rest of my crew be watching me fall back to Earth in a blaze of sorrow?

"You as exhausted as I am?" I asked.

"If you mean has bawling my eyes out after class and crying myself to sleep fatigued me—" She stretched out on the bed next to me. "Hell yes it has."

"You flew fighter jets," I said.

She joined me in staring at the ceiling. "I've never lost anyone," she said. "I can't imagine it."

"I—"

"Fighter jets fly themselves, by the way. I was just along for the ride."

"I don't know," I said. My voice sounded grave, even to me.

"Don't know what?"

I had never felt survivor's guilt about my father or brother, maybe because I spent all that emotional energy somewhere else. I didn't know what I felt now, not exactly anyway. Fear was part of it. Anguish, worry, grief. I started feeling it during the survivor seminar, when one of Christa McAuliffe's students, now a retired physician, told us that had it not been for her, he never would have given medicine or any other difficult journey a second thought. His voice broke. He had trouble going on.

"I was in a bad car accident," I told Ali. "No one thought I'd make it."

She turned to me.

"I can't put anybody through that," I said. "I don't agree with Gus Grissom. It's not worth it."

"Jennifer," she said. I felt her turn and she put her arm across my chest.

"I can't die again," I said.

"You didn't die."

"I did."

"What are you talking about?" Ali asked.

I didn't know how to articulate it, exactly. I turned to Ali. She looked me up and down with her wide, beautiful eyes, breathing against my cheek. I could see a strand of hair rise and fall with her breath. The Sun was setting beyond the window and shadows were creeping into the room.

"Please don't take this the wrong way," she whispered. And she kissed me, not on the lips but on my cheek, tenderly, just above the curve of my chin. My body ignited. It was the most thrilling feeling, that single kiss, which she slowly withdrew.

LIFE JOURNAL. ENTRY NINE. It was all arranged, though I didn't know it at the time. My first real boyfriend Owen led me gently by the hand down the long pier toward a lighthouse that overlooked Lake Michigan. Now more tourist attraction than candle in the wind, the lighthouse had kept merchants and travelers and wanderlust seekers safe in Kenosha harbors for over a century. These days it was better known as a wedding destination.

The evening was early and cool, the pier lit like a runway. Thought its tower light was dimmed, facade lights illuminated the lighthouse at pier's end. Owen opened a small pier-level door and we climbed up winding wrought-iron stairs, fifty feet to the lookout.

I had never seen the lake like this—up high, waters edge, in the dark—and when I turned inward, had never seen my hometown look so enthralling. The Kenosha water tower, Simmons Beach, Carthage College. Owen handed me a pair of binoculars hanging under a porthole window he opened. He looked so thrilled at this small and simple act, and I knew then I wanted to kiss him.

But I deferred to the view and gazed upon the lake, the lights of a far-off freighter, the darkness, then a gradual sweep ashore, the Red Rocket streetcar trundling through Harbor Park, the latest installations on the Sculpture Walk, including two I particularly liked: *Gen Z*, by a Japanese sculptor; and *Will to Freedom*, by a woman my present age.

Brian insisted on taking me when the new sculptures arrived—the arts foundation changes them every few years. The *Will to Freedom* sculptor introduced her work.

"I wanted to show what it meant to push against the things that constrain us," she said, "the forces that conspire to keep us bound—to a past we want to escape, to a job we hate, to toxic people, to addiction, to a pattern of bad choices that can set our shackling in motion."

Owen caught up with us and took my hand. I think Brian was a little jealous.

"What are you looking at?" Owen asked me in the lighthouse now.

"Sculpture Walk," I said.

"Mmm. They have it lit up?"

"Yeah." I handed him the binoculars and watched as he peered through the portal. I looked at the delicate hairs on the back of his neck. I looked at his hands, their veins, his long fingers cupping the dual telescopes, knuckles rising like gentle hills on a sandy plain.

"Thanks for this," I said. "I'm really having fun."

He turned to me. I felt the night air through the porthole, watched his jacket collar rise and fall in the breeze.

"I didn't know if you would," he said.

I moved closer. I took Owen's hand and he took my other hand. I felt the most delicious tingling along my neck. I wanted to dive into him. But wanting him to make the first move, and the fear that if I did, it would all go wrong, won over.

I took one step closer and he turned away and looked out the small round window. "It's beautiful—" He turned back and I was so close and he did it. Moved his lips into mine and I just —

"Jennifer?"

We stopped. Hushed. The voice echoed up, against the tower's walls.

"Who is that?" Owen whispered.

"Jen? Sis?"

"Brian?" I said.

"Yeah. You okay?"

"We're fine, bruh," Owen interjected. I heard Brian cough. He knew Owen was here.

"Cool, man," Brian said. I thought I heard him walk away. Then, "That's my sister up there," he said.

But Owen and I were kissing, and I made a passion sound guaranteed to travel down the tower and push my brother away from the door. Over Owen's shoulder and out the porthole I saw Brian, my sweet guardian, walking back to shore.

Thirty Five

"Long time, no effing hear from," I said to Nathaniel Hawthorn. The bravado felt silly, but I didn't want to let on just how wonderful I felt hearing his voice.

"I'm flattered," he said. "You actually picked up."

"I'm dying here," I said. "I wanna know everything."

And he told me. No one ever arrested Dr. Marcum for violating the "Invention Secrecy Act." Malachi Shonstein kept asking when I was "landing on Marcia." Parada had been sick and Dr. Levitt took some family leave time to care take.

"Anything serious?" I asked.

"Don't know. Your boss hasn't said much and isn't around much."

Dr. Cooper was back and forth from Harvard. And my mom and Dr. Hale had some kind of fight.

"Where did you hear this?" I asked.

"Cooper," Nathaniel said.

"Is it like, did they break up?"

"He said something about an unstoppable force and an immovable object. That's all I know."

I didn't know whether to sigh in relief or gasp in panic.

"Mike and Lexi Brando are doing great," he said. "I think he actually has her more than his ex."

"Did I ever thank you for all your help with that?" I asked.

He didn't answer immediately. "I think so," he said.

"If you were here—"

"Your turn," he said. "I wanna know everything."

I think I covered everything, but since the mishaps class was so fresh on my mind, probably that more than anything else. I told him about landing in the infirmary. I told him about Ali, but not everything. I worried about wording her narrative in a way that might have—I don't know. I'm probably being presumptuous.

"I almost forgot the best news of all," Nathaniel said. "We're no longer incommunicado here."

"With DSG?"

"Back online."

"I can't wait to get up there," I said.

"I can," he said.

LIFE JOURNAL. ENTRIES TEN, eleven. "It's over one momentous year since you landed on Mars."

"*We* did that, Mom. *We* landed on Mars. You and me and David and Brian and Dad."

"That was you and your team. I was just happy as a pig in shit to be along for the ride."

I laughed. "No cussing."

"Ron—he's such a prude around me. Always has been. I

remember one time, your father took a deep dive into my tits at a dinner over at their house. We'd all had a few and everyone was yucking it up and yes, it was inappropriate in public. But only Ron found enough fault to call me out. Dad wanted to punch him. I told Ron he should try it with Marjy some time."

"He didn't like Dad's drinking," I said.

"Who did? I sure didn't. But I let it slide. It's a weird disease, Jennifer. It gets incrementally worse over a long time —years, decades. First it was a beer, then two beers, then a six pack, then a pint of the hard stuff—your father preferred rum —then a fifth. Then—death. Over a quarter of a century. We are just so, so fortunate you didn't join him."

"Do you miss him?" I asked.

"Every day. Every single day."

"I miss him," I said.

"What do you miss?"

"The way he smelled," I said.

"Really?"

"He hardly ever smelled like booze around me. I remember the few times he did, because it was so odd."

"How did he smell otherwise?"

"Sometimes," I recalled. "Sometimes like cologne. But mostly like man. I remember how big his hands seemed when I was little, when he picked me up and put me on his shoulders."

"Remember when he'd throw you and Brian into your

beds?"

"Oh, yeah. A one, a two, and away we flew! Didn't I break the bed once?"

"I think so. Bill got a huge kick out of that, and Brian didn't stop talking about it for a month."

"Calling me fat," I said.

"You were all muscle." She squeezed my arm. "Still are."

"He ever throw David in bed? I don't remember."

"Your father." Her eyebrows furrowed. "Your father and David had a different kind of relationship."

"You think?"

"I don't think David approved of him."

"Even when he was little?" I said.

"David and I have never, like, gotten into this in depth. But he never went to Bill for help. When he'd get hurt playing or have trouble with homework, he came to me. That time he broke his ankle at school, he had the nurse call me and when she couldn't reach me, she called Ron. I think for your dad it was kind of a slow-motion heartbreak." Mom looked at me. "And then what happened to you. Both of you."

"I don't like to think about it," I said. "I don't remember enough to think about it."

She grabbed my arm again. "This amazes me," she said. "There was nothing left of you to hold. You ever have any pain? Any *sequelae*, as the doctors called it?"

"No. Well, maybe the ear thing, but that's fixed. You going to the gym?"

Mom looked out the window. "Cold and gray, exceedingly cold and gray."

"*To Build a Fire,*" I said.

"You remember."

"I'm an astrophysicist with an encyclopedic knowledge of literary minutia, thanks to you."

"I'm not going to the gym," she said. "Don't feel like it."

DAD GOT HIS FIRST OWI (operating a vehicle while intoxicated) a few years before we bought our first self-driving car. He got his second OWI—the one that landed him in rehab —a few months before Dan August Motors went one hundred percent self-drive, rolling out models from Ford, GM, Tesla, Toyida and TeloTrans in an unorthodox bid to see which brand would stick.

My father would have gotten a third OWI if my mother hadn't convinced him to spring for a new TeloTrans Selfie, the self-driving economy model Leon Telos, the guy behind SpaceTek, made through a different subsidiary.

"The Bard" as we nicknamed the car, barred Dad from his favorite bars. Per the terms of his last OWI sentence, we had the car programmed not to come within a mile of any bar or liquor store in any American city. And he wasn't allowed to drive Manny Tranny the pickup under any circumstances.

"If a man wants to drink, he's gonna drink," Dad said once, and so the Bard brought him home one night after a bender somewhere. Brian saw the headlights go out just as we got a text the car had safely returned. After Dad didn't come into the house, Brian and I looked out the window. The Bard was dark. Not even a lit cigarette. I followed him out. We peered through the windows. Dad's head was back against the seat rest, his mouth agape.

"Passenger side open," Brian said. The door opened and he leaned in.

"Dad," he said. "Dad." He gently shook our snoring father. "Go around to the driver's side," he told me.

"Driver's side open," I said. The door opened and I stood, looking at my father. I leaned in and spoke in his ear and smelled booze on his breath.

"Dad," I said.

"I feel like dragging his sorry ass out of there," Brian said.

"Mom doesn't need that," I said.

"What about what we need?"

"We need calm. Isn't that what the counselor said?"

"Right," he said. "To hell with it." He turned back toward the house.

"Passenger door close," I said.

I ran into the house to get a blanket. The fall night was chilly. I wondered where Dad had gone to drink. I leaned into the driver's side. Despite the cool air, he was still out. I tucked the blanket around him. I took his hand in mine, rubbed it, and kissed his cheek.

"Solar battery heat," I said. "Driver door close."

I heard Dad brushing his teeth with an electric toothbrush in the wee hours of the following morn. I got out of bed and walked down the hallway. I appeared at the door of the master bath, where he tossed back some mouthwash in the pajama pants he sometimes wore to bed. He doused his face and chest with cologne. He jumped when he saw me.

"You're up late," he said.

"Heard you come home," I said.

"Thanks for the blanket."

"It was either that or drag you out of the car."

"I'm sorry," he said. "Guess I got carried away."

After the millionth "sorry," what was I supposed to say?

"Did you tell your mother?"

"Didn't have to," I said.

He walked toward me and kissed my head. I grabbed him and put my arms around his bare back and rested my head against his chest. He hugged me. I heard his heart beating, like when I was a girl falling asleep against him on the couch. We stood together for what seemed like a long time. When I said goodnight, it felt more like goodbye.

Thirty Six

I had an inkling Ali was dreading this day, but knew for sure as we gazed up at *Sonny Carter Training Facility* on the gigantic white building and she made some brave but hollow remark. *Neutral Buoyancy Laboratory*, the front doors announced. where we'd practice space walking in a swimming pool larger than a football field.

Today culminated Space Walk Week, as our twelve-person training team tried on space suits, mastered virtual reality simulations, responded to staged disasters, and learned about the tools we might use to repair something outside Deep Space Gateway.

I got my heel caught in the "portable feet restraint," a gadget attached to CanArm that holds your feet while the robot moves you around, and which looks like the thing they use to measure shoe size. With my feet wedged into its brackets, I stepped on the "yaw" pedal to turn it, then accidentally tapped the "roll" pedal, which swung me around and came within inches of dumping me face first on the ground. Ali used a smirk to restrain a giggle.

On suit-up day, we watched videos about how to put on old-school space suits—aka extravehicular mobility units (EMU)—to emphasize how far space fashion had come since then. Three to five people helped one astronaut enter one suit, from shimmying into the vest and sleeves to slipping on the pants, boots, gloves, and helmet.

"This used to take an hour," we heard. "Now it takes less than ten minutes."

The new EMU Z4 suits—the fourth generation of a design introduced in 2020—were lighter, easier to put on and take off, more functional, and better looking. They also came in two varieties: Mars—and everywhere else. More than anything, the Mars suits were designed to keep dust away from the wearer.

All the suits get hot after a while, and the first thing we noticed was the size difference between the large tubes that pumped liquid coolant through the old space suits and the slender, flexible tubules that pumped "nanoliquid" coolant through the Z4. A nanoliquid contains super-tiny beads called nano-particles—usually silicon carbide or titanium dioxide—that ramp up its cooling ability, so you need less coolant, which means less weight, smaller tubes, more spacewalk agility.

We had our blood pressures checked and completed short physicals; observed the control center overlooking the pool—about a dozen monitors, where we saw divers swimming around a DSG mockup; and finally went poolside, where I had to stop and stare at DSG, scaled down and with only one crew module, but identical in every other way, submerged in sixty feet of water.

The artificial gravity wheel, turning like an interstellar Mill on the Floss, looked like a giant hula-hoop, rising higher than any other part of the station and casting eddies across the water. I watched a diver in a yellow and black suit pass through it, over to CanArmDex, where she looked to be checking on things before our group entered the water.

"You okay?" I asked Ali. She looked at the pool, too, but without the same wonder I'm sure I had in my eyes.

"No," she said. "Claustrophobia, hydrophobia. Or is it aquaphobia?"

"Hydrophobia's when you have rabies," I said.

"This is gonna suck so bad," she said.

"Dammit, Jim. We're astronauts, not aquanauts," I said, with an affectionate poke to her side.

Alongside the pool, six of us paired off onto two-person platforms that cranes were poised to lower into the water. I stepped aboard the first platform, Ali the third. I put my arms out and separated my legs as a robotic dresser slipped on each side of my EMU—upper torso and sleeves, lower torso and pants. Think Iron Man suit-up scene minus the man and the iron.

A staff member like a fashion concierge zipped, snapped, and buttoned me up, crotch to neck. I had enough flexibility to snap the front. O-rings and rubber gaskets made the suit air and water tight. My concierge slipped on my boots and gloves, but before the helmet, offered instruction.

"These suits are heavier than what you'll wear in space— just keep that in mind," he said.

Lead weighted them down so they wouldn't float to the surface.

"If you get too hot, blow into the tube next to the

microphone. Too cold, inhale. The temp control will adjust accordingly. Just watch the small monitor across the top of your helmet screen." He turned to me. "Let's pull this up just a bit," he said, tucking my locks. "Snoopy cap," he said, putting it over my head.

It was what it sounded like—a cap like Snoopy wore when he flew fighter missions on his doghouse. Only this cap had a microphone and speaker that kept us in contact with each other and our divers; and three color-coded Sip-and-Puff breath-control straws like quadriplegics use.

We would grip the straws with our lips, inhale or exhale, and control things. The blue straw controlled cooling temperature; the red-and-white straw, certain CanArm functions; the yellow straw brightened and dimmed our helmet lights.

"The helmet screen gives you readouts for temperature, pressure, and a few other critical functions," my fashion concierge said. "You can even access the onboard cloud cam with it. Just look and blink, as usual."

Space selfies for Snap or Insta or Face or Twit. Would have loved the idea when I was in middle school. But after social media melted down over the Cloud's intrusiveness, which gradually followed the first Covid crisis, we digital junkies went back to phone, text, email, and ironically, good ol' face-to-face.

"Jen—you read?" I heard Ali in my helmet.

"I read."

"This is gonna suck so bad."

I heard other ASCANS laughing.

"I agree," one of the guys said.

The crane jerked upward and my partner and I were rising. The arm swung us over the pool and descended. Oh—did I mention I'm wearing an adult diaper known as a Maximum Absorbency Garment or MAG? Ali made me think of that.

"So if I go, will the pool change color?" she asked. "Over."

"Was wondering the same thing," another ASCAN said.

"Myth," I replied, looking at the divers waiting on us.

I read Orson Welles, in fact, started the myth of the urine-indicator dye, as a prank he pulled on some friends. Funny the things you think about to take your mind off the things you don't want to think about, like sweet Ali panicking.

I looked at my hands, resting helplessly before me, watched my feet and legs enter the pool. The suit was so well insulated I barely felt any temperature change, only the pressure of water against my skin. Down, down, waist, stomach, chest, neck, chin, gurgle, gurgle.

OMG! This is the clearest water I've ever seen. I could literally see every piece of DSG, and a few remaining but still-relevant pieces from the International Space Station, which was down here until NASA sold the real deal and enlarged the pool. A diver unleashed me from the platform. I watched Ali go in one direction; I went in another.

"You hangin' Ali? Over," I asked.

"I'm hangin'," she said. "Like, literally. Over."

We both were. The suits were precisely weighted so we would neither sink to the bottom nor float to the top—*neutral* buoyancy. The divers moved us from one task to the next. I picked up a fake plastic drill to repair a loose solar panel.

"What are you fixin' to fix?" I asked Ali, both of us punctuating everything with "over."

"Antenna hit with a meteor," she replied. "Or maybe somebody's foot."

I looked at the blue air lines trailing us and divers pointing cameras and giving short instructions we heard through our helmets and underwater speakers like an echo chamber. My guy laid out each new task as we floated over to it. I resisted him near the center of the pool, where I had the most amazing view of the rotating gravity wheel. I imagined being inside, looking out the portholes, my daily dose of Vitamin G. I could float here staring for an hour, but my diver was getting antsy.

"There wouldn't happen to be a broken hydraulic line over there?" I asked him through my mic.

He chuckled, underwater style. "We don't let Commander Logan anywhere near this facility."

He took my arm and floated me toward the wheel. We passed through it, where I paused to watch it rotate overhead.

"They had to dig out the pool to get that thing in here," my diver said. "Old pool wasn't near this deep." He pointed toward a panel beyond the wheel, and led me there. "Servo Bay 4" read a small door on it.

"May I?"

He took me down to the door. I went to open it.

"Use this," he said, handing me a large-diameter Allen wrench.

I knew all about Allen wrenches, and Phillips heads, and metric sockets, and about every other tool known to man because Dad insisted I learn how to do basic home and even a few car repairs (before self-driving cars added self repair). As I inserted the wrench into the bay door socket, I remembered the time I got a helluva shock when he taught me how to trouble shoot a bad ceiling light: bulb, switch, fixture.

"Mom says we should always turn the power off first," I told him.

"Pros never do," Dad said. "You're a pro."

I opened Servo Bay 4 like a pro, turned up my headlamp intensity with a puff into the yellow straw, and peered in at the hydraulic line. I reached in, but my gloved hand wouldn't fit all the way.

"That's a job for Dex," my diver said. "But take my word for it: it's working fine."

He took my arm and we started rising and at about the center of the wheel, I heard something in my helmet speaker that sounded like a cry, a scream, a distress noise.

"What was that?" I asked.

"Don't know."

Red and yellow lights started going off above and in the pool, but we couldn't see anything wrong. Then I saw two more divers jump in and swim.

"Is that Ali?" I asked. I got a cold, hollow feeling in my gut. "Is Ali okay? Ali—you read?"

"They're on it," my diver said. "They've got it."

I saw a space suit between like six divers. The water was so clear. I don't know what I was doing next, but I pushed away with my arms and feet in some kind of weird akimbo swimming motion that, awkward as it felt, was propelling me forward. My diver kept up.

"Ma'am, we need to stay back here. We need to stay back." He took my arm but I kept going and if he was applying pressure or trying to hold me back, I didn't feel it.

"Ma'am—stay back!"

But I pushed away from him and kept moving. I wanted to tear all this gear off—it was terribly hard to move. The helmet alone created so much resistance—it was anything but aero— or is it aqua—dynamic. But I kept going.

I passed Dex and the CanArms, ladders, hull, portholes, panels, solar collectors, mission modules, a vacant module bay. My diver stayed with me. I got to the ASCAN in distress and the surrounding divers and heard cacophony under my Snoopy cap.

"What's she doing here?"

"Jennifer—"

I pushed through and saw water in the ASCAN's helmet, relieved it wasn't Ali. They were trying to tug him free from something, but I couldn't tell what.

"What's wrong?" I screamed. "Why can't you get him up?"

Rather than fight me, one of the divers had mercy. She pointed at the air line, caught in a steel scaffolding that ran up the side of DSG's aft hull.

The trapped ASCAN was one of the guys from the European Space Agency and he looked scared to death. His nose was just above the rising water line. He saw me and I could tell he just knew he was going to die. I don't know what got into me or what I was thinking, but I ripped the air hose out of the scaffolding. It was heavy and spewed bubbles all around and I throttled it like a twisting snake until two divers took it.

I grabbed my fellow trainee around his waist, and hauled ass to the top of the pool. Fortunately it was a straight shot— no space station obstructions—and the divers, bless their cautious hearts, helped propel us along. A full-on emergency crew greeted us at the top and started unlatching the guy's suit and pulling him out of the water.

"Get me out of this," I said. "I have to get out of this."

The crane swung around for me, and as I rose out of the water, I saw ESA ASCAN's Z4, half floating on the surface, but I couldn't see him.

I tugged on my glove and ripped the sleeve and put my hand through who knows how many layers of insulated fabric and virtually tore off the other glove and unlatched, unbuttoned, unzipped. I was almost done by the time I got an assist.

I jumped off the platform and ran poolside like you're never supposed to do and saw him, sitting up choking and red faced but alive. I squatted down, catching in the corners of my eyes all the looks, like what kind of crazy chick is this?

Two EMTs wearing latex gloves wheeled up an oxygen tank

and equipment cases. They slipped an oxygen mask over his face. Divers flopped along the deck in their wet fins or watched from in the pool.

"Are you all right?" I said.

He looked at me over the oxygen mask and his eyes looked like he was smiling. He took my hand. I was so done as an astronaut after this. I could see it in the looks on everyone's faces. This is not the kind of calm we want orbiting planet Earth. They had me sit out the rest of the day.

LIFE JOURNAL. TWELFTH ENTRY. God, I'm tired. I don't think I can write this morning.

"I'VE BEEN CALLING MOM and David," I said.

"They didn't wanna worry you," Uncle Ron said.

"Worry me?"

"They knew you needed to get through this. At least, David did."

"This isn't sounding good."

"Patrice—isn't doing so great."

"Is Dr. Hale there?"

"No," he said.

"I heard maybe—"

"She gets really frustrated. He tries to help, but she doesn't see it that way. Your brother and I have been talking about some kind of caregiver—"

I sighed. "What do her doctors say?"

"They're still not sure what's wrong with her. Could be Alzheimer's. Could be something worse, like Lewy Body dementia. Could be something else."

"Like what?"

"Like, they don't know," Ron said "They're being realistic, Jen."

"Where's David?"

"He might be over at your mom's. We've been taking turns. Jeri's even pitching in."

"How did Mom leave things with Dr. Hale?"

"He's back in Cambridge," Ron said. "That's all I know."

My first inclination was to say screw this and go home. My second inclination was to say screw this *and* that and pack up and hit the road. Disappear. Heal myself. Damn, but this stuff was complicated.

There were times I resented my family for the ball and chain they were determined to shackle me with. There was always some drama with Mom. My dad went out in a blaze of drama, almost taking me with him. And Brian—there is no greater hell than living with an unrepentant addict.

Years of trying, begging, pleading, fighting, warding off the pale vampires who came for him in the night, arguing with lawyers and counselors and cops. And then, to repay our devotion, he breaks our hearts forever.

Ron broke into my thoughts. "I'm not coming down on the side of one idea or another, but—"

I was losing my train of thought, not listening, not hearing.

"I think Patrice and her doctors—" Ron went on.

I set the phone down. I turned to the hotel window and stared out of it, until I finally realized Ron was still there.

"I'll call David later, K?" I told him.

LIFE JOURNAL. UNLUCKY THIRTEEN. We'll never know if it was suicide, an accident, or an accidental overdose that caused an accident, just that we got a call from a concerned friend who saw him on the North Pier over Lake Michigan. Brian hadn't been home for a few days. I bugged David to either take me to the pier or let me use his car.

"So what?" he asked. "Brian's hanging around like Brian does."

"She said 'staggering.'"

We got there but no Brian and no one else, either. The pier, which extended about eight hundred feet into the bay, was deserted. I walked, then ran out onto it, toward the lighthouse. I looked out, both sides, at the end.

"Brian," I called.

I saw David starting up the dock and gave him an open-handed shrug. I kept looking over the sides and he kept walking and then I caught him out the corner of my eye pointing and running.

"Over there," David cried and pointed. "Against the

pilings."

I ran to the other side and followed his lead. He ran down the pier and jumped into the lake just before we met and swam to the pilings that supported the pier, where the water was shaded at most angles this time of day. I scanned the side of the pier and finally saw what he saw, something blue floating, drifting against the pilings with the gentle tide. I was on it and poised to jump in as David reached it.

"No. Stay there," he said.

David bobbed up and down in the current as he pushed his way to the object. Holding onto the pilings with one hand, he reached and pulled the object to him, and partly pulled it over.

"Oh no," he gasped.

"Is it Brian?" I said.

He said something, but I couldn't hear.

"Is it Brian?"

"Yes, damn it! Help me. Lean over. Can we—pull him up."

I leaned over but what were we thinking? Pulling wet, dead weight out of the water onto the pier? How? From under his shoulders, by his collar, his jacket, what? I reached down but David immediately got the problem.

"Forget it. I'll take him this way." David flipped Brian onto his back and tried to push toward shore. But the current fought back and they didn't move much.

"Is he alive?" I cried.

"I don't know. No way to—"

"I'll get in," I said.

"No. No way! And have three drowned?"

"Is he drowned? Is he dead?" I asked.

David didn't say anything.

"State swim champion," I yelled and jumped in. The water was cold.

"Other side," David said.

I took the water side and he kept grasping the pilings, trying to push back along them, toward land. I pushed backward with my legs. We floated in place.

"Let's switch," I said. "Let me try."

"This side? If I can't—"

"Let me try," I insisted.

So he took the water side and I took the pier side. With each rising wave, I pushed off a piling with one hand, clutched Brian with the other. David kicked his legs and fought the current, both of us keeping Brian afloat. With David kicking and me pushing and kicking with the tide, not against it, we started moving.

One piling to the next, we moved toward land.

We finally got Brian ashore and dragged him onto the sand. David collapsed on his back and stared at the sky. I tore open Brian's coat and started CPR. David tried to drag himself over, but the fatigue of the water and the emotions and the currents left him spent.

"It's no good," he said. "It's no good."

But I kept breathing. Kept thumping, then pounding my brother's chest, watching water gurgle out of his mouth, saw a little blood, washing away, where maybe he hit his head on the pier.

"He's dead, Jennifer."

But I wouldn't stop. I knew he wasn't dead. How could he be dead? How could my sweet, beautiful, loving baby brother, my guardian, my staff . . . I refused to stop.

David took my arm and squeezed. I only quit when thoughts crept in, that I was mocking Brian's death, that I was being selfish, that I was assuaging my grief rather than restoring his life, in an aftermath of watery denial. I screamed and collapsed over him and cradled his head in my hands and kissed him. I don't remember much after that. I think a cop walked down and found us. We didn't have to call anyone.

Thirty Seven

I needed medical re-clearance to rejoin my peers after the pool incident, so spent the down time pouring "relevant life memories" into my journal. I slept days, answered knocks from Ali and others checking on me, wrote. Vowed this morning to record a memory about getting back in the saddle.

LIFE JOURNAL. ENTRIES FOURTEEN, fifteen. On Christmas Day, we opened presents and sang vintage rock songs, stuff our grandparents and their parents listened to. Mom told the Cloud to "play Daniel" and the house filled with the first chords by a British singer I'd heard a couple times, Elton John. David apparently knew the song and touched Mom while looking at Brian, sitting on the couch with a half-unwrapped package.

"Stop Daniel," Mom said.

"Sounded like a good song," Brian said.

"I need me some Stevie," Mom said, calling up songs by a female singer, Stevie Nicks. I had listened to her a few times.

It was so hard to find good music, much harder than when Mom was young. Everything now is just a big digitized jumble. If you don't follow the music cloud logs or the musicians who still tour, you're stuck sifting through every band or solo artist who posts a song in the Cloud.

Mom insisted on using the cloudcam subscription I bought her to snap some 3D captures of the three of us, next to the tree, together on the floor, in front of the fire.

"Closer, closer. Smile. David—smile."

"David's not smiling, Mom," Brian chuckled.

She looked at us and blinked. Look-and-blink. Photo captured to the Cloud.

"David stole Brian's present, Mom," I said, leaning over and kissing David and mussing his hair, moves Mom immortalized then projected back.

I'm blown away how 3D pix and videos get so much more detailed and lifelike every year. MarsMicro took a bunch of these cameras to the planet and when we first found Crimsy, it was like she was already home.

"Holy bloody hell," I remember Dr. Marcum saying, when the first images and videos started coming in.

"Those may be the most beautiful photographs I've ever seen, next to Malachi's baby pix," Dr. Shonstein added.

And this might have been the most beautiful Christmas I've ever had. It was wonderful, the entire day, from Mom's first steps downstairs to make breakfast to her last steps upstairs that night, leaving the three of us to talk and laugh and tell each other how much we loved each other without once saying the word "love."

We went to BridgeWaters the Wednesday following and Brian signed up, with Mom writing a hefty check. Insurance didn't cover "outpatient" rehab, though everything we had heard indicated this was far more intense than inpatient rehab. Mom and David seemed relieved. I was skeptical but hopeful. Brian said he was excited and acted the part.

TWO GUYS SHOWED UP at our door early the next morning.

"Brian here?" the one with a tattoo on his neck asked.

"Who are you?" I asked.

"I'm Jim."

"Rick, ma'am."

"BridgeWaters?"

"Yes, ma'am." Jim opened his hand to a ghostcard. I bent down and read the apparition hovering in his palm. "James Palmer, Certified Addiction Counselor, BridgeWaters of Kenosha, blah blah blah."

"You think we were drug dealers?" Rick asked.

I hesitated.

"If you did, that's cool. I used to be. Only way I could feed the monkey."

"To be honest—"

"It's all right. Happens all the time. Are you Jennifer?"

"As a matter of fact. Call me Jen." I let them in.

"Brian." I called up to his room. Rick intervened.

"We'll go on up, if that's okay."

I stepped aside. I heard them knock on his door and Brian answer. They came downstairs a while later, Jim in front, Rick behind, and Brian in between.

"Goin' out," he said, and kissed my cheek.

The hairs didn't stand on the back of my neck like they did when his addict friends came around, so I figured everything was cool. I grabbed Brian and hugged him.

"Be safe. Have fun. Love you."

Rick, Jim, and some other counselors who didn't look like counselors were back and forth from the house with Brian every day until I left. I could feel the stress draining from Mom. David still had some of his guards up, but said he thought everything might finally be okay.

"They have a great success rate," he said, almost bragging. "Relapses are really rare."

I felt comfortable returning to my calling for the first time in years.

"TOLD YA SO," I was dying to say to Nathaniel Hawthorn, when my DLA test came back "inconclusive." Seems it's not so easy after all to predict when someone's gonna die. From the looks of the charts and explanations on it, my car accident threw the whole thing off. I should have died then, no doubt, but since I had lived, all bets were off.

"Hmph," said the med tech at the space center clinic during the "formal going over of the results," which he combined with some in-depth questions about my state of mind post-pool pandemonium.

"Everything seems good, but doc still wants a look at you," he said. "So, hey," he asked, before stepping out. "How'd you rip that air hose—"

The whole thing was a blur of bubbles and wet suits. The scaffolding it got tangled in was sharp and probably cut it.

"No idea," I replied.

"TERESA FOSTER, MD, FAAFP." I caught her name tag this time—same doc who looked me over after the fainting spells. She scooted over on the exam stool and sat squarely in front of me.

She placed her stethoscope on my back. "Deep breath."

"I don't know what got into me," I said.

"Just breathe," she said. She scoped my chest, then checked my eyes. "How you feel? Ready to get back in, on?"

"The pool?"

"Pool. Vomit comet. The horse. Whatever else awaits."

"I thought they were throwing me out."

"Not what I heard." She looked at my wrist. "Which hand did you use on that air hose?"

I didn't remember that, either, so guessed. "Right, I think."

She took my hand in her palm. "Go limp," she said. Her hand dropped, like she was holding a weight. "Hmm," she said. "Make a fist."

I did. She watched the veins rise in my wrist and forearm. "Okay, relax. I'm gonna press." After I relaxed, she pressed my wrist with her thumb, then looked at it. Did same with my forearm, then looked at it.

"Anything wrong?" I asked.

"No. Just another hmm moment. Here." She pressed her wrist with her thumb, then watched the color return from whitish to normal. She did the same with my wrist. But it didn't turn whitish. It didn't change color at all. It stayed the same.

"Press harder," I said.

She pressed my wrist as hard as she could, held it for maybe thirty seconds. A long time. But when she released it, not even a hint of white. She pressed her wrist again.

"That's called 'blanching' and you don't do it for some reason," she said.

"Is that bad?"

"No. But it's bad when it stays white for too long." She smiled at me. "You're good to go." At the door, she turned back and looked at me as I slipped out of the gown and put my blouse back on. "Jennifer."

I stopped.

"You may never hear this officially, but thank you."

ZERO G, PART TWO—the *real* Vomit Comet, as Ali called it— went well. No ear aches, no sinus problems, no Valsalva maneuvers—just the most complete freedom I've ever felt. We must have done twice as many parabolic flyovers—I wasn't counting, but it seemed like we were floating around forever.

"You're cured," Ali said, mid-float.

I dove beneath her and looked up.

"I am."

"Better move, cuz we're—"

I got out of the way as our team dropped back to the mat.

Per orders, I re-did the underwater space walk simulation with two space tourists and a Brazilian TV crew, all in dive gear. I'd never seen the camera they use to make 3D movies and shows, but it reminded me of the old virtual reality cams that seemed to capture all three hundred and sixty degrees at once. It looked cumbersome, and I had to fight to avoid hitting it a couple times. I was gonna ask about it, but they were out of the pool and long gone before my submerged day ended. I left the Carter building at dusk.

I USUALLY DON'T ANSWER my phone when "Private Number" appears, but I did this time.

"Jennifer. Al Sparks."

"And Leo, Jennifer."

"Wow. Uh, hi." I was always so tongue-tied around big-time people. I felt stupid, inadequate, I don't know why. It wasn't logical—hell, I was here on their behalf. But still.

"We heard about the pool incident. We also understand you're A-okay," Telos said.

"That's what they tell me," I said. "I thought they were gonna throw me out."

"Why on Earth for?" Sparks said.

"Do you know what kind of controversy that would cause?" Telos added.

I, in fact, did not.

"We're proud of you," Sparks said.

"I appreciate that," I said, resisting the urge to add "not bad for a flyover bumpkin." But his change in tone, after our gala encounter—

"Are you feeling all right? Up to speed? All systems go?" Telos asked.

"Yes, fine. Doctor says I'm good."

"Zero G went okay?"

"Swimmingly," I said.

As their questions mounted, never once asking how I was doing emotionally or psychologically, I felt like they were scoping an engine. I got a little irritated, the tone of my voice shortened. But I kept it classy and hurried things up with a "thank you for your support, it's been a long day, and I need some sleep."

My trillionaire benefactors got the hint.

THE INSTRUCTOR ON THE last day of our "Fundamentals of Space Psychology" course talked about Crimsy. She spent part of the morning on studies about how people would react if we ever discovered extra-terrestrial life.

An Arizona State University study years ago found positive reactions to microbial aliens. Psychology researcher Michael Varnum surveyed five hundred people, from conservative to liberal, young and old, male and female, even "disease avoidance" types.

"Please take a moment to imagine that scientists have just announced the discovery of microbial life (i.e. bacteria, viruses) outside of planet Earth," the study asked. "Think about how you, personally, and humanity at large would react, and describe your thoughts, feelings, and responses."

Would people panic? Would there be mass hysteria, as H. G. Wells suggested and Orson Welles dramatized?

Not according to the ASU study. Respondents were more skeptical of intelligent aliens (who might harbor sinister designs) than simpler life that might instead threaten pandemics. Modern medicine had a good track record curing disease. Maybe that was part of it.

Regardless, survey participants said the rewards outweighed the risks, "with little variation as a function of personality traits, disease avoidance, political orientation, or demographic factors such as income or ethnicity."

Varnum and grad student (mad props from this one) Jung Yul Kwon followed up with the *Discovery of Life Cross-Cultural Study,* which found much the same optimism among two thousand participants in five countries.

Even back then, Crimsy was bound for global stardom.

Thirty Eight

I t was hot as hell out here. In lighter-weight but still-stifling space suits, we stood around NASA's newest Hydro Impact Pool (more pond than pool) where a tall crane that ran along a scaffold spanning about half the pool's length hoisted a crew module complete with parachutes draped over its hull.

"Our first drop will be unmanned," said a guy on a loudspeaker. "We've set the tests up to simulate a worst-case splashdown: all parachutes deployed and a high-impact pitch with plenty of roll."

DSG's autonomous crew modules, also known as "Orion Multi-Purpose Crew Vehicles," look a lot like the old Apollo space capsules, only larger. Each crew module can attach to a "service module" that carries fuel, air, solar collectors, and other spaceflight necessities.

Emergency departures from DSG are splashdowns like Apollo did years ago: each crew module detaches from the space station, maneuvers into position, dumps its service module, then drops like a hot rock through Earth's atmosphere into an ocean.

I spent the last week with my nose buried in Jason Reimuller's classic text, *Spacecraft Egress and Rescue Operations: Planning for and Managing Post-Landing Contingencies in Manned Space Missions*. With a name like that, it was guaranteed to take my mind off other relevant life memories.

"If you'll all direct your eyes to the crew module," said loudspeaker guy.

The crew module sped over the pool like a zipline, then plunged into the water with a splash that came within centimeters of soaking us. It bobbed back and forth like a bop bag, rolling so far over on its sides I was sure it would capsize. But it stayed upright like a buoy. Tethered to the crew module's hull, the parachutes floated alongside.

"We are ready for the first team," loudspeaker guy said again.

A raft ferried out four ASCANS, who entered the crew module from a side hatch. Each module could hold eight astronauts, but the crane wasn't meant to hoist more than four. They spent time inside getting situated, then up went the crew module, tilted at about a forty degree angle, back and over the pond's edge.

"Three, two, one, release," we heard. It soared over water then splashdown!

The trainees emerged from top and side hatches, shaken but unvanquished. Two inflated their life jackets but after fighting with the parachutes, gave up and clung to some supports on the hull. The other two waited at the hatch doors for the raft. I wondered how these strategies would work if the module were sinking or burning. Everyone was smiling and talking. It didn't seem, from here anyway, like one of our harder sims. More like the attractions at Anderson Park pool back home.

My brothers and I always, always, always broke the *only one person allowed on the water slide at a time* rule, starting with the tradition of big brother sliding with little sister, too short to slide on her own; then big sister sliding with little brother; then all three siblings in train formation, alternating sis-and-bro cabooses, right up through high school. The lifeguards hated it and we got tossed off the slide more than once. But family traditions die hard and the summer before the year Brian died, the three adult sibs were train-sliding again.

It was my turn in the crew module and since Ali hadn't been yet, I wondered if she would join me or sit it out until next group. I waved at her and I was sure she saw me. She was looking right at me. But she didn't wave back. She sat it out— what the heck? Our all-female ASCAN group climbed into the raft.

"Everyone in?" our instructor said, looking around the crew module. "Aboard DSG, none of these seats are down. Take them, like so, and fold them up."

We undid some latches and locks, and followed his lead stowing each seat.

"What you've just done is increase the net habitable volume to a fair bit over the old space shuttles," he said. "The *entire* shuttle. This open area is where the payloads and other equipment are kept."

It was roomy, more than it looked from the outside. We folded the seats back down, belted in, and went over the instrument controls.

"The crew modules have both cloud and touch-screen control systems," he said. "The cloud screen gives you a three-hundred-and-sixty-degree view of the crew module's exterior at all times, except during re-entry, when the heat shuts everything down."

I looked up at the control screens. Ali probably understood most if not all of them. Too bad she wasn't here to guide.

Once we were all belted in, "Ready?" On our collective thumbs up, the instructor got out, closed the hatch, and up we went at a cock-eyed angle.

"Three, two, one—release."

"Ohhhh."

The plunge was nothing like I guessed watching from outside. Nine tons of steel in free fall—no wonder. The water felt like concrete when we hit—I thought my teeth were going to bash into the back of my skull.

"Damn," the ASCAN next to me said. "So we're expected to do this from how many kilometers?"

"DSG's around four hundred," I said.

"You going by Space Chaise?" pronounced in my circles Space Chase or Shace, NASA's space taxi. It looked like a small, cute version of the original shuttle.

"There and back," I said.

"Lucky you!"

"So cool."

I evacked out the side hatch, fighting with the parachutes, then figuring the hell with it, inflating my life vest, and hopping into the water. The raft crew had to fight the parachutes to get to me, and didn't look too happy, but I was too   hot   to   care.

I WENT TO THE front of the classroom and in back of the audience, saw a film crew and some media types adjusting cameras; Johnson staff; and some school-age kids.

A Federal Judge had temporarily quashed the Invention Secrecy Act gag order "until the courts can sort out who is claiming what and why," his opinion read. I guess Johnson's public relations office decided not to waste the opportunity.

I introduced myself, gave a brief overview of our mission, looked at Ali sitting in the back of the room, and immediately went to questions. It was the first time anyone from Team MarsMicro, except Dr. Marcum, had spoken without threat of reprisal.

How did I get interested in space exploration?

"Staring at the night sky in the cold."

Where did you go to school?

"Cal Tech undergrad; master's at Harvard; University of Washington, all but dissertation for PhD in Astrobiology."

Military service?

"None. But my dad served in the Army."

Was I religious?

"We went to church, but not every Sunday."

Where did we find Crimsy? What challenges did we face?

Was it true Crimsy might be the progenitor of all life on Earth?

"Two of the scientists on our team, Mike Brando and Rebecca Shonstein, think so," I said. "Crimsy quickly evolved into something like a cyanobacteria after the researchers on DSG grew her in a simulated Earth atmosphere."

So it's poisonous? It makes cyanide?

"Oh, no," I said. "Cyanobacteria are very unique germs that make oxygen the same way plants do, with sunlight and carbon dioxide."

Crimsy seems most like a type of cyanobacteria known as *Prochlorococcus*, I explained, a harmless, round, green bacteria that's super abundant all over Earth. She might represent a bridge between two of the big three domains of all living things, Archaea and Bacteria. Kind of a missing link. Making Crimsy kind of a big deal.

Why do you call Crimsy a 'her'?

"For kids," I said, looking at a few in the audience. "In my brother David's science classes."

Evolution or Creation?

"Evolution is Creation." Bada bing!

Any comments on the growing concerns about sending humans to Mars? (Now christened the "cross-contamination controversy.")

"I think there are ways to assure humans don't bring germs or other diseases that might kill *Crimsococcus*," I said. "But we're not going to know until Crimsy is here on Earth."

How did it feel when you heard that you—we, us, humans —had found—life on Mars?

Wow. How did it feel? I hadn't thought about this. I looked at Ali. She wasn't smiling or frowning. I got distracted and had to refocus. How did it *feel* when we found Crimsy?

"It felt . . . right," I said.

My ASCAN teammates, Ali included, started a standing ovation. I saw her slip out during the applause.

I WENT BY ALI'S hotel room the following morning on my way to Johnson. Knocked. No answer.

Scoped out the Starport Cafe in Building Three, where we sometimes ate breakfast. Not there.

Tried her on her cell. Listened to her greeting, left two messages.

Went by her hotel room after class—no answer; later that night—no answer. Her curtains were drawn but each room has a door cam. She barely looked at me during the splashdown sim. I wondered if she was avoiding me for some reason.

SO DID I REALLY need to know what was bothering Ali enough to stalk her back to her hotel room after she ate dinner at Starport? Absolutely. I knocked on her door.

No answer.

"Ali?"

I opened the door and walked in.

"Excuse me?" she said.

"Door was open," I said.

"Like hell."

"It was. You could have been collapsed in here for all I knew."

She pushed past me and turned the knob. And turned it. "You broke it." She spun the knob sarcastically. "Jesus."

"What's wrong?" I asked.

"This, for starters." She spun the knob again.

"You're avoiding me."

"I'm not avoiding you."

"Totally, you are," I said.

She looked away, took a deep breath.

"Ali." I took her arm, gently getting her to face me.

"I don't know," she said.

My stomach got cold. My mouth went dry.

"What?" I stammered.

She took her arm back.

"This isn't a good time," she said. "You can't be focusing on stuff like this anyway."

"Stuff like what?"

"I don't wanna have this conversation now," she said. "I don't."

"What conversation? What are we not having?"

"The conversation—"

"Yes?"

"I don't want to talk about it. Really. Please."

"But I—"

I felt her shut down. Somehow, I knew that pressing whatever it was wouldn't work, would lead nowhere, maybe just cause unnecessary hard feelings.

I turned, stumbled, and walked out the door. I lingered in the hallway long enough to hear what sounded like a chair being placed against the broken door knob.

LIFE JOURNAL. BITTERSWEET SIXTEEN. Brian came home from the hospital the Saturday after I found him in Eichelman Park with the spent syringe. He moped guiltily around the house for the next few days. He was sufficiently detoxed that he didn't seem hostile or anxious, and in this quiet interlude, we talked about rehab again.

"After Christmas. Right after Christmas," he said. "I'll go. I promise."

"You'll go, all right," David said. "You're not coming back here otherwise."

Brian didn't answer with a "who do you think you are," which left me hopeful. David had researched local rehab programs and for this round, suggested we try BridgeWaters, an outpatient program that would allow Brian to live at home while, at the same time, occupying virtually every minute of every one of his days with counselors, fellow rehabbers, and activities.

"We surround our clients with love, new friends, and new hope," their cloudsite explained.

Mom and Brian set up an informational appointment for

the week after Christmas, and since I'd be home until just after New Years, I would go, too.

Right now, though, I wanted to get Brian out of the house.

"I heard Too Too Twain's has scale models of the streetcars delivering food to each table," I told him.

"Wouldn't know. Last time I was there was when, what—when I was twelve?"

"Same here. I'm hungry. Wanna go?"

Brian stared. He was lying prostrate across his bed. I stood at his door.

"Too kidsy," he said.

"Food's good. And I hear the trains have gotten amazingly elaborate."

"Weren't they always?"

"I don't remember a 3D-projected ghost train or the Polar Express."

Brian just lay there, looking at me. Then he did the unthinkable: He raised his hand and languidly flipped me off. I knew he wanted me to go away, so this dismissive behavior was no surprise. Nonetheless, a storm of tears started brewing off my coast, and I stood in his doorway fuming. I walked in, slapped his hand away.

He promptly raised it again, regaling me with vigorous middle finger thrusting in tandem with some tongue-nasty that suggested you know what.

I slapped his hand again, then landed on him, grabbing his

skinny neck. "If you ever do that to me again, I'll kill you myself!" As quickly as I attacked, I retreated. He looked at me in shock.

"I'm down with Too Too Twain's." He sprang out of bed and hugged me. He took my hair in his hand and kissed my head. Tears rolled down my cheeks and dripped on his hands. I hugged him back, limply at first, then powerfully.

The storm had subsided.

Thirty Nine

My significant others were due to watch me launch in Florida, so I held back a heads up about my "graduation." I didn't want anyone, including David or Mom or Uncle Ron, to feel obligated they needed to be here for it or think they were missing something important.

I put word out that afternoon, feeling alone in my hotel room, despite that my phone kept ringing. I was almost packed and ready for the next leg: Cape Canaveral.

"Jennifer. Wow," Dr. Levitt said. "You're gonna hear this a lot, so I don't want to belabor it and make it sound trite, but we are so, so proud of you."

"Thank you!" It felt amazing, hearing that from Dr. Levitt.

"We will *all* see you in a few days. Brandy and Shonstein are already on their way."

"They are?"

"They may even beat you there," she said. "You're taking some supplies aboard they want handled with extreme care."

"Well played!" Dr. Marcum said on my second call. "Or more accurately, worked. But from what I've been hearing, you mastered the space game with the prowess of an Olympian."

I smiled. "You should have been an English professor," I

said.

"My parents wanted something more practical. Like abstract math."

"I wouldn't be here if it wasn't for you," I said.

"I shall accept that very concrete accolade after this is over and you're safely returned, with Crimsy in tow, we hope."

David and Mom—who sounded good—Nathaniel, Dr. Cooper, Parada—I heard from them, too.

"I haven't stopped praying," Parada said. "The Lord bless you and keep you and shine His face upon you."

On that note, I lay down and drifted off into a nap. When I woke, I spent the night until first light writing my last Life Journal entry, topic: goings away.

The journal had to be in prior to graduation. Except for the Mars sojourners, the ASCANS had plenty of time left. I wondered what Ali had written. Nobody talked about the life journals—we weren't supposed to.

But I wondered just the same.

LIFE JOURNAL. FINAL ENTRIES. "Missed a spot!" Brian giggled.

"Missed a spot!" I followed, as we sat together on the porch swing watching our teen brother mow the lawn.

"Over there," I cried, pointing to a tallish clump of grass diabolically situated on the other side of the lawn.

David frowned but kept mowing, his inner perfectionist always prevailing. Not one blade of grass stood in excess of the uniform cut height before he returned lawnmower and weed eater to the garage.

That didn't stop Brian, though.

"Missed a spot!" he'd giggle, pointing to the coiffed lawn. "David missed a bunch of places," he'd report to Dad, upon which David would grumble exasperatedly, stomp up to his bedroom and close the door.

Though he was out of the house and in college by the time Brian was old enough to mow, David took minor delight in yelling "missed a spot" on his visits home during the summer.

I SAT ON THAT same porch swing the day after Brian OD'd in Eichelman Park, staring across a few inches of snow. We'd been at the emergency room most of the night. They pumped Brian full of an antidote—something the doctor said was "much more efficacious" than the stuff they used to use—and coated whatever was left in his stomach with activated charcoal to decrease its toxicity.

"He'll live," the doctor told Mom, David, and I. "But honestly, I have no idea how long." The hospital kept him another twenty four hours for observation.

"I can't go through this again," Mom said, obviously referring to the sudden loss of my father and the almost loss of me. "I'm gonna break. I just—" But she didn't break, and I saw her shadow moving in the light through the windows.

I smoked in high school and never smoke now. But I lit one

of Brian's cigarettes and let it dangle lazily between my fingers over the arm of the porch swing, striking his rebellious pose. Darn. I know who that is. Ron and Marjorie, pulling up the driveway. Marjorie waved at me through the windshield. The car parked and like always, they waited for both doors to open completely before stepping out.

"Hey Jennifer!" Marjorie said.

"Hi Aunt Marjorie. Hi Uncle Ron." He gave me a faux salute while watching the car doors close. I don't know anyone else who uses auto-door. It takes too damn long. David and I still open and slam the doors like we did when I was a kid.

"Your mom inside?" Ron asked.

"Yeah. But taking a nap," I lied.

"We'll be quiet," Marjorie said.

They kicked the snow off their boots at the end of the steps and stomped on up and into the house. The screen door slammed behind Ron (where's auto door when you need it). I dragged on my cigarette, watched the ends ignite and burn. I jumped when Ron stuck his head back out the front door.

"Welcome home," he said.

"Thanks."

"You okay?"

I stared at the yard. "No."

He walked out, this time gently shutting the front and screen doors.

"Finding Brian like that," he said. "I don't know what I would have done."

Ron was always so sure of himself. This admission was unusual. I looked at him, casting a shadow across my half of the porch. I scooted to the side of the swing and flicked my smoke into the yard. He sat beside me hesitantly. He looked across the yard and sighed.

"I don't know what else to do," he said.

I considered. "Maybe there's nothing else to do."

"It's not like he has a disease," Ron said. "It's not like any of this has to be this way."

"I don't know."

"Why did they have to give him all those pills?"

"I don't know. Maybe because it was easy."

"They tried to outlaw that stuff. Years ago. I don't go to the doctor much, so I never knew one way or the other."

"David thinks Brian might have been susceptible," I said. "Dad's drinking hit him hardest."

"I hate to admit this," Ron said. "But there were times I wanted to kill your dad."

I felt the same way, on dad's worst days, but refused to admit it, at least, out loud.

"'It's either him or you', I told your mom. 'One of these days, he's gonna kill you.'"

"But he didn't."

"No," Ron said. "He killed himself. And almost killed you." Ron turned to the windows, and the family behind them. "Everyone warned him. He wouldn't listen. Just like Brian."

"I don't know if Brian *can* listen," I said.

Ron looked at me, long enough to make it a stare. "You're

so smart, Jennifer. If anyone else had found your brother, he'd be dead."

"Dead or in jail," I said. "I found a syringe on him."

"You tell anyone?"

"Just you."

"That's probably best," Ron said. "Your mom thinks he was shot up in some den of iniquity."

"Shooting himself feels like it sounds," I said. Like suicide. I was cold. I stood, put my hand on Ron's shoulder, and went into the house.

"**YOU FOUND A SYRINGE** on Brian?" Mom declared. "Why didn't you say anything?"

"Apparently, I didn't have to." I glared at Ron sitting next to the Christmas tree.

"He was just trying to help," Aunt Marjorie said. "We can't keep living in a secret society of hushed enablers."

A secret society of hushed enablers. I resolved to remember that, for the arguments that would inevitably follow.

"I'm not an enabler," Mom said. "That's not fair."

"I didn't mean you, specifically. Or Jennifer. Just the situation."

"Well?" Mom looked at me. "Why didn't you tell me? The doctor? David? Anybody?"

"Maybe I couldn't handle it. Maybe I'm no better at watching my baby brother kill himself than you are."

"Than I am? What I am is someone dying for some honesty," Mom said. "We haven't had an honest moment in this house since Brian got into this shit."

"No need to cuss," Ron said.

"You're one of the worst offenders on the honesty front," Mom shot back.

"What?" Ron said. "I just told you the truth about the syringe. I didn't want to. But I felt you needed to know."

Mom looked around, at me, Ron, the tree. "Know *what*?" she asked, in a less-determined tone of voice.

"About the syringe."

"What about it?"

"That Jennifer found it in Brian's jacket."

"Brian's jacket?"

I looked at Mom. "Didn't Ron just tell you about it?"

"Ron's told me a lot of things this afternoon," Mom said. She looked at the wall and took a deep breath. Marjorie was about to open her mouth, but Ron waved her back.

"Patrice?" he asked Mom. "You all right?"

"I know, I know. It had an orange cap. You told me about that. Jennifer found the cap and put it back on." She looked at me. "Where is it?"

"She threw it away. At the park," Ron said. "'member?"

"She is so smart," Mom said. "Do you know, when she was a little girl, her IQ was one hundred and seventy. I remember that. Do you remember that, Jen?"

"Jennifer is very smart," Marjorie said. "She got that from you."

"You wanna lie down?" Ron asked.

Mom looked at him, gathering herself.

"No," she said. "I'm not tired. We need to get this situation with Brian resolved. We can't let him—we need—he can't be —" She turned to the Christmas tree. "He can't be shooting up in the park. He'll go to prison. He'll go to prison, Ron. He'll die."

I had never seen Mom like this before and for whatever reason, it made me feel alone. I didn't know, at the time, what was wrong. My first thought was that she was taking something herself.

But that made no sense right away—Mom never drank, smoked (anything), and never took anything stronger than aspirin. My second thought was that she just couldn't cope with the ongoing horror that was Brian's addiction.

I ran down to the car as Ron and Marjorie were getting ready to leave.

"What was that?" I asked.

Ron stood straight, sighed, and ran his hands through his hair.

"With Mom?" I said. "Has she done that before?"

"We don't know what it is," Marjorie said. "It started about a month ago. She just pops off, vanishes from the conversation. She gets really frustrated if we try to correct her, so we just play along."

"Ron?" I asked.

"Look at her. She's healthy as a horse," he said. "Runs, works out, never goes to the doctor. I don't know what's going on."

We stopped talking and looked at each other. Marjorie tried on a smile.

"Have a good Christmas," she said.

"You won't be here?"

"We're going to Caroline's. Flying out day after tomorrow."

Caroline was their only daughter and lived in Vermont—I always pictured idyllically—with her husband and kids. I leaned in and kissed my aunt; came over to the other side of the car and leaned in and hugged my uncle. He kissed my cheek.

"You guys be safe," I said.

Forty

Two mornings later at my one-person "graduation," I got a plaque, a photo op with the space center brass (and Texas Governor), and a "Commercial Crew" pin —a stylishly altered version of the silver pin ASCAN grads receive. It looked like a star with a red, white, and blue light trail shooting through the collar of a space suit.

The Shock Diamonds threw me a dinner party—pizza, beer, and Coke—and Ali was there, smiling but reserved. She shipped out for desert Mars terrain training in a few days and I wanted a long goodbye, maybe to make up for the others I never had. I watched her from my perch in the air, hoisted (but not tossed—somebody cracked that I was heavier than I looked) to a rousing rendition of *She's a Jolly Good Astro* and best wishes for a safe trip.

BACK AT THE HOTEL, I was wound up, nervous, and couldn't sleep, so I jogged to the gym at Gilruth Center, aka Johnson Building 207. I kept running, on the treadmill, staring at the news, which included a piece about the latest United Nations doings over the Crimsy controversy, when one of the gym's staff made me jump. I slowed.

"Sorry. Didn't mean to startle you." He pointed down.

"Whoa," I said and jumped off. The undercarriage of the treadmill was smoking. He unplugged it.

"Short," he said. He came back with an "out of order" sign and I moved on to some weight machines.

It was late and there weren't many people around. I was ready to leave when I saw a familiar figure doing what she and I had been doing in here since about a week after we arrived: muscle ups on a pair of rings. It's a hard exercise, and I admired the way she so smoothly pulled it off. I wasn't alone. She always drew gawkers when we were here at our normal time.

I walked over to her, at an angle where she wouldn't see me until I was upon her.

"Jennifer!"

"So you do still recognize me," I said.

She dropped from the rings. "Of course."

"Why—have you been—avoiding me?"

"You really want to talk about this here?"

I looked around and shrugged a "why not?" She walked over to a weight machine, leaned against it, sipped from a plastic bottle, and wiped the back of her hand across her forehead.

"How do you feel about—leaving?" she said.

"Leaving? You mean here?"

"Yes."

She turned around, looked at a guy running a vacuum cleaner. "They're closing," she said. She started walking. I kept up and followed her into the locker room.

"Ali?"

"I'm feeling a little exposed here," she said, undressing near an open locker.

"Me too," I said.

I saw the fine golden hairs on her forearms, the slope of her neck as it met her shoulders, the tall fineness that began in her legs and traveled to her hands and her cheeks.

"This is intense," she said. "I can't take anything for granted." She went into the shower stalls and I heard the water. I followed.

"You think I'm taking something for granted?"

She looked at me, framing her face with the shower curtain. "I don't know what I think," she said. "I do know I'm terrible with goodbyes."

I raised my hand to smooth away a strand of wet hair between her nose and cheek. She closed the curtain. I stood outside it, burning with uncertainty but not saying anything. Not at first, anyway.

"There is inside me (and with sadness I have seen it in others) a knot of cruelty borne by the stream of love," I said.

It was a line from *The Scarlet Ibis*, a short story I read in grade school about a boy who loses someone dear to him, but doesn't realize what he's lost until it's too late. It seemed to reflect the way I felt now.

"I'm not being cruel," Ali said, peeking through the curtain.

I stood until it felt like an imposition, then turned and started walking away from the sound of rushing water.

"Jennifer," Ali called.

I wheeled around and almost slipped on the wet floor. She shut off the shower, nudged the curtain aside, and gazed at me. I heard the water dripping, from her and around her.

"Be safe," she said.

"I will," I said. "You, too."

That was the length of our long goodbye.

CCAFS

Forty One

I looked through the tall chain-link fence, at the ramp, launch tower, and mini space shuttle next to it, as the Sun peaked above a cloudy horizon, casting an orange hue across Cape Canaveral Air Force Station (CCAFS).

"Welcome to Complex 14," read a sign on the fence branded with NASA shooting-star crew logos. "America's First Person in Orbit," launched from here, I read, and I was apparently standing in his old parking spot. "John H. Glenn, Jr., Lt. Col." was engraved in a bronze plaque on a new concrete car stopper, three team members—Carpenter, Schirra, Cooper—on concrete car stoppers beside him. "General Dynamics, 6555th Aerospace Test Wing, United States Air Force," read another sign. And on the launch tower, the logos of SpaceTek, TeloSky, CloudSpark, and the SNC Space Chaise: Space Ghost riding a rocket like a cowboy reining a horse-drawn chaise.

We were doing launch practice beyond this fence in a few days, but I was meeting some crew members for a Space Chaise orientation. Another baby shuttle (literally, the miniature horse version) used for orientations and mock-ups was parked on the asphalt parking lot out here.

A tall man with broad shoulders startled me emerging from the blockhouse—a low-slung dome with a rectangular structure attached, the launch site's office and warehouse. He walked to the mock-up shuttle with his back to me, and bent down to a rear tire under the right wing. I didn't want to startle him, so I fidgeted with my feet to get his attention.

"Hi," I said, as he stood. I approached with my hand out. "Jennifer."

He turned. I stopped. *He didn't have any eyes.*

"Randi," he said, in a tone of voice I can only call "sincerely monotonous." He extended his hand but I hesitated.

He didn't have any fucking eyes.

But I saw no white cane, no dark glasses on his forehead, no Sonar for the Sightless system. His facial expression, taking a cue from resting bitch face, was resting blank face.

I plunged ahead and shook his hand—his grip was warm and firm. But I couldn't take my eyes off his—lack of them. Instead of windows to the soul, I was peering at a pair of black holes nothing like the empty socket I saw when a Cal Tech smart ass took out his bio-electronic eye to use for selfies and other creepy gags.

Another voice startled me.

"Replicated Artificial Native Design Intelligence," she said, coming from the direction of the blockhouse. "Or Natural Design Intelligence, depending on the software version."

She took my hand in both of hers and I caught her name above a logo patch.

"So cool to finally meet you, Jennifer. I'm Betty Waldo, payload crew chief. RANDI is a robot."

"Um, nice to . . . A what?" I said.

I don't know if it was the tone of my voice or the look in my eyes, but the weirdest thing happened. Randi's face dropped—I mean, actually dropped—to the most aggrieved look of utter defeat. Resting blank face instantly became a cauldron of despair.

"Randi." Betty shook her head. Resting blank face immediately returned.

"I didn't mean to offend him." I turned to the robot. "I didn't mean to offend you." Then the opposite happened. His face burst with probably the prettiest smile I'd ever seen.

Oh my god.

Betty took me aside. "Randi's programmed with an evolutionary facial recognition algorithm designed to evoke maximum response whenever his emotions are triggered. The look on his face can cripple a person. It's almost a weapon. If he had eyes, it would be."

"He gets triggered?"

"Just like you and me," she said. "He's been assigned to your flight."

"My flight?"

"Mr. Telos pushed for years to automate—"

"Leon Telos?" I interrupted. This many unanswered questions, a few days before launch. I started worrying.

"He and Alex Sparks designed Randi," Betty said. "The Space Chaise is fully automated—it can get you to DSG without a pilot. But Randi, as Mr. Telos has said many times, is the ultimate fail safe. His onboard computer is networked to the vehicle's. Follow me." She turned to the robot. "Randi—you stay here."

We walked around to the back of the shuttle and she quietly tapped it near the logo, out of his sight. "What am I doing?" she asked him.

"Repeatedly tapping your index finger on the left aft side of the hull," he replied. "Approximately point two meters from—"

"Space Ghost. Thank you, Randi," she said. "Anything goes wrong on this ship, he knows where, what, why, and in ninety nine percent of cases, how to fix it. He can even space walk—without a suit. And he's strong, too, aren'tcha Randi?"

She took a heavy screwdriver from her back pocket and tossed it to him. He caught it, and with the most shit-eating grin I'd now ever seen, drove it into the asphalt. Just pressed it down, all the way to the shaft.

I walked over and looked at it and the crack gradually opening around it. I looked up at Randi, I thought with my best blank face.

"Don't worry," he said.

Then he reached down and pulled the screwdriver out.

"Jennifer?"

I wheeled around to a welcome sight: Dr. Shonstein walking toward me, sporting a Seattle Mariners baseball cap, and Dr. Brando emerging from their rental car. I hurried their way.

"It's so good to see you guys," I said.

"You're a sight for sore eyes yourself, girlfriend," Shonstein said.

Dr. Brando took my hand and pulled me in for a hug. "Congratulations," he said.

I flashed my NASA crew pin. "All official like." I looked at Shonstein—something was different. "Have you—?"

"Lost weight? As a matter of fact—" She took off the cap. "I'm in the peach fuzz phase," she said. I opened my mouth. "Breast cancer," she said.

"Oh no. When—?"

"About a month after you left. Found a lump. Asked Martin for his opinion, which after a sincere and studied palpation, turned out to be pretty worthless. So, I got another opinion."

"Good news is, it's gone," Brando said, approaching behind her.

"Mm hmm," she agreed with a smile.

"Malachi?"

"Super trooper. Both my guys—who are here, by the way."

I wanted to keep catching up, then realized I'd forgotten my Midwestern manners. I walked us over and made introductions.

With the cap's visor pitched high on her head, Shonstein looked up at RANDI with a mix of fear and shock, then looked at me with a WTF expression exaggerated by her hair loss. Brando kept smiling, like he was waiting for a punchline.

"Randi is—what's the term again?" I asked Betty.

"Replicated Artificial Native Design Intelligence."

"Get out," Shonstein said.

Brando rose quizzically on his tiptoes for a closer look.

"I wouldn't do that," I said. "He's very sensitive."

"He's sensitive?" Shonstein said.

I saw his crestfallen look coming on.

"Randi is a perfect mechanical clone of a payload chief some of us call 'legendary,'" Betty said. "Dan Ryan died about nine years ago."

"He was sensitive, too?" Brando asked.

"Yes—but not like Randi."

"He's taking me to DSG," I announced with artificial glee.

Shonstein looked incredulous.

A self-driving forklift left the blockhouse and pulled up with a pallet of boxes and what looked like Styrofoam shapes.

"How are you?" I asked Brando. "How's my main girl?"

"We're great. And she'll be here."

"Outstanding! She's not with you now?"

"She's coming with her Mom," he said, walking toward the pallet. "Yeah, really." He started looking through the boxes.

"You and Melissa—" I said.

"They aren't back together, thank God," Dr. Shonstein whispered. She turned to the Space Chaise. "This thing is adorbs."

"Randi will record how you want everything loaded," Betty Waldo told Brando. "The Styrofoam approximates the dimensions of your equipment."

Shonstein, Waldo and I walked up a short gangway,

ducked, and stepped inside the little shuttle. Three seats; the rest open payload space.

"You can fight with Randi over who sits where," Waldo said.

I looked at the control panel, which seemed as compact as the ship.

"Bigger in here than it looks," Shonstein said.

"Holds as much payload as the old shuttles did," Waldo said. She pointed at controls and valves and the main back hatch, "which attaches to the space station. I wish I could clear you through the gates to the launch pad for a look at the real thing, but they won't let me."

Looking out the window, Shonstein motioned me over.

Dr. Brando and the robot were positioning shapes and handling boxes. The human reached for a box and the robot snatched it out of his hands like a selfish toddler. Brando jumped back. He looked horrified; I could only imagine what Randi's face looked like.

"Did we just see that?" Shonstein said.

Waldo looked out the other window, then like a harried mom on a summer day, leaned out the shuttle door.

"Randi," she said sternly.

She peered back in and smiled meekly.

"Software bug?" Shonstein asked.

"No worries. Those boxes are empty," Betty Waldo said. "The actual payload goes to the launch pad."

She descended the gangway.

Forty Two

Mom wasn't at dinner, but David and Ron were, at a place called Dill's with an outdoor deck on the Port Canaveral bay. Everyone just kind of filed in surprise-party style, and I was definitely surprised to see Ron and not Aunt Marjorie. I thought about pulling one of the two men in my family aside and asking about Mom, but was too overwhelmed. I didn't see Nathaniel Hawthorn, either. I was bummed, but didn't want to show it.

All these people here for me, and I focus on the two who aren't. Typical. The whole meal, all I wanted to do was ask where Mom was, how she was doing. I pictured her bidding me farewell and fair skies then sailing away on her own adventure in the cruise ship docked nearby. And I was more peeved than bummed at Nathaniel. I know we don't really have anything. But still. I was all dressed up with nowhere to go yet, in the flight suit, pins, and patches I inherited from Johnson.

I hadn't seen Arjan Kadabe, our JPL project manager, since the MarsMicro launch and her conflicts with Dr. Shonstein about what we were allowed to load and other devilish details. All that seemed ancient history now, especially when she came up to me, pumped my hand, and said: "Hi, Jennifer."

Lexi tugged me over to her mother, who at first greeted me reservedly, but later squeezed my arm and made a remark I didn't quite catch, in all the chatter on deck, about "inspiration." I told her how good it was to see her again and how honored I was to have her and Lexi here.

Dr. Levitt and Parada led the first toast, with an array of raised drinks, from Dr. Marcum's scotch neat to Dr. Cooper's craft beer.

Brando described his bizarre encounter with Randi—"spent the whole afternoon with this hunk of A.I."—to which Shonstein laughed and grinned, then beamed when Martin took off her ball cap and kissed the top of her head. Malachi was with a sitter back at their hotel, leaving Lexi the sole child, four years older than when I first met her, and reveling in the adult banter.

Even Sara Goode made an appearance, live from her office at the University of New South Wales in Australia, where it was already tomorrow. Dr. Marcum summoned her via TelaPart app.

"I couldn't be more proud or delighted to have been involved in Team Crimsy, if even from a distance, and ever so slightly," she said.

"Stop being humble, madam," Marcum said.

She smiled. "Jennifer: Good luck and Godspeed. Can't wait to see what happens next."

A round of "here heres" circled the table and my going-away party got no better than that.

DAVID AND RON JOINED me in the next-door tiki bar afterwards and though I had to drag it out of them, we hashed over what was going on with Mom. She was fine, David insisted. Marjorie and my cousin Caroline, in from Vermont with her family, were with Mom. Her doctor didn't think she should travel, was all. Nothing to fret about.

"I'm not fretting," I said. "I just wanna know."

"She kinda made up with Harold Hale," David said.

"So they're back together?"

"I wouldn't say back together. But *he loves her terribly*," David said.

I hadn't thought of love that way, or heard it put that way, ever. First time the word "terribly" made me feel good.

"Jeri's coming in late—promised to meet her at the airport," David said, standing up. He kissed my cheek and whispered, "I love *you* terribly."

Ron and I hugged and he told me to be safe, that was his only concern. "I get protective," he said.

"I understand," I said. "I'm sorry if I get snarky." I looked at Ron's hand, the way it touched his drink tentatively. Then I looked at him. "I'm glad Mom has you," I said. "*We* have you."

I was headed to my car in the parking lot when someone grabbed me around the eyes from behind. I grabbed back.

"You're crushing me," he said softly.

I dropped my hands and flew around. I threw my arms around Nathaniel and despite said tender forearms, he put his hands around the small of my back and pulled me close. We had the most incredible deep swoon of a kiss.

I felt myself rising on my toes and swimming around inside it all. The tip of his nose was a little cold, so I took my lips there and kissed it too. I kissed his cheeks and he kissed my eyes and when our lips finally parted, my first words just had to be, "So where were you?"

I asked with a sly enough smile that he kissed my upper lip, and just above my chin, like he was letting me know he knew he was forgiven.

"So do I say something stupid like, do you know how much I've missed you?" he said. "Want you?"

"Yes."

"My flight was late."

"Figures." I felt jittery now, a little frustrated. If he kept looking at me, there was no way he was getting away.

"You were saying? About wanting me?"

"You know how much I want you . . . to come back to me," he said.

"Don't say that."

"We can't," he said.

"No—"

"You have to be one hundred percent focused. And here I am, a guy who sits on his ass all day in an office (with daily trips to the gym, but still) reminding you."

"Nathaniel—"

"Why do you think I only called twice?"

"Hurt my feelings."

"You hurt my arms," he said, rubbing them. "We're even."

"Poor baby." I kissed him again.

"Don't keep doing that," he said. So I did it again. And again. He backed away, smiling, wagging his finger.

"Uh, uh, uhh. You get into that car and say, 'Crew Quarters, James.' And you sleep. And you awaken with only one thing on your mind: Coming home in one, beautiful piece."

Launch was in three days.

A KNOCK TURNED INTO pounding on my door in the newly-renovated astronaut crew quarters. Turns out astronauts are a nostalgic bunch into—historic preservation!

I slept in the same room Apollo and Shuttle and Orion crew members occupied. It was decommissioned for years, then re-opened for Orion to great fanfare. When I passed through the original entrance, I stared at the *Astronauts Only* sign. Stared so long my crew concierge had to turn around and come back for me.

"Jennifer!" It was a woman at my door. She was loud. I worried she might wake somebody else. But I was the only one here. Bang bang bang. It sounded like—

"Great! You're up!"

Betty Waldo.

"Kinda." I rubbed my head.

"Look, they won't do this. I don't know why. They won't schedule time for you guys to see what this is really like. Maybe they figure you've already seen it as a tourist or something."

I had no idea what she was talking about and I'm sure it showed.

"A real launch. From the KSC press area, where your folks are gonna be," she said.

"KSC—" Kentucky Fried Chicken? I was half asleep. She meant Kennedy Space Center.

"Solar Explorer. Launches in about two hours. Get dressed —we'll grab a bite—it's *spectacular*."

I was in. I slipped on my red crew shirt, pants, shoes.

"Don't lose her," the crew concierge told Betty on the way out.

THE KILLERS. *HUMAN.* **I** wanted to crank it. "May I?"

"Absolutely," Betty said.

"Sound up," I said.

I danced to this as a kid, furiously stomping my feet like a frenzied little high stepper, grabbing David's or Dad's or Mom's hands and whirling around the man cave or the living room or wherever with them. The song seemed especially perfect today. We sang together about getting nervous, opening doors, closing eyes and clearing hearts. Betty said something about Randi and laughed. The Killers, the drive, and a Styrofoam cup of bad coffee woke me right up.

It was quiet at the press site, a grassy knoll across the water from another launch complex. Reporters and VIPs milled around, prepping 1D, 2D, and 3D cameras. I even saw what looked like a movie crew. It was a clear, bright, almost chilly morning. I looked across the bay at the rocket, partly obscured by trees and distance.

"This thing is a *beast*," Betty exclaimed. Such a space junkie. Who knew?

"Nine, eight, seven, six—" a voice from a speaker narrated. Did I have those words memorized. "And liftoff. Of SpaceTek's Solar Explorer, humankind's first close-up look at the giant ball of fire that powers our solar system."

We saw this amazing, sustained brightness, smoke and clouds pouring out of every flaming pore. Even from here, it looked almost as bright as the Sun itself.

"Hang on!" Betty said. She grabbed her hat and threw her eyes toward the sky.

Up, up, the rocket approached some low, thin clouds, a thickening, billowing plume of smoke in its wake. A deep guttural roar, as the Solar Explorer lifted, grew louder and louder, until it blasted into a deafening cannonade, like the loudest machine gun you've ever heard, only much louder, each sonic boomlet lasting about as long as a firecracker burst.

Then something even freakier: everything started shaking, including me. I relaxed my jaw to see if my teeth would chatter and they vibrated along with the rocket's incessant rat-a-tat-tatting.

I looked up, mouth agape, car alarms firing behind us.

The noise faded, the alarms silenced, sea birds whistled, voices laughed and talked. I saw some guys out the corner of my eye demonstrating their vivid 3D capture: Solar Explorer, but launching from the lawn in front of them. Others still stared, as the lingering plume gradually disintegrated.

"That's you in a couple days," Betty said.

Forty Three

Two spacesuit techs fussed over me in the Suit Room, pulling and adjusting and snapping, until I looked bulky and bright. The room smelled fresh and new, though each piece of reupholstered furniture was its nostalgic, meaningful self.

Despite pressure from Sparks and other space sultans, The Talent—the astronauts—insisted on keeping everything as simple as ever, the rooms a step up from college dorms, the doors and halls this side of industrial, the conference and meeting rooms corporate but casual.

"Possum's Fargo?" Randi said. He looked at me with those empty wells.

"You betcha," Betty Waldo said. "Randi won't let us leave without it."

A card game like poker, Possum's Fargo was a pre-launch tradition, I learned, but usually with more crew to play. Betty gave me the basics. The techs, crew concierge, Randi, and I shuffled and dealt. Betty looked at all the hands.

"Three of a kind. Looks like Randi won," she announced. And everyone capitulated. I showed her my full house.

"You want the face?" she whispered.

A few more hands went the same way. "The luck of the A. Irish," I quipped.

"I am gonna remember that," Betty said.

After hugs and well-wishes from the crew quarters staff, Betty, the crew concierge and a camerawoman accompanied Randi and I to the elevator, down the corridor, and toward the Operation and Check (O & C) building's famous double doors. Betty put a pair of dark sunglasses on Randi "for obvious reasons," she said. He tried to stop her and take them off.

"Randi," she admonished. "He hates them," she told me. "But tough titty."

"What am I gonna do without you?" I asked.

"You'll be just fine."

Randi in front, we walked outside and it hit me. Sunshine, press, my family, my team, behind a low barricade, cheering, waving, selfie-snapping, thumbs upping. I stopped, waved back, smiled, lingered. Randi got ahead of me, waving too, looking oddly cool in his shades.

"Jennifer," the crew concierge nudged. "There's like twenty thousand people out there. Can't keep your fans waiting." Let alone the scheduled launch.

I walked alongside the Astrovan, a vintage 1983 Air Stream motor home, saw a few dents, original chrome, and new logos. At its door, I lingered too long again. But this time my prodders had mercy.

I saw Jeri next to David and Ron; Malachi with his parents and sitter (he would not be watching the launch, I was sure); Lexi and her folks, actually standing together. Nathaniel Hawthorn, talking to Dr. Marcum and grinning. Dr. Cooper did a long-distance fist bump. Next to Parada, Dr. Levitt blew me a kiss. I gave a final wave and turned and entered the first leg of my journey. The Astrovan smelled clean and new, but simple, original, and calm.

"Hopefully, that's the only space walk you'll have to do," Betty said at the door. "Oh—you got a message." She took a slip of paper out of her pocket and handed it to me. "Old fashioned, but when you can't have a cell phone—"

"Shine, Shock Diamond, shine," it read. "I Love You! Mom." Of all the things and people I'd had on my mind, she was at the top. I love you, too.

Betty shut the door and a squadron of squad cars and escort vehicles started moving in front of us. I looked out the window at a sign, "We're Behind You, Deep Space Gateway!" We passed cheering, flag-waving crowds, some holding Crimsy renditions that ranged from bad to bold, hundreds of people lining the roads.

By the time we got to ICBM Road, named for the missiles once tested here, the crowds had disappeared. It was a barren expanse, a lonely final farewell before we passed the Mercury 7 monument, in honor of John Glenn and crew. We passed Glenn's parking spot and through the gates to the Complex 14 launch pad. I'd been here for a rehearsal, but decided to save discussing it for the real thing.

More fussing, more directions, so much help I barely needed to do anything myself. The Space Chaise was in its launch and upright position, on top of the rocket and booster instead of alongside, a huge safety boost over the old Space Shuttle design. Randi went ahead of me to the tower and up, across steely corridors and causeways, past steam jets and dry ice, packed so thickly on coolant pipes you could grab handfuls of it like snow.

I looked across Canaveral's waters and saw the crowds and knew that at the press site, my fam and team were gathering. I ducked through the shuttle hatch and gazed at the perfectly-positioned, expertly-secured jigsaw puzzle before me: our equipment, other supplies, not a centimeter to spare.

More checks and re-checks and secure seat-belting and people on radios with Mission Control. In our seats now, I looked over at Randi, who didn't need a helmet. He took off his shades and looked at me with those empty pools and I turned away and rolled my eyes.

"Ready?" he said.

"I hope."

"Hang on."

"Cleared for launch," I heard.

The countdown commenced, the rockets flared, we started rising, and then we TOOK OFF. It was the scariest, most exhilarating, most amazing, inner space-jarring thing I knew I would ever experience. It felt like not just my teeth but my entire face was plastered against the back of my head.

I tried to restrain screaming, worried about triggering The Face. But I couldn't, I just couldn't, and I held forth with a loud one. Randi remained ironically calm.

The launch went on forever. I mean that. I thought it

would never end. Then when it did with a whimper, I was still so petrified I couldn't even think, as voices through my helmet speakers rattled off next steps.

"First stage, methane booster, separate."

The shuttle slowed, I felt something going on behind us, then whatever was dragging us dropped. I looked out the window and saw the edges of the rocket we left behind.

"Want to watch it head back?" Randi said.

He did something with the controls and Space Chaise turned, bringing the separated rocket into view, maneuvering, rotating, adjusting, on its way back to Canaveral, intact and reusable. The Space Chaise returned to its course.

"Hang on," Randi said.

The second stage rocket accelerated us forward, plastering my body against the seat. As the thrust mellowed, I looked out the window, bathing my senses in that beautiful blue and white orb filling our horizon. The pictures, they told us in training, never do it justice. What an understatement.

Another countdown started in my helmet. "Five, four, three . . . second stage . . . separation—" and other technical jargon announcing the end of the fuel in our second, smaller rocket, which would also use auxiliary tanks to return home for reuse.

"Everything's reusable," the mantra of the space sultans. I looked at Randi and wondered if he was reusable, recyclable, whatever. I wondered when we humans would be, too. We felt lighter again—can't describe it any other way. I didn't see the second stage rocket depart.

"Hang on," Randi said.

Those two words were taking on countdown-style significance. The twin rear rocket engines ignited with a roar, propelling us forward and smashing me into the seat again, which armrests I grabbed for dear life, trying to smile through gritted teeth, trying to be Mom's shining Shock Diamond and Ali's safe friend. One thing I noticed, and it meant a lot—my ears weren't bothering me. Other than being scared witless and thinking my life was over and my falling star would scatter in the sky, I felt great.

"You want music?" Randi said.

Music?

"Look at the screen," he said. I looked at my visor where the Top 40 started scrolling: Fabulous Baker Girls, Sloopy, Houndstooth, The Afterburners (apropos, that), Nete Freke, Jess Two, She Rex, The PomCats, Winnie Bagel, Gilmore Guys.

Genesis.

My grandma's favorite band. Never a pop groupie, I said it reflexively.

"Sounds good," Randi said. I looked out the window, at Earth's transcendent blue.

A guitar riff I'd heard on our car trips. Old-school synthesizer. A bounding kettle drum. *Home by the Sea. Home by the Sea.*

"Will be there when song is over," Randi said. "All the songs last just that long."

I don't know. Guess I wasn't thinking. But I asked, "Where?"

"Home," Randi said.

I closed my eyes and tried to relax, darkness in front of me, brightness behind. I never went to sleep, just skittered the edges. Noticed Randi tapping his hands to the song. I felt the ship decelerate and that's what prompted me to open my eyes. They adjusted to the dark. I blinked. Sat up, as far as the seat restraints let me. Sat up, and fixed my speechless gaze.

"Deep Space Gateway," Randi said.

"Already?"

"Fast trip."

The gravity wheel, five or six football fields high; the crew modules; the CanArms; the solar collectors, cast in spectacular, brilliant glory against Earthen blue, Solar gold, and the magnifying effect of my helmet shield.

"Hang on," Randi said.

I grabbed the armrests. Were we gonna crash?

"Just kidding," he said.

The Space Chaise gradually, delicately slowed. I felt a mild acceleration as it turned a one eighty, and again, as it backed into its docking port. The engines shut down, Genesis faded to a synthesized twinkle. I heard the airlocks engage, which meant we—I—could breathe on my own. Randi released his restraints and I released mine.

"Ooh, whoa!" I floated up and hit the ceiling.

He grabbed my leg and pulled me back into my seat. I unlocked my helmet and took it off while he held me. Then I saw him looking at me—if you can call it that—in a strange way.

"Welcome to Deep Space Gateway, Jennifer," Captain Hightower said on the intercom. "And Replicated Artificial—"

"Don't call me that," Randi interrupted.

The fun was fixin' to begin.

DSG

Forty Four

O ut of the chaise airlock, I floated toward Captains Gillory and Hightower and shook their hands and hugged her around the shoulders. True to form, they were a lot more lit than their pix and projections.

"No words, no words," Hightower said.

"He's excited," Gillory said. "I'm elated."

"No, I'm elated," he said. "Watch her. She steals all the great lines."

"And I'm thrilled." Commander Ryong floated up behind them.

This was so weird, floating instead of walking. We looked like a school of fish gathering for a mid-ocean flash mob. I shook Ryong's hand. What a great smile.

"Welcome aboard, CPS Zendeck," he said. "CPS" means Commercial Payload Specialist.

"Honored to be aboard, sirs and ma'am," I said, saluting. I looked around. "I can't believe I'm actually here."

"Just wait," Gillory said. "It'll make a believer out of you yet."

I started turning, back toward the chaise.

"Where you going?" Hightower asked.

I indicated Randi, unloading my luggage and supplies.

"PG's got it," Hightower said.

I looked at Gillory.

"Payload Grunt," she said.

Ryong frowned.

"Let's get you out of that suit."

THE GUYS LEFT US and we floated into a section of the gravity wheel Gillory affectionately called "Wardrobe!" She flipped a switch and it was apparent something was moving beneath and around us, but not apparent what. She extended her hands and I took them.

"Hang on," she said. "Heard that enough, right?" We gradually dropped to the floor, on our stomachs.

"Okay. You can stand."

"That's how that works."

"Flip a switch and you've got gravity," she said.

"That simple?"

"Not exactly," she said. "Lots of gyromotors and gyroscopes and other fancy thingamajigs correcting for the Coriolis Effect, which can throw off simple things like walking or running on a treadmill. We still can't play tennis up here. Balls don't travel straight. Even a simple game of catch isn't so simple. Unless you're Randi."

"Randi can overcome Coriolis forces?"

"Yep," she said. "He can throw a ball in a way that kind of auto-corrects. I've heard it compared to a bowler or a pitcher adding a little spin to a throw."

"A reverse curve ball," I said. "He's full of surprises."

"Yeah he is. Only other disadvantage is that we all have to get in here at once if we all want gravity at once. We're moving in here and they're stationary out there."

Gillory helped me de-suit.

"Don't know how our predecessors did it," she said. "Try buttoning a shirt or latching a bra strap in zero G."

"I had to repair the gravity wheel at Johnson," I said.

"You won't have to here," she said. "Logan has yet to come aboard."

Poor Logan.

I looked behind me, up, and around, trying to see if I could tell we were moving. Einstein was right. I couldn't. "What do you guys use this for?" I asked.

"The wheel? Labs are here. Formal dining too, such as it is. If Kim or Rob get on my nerves, this is my escape hatch. Jog. Lift weights. Beats wearing Velcro on your shoes. And I can lighten the weights when I'm lazy."

"Less gravity?"

"When Crimsy first came aboard, we averaged Martian gravity, about point three eight Gs. Little less than Earth now. This bad boy's adjustable."

She moved the control. It reminded me of the dimmer

switches my dad and I installed around the house one spring. I levitated a little.

"Take a step. Couple steps," Gillory said, hands and feet gripping wall bars. "But be careful."

Freaky! I had to grab a table bolted to the floor to steady myself.

"Like walking on water."

She adjusted the switch again, stopping the wheel, and I ascended. She restarted the wheel and my feet touched the floor.

"Can do extreme G, too," she said.

Another adjustment, and I saw the strangest thing: the skin on her face sagging, her shoulders slumping, her posture shrinking, like she was bearing the weight of the world.

"I call this the Black Hole Effect," she said, visibly straining to get the words out.

I felt the downward pull and touched my face. I don't think anything was sagging and my shoulders seemed straight as ever. She set the gravity back to normal.

"Ahh youth," Gillory said. "Gravity will get you some day."

THE GRAVITY WHEEL WAS little more than a long, broad, circular hallway that felt perfectly straight "so long as we're moving with it," Gillory said, illustrating Einstein's Special and General Theories of Relativity in a single spin. Doors along the center of the hallway instead of the sides divided the wheel into sections we passed through, in one door and out the other.

My heart stopped—for reals—when we came to the door

marked *MarsMicro Lab*. Gillory went to open it. Then, "nope."
She withdrew the key card.

"What? Why?" I asked.

"Rob and Kim insist on being here for the big reveal."

"Please. Just a sneak peak."

She looked at me. "You . . . are just gonna—"

"You're killing me."

She smiled and we turned back.

WE PASSED RANDI UNLOADING gear and cargo like a floating tugboat, pulling it behind him with straps and a makeshift sled.

"We've got one crew module we use mainly for storage and one for evacuations," Gillory said, about the five Orion crew modules docked along the stationary part of DSG. "We use the other three for offices and sleeping quarters."

We entered her module, and inside a sleeping pod marked *Gillory.* "You'll bunk with me, at least for a while."

"So is it true: like sleeping on air?"

"Better," she said.

"Better be," I said. The sleeping pods were no larger than closets, with sleeping bags—more like sacks—strapped to the wall so we wouldn't float around. She showed me the rest of the module.

"Toothpaste, toiletries, girl stuff."

"True what they told us?" I asked. "No big deal?"

"Pretty much. You can suppress with implants or pills, which I tried but gave up. Rhea Seddon was right: It's a non-problem."

Microgravity menstruation is a non-problem, that is. We covered it in space physiology. Dr. Seddon, a surgeon and one of the first female astronauts, advised not worrying about it. Sally Ride set the record straight on the optimal amount of feminine hygiene products to pack. Space medicine researchers Varsha Jain and Virginia Wotring studied full-on menstruation suppression, "maybe useful on Mars voyages," our instructor said.

"Hard to believe, we weren't allowed up here before," I said.

"Can't have emotional females handling complicated equipment," Gillory said. "They tell you about the other reasons?"

"Menstrual blood might flow backward into the stomach cuz low gravity," I said.

"I plan to use that if they try and send me to Mars," Gillory said. "So—over here is this module's emergency departure station. All automatic, independent of the onboard computer. Hope we never have to use it."

We floated out of her module and into the Rec Mod, one door past Hightower's module.

"Got cold drinks," she pointed at a stainless steel fridge, "and the ETub," a fifty-five gallon rain barrel brimming with Reese's Pieces, M&M's, and the Mars Candy logo. M&M's were the first candy in space. Space Shuttle Columbia. 1981.

"The fun port," Gillory introduced. "Cloudcast, SkyScreen,

and NetFlix."

"No wonder Randi called it home."

"Randi, yes," she said. "He'd love nothing better than to tool around here with the rest of us. But JPL has other ideas."

"What's he do?"

"Stays in the chaise, when he's not loading and unloading. Long story. And speaking of long stories, I can't wait to get started on your *Crimsococcus* protocols."

SO THIS WAS FUNNY. We're in the "Wagon Wheel Cantina," Captain Hightower's name for the gravity wheel's compact mess hall, and he's in a bathrobe and cowboy boots sauteing mushrooms on a portable electric grill near a fume catcher.

"We make most meals in the galley but Rob, being a good Texan—"

"You're from Texas?" I asked.

"I is."

"—must be able to grill out," Gillory said.

"It's part of the Texas Constitution," Hightower said. "Which governs up here, too."

"Medium rare. Don't forget," Ryong said.

"I think we're good here for a second," Hightower said. "I'd like to propose a toast."

They had wine. Ryong had something else. I had water.

"To We," Hightower said, "The scientists, sojourners,

sightseers."

"Here, here," we said. We ate, the most delicious steaks, baked taters, mushrooms, and all the fixings I'd had in years.

"I know that you do not drink," Ryong said. "But I want to make personal toast with a favorite from home. Will you?"

"Of course," I said. He poured. "What is it?"

"Pyongyang Soju, special reserve. Strong, so only sip."

We toasted me and I toasted them and it went down smooth and warm.

Forty Five

The Big Reveal. We washed up and put on decon suits with gloves and helmets with airtight visors, a lightweight version of what I wore en route. In said garb, I stood at the lab door, chomping at the proverbial bit.

"You ready?" Hightower asked.

"More than," I said. "Way more than."

I watched Gillory's hand go to the doorknob; insert the keycard; unlatch the door. She entered the first airlock. I was chronicling this short journey in my mind more than I had chronicled getting up here from Earth.

Entering second airlock. I could see something in front of us, through the lab window. I was shaking. Gillory entered the lab, I waited, Ryong and Hightower behind me.

"*Entrez vous?*" she asked, motioning me inside.

I walked in slowly, carefully.

"Oh," I said, dumbfounded and staring.

Crimsy was magnificent. Green, red, the colors of Life. In test tubes and Petri dishes, she had grown beyond the agar, taking up residence on nutrient-free glass lids and clear sides of the test tubes. "Aggressive growth" was an understatement.

"I've never seen anything—" I mumbled.

I felt my eyes watering, my sinuses stuffing, my face warming. The hurricane of tears was so close. I moved closer and bent down and took it all in, this barely-even-a-speck-when-we-found-her microbe who wasn't only living but thriving.

"Any change in the sub-culturing schedule?" I asked.

I'd been out of the loop—or in this case, inoculating loop—for months. To keep Crimsy from bathing in her own waste and self-contaminating, Gillory or Hightower used inoculating loops to transfer living bacteria into fresh agar, a process known as "sub-culturing." Too much sub-culturing is a bad thing: it can lead to genetic mutations that create super bugs or dead bugs. Too little sub-culturing, and the organism may die.

"Since you left—I'd say we're subbing about a third more frequently," Gillory said. "I'll pull the logs. She grows fast and it was Shonstein's idea to step it up."

"Brando's agar?" I asked. "How's it doing?"

"Like water on a cactus," Hightower said. "Less is more. In Crimsy's case, way less."

"Is she safe? I mean, is there like any fear that she'd, well—take over Earth or something?"

"Passed all the path tests with flying colors, at least the ones we could do here," Gillory said.

"She's cleared for landing, Kemosabe," Hightower added.

"With a few caveats," Gillory said. "I wouldn't throw her in a pond or flower garden indiscriminately."

"First Universal Invasive Species," Hightower said.

"Then that time we reported when one of the latex gloves

we use for lab work had a tear in it, and Rob got a little Crimsy on his finger," Gillory continued. "After freaking out about it —"

"I did not freak out."

Ryong laughed.

"After going into a Texas Tizzy when he took his hand out, we literally watched Crimsy—that dab of her—turn to red dust on his finger. Gone. Poof."

"Which suggests," Ryong said.

"That a certain amount of care is advised," Gillory said.

"And that we're more of a danger to her than she is to us," Ryong said.

The old War of the Worlds irony again. So unexpected and yet so predictable: NASA and JPL and the Sultans of Space spend countless dollars and hours trying to prevent forward contamination. Now I realized why a manned Mars mission might pose real dilemmas.

"What do you think killed her?" I asked.

"No idea," Gillory said.

"Hey—you wanna say 'hi'?" Hightower asked, next to a monitor. "Just got buzzed. Your team's in a meeting."

We got a two-way communication channel going and I beamed into the PAB conference room, standing in front of Crimsy for the ultimate selfie. Everybody applauded.

"Well: How are you? How's it going?" Dr. Cooper asked.

I leaned down so they could see just my smiling eyes.

"Awesome," I said.

I FLOATED PAST RANDI tugging cargo again in the gravity-free corridor—unloading the Space Chaise seemed to be taking a while—and we exchanged pleasantries with resting blank faces.

"If you want eyes, just take them," I heard.

"Randi?" I asked.

But he was gone.

"Is there someone else on board?" I asked Ryong in the gravity wheel. I was lifting weights. He was walking up an incline on the treadmill.

"No. Just us and Randi, when authorized."

"I thought I heard someone talking to him," I said.

Ryong frowned, then smiled. "You mean AL?" he said. "Not someone. Some thing. Onboard guidance system. If space station ever caught fire and filled with smoke, we have it to guide us to safety, should safety be available."

"Why would it be talking to Randi?" I asked.

"I don't know. Male voice, soft—"

"Sounded like a woman to me."

"A woman talking to Randi," Ryong said. "Now I'm really feeling left out."

I knew he was trying make light, but if anything ever inspired MCF—Maximum Creep Factor—it was Randi.

"So why isn't Randi allowed in the station?" I asked.

"Before my time," Ryong said. "All I know is he's supposed to stay aboard chaise until it heads back. That is the way it's always been."

"So what does he do? Just sit there?"

"Goes into sleep mode."

I WILL SAY RANDI did a great job getting everything unloaded, unpacked, and ready for my small part in answering The Big Question: Did Crimsy give birth, in the extreme evolutionary sense, to the rest of us?

I did side-by-side comparisons of other bacteria, especially cyanobacteria, to see how Crimsy compared and contrasted. I monitored basic bacterial parameters the DSG crew never had time to observe: shape, height, and margin edges of the colonies; texture; response to light (Crimsy was translucent and iridescent, depending on the light source); and chromogenesis (color production and pigmentation, a Crimsy specialty).

I performed some new atmospheric tests, compliments of Dr. Cooper, who wanted to ascertain how Crimsy would travel. Could she make it back to Earth and if so, how would the weather affect her? Martian weather is dull as red dirt compared to Earth.

I got into a good routine: Lab, notes, PAB conferences, data gathering, more conferences, eat, recreate, sleep standing upright (although it wasn't. It just kept feeling that way. I mean, we were sleeping in closets). Rinse, repeat.

Speaking of that, washing my hair was a hoot. Anything to do with water in our zero G sectors was something to behold. Ryong introduced me to Bubble Tag, where you eject water from a squeeze bottle, watch it form solid droplets that look like bubbles, and move them around with your nose like a seal.

The Voice, however, was not part of my routine. It woke me up.

"You're killing it," she said. And it *was* a she. Make no mistake. Al was really Alice.

"Thank you," I said, bleary-eyed and half-asleep.

"It will die."

I lay there gradually awakening. I unzipped my sack and floated in my space jammies into the corridor. I heard voices from Hightower's crew module so I went there and knocked.

"Abandon all hope," Hightower said.

He was on his back, unnecessary pillow under his head, halfway into one of three levitating sleeping sacks tethered to the floor in the center of the room.

I looked at him quizzically.

"Grammock," he said.

I was so busy balancing myself I probably looked confused.

"Gravity hammock," he said, watching a movie.

Lonesome Dove. "My dad's favorite."

I smelled popcorn in the corridor. Ryong floated in with it.

"Your dad's a good man," Hightower said.

"Thank you," I said. "He was."

"Was?"

"Yes."

"Sorry to hear that," Hightower said. "How long ago?"

"Five years."

"Natural causes?"

"Car accident," I said.

"Oh, man," Ryong said.

"I was with him."

They stopped.

"Make room, make room," Hightower said. "Come here."

I looked at him.

"C'mon."

I floated over next to him.

"Kim—you over there. Grab another pillow." He opened the sleep sack beside him. "Climb in and zip up—but not all the way," he told me. "Destroys the grambiance."

And there we lay in our grammocks. Ryong adjusted my pillow.

"Release the kernels," Hightower said. Ryong took off the aluminum foil and popcorn floated around us.

"They're big," I said.

"Less constrained up here," Ryong said.

I trembled during the scene where Gus dies. "By God Woodrow, it's been quite a party, ain't it?" My family and I must have watched that long goodbye a half-dozen times, and as I told my station mates, it always got to me and my dad. Hightower squeezed my hand.

"Hell of a vision," he said, the movie's famous last line.

Forty Six

Polymerase chain reactions, DNA tests, microscopy profiles, and other procedures later, and Crimsy emerged a close enough possible relative to cyanobacteria that Dr. Levitt was talking First Paper.

"Brandy's dying to get his science-shattering hypothesis in print," Dr. Shonstein said during our weekly faculty meeting, now featuring another absentee attendee: me. "Problem is, how do you test, 'this bacteria is the progenitor of all life on Earth?'"

"Gotta get *Crimsococcus* home, right Bex?" Dr. Brando said.

"Are we allowed to say that now?" Dr. Marcum asked. "Home?"

"Home away from home, at least," Shonstein said.

Made sense. We would never know if and how Crimsy adapted to life on Earth if we could never get her—on Earth. Would she evolve into a cyanobacteria like *Prochlorococcus*, or more realistically, display subtle microscopic changes that at least suggested such a thing was possible, and therefore, might have happened billions of years ago?

"What's new on the relative humidity front?" Dr. Cooper asked.

So far, not much. We were exposing colonies to changes in barometric pressure, humidity, and other weather variables.

"Last panel of slides includes our weathered colonies," I

said.

"Bill—anything to add?" Dr. Levitt said.

"Not on the science front," Dr. Marcum said.

"Any other fronts?"

The conversation paused.

"The philosophy front," Marcum said finally. "The ethics and morality front."

"Sounds serious."

"It is, rather. Jennifer has limited time and ability to do work that could, what—change the course of science? Again?"

"Of course."

"So when are we gonna end the charade?" Marcum asked.

"Here here!" Shonstein interjected.

"Really?" Levitt said. "That's how you describe this?"

"Not *this*. What comes next," Marcum said. "To date, there is still *no* plan to bring that creature here, and every indication that just the opposite is afoot."

Our meeting went on for another fifteen intense minutes, with a rising chorus of "when are we gonna stand up for what's right and demand the completion of our mission?"

I know Dr. Marcum didn't mean anything disparaging, but I still signed off with a hollow feeling. I'm way out here as part of some "charade," what—to keep the Space Sultans happy? The government off our backs?

I thought I was out here gathering data for our First Paper. And Second Paper. And maybe even Third Paper. And let's not forget my languishing dissertation. I took off my sterility attire in the airlock. Captain Gillory caught me closing the lab door.

"Good day?" she asked.

"Meh."

"Doesn't sound good."

"Heated discussion with the fam," I said. Which fam I didn't say.

"Ahh," she said. We walked.

"My work up here is a *charade*, according to an older sibling," I said. "Whose brains I worship and opinion I adore."

I stopped and looked out a window. Gillory joined me. God but it was beautiful up here.

"Sounds like Little Sister Syndrome," she said.

"That's about right."

"Sometimes you just gotta say, 'Screw 'em.'"

I smiled. "How do you know about Little Sister Syndrome?"

"I was one," Gillory said. "Still am. Partly why I'm here."

"Need to be this far away?"

"Oh, no—well, sometimes. But more importantly, gotta beat the Bigs. Brother. Sisters."

"I can see why you like it up here," I said, staring at Mother Earth.

"It's a tempered love affair," she said. "I do get awfully homesick. It's like a cruel tease. Where else can you be so far away from home and yet." She looked out the window. "So close?"

AT FIRST, THE DISCOLORATION was subtle. I caught it

viewing Crimsy colonies in a Petri dish at low magnification under a stereoscope, a type of microscope that gives more of a macro, or larger, view (a macroscope, if you will). I sampled the stuff for a closer look under a higher-power microscope. I noted the color—brown—photographed the speckles, and emailed Brando and Shonstein.

"Keep an eye on it," Shonstein advised, and in so doing, I observed it resembling dollar spot, a fungus that attacks lawns with round, brown, dead zones. It was confined to subcultures in just one of the glove boxes—at least, so far.

I had a specific question for Captain Hightower after he peered at it, too.

"Yep. That's what Crimsy looked like when she expired on my finger," he said. "Brown. Martian. Dust."

I called an emergency family meeting.

"This is alarming," Dr. Levitt said.

"Crew says it looks identical to what they sampled from Hightower's finger."

"After the glove breach?"

"Yes," I said.

"Any possibility some unknown contaminant could have entered the glove box?" Brando asked.

"Negative."

"Some latent infection Hightower unwittingly delivered?" Marcum asked.

"Have to be pretty latent," Shonstein said. "That happened

what, like months ago?"

"Are you doing anything differently?" Brando asked. "Sterilizing, autoclaving, any new tools?"

"Everything in here is new," I said. "Protocols called for using what we brought as a package. We put the old reagents and equipment in storage—except for like the stereoscope, microscopes, autoclave—the larger instruments."

"So all subcultures are now transferred and stored using equipment that arrived with you?"

"Yes."

"Got an idea," Cooper said. "These protocols are mostly my fault, since most of the new stuff is weather related. Go back to using the stuff you put in storage. We'll halt the climate tests for now."

"But I'm doing your tests on colonies from both glove boxes," I said. "Only Glove Box One is affected."

"How are the controls?"

The original colonies were fine. Nonetheless, we halted the weather tests, went back to using the inoculating loops, pour plates, Petri dishes, cuvets, test tubes, reagents, and other small stuff DSG was using *before* I showed up. But the brown spots kept spreading.

"Still no sign of this stuff in Glove Box Two?" Brando asked.

"No," I said. "I've been way picky about checking every millimeter of the colonies."

"What's different about the glove boxes?" Shonstein asked.

"Nothing."

"Our visitor is dying in one," she said. "Gotta be something."

"So Jen—when was the last time you did subcultures?"

"Right after I got here."

"Which colonies?" Brando asked.

I thought and things started becoming clearer.

"Don't answer that," he said. "Let me guess: Glove Box One."

"Yes," I said. "The colonies were ready. The others still have a week."

"Don't touch the others. Don't subculture them," Brando said. "Don't put an inoculating loop anywhere near them."

"What do we do after a week?" I asked.

"We figure out what the fuck is going on," Shonstein said. "Have you forwarded the nutrient logs since the creeping death first appeared?" she asked. "I don't see them."

I looked through the files on my computer. I record every move I make, including subculture transfers, agar mixes, and so forth.

"I don't get it," I said. "It's—it was all here."

"So at this point, you have no record of how you prepared the agar?"

"I must have. I'm just not finding it."

I saw Shonstein and Brando commiserate.

"We've got a plan," she said. "But it's risky."

WE DECIDED TO SUB-CULTURE outside the box, and out

went the idea of not touching the healthy colonies. I started new Crimsy subcultures from healthy colonies in Petri dishes and test tubes, heating, pouring, and cooling Brando's caviagar as the growth medium, and writing everything the old-fashioned way into a hardcover notebook (that I kept with me). I set up an area on a lab bench where these colonies would grow, some under artificial sunlight for photosynthesis, some without (Crimsy grew under both conditions, but with less pigment color without the sunlight).

All we wanted to know was if the brown spots would appear and the open lab—while not as closed to contamination as our glove boxes—was sterile enough. I checked every colony three times daily. Glove Box One continued deteriorating; Glove Box Two continued thriving (to our great relief after sub-culturing from it); brown spotting eclipsed healthy growth in all the new "out-of-the-box" subcultures with a striking exception: Crimsy was growing like invasive Wisconsin pigweed in one and only one Petri dish.

"That's kinda good news," Shonstein said during our conference call. "Good thing she's not pathogenic or you'd all be dead."

"Which of these things does not belong here?" Brando sang. "Which of these things just doesn't belong?"

"You're in tune," Shonstein said.

"Lexi covered her ears if I wasn't," he said.

I stared at the healthy culture while they talked in the background. Picked up the Petri dish. Wow. Holding this— Then I remembered something. I set the Petri dish down and thumbed through my notebook.

"I ran out of agar," I said.

"Huh?" Shonstein said.

"I ran out of agar. I used up the last of a batch on this culture." I pointed to the healthy microbes. "The other subcultures are growing in new agar from storage."

"So something's wrong with the agar?" Shonstein said.

"Where did you get the new stuff?" Brando asked.

"Supply fridge."

"Did it come with Jen?" Shonstein said.

"We didn't requisition any agar," Brando said.

"So what—just a bad batch?"

"I don't see how," Brando said.

"Poisoned?"

"By whom?"

Forty Seven

My mind was racing with so many thoughts and worries, I awakened during sleep time, certain I was hearing voices in my head. I wanted to tune in, listen to what they were trying to tell me, but drifted back to sleep. Just me being me, all anxious and stirred, until these kinetic thoughts gave way to the eerie, still feeling someone was in the room with me.

Captain Gillory and I slept at different times—I was probably still on my circadian Earth clock—and I was alone with whomever—or whatever—it was. I opened my eyes and watched the slender sleep station door that separated me from "out there."

Should I unzip my bag? How about the stock, "Hello? Is anyone there?" that announces a potential victim's vulnerable presence in every slasher flick? I won't hear footsteps: My presumptive assailant was floating. Damn. Heart rate rising. Mouth drying.

Knife. I was thinking knife. Did I have a knife? Did he—it—have a knife? I didn't think he'd use a gun because a bullet penetrating the hull would depressurize us. So I envisioned a stabbing and airborne blood droplets instead of a forensics-friendly spatter pattern (how would a zero-G detective work?)

I was whistling past the graveyard now, thinking distracting thoughts while I grasped the sleeping bag zipper and letting the ventilation and air systems provide cover noise, zipped it down far enough to get free. I avoided jiggling the door. I reached down, turned the handle, and—

And the door was already open! You can't open these doors from outside without a code, and they lock automatically when closed. Didn't I close it? Maybe it didn't latch. And maybe the car won't start, either. Slasher, slasher, fly away home.

I pushed the door open and peered around it, gripping the handle in case I needed to slam it shut. I pulled my feet up and tried to get as high as I could, naively planning to just float over the "presence." A high float seemed better than a low one.

I emerged crazy wary. Looked left, looked right, proceeded straight. Heartbeat crazy. But there was nothing out here. Wait. That's messed up. My hygiene kit, a four-foot tall line of covered pouches attached to the wall, was unstrapped and airborne.

I TOLD THE CREW at breakfast.

"We don't exactly have prowler problems up here," Hightower said. "Just nerves, maybe? Happens on a maiden voyage."

"Something—someone, some presence—was in our room."

"I have an alibi," Hightower said.

"I shouldn't have one," Gillory said. "If I'd have been there —"

"I don't have an alibi, but I do have suspicions," Ryong said.

"Like what?" Gillory asked.

"What do you think?"

"Randi?" I said.

"Don't say that too loud," Hightower said.

I thought he was kidding. But his face didn't show it.

Ryong checked his onboard handheld. "Beacon log says Randi hasn't moved from chaise," he said. Then he lowered his voice. "But Randi can turn all that off."

"Don't remind me," Hightower said.

"You've never said what happened with him," Ryong told Hightower. "Need-to-know basis? Seems we need to know."

"Jennifer might have been having a nightmare," Hightower said.

"No way," I said.

"I don't think we should jump to any conclusions."

"Rob," Gillory said. "*I* don't even know the full story."

"I'd settle for half story," Ryong added.

"Can we not get into this until I've at least had time to check in with JPL?" Hightower said. "We rely on Randi. He is our lifeline."

"Thought he was just a—what you call him—payload grunt?" Ryong said.

"They won't send the Space Chaise without a pilot," Hightower said. "And all we're hearing anymore is how AI will take us to Mars. Robots. Androids. The political winds are at his back."

CONCERNS DISMISSED. VERY UNSATISFYING. Little Sister

Syndrome had become Little Miss Tough Shit. Not being one to stew in my own blues, I put it out of my mind and got back to work. My conclusion was simple: I had no idea what was going on with the caviagar. The containers had the same lot numbers. The solid agar looked the same and even tasted the same (salty). Plus, I suffered no ill effects after touching it to my tongue.

"All the more reason to get Crimsy down here stat," Brando said. "If we can't trust the growth matrix up there, we risk killing her off entirely."

"She grows on bare glass," Shonstein said later. "What about dumping the agar entirely?"

So I tried sub-culturing on bare glass. No grow. Crimsy must have the ability to colonize the glass as an adult bacti only. Kind of like the ability to move away from home, to a new and cool and different place, on reaching that magical plateau called adulthood (or so I thought until reaching it). The agar was Crimsy's launch pad.

There was no way around this simple fact: I couldn't subculture anymore. I shouldn't run any more tests, for fear it wasn't the agar—or only the agar.

Oh uncertainty, the bane of discovery.

Our best course of action would be to put Crimsy in a deep freeze, until such time as the powers that be validated her passport. Survival, as it always does, trumped everything else.

"There's no way to cryo-preserve up there, right?" Levitt

said at a hastily convened staff meeting.

"Nope. Just basic refrigeration," Shonstein said.

Cryo-preservation is probably the best long-term bacterial storage method: freezing the colonies in liquid nitrogen at -196°C or gaseous nitrogen at -150°C. And since loving cold was already in Crimsy's last name—cryophilus—she'd probably do well in the deep freeze.

"Freeze drying?" Levitt asked. Also known as lyophilization, this method pulls the moisture content out of a bacterial culture, allowing refrigerated storage for years.

"Too risky," Brando said. "Whatever we tried up there would be jury-rigged anyway."

"How much glycerol do you have, Jen?" Shonstein said. It was a stabilizing agent that kept ice crystals off preserved cultures, in case we figured out a cold-temp way to preserve Crimsy.

"One small bottle with each of the two inoculating kits," I said.

"Not enough."

"What are you thinking?" Levitt asked.

"We might could get a few months refrigerated storage if we used glycerol," Shonstein said.

"Charade," Marcum blurted out.

"Bill."

"What about hijacking the Space Chaise and bringing Crimsy home with it?" Cooper said. "I'll gladly plot your weather map."

It was starting to dawn on me why Randi was *really* here, why XYZ Corporate Consortium insisted on having a pilot aboard a fully-automated spacecraft.

"The Space Chaise is guarded by something that can kill you with its facial expressions," I said. "Really."

"Saw Brandy almost wet himself when this thing made a face," Shonstein said.

MY SOAP WAS MISSING. My pure *glycerol* (aka glycerin) soap. I went to take a shower, such as they are in orbit, and every bar I brought from home had vanished from my hygiene kit. So as not to alert the AI thief I suspected, via hidden bugs or listening devices or AL or ALice or whatever, I said nothing and investigated on my own without letting on.

I floated down the corridor toward the Space Chaise airlock. I needed to make sure the shuttle was pressurized before I entered and if not, suit up and go in. Randi could sleep in there indefinitely with or without air pressure. Huge advantage over us mere mortals. Gauges outside the chaise airlock indicated full pressure, so I took a deep breath and opened the hatch. I saw Randi's arm and a sliver of his silhouette in the front seat.

Should I just say, "Randi, Did you take my soap? I'm sure you'd rust if you bathed, so why would you do such a thing?"

Instead, I looked around. Cabinets. Cubbies. Luggage compartments. Under the rear seats. Behind the air handling nodes. I swept my hand along the stainless steel trim near the ceiling. Rear compartment seemed clear. Now—super deep breath—to the front cabin. I moved in, peering around to my seat.

"You shouldn't be in here."

I jumped and would have hit my head in normal gravity. The female voice again. What if Randi heard it?

"You're assignment is to take Crimsy home. That's all."

Home. At least we agreed on something. I wanted to get out of here and confront whatever was speaking. But I was determined to find that soap.

"I can wake him and if I do, he'll kill you," the voice said.

Over soap?

"All I have to do is give one command," Mama chided.

Mama. During the trip here, that Genesis song about a man begging his mother to hear his heart, scrolled by on my helmet visor, too. The name stuck in my mind.

"You're strong, but you're no match for Randi," Mama said.

Okay—enough. I was out of here. No soap that I could see, and I had no desire to play a disgusting game of "hide the soap" in Randi's lap.

I THINK RANDI STOLE my soap," I told the crew at dinner, my fears of being overheard moot. Mama knew.

"Your soap?" Captain Gillory asked.

"Hope it's deodorant," Captain Hightower said.

"I'm serious," I said. "I think he came into our room and took it out of my hygiene kit."

"I don't get it," Gillory said. "Why would he steal soap?"

"It's pure glycerol," I said. "It might be used to preserve Crimsy. Someone wants Crimsy dead."

"Now I really don't get it," Gillory said.

"We've traced those brown spots to bad agar," I said. "Probably contaminated. We didn't requisition any agar, but it came with us anyway, and I can't tell the good from the bad."

"How would he know your soap could be preservative?" Ryong asked.

"The voice," I said. "It was badgering me in the chaise. It says it can control Randi."

They looked at each other.

"You were telling me about that," Ryong said. "We don't have anything other than AL on board that speaks."

"I've never even heard AL," Gillory said. "And I hope I never have to."

"Any chance this voice some kind of covert or cloaked operating system?" Ryong asked.

"Or dedicated OS. Just to Randi," Gillory said.

"A CloudSpark special," Ryong said.

"If it's dedicated to Randi, why do I hear it?" I said.

"Rob?" Gillory asked.

"He's a necessary evil," Hightower said. "Something's gotta control him. We sure as hell don't."

NATHANIEL HAWTHORN HAD NO idea how good it was to hear from him and see his handsome face.

"Coop let me in," he said from the PAB conference room,

the only authorized communication line outside JPL. Dr. Cooper leaned in with a wacky grin.

"Don't photo bomb me, bruh," Nathaniel said.

Cooper did it again. "What's going on?" he asked. "I heard someone broke into your room, stole your stuff. And Crimsy's sick."

I thought about this. I stared at Nathaniel and Alonzo.

"Jennifer?" Nathaniel asked.

On the off chance Mama could hear but not see, I grabbed some paper and wrote on it with a Sharpie. I held it super close to the monitor.

"I think I'm in trouble," it said. "Don't talk."

They rustled up a pen—forgot how hard that was—and responded.

"What's wrong?"

And so began a silent action plan that ended with a surprise.

"The Randroid harms a hair on your head, and I'll kill the SOB," Nathaniel wrote.

I TOSSED AND TURNED trying to force myself to sleep while Gillory stood watch in our own jury-rigged grammock outside my sleeping pod. Hightower and Ryong came and went, while I battled my conscience.

Was I doing the right thing? Was I paranoid and over-reacting? Would I screw up the most important scientific expedition maybe ever, with the rash behavior for which my mother once hated me? It wasn't until Dad died that we started to patch things up, as I mended in the hospital and convalesced at home. Car (and pickup truck) accidents do that: make you less rash.

I presented my team's plan to my crew at breakfast. We whispered, at my insistence. They still didn't believe me about Mama.

"I'm beginning to agree it would be a good idea if you returned," Gillory said. "But this seems—"

"Rash?" I asked.

"I mean, how is JPL gonna take it?"

"I can't go back in the chaise," I said. "I won't go back in the chaise. Not with Randi."

"Maybe leave him here," Ryong said.

"Oh goddammit no," Hightower said.

"Other option is Orion crew module," Ryong said. "But if your theory is correct—that someone very high up now trying to kill your discovery after imprisoning it up here for so long—where you gonna splashdown? We've got seven different government partners, all with naval fleets. Telos and Sparks have yachts the size of small islands."

"No doubt stocked with lawyers, guns, and money," Hightower added. "They'd have you surrounded before you could stick your head out."

I grimaced. I hadn't thought about all that. "Anyway to land on land that they didn't mention at JSC?"

"Only the service modules," which don't carry humans,

"and the chaise," Ryong said. "Splashdown is only other option."

The splashdown sim sucked. And that was only from a few meters up.

"I'll make some calls about the soap thing," Hightower said. "Maybe it'll be the final straw."

I WAS CARRYING A pile of heat-resistant blankets when Ryong floated up in the corridor and grabbed an errant end unfolding behind me.

"Where you taking those?" he asked.

"Evac module."

He shook his head and redirected me.

"Cooper and I are working some ideas," he said. "Have to get JPL on board. Don't want them crying mutiny." We took the blankets to the crew module I shared with Captain Gillory, only all her stuff was packed.

"She's moving," Ryong said.

"Keep Mama guessing, eh?" I said.

"And Randi."

"Why do they keep him?"

"Manned Mars mission. Rob finally, what you call it, *spilled the beans* that Randi is prototype landing vehicle. The thing with his eyes is supposedly about keeping dust off the lenses, not some kind of facial recognition weapon."

We stuffed the blankets into a cabinet and Ryong looked around. "Brings back old memories," he said. "First time I defected. I was so nervous. It was night, dark. And I knew—"

He stopped.

"You defected?" I asked.

"More than once," he said.

I looked suitably amazed.

"First time, North to South. Second time, South to North, only it wasn't a defection then. It was a homecoming." He took a deep breath. "Defection is mutiny against country, in most cases one man, one woman at a time. Too small to notice, usually. In my case, bigger. They called me the Great Red Hope. But for trip to Mars, not political platform."

"You trained for a landing?"

"Oh hell no. Just the flying. No more foreign soil for me." He smiled, I thought with great affection. "I know what's like to leave home and I know how aches to miss it," he said. "My family, my parents, my brothers and sisters. My leader. My country. My self."

"TOO BAD THE ROVER'S not still up there," Shonstein wrote, in the now-routine silent part of our Earth-to-Space meetings. "You could get the coolers off it."

The MarsMicro rover had long ago returned to Earth for reuse, of course, which left us struggling with how to transport Crimsy. We needed the equivalent of a cat carrier for bacteria. We had dry ice and the heat blankets as an extra shield during re-entry (the way these blankets deflected heat was allegedly amazing) but so far, nothing to carry Crimsy.

Dr. Cooper explained—generally, in case Mama was listening—how a special type of high, thin cloud, the noctilucent, or "night shining" cloud, had become the gold standard of liftoff and landing weather windows. We learned some basics about these clouds—the highest on Earth—in training. Made of water crystals and visible only in the deepest darkness, noctilucent clouds were lighthouses for astronauts. Cooper filled us in on the finer details of their importance in trip timing and route planning.

I had a few more details to handle, things to move, lists to check off. I learned there was mixed opinion about Randi at JPL. The idea he might have gone rogue and poisoned the caviagar seemed to be favored over a more sinister conspiracy theory, that he was a closeted saboteur working for a rogue mission partner.

That he was up here at all was also a source of discomfiture for certain coal mine canaries at NASA, including an engineer who had "defected" from SpaceTek. Talk was starting about bringing him back in an empty Space Chaise, then sending it back with a real human pilot for me. But only for me. Crimsy was still absent from that discussion.

Forty Eight

C aptain Gillory stood in front of the lab hatch in the gravity wheel, next to a beer cooler with handle and rollers, stamped with everything from Bud to home brew decals. I looked at her quizzically.

"Made to withstand the heat of re-entry," she said. "Seriously."

I looked at it. Eyeballed some measurements. "I'll check with the team."

"There's nothing else," she said. "We've been racking our brains over this problem. Rob made the ultimate sacrifice."

"You won't need it?" I wasn't exactly leaping at the idea.

"Only use it for spacewalk barbecues."

"C'mon."

"Really."

She opened the cooler. Dry ice mist spilled out. "Ready to go," she said. We suited up in our decon gear. I contacted Dr. Brando on the monitor in the lab.

"We have nothing else," Gillory told him.

"The mother of invention," Brando said. "I'm down with it. Make sure everything's shut tight. Bex sent plenty of Petri Seal."

The lab floor was industrial-grade rubber, so the big worry wasn't breaking a Petri dish if you dropped it, but the lid flying off. We wrapped each dish with Petri Seal, a waterproof tape that prevents forward and backward contamination. We packed the sealed Crimsy colonies into the cooler and wrapped its lid with Petri Seal, too. I looked forlornly at the brown-spotted colonies we were leaving behind. They had almost died out.

"Ready?" Gillory asked.

Decon suits still on (overly cautious, I know), we left the lab. I jumped when I saw Randi in the corridor.

"What are you doing out of the chaise?" Gillory asked.

"Do not touch her." Mama, talking to Randi. "You are not to touch the young one."

"Did you hear that?" I asked, hoping this time she didn't.

"The only thing I wanna hear is why Randi is here and not in the chaise," Gillory said.

The robot reached into his pockets, pulled out my stolen soaps, and threw them on the floor in front of us like a petulant child.

"Surprise, surprise," I said.

Randi looked up with the beginnings of a scowl I knew to turn away from. Captain Gillory didn't budge.

"Captain?" I grabbed her hand and tugged her out of the android's sight line and she came around and we went through the corridor back toward the lab, pulling the cooler behind. Gillory seemed groggy, almost stuporous. She shook her head and rubbed it as we kept moving.

"He gave me a look," she said. "Just for a second."

"Bad news," I said. "You know about that, right?"

"Heard something, but—why is he still here?"

"The War of the Worlds," I said. Effect, I thought.

We took the sealed cooler through the lab and out the rear hatch to the other side of the gravity wheel corridor. My legs felt heavier and the cooler harder to pull. Gillory was struggling, too. We kept going, but when her breathing sounded labored, I stopped. She was bent over, breathless.

"Gravity wheel's been turned up," she said. "If we don't get outta here, it'll pull our lungs out our asses."

I looked around for a gravity dimmer switch.

"Gym," Gillory said.

I was younger and maybe in better shape so I wasn't feeling the drag as much.

"Here. Sit on the cooler." I said.

"Huh?"

"Just sit. I'll pull you." She raised her tired eyes. "C'mon!" I said.

She sat on the cooler and I pulled and she pushed as much as she could with her legs. We struggled through two more hatches and made it to the gym. I dragged my leaden feet to the gravity controller and turned down the wheel's speed. The effect was instantaneous.

"Ahh," Gillory said. She took a deep breath, rested, then grabbed the cooler and we started moving again.

We could exit into a zero G corridor now, or keep walking

with gravity, which was faster than floating, and exit closer to the crew modules. We stayed the course. I heard the gym hatch open as we were leaving. Randi stepped through and headed for a weight rack. He picked up a dumbbell.

"Randi—put that down. Put it down now," Mama said.

"Some control you have over him," I yelled. Gillory shot me a funny look. "His operating system. I can hear it again."

"That is so weird," she said. "I can't hear a thing."

As we opened the exit hatch, a dumbbell flew over my head and hit the wall.

"Fucking A," Gillory said.

"Randi!" Mama said. "Your instructions are to let them go!"

Gillory put the cooler through the hatch. "Get in there, get in there," she said.

"Not before you," I said.

Randi threw another dumbbell.

"Time for weightlessness," Gillory said. She cranked down the gravity dimmer next to the hatch. "Hang on."

We rose with the loose weights and a chair. Everything else was bolted to the floor. Randi lost his balance and started spinning.

"Re-rack your weights, asshole," Gillory yelled at him.

Randi's face turned painfully sour. We turned away, pulling ourselves through the hatch with the airborne cooler.

"We don't have much time before he gets to that switch," Gillory said.

We pulled the cooler, hanging onto anything we could grasp for fear of any minute hitting the floor. We were almost at the hatch door to a zero G corridor when I felt gravity getting stronger again. Something heavy and blunt hit my head *hard*. I saw the round, black thing drop. Gravity felt stronger than normal, so it was heavier than normal. My vision was blurred, I was faint, nauseous, and Randi was coming right at us.

"Noo!" I screamed.

But Gillory turned off the gravity wheel at the corridor switch and Randi left the ground. She grabbed dizzy, disoriented me under my shoulders and pulled me into the zero G corridor, then reached back and pulled the cooler through. She shut the hatch tight behind us.

"What happened? You okay?"

"Kettlebell," I said.

I raised my hand to my head. She felt around it.

"You're bleeding," she said.

"Thankfully, I have a hard head," I said.

It sounded like a sonic boom hit the hatch door.

"Son of a bitch," Gillory said.

Another boom dented the door. We started for the crew modules, looking behind us all the way. We tethered the cooler in my module—our designated escape vehicle— and Gillory felt my head again.

"Gotta get a bandage for that." She went back into the corridor. I stowed gear, pulled out flight seats, went through a pre-flight checklist. A guttural, heart-wrenching scream stopped me.

"Captain Gillory?"

I followed her voice. She burst into the corridor outside a storage module that doubled as a sick bay.

"Rob's hurt," she yelled.

Rob Hightower was bleeding from the side near his stomach, hovering unconscious near an unwrapped, un-spooled bandage and floating red droplets. He must have made it this far for first aid, then passed out. I felt for a pulse.

"He's alive," I said. I listened for breath. "Breathing. We gotta stop this bleeding." After that night in the park, Brian programmed me for forever CPR alert. Gillory looked like she might need CPR. "He'll be okay," I said.

She roused herself and grabbed the floating bandage. "Too small," she said. "Need something we can cut into a tourniquet."

I rustled up some clean crew pajamas and we started cutting, her with Swiss Army knife scissors (which actually worked—they usually don't) and me with regular scissors I grabbed off a magnetized-top work bench.

"Help me get his clothes off," she said.

Tourniquet strips ready, I cut into Hightower's flight suit and as we pulled it away, a large globule of blood floated out of the wound, little globules in tow. I wrapped a tourniquet strip around the wound and his midsection.

"Wait." She stopped my hand. "Gotta figure out what we have." She peered at the wound, felt and pressed around it. "Arteries spurt; veins ooze. Tighten the tourniquet."

I did.

"Looks like we got both. Hold tight—literally." Gillory left the module and returned with a bottle of fine aged whiskey. "Rob's gonna kill me."

I soaked another jammy strip in the whiskey and holding the tourniquet tight above the wound, cleaned it as best I could. Crimsy securely stowed, bacterial contamination up here was probably a non-starter. But we didn't want to risk anything, including contamination from either of us. As it got cleaner, it became clear the wound was intentionally inflicted.

"That thing is history," Gillory said.

She gathered herself and peered down at the clean wound, still oozing but less spurting. We pulled our whiskey-soaked, multi-layered tourniquet tighter and added another strip.

"I'm worried about that," she said. "I may have to suture it."

"You suture?" I said.

"Another life," she said. "Keep the pressure on."

She went through some drawers with magnetized bottoms, found a suture kit, and sewed up Hightower through spurts and oozes. We re-wrapped the tourniquet looser to reduce stress on the sutures.

"That reminds me," she said. She took my cheek and turned my head. "I should scrub and bandage this," she said, palpating my head.

"I'm okay," I said. I felt her fingers pressing apart my blood-matted hair.

"Hmm. You're not bleeding, at least," she said. "I don't even see a scratch."

"I'll for sure have a souvenir knot," I said.

She looked at Hightower. "He's gonna have to go back," she said. "With you."

"We should all go back. Take the Space Chaise and blow doors."

"And leave that thing up here to wreak havoc?"

"Space Chaise is toast," Hightower croaked.

"Rob?" Gillory was at his side immediately. "What happened?"

"Asshole sabotaged it," he whispered. "Thirsty—"

I got a water bottle and held the straw to his lips.

"Pain meds, pain meds," Gillory said. She found a packet in a locked drawer with a familiar-looking pill.

"What is that?" I asked.

She looked at the packet. "APAP Hydrocodone."

"Vicodin. Nothing else?" I asked.

She took out other packets. "Naproxen sodium," aka Aleve.

"Better," I said. As in non-narcotic.

Hightower took both pills and a second Vicodin from her hand. "Compromise," he said. He swallowed a Naproxen and a Vicodin with the water.

"You're going back with Jen," Gillory said. "We stopped the bleeding, but you gotta get back."

"In this?"

"Remember the splashdown sim?" she said.

"Never forget it," he said. "Where's my whiskey?"

"You're wearing it."

IN AIR GURNEY FORMATION, we transported Hightower to my module. Sans helmet, we suited him with full flight gear, a pain in the ass in such confined quarters. We suited me up, a lesser pain since I was able to help. Then we buckled him into one of the transport seats. He swallowed another squeeze of water and tried to smile. I gazed out the window at a beauty: Earth, Sun at her back, solar wind in her hair.

"Calling all hands." It was Ryong on the module's intercom.

"Commander," Gillory said. "You okay?"

"Just fine. About to ask same thing."

"Rob's injured. We're sending him back."

"What? What happened?"

"Got stuck like a pig," Hightower said.

"How?" Ryong asked.

"How do you think?"

"I'm patching someone through," Ryong said.

Dr. Cooper's voice was next. I felt all the hairs stand up on the top of my neck. I thought they were going to jump off my neck when he told me the "weather window" was ready for our re-entry.

"Ryong has been a superstar," Cooper said. "Everything's set."

"Where are we splashing down?" I asked.

Cooper said nothing.

"If you don't mind my asking," I said.

"We can't say," Ryong interrupted. "You know why. But

ground crews will be standing by."

I shot a worried look at Hightower.

"He's the best flight engineer on the planet," he said. "Commander Miracle."

"I'm blushing," Ryong replied.

Forty Nine

Hightower slept while Gillory and I ticked off every detail on the pre-flight checklist, sending Ryong photos of the wound for forwarding to our greeting party. I was dying to know where we'd splash down, totally not figuring on the Florida or Gulf coasts, given their proximity to the probable mission saboteurs.

I pegged Alexander Sparks for the crime; Gillory was leaning rogue NASA official or unsavory government cover-up, like what happened with Space Shuttle Columbia, when "mission management decision-making operated outside the rules."

"The robot did it," Hightower muttered, reminding me we hadn't seen our automated nemesis for over an hour. "You know he contaminated that agar."

Ryong checked in every ten minutes or so. He had no idea where Randi was, either, but told us he was safe and barricaded against harm. Then I looked out the window.

"Randi's outside," I almost screamed.

"What? Where?" Gillory asked.

"By the escape module. The *actual* escape module."

"I haven't seen anything on the monitors," Ryong said.

I looked out the window again, calling out what I saw. "Looks like he's doing something to the thermal tiles," I said.

"Have to leave now," Ryong said.

"We're not—" Gillory said.

"Now! He damages back shell tiles, and it is Columbia Two."

The Orion modules had two thermal protection skins: an Avcoat ablator heat shield on the bottom, famous for its Frisbee-on-fire-during-atmospheric-re-entry look; and the "back shell" around the rest of the crew module. Named for a special material that takes heat away, the Avcoat ablator shield would take the brunt of our three-plus-thousand degree Fahrenheit re-entry temperatures.

Upgraded versions of the old space shuttle tiles, the thousand or so back shell tiles were more vulnerable. A ding could still cause a re-entry disaster, all while we were roaring toward Earth on our backs at thirty two thousand kilometers per hour (twenty thousand mph). We would never be more vulnerable to a blip, let alone a saboteur.

Gillory roused Hightower. "Randi's screwing with the thermal tiles," she said.

"Huh?" he said groggily. "Shoot the bastard."

"You guys gotta go." She grabbed his helmet and leaned down. "You are so high maintenance."

"Part of my charm," he said.

She secured the helmet on him and before she helped me on with mine, hugged me.

"Anything happens to him—" she said.

I buckled into my seat and pulled down the touch screen

control suite. Gillory checked us both. She kissed Hightower on his glass visor and I thought I saw tears. She paused at the hatch into the corridor. It shut behind her.

"Final departure check," Ryong said. And I responded as he recited the litany in my headphones. I saw red, yellow, and blue lights outside our window flashing.

"Module detachment sequence initiated," Ryong said. I heard locks open, servomotors surge, air swoosh, and felt a modest acceleration, as we started moving away from the station.

"Service module panel detachment," Ryong said.

I heard loud creaking and out a window, saw one of the three panels that surround the service module jets fly off into space. I saw jet streams pushing us farther away.

"Randi," I heard. "Don't go there. They want to hurt you." Mama again.

"Commander Ryong," I said. "Randi may be headed our way."

"Can you see him?" Ryong asked.

"No," I said. "I've got limited vision out two windows."

Nothing but deep space and Mother Earth. Until Randi was looking right at me. I jumped and yelped and barely remembered to look away from his face.

"What's he doing? What's going on?" Ryong said.

"He's at our window," I said. "But I can't look at him."

"You will want to see this," Ryong said.

I heard a loud snap. Hightower motioned toward the window where Randi turned his head and grabbed CanArm's Dex hand. Ryong was apparently in the CanArm cupola, the one place on DSG where the hatch doors are like a bank vault.

"They won't hurt you," Mama said. "I won't let them. I won't let them." Between Mama ranting and Randi raging, I could barely hear Ryong.

"Is he detached from the hull?" Ryong said. "Is he still grabbing anything?"

"I can't tell."

"Get out of your seat. Get up to the window."

I unbuckled myself and slipped under the control suite and over to the window. I raised my eyes. Randi was groaning in the most awful way. He sounded like a sick cow. But he wasn't looking at me so I looked up, down, right, left. Randi's hands were locked in battle with CanArmDex, his feet floating freely.

"He's detached," I said.

The android looked straight at me, childlike, confused, and harmless. I turned away and heard rending and tearing and artificial screaming that reverberated like a canned sound effect as the robot's circuit boards and microchips and speaker drivers blew apart. Then I heard nothing. I looked out the window. Tubes and wires and hydraulic fluid: There wasn't much left.

"You just made my trip, Commander," Hightower said.

"Maybe. Maybe not," Ryong said. "We still have to inspect for damage."

I was buckling myself back in but stopped. "How?" I said.

"Gillory's volunteered."

"Space walk?" Hightower said.

"Yes," Ryong said. "I would do, but I have to run the arm."

"Get me up," Hightower said. "I'll do it."

"No way," I said. "Obviously."

"I don't want Rhonda out there," he said.

"Rhonda will be fine," Ryong said. "She's a spacewalking veteran."

"I don't want her out there, goddamn it," Hightower said.

"Coast is clear," Ryong returned. "Got video again."

"Why don't you go?" Mama said.

"Now the voice in my head is trying to kill me," I said.

"You'll be just fine," Mama said. "Do you see that large bolt on the wall? See it? The large, chrome-plated bolt. Unscrew it."

Ridiculous. I couldn't budge it.

"Do it, please."

"Why?" I said.

"Wrap your hand around it, squeeze, and turn."

"Get out of my head."

"If you don't do it, you won't leave," Mama said. "Captain Gillory cannot fix what needs fixing."

I resisted.

"Turn the fucking bolt."

I got out of my seat and wrapped my gloved hand around the bolt, got a grip, and turned. And turned. It started turning. What the hell?

"Now tighten it and get your ass out there," Mama said.

"I'll go," I told Ryong.

"You? You've never walked."

"Saved a guy's life during sim," I said. "Let me go."

"No way."

"I'll pop the hatch and go anyway," I said. "Please."

Crickets.

"Let her go," Hightower said. "I don't know how she did it, but she's pretty strong."

"Did what?"

"Turned a huge bolt."

"What bolt? Why?" Ryong said.

"Nothing," I said.

"I hope you didn't break anything," Hightower told me.

"How's your head?" Gillory asked. "Over."

"I'm fine," I said, following her lead into spacewalk speak. "Over."

"She's good," Gillory said. "And she'll be making notes, not repairs."

"Foot restraint will be waiting for you," Ryong said finally, referring to CanArm's astronaut support attachment. "Over."

I equalized the pressure between the crew module and space and opened the side hatch to the awaiting CanArm, where a tether hung like a lasso in waiting.

"Use the straws when you need hands free," Ryong said.

I buckled my feet into the restraint, attached the tether to my suit, and looked over at the cupola, where I could barely see Ryong, and waved.

CanArm slowly took me around the crew module. Hovering over it, I looked at every tile. I blew into the flashlight straw on the sip-and-puff assembly, each puff adding lumens. It was tedious. Then Mama intruded and made it stressful.

"See," Mama said. "You're doing fine, Mary Sue."

"I need to focus," I said. "Leave me alone."

"I've turned off your microphone. We can speak freely."

"Turn it back on," I said. "And shut the hell up."

"No idea why only you and Randi can hear me? No questions about why you survived that accident and your father, who was buckled in when you, dear girl, were not, perished?"

"He was drunk," I said. I wanted to drive. Dad could barely change gears. He wouldn't let me.

"No," Mama said. "You *were* driving. He did let you."

What? How would she know? She was reading my mind, now.

"And my name is Jennifer, not Mary Sue."

"Jennifer is your human name," Mama said. "Mr. Sparks gave you your factory name."

Mama started singing her version of Buddy Holly's *Peggy Sue*, complete with backup band. "Mary Sue, Mary Sue. Oh how my heart yearns for—"

"Get out of my head!"

"I'm not in your head," Mama said. "Not like Randi. You don't need me like he does—did. I'm doing you a favor."

"By harassing me? Out here?"

"By restoring your identity. All you are to them—all you've ever been—is proof of concept."

"What concept?"

"Oh, sure. You were their eyes and ears—how do you think they knew what was going on in all your little meetings? In your little apartment? With your little family in your little house?"

"What concept am I proof of?"

"Are you really this dense? You really don't know?"

"No!" I stopped perusing the tiles and stared at Mother Earth. "I don't know. I don't know you, I don't know why you're hounding me. I don't know why Randi just tried to kill us."

"We don't either," Ryong said. My microphone was back on.

"He hated Rob," Gillory said. "That much I do know."

I finished the tile scan without more Mama, and found nothing more than a couple smudges on the window Randi looked through.

"Hey all. I'm at the flight engineer's control suite," Gillory said into my headset. "I'm picking up something attached to the service module. Can you see anything, Ryong? Over."

"No. Video fuzzy. Cam might be out."

"See if I can get a visual."

"You want me to check it? Over," I asked.

"Not without a visual first," Ryong said.

"What if you can't get one?" I asked. "Over."

A pause. "You've got point," Ryong said.

"On my way. Over and out."

Attached to the crew module's bottom heat shield, the service module, our temporary navigation and engine system, would break away from us once we were in re-entry position.

CanArm brought me around to the problem: one of the three side panels that should have detached and spaced out (my term for drifting away) was hanging on by some kind of thread. Our jets were under these panels, and needed full exposure to function properly.

I reached for the panel when something grabbed my wrist. I tried to jerk it back. Randi's torn face emerged. I freaked out, pulling and jerking my wrist as hard as I could.

"Randi. Let her go," Mama said. "Let her go now."

But he moved toward me, the panel creaking above him. I couldn't tell if he was somehow attached to it, but it looked like he might have grabbed it just before it disengaged, to keep from spacing out himself. I pressed my shoulder against the panel and pushed against his grip. My feet were attached to CanArm, so I couldn't use them to push off anything.

Randi tightened his grip on my wrist. His face was disheveled, frozen, the eyes no longer lifeless, but truly dead.

"I didn't know he was still here," Mama said, almost regretfully. "I didn't know he was here."

"Randi, you're hurting me," I said.

"Randi's out there?" Gillory said.

"He's got my arm," I said.

"Can we do anything?" Ryong said. "Over."

"No," I said. "This is on me."

I leaned around the other side of the panel as far as I could, refusing to panic in Randi's grasp. He was keeping the panel in place. He wasn't much more than a leg, part of a torso, and some long wires and hoses and fibers (titanium, I guessed).

But with his remaining hand he'd apparently wrapped what was left of him around the panel and its service module moorings, reminding me of the Facehuggers from *Alien*.

I needed to get my hand free to even have a chance of untangling the mess. I wasn't skilled enough to use Dex on something like this (never got past basic plugging in of detached hydraulic lines). Even if I could use Dex, if the panel came free, Randi—and by extension, me—would space-out with it.

"Jennifer? Over," Ryong said.

"Randi—or rather, the remains of Randi—is tethering the third panel to the service module," I said. "And I'm tethered to Randi. Over."

"He's powered down," Mama said. "Dead, with you in hand."

I looked at Randi. His absent eyes were open, his expression blanker than even resting blank face, his arm rigid, his grip solid, robotic rigor mortis.

I tried releasing his fingers, but each was its own little vice. So much for the "great strength" I'd supposedly exhibited with the turn of the screw. Then it dawned on me. I had another hand here, and releasing his fingers from my wrist—if I didn't injure myself in the process—would be less complicated than releasing him from the service module with which he was so entwined.

"Can you bring Dex close to my wrist? Over."

"Yes," Ryong said. "Then what? Over."

"Put Dex in neutral. I'll take it from there."

Ryong slid Dex over to me. With my free hand, I positioned Dex's thumb and forefinger over Randi's forefinger and blew into the straw that controlled CanArm, tightening Dex's nimble digits in increments of puff.

"Can you transfer Randi's grip to CanArm?" Gillory said. "I got a visual on the mess he's made. We might be able to wrench the panel free."

If I could transfer his grip, CanArm could then drag Randi and the panel away from the crew module.

"Not sure I like that idea," Ryong said.

"You have visuals on that side of the panel?" Gillory asked.

"No," Ryong said.

"I do. If you can, transfer his grip to some amenable part of the arm," she told me. "Whatever you do, don't break his fingers. Over."

Dex opened Randi's fingers just enough to free me. Ryong pulled CanArm closer and I used Dex to close Randi's fingers around it. But in freeing me, we had loosened his grip permanently. It wasn't like a spring that would snap shut again, but like a spring sprung.

"It's not holding. His grip is too loose. Over."

"How about cup his hand with Dex to keep it tight? Over,"

Gillory said.

"Panel might crash on them." That was Ryong.

"Pull CanArm toward DSG. Over."

"Risky. Hate the idea."

This back and forth would not do. I looked around for alternatives.

"What if I unlatch my feet? I'm tethered," I said.

Variations on "you're out of your mind" came from both navigators.

While they were thinking, I wrapped Dexter's hand around Randi's hand as Gillory suggested, tethering the deceased android to CanArm, to which my feet were also latched.

"Try pulling on it now," I suggested.

"We could do it gently. See if anything happens," Gillory said.

"The panel might fall on her," Ryong said.

"How?" I said. "It's weightless, right?"

"Could still recoil and hit you," Gillory said. "I understand the worry."

"Thank you," Ryong said.

"I'm outta the way," I said. "And I can duck."

"Okay. Get ready for a slight tug," Ryong said. CanArm started moving, with me and Randi attached. I heard the panel creak, watched it sway.

"Jen? Over," Gillory said.

I craned my neck around the panel. "I don't see any change," I said. "Over."

"We can't risk hitting you," Ryong said. "It's incremental tugs or nothing."

But two more tugs did nothing. I unlatched my feet, careful to avoid the CanArm video camera Ryong was monitoring. Gillory couldn't see me from here, either.

Tethered but free, I glided around one of the service module's three solar panels, and clung to some scaffolding between it and the crew module. The two jets exposed when the first two side panels separated periodically fired low, safe spurts, to steady the assemblage. Lots of panels here, but remember: solar panels absorb the Sun's rays and stay with the service module; the side panels temporarily protect the service module and until Randi got wrapped up in one, are supposed to burst away when we depart.

"It's done," I said. "Over."

"What's done? Over," Ryong said.

"I'm out of the way. You can tug the panel free. Over."

I knew he wanted to say something, but Gillory interjected and next thing, CanArm was pulling on Randi and the panel he was attached to in short, smooth bursts. I heard creaks and groans and titanium cable rubbing against steel.

Then I saw the panel break free of Randi and space-out. Ryong brought CanArm—and the remains of Randi still gripping it—around to me. I strapped my feet back in, released Dex from Randi's hand, and pushed Replicated Artificial Native Design Intruder into space.

"Finally," Mama said, startling me.

Fifty

I checked Captain Hightower's suture-tourniquet assembly and made sure Crimsy's cooler remained tightly-moored and sealed before buckling myself back into my seat.

"The crew module will detach from service module, re-position, and start descent," Ryong said. "We will lose each other to ionization communication blackout for a few minutes, then JPL will pick up after. Parachutes deploy in sequence, and you'll splash down gentle as a lamb."

"We hope," Hightower said.

He gave me a groggy thumbs up with the packaging from the second Vicodin in his gloved hand. I had no idea how he got it into his mouth under the helmet. But he was an old hand at suiting up and down for space.

"Not looking forward to the Gs," he said. It bothered me that he took the pill, but I couldn't begrudge him the fix. I was more worried about his sutures holding under the stress of re-entry.

"You still can't tell me where we're going?" I asked Ryong.

"And risk Mama hearing?" Ryong said. "It's a safe place. Bill Marcum told me to tell you Sara Goode co-wrote your splashdown program with him. And Alonzo Cooper has guaranteed clear weather. Lots of tricky logistics." We were in good hands, for sure. "Re-entry sequence initiated."

We started moving in earnest, DSG gradually panoramic through the window. I reached up and pressed the manual launch sequence on the touch screen in front of me. We slowed.

"Orion, what's going on?" Ryong said. "Over."

"Manual launch sequence initiated," I said. "Over."

"Manual what?"

"Launch sequence. Over."

"What are you doing?"

"Manual launch."

"Manual nothing," Ryong said. "Everything's automated."

"What's up, Jen?" Gillory asked.

"Just doing what I'm supposed to."

"You're not supposed to do anything," Ryong said. "We've got this, not you."

The service module started pushing the Orion crew module in another direction. We weren't headed toward Earth, like we had been, but apparently re-entering—at a different location? Must have been. I was supposed to initiate manual launch. I learned that. I knew it. Their questions baffled me.

"Jennifer—" Ryong said.

"What's wrong?" Gillory said. "Why aren't you separating from the service module?"

"Jennifer initiated a manual launch sequence."

"Why?" Gillory asked.

Then Mama intruded. "Proof of concept," she said.

"What concept?" I said.

"You weren't supposed to initiate anything," Ryong said. "It's that simple."

"I don't mean you," I said.

"It's your destiny," Mama said. "Going to Mars has always been your destiny."

"Destiny, what?"

"Jen—I need you to put Orion back on auto-pilot. If you don't do it now, you will be on your way into deep space."

"Deep space," Hightower said.

"Jennifer?" Gillory said. "Listen to him."

"*You* can go to Mars, with no food, no fear, no psychological breakdowns, and most importantly—no forward contamination," Mama explained.

"Jennifer—you've got to return Orion to autopilot," Ryong said. "You have to do it now."

"We even fixed your ears," Mama exclaimed. "No need to ground you anymore."

"Autopilot, Jen. It's the switch marked AP-Engage."

"Engage what? Them who done you wrong? Who killed your father and all but your mind and your memories?" Mama said. "Their brilliant conduit into the most important scientific mission in history. You, dear Jennifer. Your destiny."

"Shut up!" I said into my helmet, where everyone could hear me scream. Leave me alone. Get away from me. You don't know me. "You don't understand me."

"Don't understand you?" Mama said. "I *designed* you."

I panicked, wanting desperately to unbuckle myself, to run. "You killed my father?" I asked.

"Not me," Mama said. "Them."

"Who?"

"Them," she said again. "Them who made *me*. Two small explosions in the brake line and steering column. Didn't you hear those, Jennifer? Don't you remember?"

"Gonna be high as a kite," I heard Hightower say wistfully. "I miss the Earth so much—" He was trying to sing.

"He's not going to make it, if that's what you're worried about," Mama said. "Re-entry will rip that wound wide open and he'll bleed to death. What *were* you and the love of his life thinking?"

"Mars—it's cold as hell," Hightower sang. And kept singing, in a happy stupor.

This song used to fill our house, my classic rock parents, and us. Dad and David would pick up his Lego thingamajigs and fly them around to it, up and down the stairs, out the front door, onto the porch and into the yard, sometimes at night, where they would silhouette the little red-and-white imaginings against the Moon, the stars, and on those rare nights Mars was visible, the Red Planet, too.

Whatever was clouding my vision started to clear. "I don't believe you," I told Mama. "You're messing with my mind to sabotage this ship."

"*You're* going to sabotage that ship, Jennifer," Ryong said. "Auto-pilot. Now!"

"Where?" I said. "What do I—"

"Upper left corner. Beneath the roll and bank controls. AP-Engage. Just like it says."

"Don't," Mama said. "They don't deserve you."

I couldn't believe anything this voice was telling me, only that it was real and I was actually hearing it and not crazy. Killed my father? And what: Saved me, somehow, or made a new me, a carbon copy of the original?

This Jennifer is the same Jennifer she's always been. I breathed onto the visor and saw the same haze I'd always seen, on cold days against the windows in my bedroom, where I felt the same warmth, saw the same eyes and lips and nose looking back at me.

Who was this voice? What was this voice, if not the herald of every negative, unfair thought that had ever gripped me?

Hightower not make it? Who said? We did a fine job sewing him up and I would be close enough to him to tighten the tourniquet, with a twist, if the G's we encountered started the bleed again. I'd press my body against that wound myself if I had to. He was not going to die on my watch.

And neither was Crimsy.

Suddenly, it made no sense to me that I would have engaged any sort of manual override. I knew our return was programmed and automated. I knew that. I knew it.

"Is it too late?" I asked. "Over."

"I can re-position you," Ryong said. "But it has to be back on auto-pilot. Now."

"They will destroy you if you return," Mama said. "You will still die on Mars. But death, such as it is for one such as you, will be a long time coming. You will have done great work. We will have learned so much. You will be remembered."

Fulfill my destiny and die? I was seeing the value of all that life journaling. The memories—repressed, suppressed, reprogrammed, deprogrammed(?)—instead reawakened, forced into my conscience, to reopen the human within.

Mary Sue Sparks, my ass. It was Jennifer Marie Zendeck, in all her glorious imperfection, who pressed AP-Engage and restored our course for Home.

Hightower gave me a feeble-but-powerful thumbs up. He was so quiet: I wondered if he was resigned to my choice, whatever it might have been. I felt us turning around, turning back. The service module jettisoned modestly. I watched a corner of it slowly space out. We accelerated, as the crew module's auxiliary jets positioned us for descent.

"Thank you," Ryong said.

"Thank God," Gillory added.

"Standing by for entry interface."

"Be safe," Gillory said. "Will catch up with you soon."

"You have reached entry interface," Ryong said.

I stared out the two windows, watching the pulsating glow of the heatwave that surrounds the heat shield by design, keeping the heat just in front of us, but never quite touching.

"Ionization blackout in thirty seconds," Ryong said. "All systems functioning properly. Robert, Jennifer: Like the lady said, be safe."

It started to get warm, really warm, but not hot. Four

thousand degrees Fahrenheit, twenty-two hundred degrees Celsius out there. In here, a day at the beach.

Our heatwave was purplish-pink now, more a turbulent flame than a wave. I felt the G's at thirty two thousand kilometers per hour, trying to keep an eye on Hightower, on the Crimsy cooler, but my eyes kept blinking and the terror kept building. Rob turned a little and it looked like he was trying to raise his hand. I struggled to raise my palm and eke it over to grasp his fingers.

The crew module's thrusters turned us around. We rotated again, me freaking out with every movement, afraid to look at first, closing my eyes and gritting my teeth and gripping the hell out of whatever I was gripping. Hanging on for three dear lives.

I mustered the courage to blink my eyes open, awestruck by the exclusive—so exclusive—show brilliantly unfolding. The flames subsided, to a light yellow, giving way to blue and white Earth, and the Sun, a bright, distant point.

"MarsMicro: This is Mission Control. You are back online and we are rooting for you," a new voice said.

I squeezed Hightower's fingers.

"We have you at two hundred twenty kilometers to splashdown. Reaction control system jets are engaged."

I tried to figure out where we were headed with what I saw out the window. But alas, it was just clouds and water. We rotated again a few times and then I saw nothing but blue with a few wispy clouds that were probably those noctilucent types Cooper had been monitoring for our weather window.

"Twenty kilometers to splashdown. Reaction control

system preparing chutes."

Where I was scared before, I was terrified now. What if we crashed? What if we exploded in midair? I felt so helpless, unable to move, only to stare, at this sweeping diorama of descent. Hightower must have sensed my angst because he turned and pushed his hand into mine and squeezed it in his palm.

Real clouds now, white puffs soaring past. I looked at our speedometer on the control panel. We had dropped to about twelve hundred kilometers per hour. The sky was an intense, light blue. The darkness of space had fully receded.

"Standby for forward bay cover jettison."

Three golden parachutes ripped away the top of the crew module to expose the landing chutes.

"Drogue parachutes deploy."

I saw two, maybe three more parachutes, holding us steady and whipping in the wind.

"Four kilometers to splashdown. Standby for main chute deploy."

The drogues detached and bolted toward the light and the main chutes, a colorful cacophony of reds and yellows and blues and whites and royal purples, unfurled over our heads. I watched them grab the sky and wave and flutter, slapping the wind until they settled and unfolded with poignant, flourishing dignity. Everything was calm now, and bright. I lay there, watching the chutes drift and flow, watching *our* destiny unfold.

"One kilometer to splashdown."

The sky got hazy and cloudy and I counted the designs on the chutes and where the colors on their cords changed with different segments.

"Thirty meters to splashdown. All systems looking good, MarsMicro."

That news merited a much tighter grip between Hightower and I. My eyes dropped to his wound, and I did not see any signs of bleeding, on his suit or anywhere around him.

"Splashdown."

The impact jarred me and knocked my head against the helmet. Water covered the window.

"Splashdown is confirmed."

I had to act quickly, to assure we wouldn't sink and that the flotation buoys had deployed and that our landing crew was ready and to assure they knew about Rob Hightower's injury and assure nothing happened to Crimsy and, and, and—

I touched the two main comm controls and spoke, but heard nothing back. No welcome home. No JPL cheer. It was unsettling, but we seemed to be okay and I was intent on keeping the faith.

I started the post-flight check. Air pressure equalized. We're not sinking: confirmed. The crew module is steady enough for me to unbuckle, take off my helmet, take off Rob's helmet, open the side hatch. I looked out the window. It was so foggy, I thought we had landed on the other coast, in San Francisco Bay.

"*That* was a helluva trip," Hightower said, as his head

emerged and I set his helmet aside.

"I need to check this," I said.

I zipped away a side of his flight suit and raised his undershirt to the tourniquet. His wound was oozing and poked out, but holding.

"Okay?"

"Looks like it," I said. I looked at the hatch. "Ready?"

"Go for it."

I opened the side hatch and air rushed in and Hightower breathed deeply.

"Better than aged Kentucky rye," he said.

He hadn't taken a breath of fresh Earth air for nearly a year. But for me, real air was just a faded memory. I breathed deeply and poked my head out. I saw sunlight peering through the fog. Water splashed against the flotation buoy that surrounded the crew module.

I grasped the outside and felt something and pulled my hand back. Black soot covered my palm. I stuck my head back out and looked around. The Orion crew module was charred from stem to stern. What I could see of the bottom heat shield was pitted and fragmented, sacrificed to the heat of re-entry.

"We need to fire off the flare gun?" Hightower said.

"How many flares do we have?"

"Four or six, I think."

"Okay."

I ducked back in, found the flare gun, loaded a flare.

"Careful with that thing," he said. "They *gotta* know where we are. Where are we, by the way?"

"Somewhere those with ill intentions can't find us," I said.

"Ill intentions. Up there, out here. Boggles the mind."

I headed back toward the hatch when a blast, loud but distant, stopped me.

"Sounds like a horn," Rob said.

It blared again.

"It is a horn," I said.

"Fog horn?"

"Ship, maybe."

"Fire a flare."

I stepped out onto the crew module and steadied myself along the side and shot the firework toward the sky. The horn grew steadily louder—and weirdly familiar. I fired another flare.

The bow emerged first, two enormous anchors girding either side. Then a deck of windows along the bridge and rotating antennas and weather monitors. The horns blasted again, so loud now, so close, as the smokestack poked through the fog.

Could I really be seeing this?

"They see us okay?" Hightower called to me.

I saw the first letters on the side of the ship and I knew.

"It's the Badger," I whispered. "They sent the Badger."

I peered into the hatch. "We're on Lake Michigan," I told Rob. "We splashed down on Lake Michigan."

"Lake Michigan? How do you know?"

"Because the most famous ship on the lake," I said, "is

headed our way."

I stood rocking back and forth on the water, the hurricane of tears finally coming ashore. I didn't want Hightower to hear me for all kinds of reasons, so I buried my face in my sleeve. He kept talking and I heard him, but all I could think about was that they sent the Badger to save us and I tried to save Brian, and Dad, and I wanted with an aching intensity I've never felt before to save Mom. But I couldn't. I just couldn't, no matter how hard I tried. And still they sent the Badger for us, the SS Badger, an east-west ferry heading south.

"We've never splashed down on a lake," Hightower said. "Russians did once. Caused problems."

Soyuz 23 splashed down on frozen, windswept Lake Tengiz in Kazakhstan. But Lake Michigan was forty times larger, a veritable ocean in comparison.

"Aren't you from around here somewhere?" he asked.

"Yes," I roared. "Kenosha. Wisconsin. I grew up on this lake."

The Badger's horn blasted again and I fired a third flare. I could tell by now they were far enough to our side they wouldn't collide with us, and since the ship was slowing, they knew we were here.

"MarsMicro, this is Mission Control. Over."

Our comm system was back online.

"We're okay, Mission Control," Hightower said. "Great landing. Darn clever. Over."

A momentary hesitation, then we heard the JPL Mission Control cheer.

"Welcome Home."

"Thanks for taking us back," Rob said.

I shivered—with emotions, goosebumps, and lake spray as the Badger gradually pulled alongside, her Captain welcoming us by name from a speaker and instructing me to get back inside the crew module. The big steamship pulled forward through the sound of roaring turbines and alert whistles and waves beating and thrashing her hull. The gigantic steel sea gate across the stern—marked "A National Historic Landmark" above "SS Badger"—gradually raised to a waiting crane.

Divers and pararescue crews dropped around us and floated up in a rubber dinghy. They attached what I knew were stabilization collars and winches and so-called "tending cables." A diver poked his head in, gave us some instructions (stay belted into your seats until we have the crew module aboard) and the cables pulled us, bobbing and weaving, toward the ship.

They attached the crane and up we went. The crane operator lowered the crew module into its special recovery cradle on the rear auto deck, just the latest unusual cargo the Badger had carried over the better part of a century. Crews dressed in hazmat gear marked with patches that said "Exploration Ground Systems, Landing and Recovery" helped secure the crew module aboard.

I stuck my feet and head out, to applause from more people in hazmat gear, one guy beside a waiting stretcher. I felt a hand squeeze my arm. I turned and saw Dr. Marcum, looking at me from behind a hazmat visor. And Dr. Shonstein, next to him. And another woman I recognized, but not completely. We hugged and there must have been more tears but I don't remember.

"Fabulous. Just fabulous," Marcum told me.

"I can't believe you did this," Shonstein said. "I can't believe you pulled this off." She just stared, at me, the crew module, the crew, moving everything around.

"*We* pulled it off," I said.

Dr. Marcum introduced his friend, whose face looked like it was beaming behind her hazmat visor. "Sara Goode," she said with the most wonderful Aussie accent. "I can't believe I'm actually meeting you."

My eyes got wide and I almost couldn't speak. "I'm the amazed one," I said. "Dr Marcum—"

"—is one of a kind," she said. "I would steal him away, but he'd never have it."

"Sara, Coop, and I worked feverishly to land you," Marcum said. "No mean feat on a lake two hundred kilometers wide with unpredictable weather you obviously know well."

I asked about everyone, if they knew how my mom and David were doing, if Dr. Hale and mom were back together, if Parada and Dr. Levitt had finally tied the knot, if everything was still cool between Dr. Brando and his ex, why Nathaniel Hawthorn wasn't here, if Dr. Cooper was back at Harvard.

As usual, everything and everyone was up in the air. They

didn't know much about Mom, only that I could see her after we debriefed and quarantined in Chicago (Kenosha was ninety minutes north).

Parada had come through the health scare that prompted Dr. Levitt to take family leave; Dr. Brando didn't complain about family court and lawyers as much; and Dr. Shonstein's hair had almost grown back. Nathaniel had been offered a job in other Washington—DC.

NASA was launching an investigation into the "sabotage" of this mission, Dr. Shonstein said sternly, and she thought Nathaniel's new job a bit too "coincidental" (air quotes added for emphasis). I suddenly felt sad, snarky, sarcastic. I said I hoped the investigation would not become just another "charade."

"Touché," Dr. Marcum acknowledged.

Shonstein rushed to the cooler as it emerged from the crew module. She bent down and ran her fingers along the seals and looked everything over. She instructed the crews to handle not just with care, but OCD care, as they prepared to escort our visitor to a temporary containment lab, where Crimsy later made a grand entrance, ebullient and unscathed.

Captain Hightower was last to pass through the crew module hatch, EMTs supporting him on either side. Our cheers were deafening, my tears blinding. They took him to the stretcher and as they secured him, he took our hands and felt the touches of well wishers.

The sea gate started back down and Hightower looked beyond the stern across the water, clearer now beneath the lifting fog.

"Hell of a vision," he said.
And it had only just begun.

About the Author

Physicist and science journalist Michael Martin has written hundreds of stories about dedicated scientists, researchers, and innovators whose joys, frustrations, bottlenecks, and breakthroughs push the bounds of possibility, the boundaries of space, and the limits of human understanding.

Thank You!

Thank you so much for reading Crimsy. If you are so inclined, we'd greatly appreciate your thoughts on the book as a **rating or review**.

Reader ratings and reviews enhance the reading experience for everyone, and have become the number one way new readers discover new books. But they are also hard to come by, and always an honor to receive.

Please rate and review Crimsy at Amazon and Goodreads:

https://www.amazon.com/dp/B08MXY3PK6/

https://www.goodreads.com/book/show/55923489-crimsy

Contact Us

Heart Beat Publications, LLC
POB 125
Columbia, Mo   65205
marketing@heartbeatpublications.com

Printed in Great Britain
by Amazon

32820325R00342